*THE*

# RABBIT

*AND THE*

# RAVEN

*BOOK TWO IN THE SOLAS BEIR TRILOGY*

## MELISSA ESKUE OUSLEY

Castle Garden
PUBLICATIONS
Renton, Washington

This is a work of fiction. All of the characters, names, incidents, organizations, and dialogue in this book are either products of the author's imagination or are used fictitiously.

Castle Garden Publications
an imprint of Gazebo Gardens Publishing
www.GazeboGardensPublishing.com

Edited by
Laura Meehan, S. C. Moore, and C. E. Moore
Cover Art by Aaron Cheney

Printed in the United States of America.
Copyright 2013

978-1-938281-34-1  (hardcover)
978-1-938281-35-8  (paperback)
978-1-938281-36-5    (e-book)

Library of Congress Control Number: 2013942734

For my Father,
who makes all things work together for my good,
and for my mom,
for her unconditional love and support.

# ACKNOWLEDGMENTS

My appreciation to Shelley and Caitlyn Moore of Gazebo Gardens Publishing for everything you've done to make this series possible. It is a pleasure to work with you and I can't thank you enough for your guidance, editing, encouragement, and friendship.

Thank you to the ever brilliant Laura Meehan and Indigo Editing and Publishing for editing the manuscript. I appreciate your much needed advice in making revisions, and your wonderful support and sense of humor. You are amazing.

My gratitude to Aaron Cheney for another stunning book cover—your artwork is fantastic.

My appreciation to my beautiful family and friends who have been so steadfast in their support. Thank you for your encouragement and for coming with me on this adventure.

To the readers and bloggers and who have helped spread the word about *The Solas Beir Trilogy*: you people rock. In the *Alchemist*, Paulo Coelho writes, "When you want something, all the universe conspires in helping you achieve it." My thanks to all of you for conspiring with me.

"With the publication of her second YA novel, *The Rabbit and the Raven*, Melissa Eskue Ousley effortlessly maintains the action and story flow that so well defined *Sign of the Throne*. She has extended her well-deserved reputation for storytelling, the rendition of that story, into the exacting artistry of the printed page, and it goes without saying that the plaudits accorded Ms. Ousley in the first installment of this series most definitely appertain to *The Rabbit and the Raven*. If she continues to follow the standards she has thus far set for herself and her writing to the third book of this series, *The Sower Comes*, Melissa Eskue Ousley will undoubtedly achieve a literary trifecta."

--Howard Parsons, *Parsons' Rant*

"When reading a great trilogy it is so exciting to pick up the second book of a series and get a feeling of visiting old friends. This is how I felt when I began reading Book Two in *The Solas Beir Trilogy, The Rabbit and The Raven*. Melissa Ousley creates with her pen a world you want to enter—her characters leap off the page and take you on their adventures. Each conflict the characters experience, I felt I was strapping on my sword to help them battle through each challenge. The most important quality of a well written book is the ability to help the reader see the story through the eyes of all the characters. Melissa truly has this ability to illustrate a compelling story."

--Deborah, *Goodreads*

"Melissa Eskue Ousley's second book in the Solas Beir Trilogy, *The Rabbit and the Raven* has ramped up the conflict, raised the stakes and increased the peril to the human realm as well as Cai Terenmare. The fate of the world is resting heavily on the shoulders of mere teens, new to their powers and their heritage. Will the allure of the dark side be their downfall? Once again, a job well done, well written and magnetic by this talented author who deftly travels that fine, yet twisted line of magical YA fantasy!"

--Dianne, *Tome Tender*

"Tynan Tierney is a most excellent villain. One minute I was almost sympathizing with him, then the next I understood why he was the villain of this story. I think he is very well written. He is almost one of my fave characters. Did I just say that? Or should I say he is one of my fave villains? He does know how to manipulate his minions like a true puppet master....A fantasy adventure with endearing characters, a villain that is quite unpredictable and a cast of fantasy creatures that go bump in the night. I am left tapping my foot for the third installment."

--Michelle Auricht, *Novels on the Run*, Australia

"Melissa Eskue Ousley has outdone herself with *The Rabbit and the Raven*. Beautifully written it begins exactly where *Sign of the Throne* left off. From the first page I was hooked. Ousley's descriptions are so vivid you almost feel as though you are watching a movie rather than reading a book."

--Amber, *Goodreads*

"Melissa Eskue Ousley's *The Rabbit and the Raven* is the perfect continuation of the *Solas Bier Trilogy*. Ousley takes the readers on an exciting journey to the outer edges of Cai Terenmare as Abby and David try to secure the support of the oracles in the fight against Tierney and his followers. Readers will fall in love with the rich and vivid world that Ousley has brought to life in the pages of *The Rabbit and the Raven* as they uncover its dark secrets. Abby and David's relationship is tested as dark forces threaten not only their lives but the lives of everyone they love. *The Rabbit and the Raven* is guaranteed to pull the reader in and maintain its hold long after the end of the novel. Melissa Eskue Ousley delivers a beautifully written novel that is imaginative, captivating, compelling, and exciting; it's a must read."

--Kira Watson, *My Dear Bibiophage*

"I loved it, loved it, and loved it. The writing was really great. I think Melissa did a really great job with *The Rabbit and the Raven* from start to finish. I really liked how it started where book one left off. I found it very hard to put this story down. I just wanted to keep turning the pages."

--Johnnie-Marie Howard, *Whispered Thoughts*

"Melissa Eskue Ousley has done it again. Give yourself some uninterrupted days to read this book, because there is no way you're going to be sleeping once you start. You know it's a good book when you start rooting for the characters only to realize that everyone in the library is giving you a weird look because you actually cheered out loud. You will get sucked into this story, and you will be left eager for the next book! In most trilogies, I am interested in the first book but don't care much for the following second and third; The Rabbit and the Raven, however, is not like other books. This book made the story grow. You still get the romantic tension, you still get the fear for the characters in tense situations, you still get an incredible story. Also, this is a great clean book! You still get all the romance and the action without the gory details…and Ousley's story telling is absolutely breath-taking."

--Cyndi, *Goodreads*

# ESCAPE FROM THE WASTELAND

The walls of the large, wood-paneled room in the dilapidated Newcastle Beach mansion were dominated by floor to ceiling mirrors in gilded frames, all shattered, save one. Piercing through the glass dome on the rooftop, the moonlight created a perfect circle of bright white light on the hardwood floor inside the otherwise darkened room. There was a stillness in the air, as if the entire world were holding its breath. It was an electric tension, the kind of silence that precedes a thunderstorm; a prickle of static anticipation. A single particle of dust hung frozen in the beam of moonlight, suspended motionless, as if it too were waiting.

The circle of light dimmed for a second—a brief flickering that could have been the wind pushing a wispy cloud across the face of the harvest moon. Then a low rumble emanated from the bowels of the mansion, followed by a sharp crack. The dome imploded in a shower of glittering glass shards, littering the circle of light with razor-edged droplets, ringing out like chimes against the floorboards.

Two lithe figures, dark as night, leapt nimbly through the rain of glass, materializing from nowhere. The larger figure took the lead, walking with long strides toward the empty doorframe with dangling hinges. The smaller figure hesitated, taking the time to tuck something into the folds of a gown, something round with a metallic glint that flashed in the light, and then, with quick, graceful steps, hurried to catch up.

ဆဘ႓ဆဘ႓ဆဘ႓

"You know we're dead, don't you?" Jon asked Abby.

Abby gave him a look, but didn't answer. Instead, she finished pulling on her boots and then buckled a belt around her waist. Hanging from the belt was a sword, sheathed for now, which she hoped she wouldn't have to use anytime soon. During the last encounter she'd had with the Kruorumbrae—in the not-so-distant past—things hadn't gone so well. Technically, the good guys had won that round, saving David Corbin and ensuring he became Solas Beir. But no victory comes without a price, and both Abby and Jon had paid dearly.

"I'm serious, Abby," Jon said. "My mom is going to kill me for scaring her to death. She has no idea where we are or if we're okay."

"I know," Abby muttered, scowling.

Jon took her expression in and then retreated to the other side of the armory to retrieve his own belt and sword. She felt guilty for being grumpy with him, but she had a lot on her mind.

He rubbed his arm absently before picking up his belt. Now healed, it had been shattered when the beast, Calder, ripped a heavy wooden door from its hinges and hurled it across the room like a discus. Abby had nearly died from the creature tearing her torso open with its claws. The attack was meant for David, but Abby pushed him out of the way and took the blow.

2

She had survived. Calder...not so much. Abby's silver blade had found purchase in the beast's belly, and Calder's nasty little friends had finished the job. So much for loyalty.

They'd barely made it safely through the portal into Cai Terenmare after the attack. If it hadn't been for the healing pool in the ancient, magical world, Abby would not have survived, and even Jon's injury would have needed surgery and months of therapy. In spite of her near-fatal injuries, there was no question that Abby would do it all again if she had to. Truth was, she was madly in love with David. She would have walked through an inferno to save him, though thankfully it hadn't quite come to that. Still, she would rather not be tackled by a giant cat monster from hell twice in the same week. Abby was certain that Jon would agree, that given more cheerful options, he too would rather not stare death in the face again. And yet, here he was, arming himself.

There was a reason he was her best friend. *Sure, he can be really irritating at times, but he's always there when it counts,* she thought. And now that Tynan Tierney, the man who called himself the Kruor um Beir, the King of Blood and Shadows, had escaped from his desert prison in another dimension, Abby needed Jon more than ever. It was supposed to be impossible to escape the Wasteland, with its endless dunes of scarlet sand. *Apparently it's not.*

Abby heard the sound of metal sliding against metal and glanced over to see Jon drawing his sword from the silver scabbard hanging from his belt.

Gingerly, he ran his fingers along the length of the blade. "Yep, she's gonna skin me alive," he muttered to himself.

If Abby hadn't been mentally preparing for battle, she would have thought Jon's fears about going home almost funny.

Never mind legions of bloodthirsty cat goblins; he was worried about how his mom would react to his disappearing act.

It had been little more than twenty-four hours since they left home, but considering everything that had happened, it felt like they had been in the kingdom of Cai Terenmare for much longer. Their going missing for an entire night and into the next one would be killing their parents, even though Abby and Jon had some pretty compelling reasons for being gone. Abby knew how her mother would react. She would be worried sick until Abby came home, and then she would be steaming mad.

She'd say, "Why didn't you at least call?"

*Well, Mom, funny thing: cell phones don't really get signals in a parallel dimension.*

"And what—you couldn't pick up the phone before you left?"

*Yeah, we were kinda busy trying not to be eaten. Sorry.*

Abby thought things might be worse for Jon though. For all his bravado about being this mischievous boy who could charm his way out of anything, he and his mother were really close, and he hated to disappoint her. His father had never been part of the picture, and even though Abby's dad had tried to fill the void, stepping up as a father figure to the son of his wife's best friend, it was Jonathon and Blanca Reyes against the world. Except, of course, when it was Jonathon Reyes and Abigail Brown against the world. When Jon was on your side, he was for you completely. Abby loved that about him.

Right now, Jon was sitting on a bench in the armory, inspecting his sword, holding it out to test its weight, but Abby knew what he was really doing was waiting for her. Jon knew his best friend well enough to know that she needed space from time to time. He had learned not to push Abby's need for reflection before any battle, whether it was the impending doom of a math test or slaying a demonic shape-shifting beast intent on devouring your soul. Her sense of humor always returned eventually.

And so it did—Abby tried to make amends for her grumpiness by drawing her sword and play-hitting his, bringing Jon out of his own reverie.

He rose to his feet. "Hey there—watch it! What are you doing?"

"Sparring," Abby smiled. "We need a little practice if we're going back out there."

"A *little?*" Jon asked, raising his eyebrows. "Looks like you need more than a little."

"Oh really?" Her sword clanged against his as she swung at him again. "I can take you down."

He laughed. "Oh, I don't think so. And don't be starting something you can't finish, Abigail."

Abby wrinkled her nose. Jon always called her Abigail when he wanted to annoy her. "Who says I can't?" she asked.

"All right then. Have it your way." Smiling impishly, Jon grabbed Abby's belt and pulled her closer, growling, "C'mere, me lusty beauty..."

Giggling, Abby twisted away from his grasp and hit his sword again. She leapt back and readied for another strike. Then she stopped. "Wait—are you speaking *pirate?*"

The devilish grin on his face faded. He lowered his sword midswing and looked at her. "Maybe. What if I was?"

She burst out laughing. "Ooooh, you are such a nerd."

Jon pouted as if he were wounded. "I'm a nerd? This from the girl who framed her zombie apocalypse survival plan *and*

5

who hoards toilet paper, just in case." This last part he punctuated with a grin and another playful clang of his sword.

ଊ୕ଊ୕ଊ୕

Standing in the armory's doorway, David watched as Abby and Jon sparred. It was definitely more a battle of wit than skill. "You two know how to use those?"

"Not a clue," Abby said, slashing the air in front of her a bit too cheerfully, considering her weapon was sharp enough to slice her fingers off.

"I watch samurai movies a lot," offered Jon. "Does that help?"

David laughed. "Not in the least." He eyed Abby in her tightly fitted black leather leggings and billowy cerulean tunic, which was cinched at the waist with her belt. He wondered if she had any idea what that shade of blue did to her eyes. She must have, just like she had to know the effect those eyes of hers had on him. "You look pretty cute like that, you know."

"Awww, thanks Corbin. That's what I was going for," quipped Jon.

David rolled his eyes. "Adorable, Reyes. Is he always this precious?"

Abby laughed. "Only when he's awake. So when you say cute—you mean menacing, right?" Abby held out her sword, trying her best to look intimidating.

"Oh yes. Very femme fatale." David sidestepped the sword and put his hands around Abby's waist, drawing her close. A stray curl fell forward into her face and he gently pushed it aside, stroking her forehead and cheek as he tucked it behind her ear. He felt the increasingly familiar prickle of electricity as he touched her skin. He wondered if she felt something similar, because she lowered her sword, disarmed.

ஐ‍ℭஐℭஐℭ

As David moved in closer to kiss Abby, Jon turned away, suddenly feeling the need to look anywhere else. He pretended to be interested in inspecting the objects on sturdy iron hooks lining the wall. There was a fascinating array of weaponry, as well as armor made of surprisingly tough leather designed to protect the neck, chest, abdomen, and thighs. He took down a breastplate. It was lighter than he had imagined it would be, but stronger than leather from his world; it seemed almost as impenetrable as steel. He put it back on the hook, killing time to avoid an awkward glimpse of the happy couple. If he could have teleported himself into the next room, he would have.

It wasn't that he was jealous—he'd given his blessing to the whole Abby and David thing, after all. True, he and Abby had some history together—after an attempt at dating two years prior, they had concluded that they were better off staying best friends. Or at least Abby had; he might have been willing to give it another shot, but he wasn't willing to risk pushing her away by pursuing her. And she was obviously smitten with David Corbin.

Abby and David had been pretty much inseparable after all that had happened, and Jon had to admit that Abby looked happier with David than she had ever been with him, even if that stung his heart and his pride. For Abby, he was willing to make friends with the guy. Abby would always be special to him, even if she was with someone else.

7

He thought about *his* potential someone else—Marisol Cassidy. Not only was she gorgeous, but she was smart and funny too. He was surprised at how easy it was to talk to her. When they had first met, he assumed that a beautiful girl like her would never, ever give a guy like him a chance, especially since she was from such a wealthy Newcastle Beach family. Sure, he was intelligent and—in his own humble opinion—a fairly witty, good-looking guy. But at the end of the day, he was still just the working-class lifeguard at a fancy country club. Not that any of that would have stopped him from taking the chance. Rejection wasn't nearly as scary as never taking a risk.

And it seemed to have paid off. He and Marisol had spent several memorable hours together at the Autumn Ball. That was before the night all hell broke loose and Jon, Abby, David, and the Buchan family fled into Cai Terenmare, running from the Shadows. He wondered if Marisol had enjoyed their evening together as much as he had—if she was thinking about him as much as he was thinking about her. He hoped she was okay, that nothing bad had happened while he was in this world. He hoped he would get to see her again.

Suddenly, Jon felt very anxious to get going—to get home, make sure his mom was safe, and call Marisol. He turned back to Abby and David.

*No, it isn't jealousy,* he decided. It was that their relationship was so new and yet they already seemed so connected. David seemed to be able to reach Abby in a way that no one else could. And...they were getting a little freer with those public displays of affection. Jon felt like the proverbial third wheel. He cleared his throat.

Abby pulled away from David, her cheeks a little red. "Sorry, Jon." She turned and stood with her back to David.

8

He wrapped his arms around her, not exactly looking repentant, but not quite as intimately entwined with Abby either.

"Not to interrupt, but it's just a little bit awkward over here..." Jon inspected his sword, testing the sharpness of the blade before braving a look in their direction. "And not to rush, but shouldn't we be getting home?"

"Yes," David replied. "That's actually why I came down here in the first place. Then I got distracted." He smiled at Abby, a devious look in his pale blue eyes. "I talked with Cael about going back."

"What did he say?" Abby asked.

"He didn't like the idea," David answered. "If Tierney is free, he could be anywhere—here in Cai Terenmare or in your world. Odds are, he'll be in yours, somewhere in Santa Linda. After that much time in prison, the first thing he will want to do is feed, and he'll be looking for easy prey."

Jon shuddered. If Calder was as big and ruthless as a mad bull, what would Tierney be like? And how many people would die before his hunger was satisfied? He sheathed his sword angrily. "Well, if that's the case, all the more reason we need to get back. Our families are sitting ducks. I don't care what Cael says, I'm going."

"Hold on—I'm not done." David put his hand on Jon's shoulder to keep him from marching out the door. "I said he didn't like the idea. I didn't say we couldn't go back. Yes, Cael advised against it, but he said that if we insisted on going, he would accompany us. Oh, and he also mentioned we would be fools to go without learning any combat skills, and that we should at least strap on some armor if we were hell-bent on meeting our deaths. I've kind of paraphrased it a bit, but you get the idea. There was some cursing involved." David pulled down armor for Abby and helped her put it on.

"Touché." Jon pulled down a chest plate for himself, fastening it over the armor he was already wearing. After their last encounter with the Shadows, Jon saw no need to offer himself up on a platter.

Marisol Cassidy had the distinct feeling she was being watched. She couldn't explain it, but she was definitely getting creeped out, and the feeling was growing by the minute. She felt silly and paranoid. She was supposed to be having a good time.

She looked around at her friends, sitting on driftwood logs around the bonfire on the beach. The usual gang was present: a mixed group of guys and girls, mostly seniors with a smattering of the more popular juniors from Marisol's affluent, private high school. It was a beautiful November night. After the hard rain the night before, the skies were clear and the moon was bright. It was the kind of full moon that was a warm yellow, almost orange, and it seemed larger than usual, lighting the night like the sphere of a giant Chinese paper lantern.

"Beer?"

Marisol startled when Tyler flopped down on the sand next to her, offering her a brown glass bottle, retrieved from the cooler he'd brought. Ty was a surfer and looked every bit the part, with an easy smile; lean, muscular body; and devil-may-care shaggy blond hair falling into his eyes.

Marisol shook her head. "No thanks." She forced a smile. "Not tonight."

"No worries," Ty smiled, and took a swig from his own beer. "Can't believe our senior year is almost halfway over."

She laughed. "Yeah, it's crazy. Time flies."

Ty nodded. "It's kinda sad. Have to make the most of the time we have left, you know?"

Marisol forced another smile. Although she outwardly shared her friend's sentiment that the end of their high school career was a great tragedy, secretly she was glad. She was tired—tired of high school, but mostly tired of the games.

Tyler scooted up onto the driftwood log to sit closer to Marisol. The smell of beer on his breath was almost masked by his cologne, which he'd apparently laid on heavier than usual. Marisol couldn't quite identify which brand it was, Drakkar Noir possibly, but whatever it was, he seemed to have bathed in it. Her nose began to itch and she fought back a sneeze.

Tyler took another long drink, put his hand on her leg, and looked at her meaningfully. "You know, we could…"

Marisol didn't let him finish. She shook her head. "Like I said, no thanks. Not tonight."

☙❧☙❧☙❧

"I wish you would not go," Eulalia said to Cael. After David had gone to speak with his friends, the queen had pulled Cael into her chamber and closed the door.

"You know I must," Cael said. He always strived to maintain an air of dignity and authority in his position as first knight. He was a soldier, trained to keep his emotions in check. Even now, his gaze was stoic. But she knew she had always been his weakness. As he stared into her pale blue eyes, his demeanor softened. He pulled her into his arms. "Your son is determined to go with or without me. I must do everything in my power to keep him safe."

"Of course," Eulalia nodded. "Of course I want him to be protected." She rested her head against his chest. "But you and I have had so little time together. There is much I need to tell you, so much I hid from you while my husband was alive."

Cael cupped her chin, gently tilting her head up so he could see her face.

She took a breath to steady herself and continued. "I never told you, but when we were young and Ardal chose me as queen, I considered running away with you."

"You did?" He looked shocked.

She nodded. "I always thought you would be the one I would marry. We grew up together. You were everything to me."

Cael ran his fingers along the length of one of her dark tresses and sighed. "Perhaps we should have run away."

Eulalia shook her head and smiled sadly. "It would not have done for the Solas Beir's betrothed to be with another. I had a duty to fulfill, as did you. But now there is a new Solas Beir seated on the throne, and I can finally speak the truth."

"I am listening," Cael whispered, his eyes locked on hers.

"Ardal's sudden attention surprised me. Lucia was supposed to become queen, not me. What did I know of ruling a kingdom? I was just a girl. Lucia was the one everyone looked to for wisdom." Eulalia frowned, remembering.

She was aware that people thought she was lovely, but she had always thought of Lucia as being the greater beauty. Lucia was statuesque, with the face of an angel and silvery blonde hair. Lucia was the one who had carried herself with the confidence and poise befitting a queen, the one who always knew what to say and do.

"I could not understand Ardal's reasons for choosing me, but I knew I could not refuse him. Instead I had to deny my love for you. Eventually I did find love for Ardal and peace about my new role. But even after he was murdered, I kept my feelings for you to myself, even though you said you still cared for me. I still felt bound by duty to my kingdom and to my son. I pushed you away. The truth is, what I felt for you never died. While I was in exile, those feelings only grew. That is what allowed me to walk with you in your dreams, even from the distance of another world."

Cael stopped her with a kiss. When he released her, she could see the weariness in his deep brown eyes. "So many years have I waited for you."

"I know I have caused you great sorrow," she whispered, looking away.

"You are worth it," he assured her, cradling her cheek against his palm, giving her the courage to look back at him. "And when I return, we will wait no longer."

Eulalia looked up at him, and he smiled. She kissed him tenderly. "Promise me, then. Promise me you will return safely, and promise you will protect my son and his friends. Bring them back to me."

"I promise I will."

&#8258;&#8450;&#8459;&#8258;&#8450;&#8459;&#8258;&#8450;&#8459;

"Here's the plan," David explained, "we cross through the portal with Cael, get your families as quickly and quietly as possible, and try not to attract attention. My mother will stay here with the rest of the guard, her thoughts locked on Cael's in case we need backup. She wanted to send more soldiers with us, but Cael thought we would be less conspicuous if it was just the four of us."

"Eulalia will sense if we're in trouble?" Jon asked.

David nodded, thinking about the connection between Cael and Eulalia, the way Cael looked at his mother—how he had held her when they realized Lucia had a tool she could use to free Tierney. David had grown up not knowing his mother, Eulalia, the Dowager Queen. His father, Ardal, the last Solas Beir, had been assassinated soon after David was born. David was getting to know Eulalia and had learned some things about his mother's life, but he hadn't decided what to make of Cael yet.

Cael treated David with respect, but to David, it felt like Cael was the one in authority. The man had been tried in battle and it showed. At first glance, he was just a well-toned man in his mid-thirties; but the look in his eyes and the long scar running from his jaw to his neck told a different story.

Although David respected Cael, he wasn't sure how he felt about the idea of Cael courting his mother. It wasn't like he knew either of them well enough to have a right to an opinion about their relationship. It was one of those things he could focus on later, after he had figured out the rest of his new life in Cai Terenmare. Right now he had bigger fish to fry.

David ran his fingers through his dark, somewhat unruly hair. He was grateful that Cael was willing to come with them. He was only just discovering his power as Solas Beir, and knew he wasn't yet ready to face the greatest enemy this world had known. David pulled down some armor for himself and checked to make sure Abby's fit well enough to keep her safe. "Come on," he said. "Time to meet up with Cael."

ᘓᘓᘓᘓᘓᘓ

Marisol watched the easy smile vanish from Ty's face.

"It's cool," he muttered. "Whatever." Standing abruptly, he walked around to the other side of the fire, where Emily sat strumming her guitar.

Emily smiled as he sat, and Marisol wondered if he'd have better luck with a fellow surfer. Em certainly had more in common with Tyler than she did.

She felt bad for turning him down. He was a sweet guy—but he wasn't entirely sober. Still, she hadn't meant to hurt his feelings. She really hated conflict. Her natural defense was to yield, giving someone else the right of way. It wasn't that she wasn't willing to stand up for what she believed in; she just didn't see the point in fighting about trivial things. The irony, she reflected, was that she wanted to study law. She had a feeling she was going to have to get comfortable with conflict, and quickly. Maybe if she could find an area in the field that she was passionate enough about, she would stop letting people steamroll her.

She'd been steamrolled a lot lately. Most of it had to do with her mother. The world-famous Esperanza Garcia had been one of the all-time most bankable supermodels. Being that much of a household name came with a whole slew of stories publicized in the tabloids. Her history of eating disorders, her leaving modeling for painting, her sudden marriage to Marisol's father (a wealthy, if considerably less-well-known, businessman from Dublin), their recent divorce, and the fact that Esperanza was as far from Newcastle Beach as she could get. She was focused on her new life, her boyfriend who was twenty years younger, and her exhibition at the Guggenheim Museum Bilbao in Spain.

The only part of Esperanza Garcia's life that had remained sacred and relatively private was Marisol. Both Marisol's mother and father had valued protection for their daughter, and there were few photographs published of the family together. Esperanza almost never appeared at public events with her daughter. Marisol appreciated that, but she hated it too, because it felt almost as if she didn't exist—especially now that her mom's calls were growing more infrequent and her dad had become more immersed in his work.

Marisol found herself worrying about many things. Was her dad avoiding her because she reminded him of her mother? Was it so painful that she physically resembled Esperanza that it was driving a wedge between them? Or—and this was somehow worse—did he just not care anymore? He seemed apathetic about everything these days, except for his financial investments.

As for her mother, Marisol had mixed feelings. She hated her for leaving and yet, she was glad she was gone, glad her parents had stopped yelling at each other and were at least being civil now that there was an ocean between them.

The other thing she hated about her mother was her former eating disorder. Even now, Esperanza was too thin, and because of her struggle with the disease, everyone assumed that she was still battling anorexia and that Marisol would follow suit.

Marisol was not too thin. She watched Michal and Monroe flirting with boys around the bonfire, and compared their bodies to hers. Her friends were stick-thin, and they were constantly urging Marisol to lose weight. It wasn't that their criticisms were malevolent—or at least, Marisol hoped they weren't. It just seemed like they were always pressuring her, trying to fix her. Marisol didn't need to be fixed. Her weight was fine. *I'm perfectly healthy, thank you very much.*

But because of her mother's history and the way her friends looked, well-meaning adults often tried to intervene, adding to the pressure, because they assumed that if she wasn't anorexic, she must be bulimic. She was neither, although denial only seemed to reinforce the assumptions. Marisol tried very hard not to focus on her weight. The hard part was that as much as she tried not to think about it, everyone around her insisted on talking about it. She just wished they would leave her alone.

She thought she heard her name and looked up. Yep, she'd heard right. Michal and some new guy from school she wanted to impress were looking over at her. Joe, was it? Marisol couldn't remember the guy's last name, but it didn't matter. Why *she* was the topic of interest for Michal and Joe what's-his-name, Marisol didn't know, but she guessed it wasn't for her benefit.

Michal, her best friend (well, *a* friend at least—perhaps *best* was pushing it), was one of the reasons Marisol had grown tired of high school. Michal could be moody at the best of times, and lately, it seemed like she was always irritated, constantly using Marisol as her personal doormat. Michal had been rather testy with Monroe, their other *best* friend, as well, but Monroe had always been better at deflecting the negativity, basically leaving Marisol in the line of fire.

Michal said something Marisol couldn't quite hear. She leaned forward and managed to catch a single word: "Jon." She groaned. Whatever they were talking about, it probably had to do with all the time Marisol had spent with Jonathon Reyes at the Newcastle Beach Inn's Autumn Ball.

Michal despised Jon. She would have insisted that it was because she was so out of Jon's league; Michal was disgusted by his audacity to hit on her. But Marisol suspected it was because he had the gall to flirt with Monroe and her as well, rather than make Michal the sole focus of his attention. Even if Michal didn't want Jon, she couldn't stand not being in the center of things. The universe *did* revolve around her, after all. And nothing captured Michal's attention more than someone else being in the spotlight. Marisol was sure that Jon's recent favoring of her over Michal reinforced this.

Marisol didn't get why Michal had to be so mean about Jon—there was nothing wrong with him. Jon was cute and he made her laugh. It felt good to talk to him. There was no pressure like there was when she hung out with other people. People like Michal.

Michal glanced over, saw Marisol looking her way, and returned to her conversation. The guy apparently said something particularly witty, because Michal rewarded him with a high-pitched laugh, tucking a strand of her long blond hair behind her ear.

Annoyed, Marisol turned away. *I really need to get out of here...go someplace to clear my head.*

The bonfire was on the stretch of shoreline just outside the Newcastle Beach Inn. Marisol considered taking a walk around the inn's garden path. The stone steps leading to the path were close, and it would be safer to walk around the inn than down an isolated part of the beach. The beach in Newcastle was relatively shielded from crime because of the affluent neighborhood and a stone wall that defined its boundaries. Across the wall though, in

Santa Linda, the beaches had a bad reputation as gang hangouts and hotspots for late night drug deals. De Luna Beach, the area just north of the Newcastle wall, was not a good place for a young woman to walk alone after dark.

Marisol turned her attention back to the inn and something caught her attention. There was that creepy feeling again; she shivered and her arms broke out in goose bumps. Something bright and reflective was in the hedge near the inn. She stared at the pair of crimson lights, trying to discern what they were.

Suddenly, the lights blinked out and Marisol realized she had been right all along—something *was* watching her. She heard the breaking of twigs and branches as whatever it was scurried away like it had been caught doing something mischievous. By the noise it made, the thing with the red eyes seemed to be headed for the blackness of a grove of trees growing between the fortress-like wall of the inn and the beach, just south of the stone steps.

If it was an animal, it sounded big. *A raccoon?* No, she had seen raccoons around before. They were rare in Newcastle Beach and they were generally stealthier. A raccoon would not have made that kind of noise going through bushes. *And raccoon eyes don't glow red.* With this realization, she stood up and backed away, instinctively trying to put some distance between herself and the hedge.

"What's wrong?" Monroe asked. Marisol jumped—she hadn't even noticed that Monroe had sat down beside her.

"I saw something—there was something in the bushes." Marisol pointed. "It went into the trees."

"What was it?" Monroe rose to her feet as well. She brushed her dark, curly bangs away from her face, and then shielded her eyes from the glare of the firelight and peered into the dark grove.

"Some kind of..." Marisol hesitated, searching for the correct word. "...creature. It looked like it had glowing red eyes." She shivered again.

Michal and her adoring fan Joe came over to see what Marisol was pointing at.

"What's going on?" Joe asked, adjusting the collar of his polo and flashing a cocky grin. He was a nice-looking guy; broad-shouldered and clean-cut, his strawberry-blond hair kept short and neat. A little too preppy for Marisol's tastes, but Michal's parents would probably adore him, especially if he joined them to play tennis at the inn.

"Marisol thought she saw some kind of weird creature in the bushes," Monroe explained. Her brown eyes were wide with curiosity as she scanned the trees.

"An animal? Hmm, I'll check it out," Joe said, his voice cavalier. He started to walk toward the bushes.

"No—don't!" Marisol said, grabbing Joe's arm to stop him. "I don't think it was a regular kind of animal. It was big—really big. It made a lot of noise as it went into the trees over there. And it had these evil red eyes."

"Evil red eyes?" Michal asked, incredulous, crossing her arms. "Are you *serious*? Come on, Marisol." She laughed. Joe and Monroe joined her.

Marisol didn't. She was very afraid, and she didn't know why. She didn't even attempt to hide it.

"Don't worry, Marisol," Joe consoled her, patting her hand as he pried his arm from her grasp. "There's nothing to be afraid of."

His tone sounded patronizing, but Marisol could see by the expression on his face that he didn't say it to be unkind. He was being sincere. That—and he *really* wanted to impress Michal. Apparently this was an attempt at chivalry.

"Just you wait," Joe said. "You'll laugh when I return with some hyper, drooling puppy on my heels. I'm kind of an animal whisperer." He winked and gave Michal a quick peck on the cheek. "Be right back." He strode confidently into the grove of trees, vanishing into the blackness.

ರುಞಭುಞಭುಞ

The goodbyes at the portal were solemn. David, Abby, Jon, and Cael each wore thick leather armor and carried a silver sword.

Abby shifted in her armor. The leg coverings fit well, but her chest plate felt a bit awkward; it was a size too large and built for a man's frame. It wasn't too heavy yet, but she sensed that she would have to build up her strength were she to wear it for any length of time, or she'd tire quickly.

Eulalia and Nysa came to see them off, along with a small group of soldiers reporting for duty to relieve their comrades standing guard at the floor-to-ceiling gilded mirror portal.

Eulalia embraced Cael. "Come back soon," she whispered with tears in her eyes.

"I will," he replied stoically.

Abby wondered how he felt about the fact that he would be away from Eulalia yet again. Hopefully they would all be back before the night was over.

Eulalia gave Jon a polite hug, and then laughed at herself as she pulled David and Abby together into a more affectionate and clumsy one.

Nysa, usually bubbling over with joy and laughter, was uncharacteristically quiet. By the frightened look on the tiny nixie's face, Abby sensed Nysa was remembering being attacked and was worried for their safety.

Abby felt a flash of guilt. If not for her, Nysa never would have taken the silver hand mirror from Cael's leather satchel and Lucia never would have gotten her hands on it to free Tierney. It wasn't Abby's fault, but still—she felt responsible for the nixie.

Nysa had about a hundred years on Abby's eighteen, but she was an innocent. In faery years, Nysa was still a child, and she could not have foreseen the consequences of her actions. Nysa had only been trying to help, but the nixie had almost died, all because she was trying to protect Abby. The whole debacle had almost gone down like a Greek tragedy.

The thought that the Kruorumbrae would attack someone like Nysa underscored their ruthlessness. The Shadows were evil, pure and simple, with *nada* in the department of redeeming qualities. And if Nysa had been vulnerable, what would the creatures do to Abby's little brother? Her parents? She had to get to her family before the Kruorumbrae did and bring them to safety in this world. If she had to battle a whole army of Shadows in the process, so be it.

Walking through the portal was akin to being smushed through Jell-O, but without the mess. The glossy surface of the mirror gave way to a gelatinous substance, which sucked gently at their bodies, requiring some effort for those unpracticed in traveling between worlds.

Abby cautiously emerged through the mirror on the other side, preceded by Cael, Jon, and David. The mirrored hall they entered was empty and unnervingly quiet. There was absolutely no sound—no night insects chirping or flapping velvet wings, not even the movement of air. Nobody spoke. The air in the room felt stagnant and heavy. Abby was tense—she felt an oppressive weight on her shoulders, diminishing her resolve to fight. It was difficult to breathe.

She looked around the room, remembering the last time she was there, surrounded by hordes of hungry goblin-like Kruorumbrae, who favored the form of ink-black shadow cats with frighteningly wide, toothy smiles. She couldn't help but relive the moment when Calder launched himself at David, and she'd pushed him through the portal a mere instant before the beast was on top of her. The image was burned in her memory. She remembered slicing pain as his talons ripped her stomach open, the weight of him crushing the air from her lungs, the sulfuric smell of his breath. After that, her memories faded, blocked by the pain. Maybe that was for the best. Perhaps it was her body's way of dealing with extreme trauma. She prayed that history would not repeat itself.

Once inside the dark mass of trees, Joe heard a number of scurrying sounds. It was difficult to tell where the noise was coming from—maybe there was more than one dog. He crouched down and whistled, trying to peer into the dark undergrowth. "Here, boy…come on out, little puppy. I won't hurt you." A rustle came from just behind him. Joe stood and turned, grinning. "There you are—" The sentence caught in his throat.

Standing before him was the most stunning woman he had ever seen. Her beauty made him want to weep; it was sweetly painful to look at her. Something deep within him knew she was not human, had *never* been human, and was not of this world. It was her eyes—they were otherworldly and dark, unnaturally dark, and spoke of ages long past, beyond anything Joe could imagine. Her hair, in contrast to her eyes, was a silvery blond that glowed like moonlight incarnate, almost matching the simple silvery sheath she wore. It was a light garment that fell to her ankles, enfolding her lithe but lovely body.

Michal and the beach became a forgotten dream. The world outside the grove ceased to exist. Only the woman was real. Only the woman mattered.

# NEWCASTLE BEACH

Watching Abby take in the room, David could guess what she was thinking about. He knew that remembering the horror of that night would only make her fear grow. "Don't think about it," he whispered as he wrapped his arms protectively around her.

She looked up at him, terror in her eyes. "How can I not?"

His grip on her tightened; he wished he could shield her from everything, even her fear. "I know—but just don't."

Abby shifted in his embrace, turning to press her cheek against David's chest.

He could feel the beat of her heart speeding up, and sensed that her fear was rising to panic. He couldn't blame her. What if the Kruorumbrae had returned? David held her and kissed the top of her head, brushing his lips against her hair, trying to reassure her. "It's okay, Abby—everything will be okay. I'm here and I won't let anything hurt you. I promise."

Abby looked up at his face. "I'm sorry. I just...coming back here and remembering..." She buried her head against his chest again.

25

"Shhhh. It's all right," David whispered, stroking her hair. "It's okay to be scared. What happened to you was terrible. You were so, so very strong. Today it's my turn. Okay?"

"Okay." It was a strangled whisper, like she was trying not to cry.

He couldn't tell if she succeeded, because her face was hidden, pressed against him. "We'll just take it step by step, face whatever comes as it comes. Let's focus on getting to your parents' house, and only that. If something happens, we'll deal with it then," he said.

"Okay." Her voice was stronger this time, calmer.

He placed his hand on her cheek, coaxing her out. "I love you, Abby."

She looked up at him, her eyes glistening from the tears she was holding in. "I love you too." She smiled weakly. Then she wrapped her arms around his neck, stretched up on tiptoe, and kissed him hard, as if she would never let him go, as if she were afraid she would have to.

ଽଠଔଽଠଔଽଠଔ

Jon and Cael were on their guard, scanning the room for any sign that something might be waiting to ambush them.

Jon pointed at the moonlit circle of broken glass. "So, what happened here?"

Cael was studying the shattered dome. Jon saw his knuckles turn white as his grip on his sword tightened. It wasn't a reassuring response. "They've come through," Cael said. "Tierney is already here."

Jon felt his face drain of blood. The reality of it, of facing something far worse than the shadow monsters they had already encountered, chilled him. Primal terror was close, the kind you feel when you are small and afraid of the dark, knowing something bad is there but feeling too afraid to find out what. It threatened to paralyze him, and he forcefully pushed it aside. He had to get home to his mom. David was right. *Focus on one thing at a time, on getting home.*

ဆာလ္ဆာလ္ဆာလ္

Michal was annoyed. She stared at the trees, scowling, her hands on her hips. *What's the deal?* Joe should have been back already. *What is he, lost? Come on—those trees are thick, but not that thick.* The grove was bushy, yes; covered with vines, yes; dark and creepy, oh yes. But the thicket was also small—you'd have to be an idiot to get lost in there.

Maybe Joe was the one who was thick. She sighed, disgusted. *Boys!* She'd have to go in there. She thought about it. *On second thought, maybe Joe isn't an idiot.* Maybe he had gone in there hoping to get away from the crowd, thinking she would catch on and join him. Well, if that was the case, he certainly didn't communicate it very well. It wasn't like she could read his mind. She stood up, brushing sand from her miniskirt, and began to walk toward the grove.

"Michal?" Monroe called.

Michal turned around. "What?"

"Where are you going?" Monroe asked. She looked clueless, twirling one of her curls around her finger as she sat on the driftwood log. On the sand in front of her were sweeping cursive letters. She'd been writing her initials in the sand with her toes, killing time while they waited for Joe to come back.

"I think Joe got lost. I'm going to see what's taking him so long," Michal responded, more irritated than before. She was annoyed at Joe for making her go after him into the dense, creepy grove, even if it was for some pathetic attempt at romance. And she was annoyed at Monroe for making her explain what should have been obvious. Not that she was surprised—with Monroe, that was par for the course.

"I don't think that's a good idea," Marisol warned.

She looked scared, but that only irritated Michal more, as she remembered it was Marisol who had started this whole thing with her silly, superstitious, "I think we're being watched," bit. Her general feeling of annoyance was chiseled down to a fine, focused point of anger. It had actually been a fun night until Marisol wrecked it by being a psycho. Michal waved her hand dismissively, turned back toward the grove, and kept walking.

She stepped into the trees, passing through a veil of vines, pushing them aside like a curtain. They fell back into place as she moved past them. Ahead, in the dark, was a large fallen tree. She climbed over it, lifting one leg and then the other, trying not to think about what kind of creepy-crawlies might be living on it. That would be the perfect end to the night, wouldn't it? Something nasty with too many legs crawling over her bare skin. Her hand brushed into a spider web stretching from the log to an overhanging bush, and she squirmed, holding in a scream while flapping her hand around in a futile attempt to shake off the web. This was *so* not okay. Joe was probably close by, enjoying this little show. If he was, he was a dead man.

ᚼᚲᚱᚲᚱᚼᚲᚱ

28

The second worst thing Abby, David, Jon, and Cael encountered on the walk home was the Buchans' SUV, upside down on the grounds of the ruined mansion, one wheel spinning as though something had been sitting on it and had just jumped off. There was a moment where they all looked around frantically, and then a moment of surprise when nothing sprang out at them.

"I thought all the chaos caused by the Kruorumbrae was supposed to magically disappear," Abby mused. On the day of his coronation, David had mentioned that a spell would overtake Newcastle Beach and erase evidence of the existence of Cai Terenmare and its inhabitants, good and evil.

David frowned. "As far as I know, the spell is already in effect. This must have just happened."

"Best not to linger then," Cael said, leading the way to the estate's gates.

It was eerie—that feeling that something evil was close and just out of sight, something that could attack at any moment, but didn't. Abby couldn't figure it out. She felt like they were being watched, but she didn't understand why they weren't being attacked. It didn't make sense. *Where are Tierney and Lucia? Where are the Kruorumbrae?*

The worst thing Abby saw was the look on Jon's mother's face.

ಬಂಧ ಬಂಧ ಬಂಧ

Blanca Reyes was staring out the living room window of the Browns' house. When Jon and Abby hadn't come home, she, Bethany, and Frank had begun to worry, and by six in the morning, they'd called the police.

An officer had stopped by three slow and agonizing hours later, asking a lot of questions and assuring them that, in most cases, missing teens turned up in a few hours. Blanca didn't like his tone—he seemed dismissive, making it seem like she was being overbearing and that Jon and Abby had run away together in some rebellious attempt at romance. But she knew her son, and he obviously didn't. In fact, she didn't think *Officer Not Helpful* knew much about kids at all.

Blanca was thinking about this when she saw them walk up the drive—first Jon, then Abby, holding hands with a boy with dark, curly hair, and finally, a rugged-looking older man. Her focus, though, was on her son, and as their eyes met, her despair gave way to joy, and the tears she had been holding back for hours broke free. She was out the door in an instant, flying down the front steps, running to him. *It's funny,* she thought, *how fast you can run to your child.*

Her mind returned to a memory of Jonathon at three years old, encountering a rattlesnake in the backyard. It was one of those California summers when rodent populations soared and snakes grew bold in reaping the bounty. She was indoors, but his scream of terror pierced her soul, and she knew, without needing to see, what the scream meant. It launched her into instinctive action. She ran out the back door, scooped him out of harm's way, deposited him safely on the back steps, and in the same fluid motion, grabbed a garden hoe and hacked the thing's head off.

It had surprised her. She hadn't known she could move like that. It gave her new confidence about raising her son. When she had realized that she would be doing it alone, that Jon's father wanted no part of their lives, she had been terrified.

The snake incident gave her new insight—she was strong. She could do this.

Now, holding her tall, almost-grown son, Blanca wept.

Jon wrapped his arms around her, repeating over and over, "Mom, I'm sorry, I am *so* sorry…"

ℰℭℰℭℰℭ

Abby's parents were coming down the steps, hurrying to enfold her in their arms. "Abby! Oh Abby, we were so worried!" Bethany Brown cried.

Abby was surprised. Where was her mother's "Where have you been, young lady" speech?

"I'm sorry, Mom." She hugged her mom and dad tight. She saw that her little brother was watching from the steps. He was only ten, and Abby could sense that he had been scared too. She felt so guilty.

David seemed to feel guilty as well. "I'm sorry, Mr. and Mrs. Brown, and Ms. Reyes," he said. "We *really* didn't mean to worry you."

Cael looked nervous, but not about the family reunion. Abby thought perhaps he too had the keen sense that they were being watched and followed.

"Solas Beir, I suggest we finish what we came to do and return to Cai Terenmare. If Tierney knows you are here…" he warned.

He didn't have to finish the sentence. If Tierney had found out the Solas Beir had left Cai Terenmare, it was only a matter of time before they would all be dead.

31

"Let's get out of the open and inside the house," Abby urged, grabbing David's hand and tugging him toward her front door.

Once inside, Abby and Jon introduced David and Cael.

"So this is the mysterious David Corbin," Abby's mother mused, shooting her a not-so-subtle wink.

Abby didn't mind, but there would be time to update her mom on her love life later. She tried to quickly tell her story about all that had happened since their disappearance, in as believable a manner as possible.

Abby experienced a feeling of déjà vu, remembering when she had told David a similar tale of everything she had learned from Eulalia: the existence of Cai Terenmare, the magical, silver nautilus necklace known as the Sign of the Throne, and the fact that David was Eulalia's son and the next Solas Beir. With David, she had been terrified that he wouldn't believe her and she would lose him for good.

She was less worried about being believed now, especially since she had Jon, David, and Cael to corroborate her tale. Abby watched her parents' initial expressions of shock soften as they listened. Abby's mother seemed to be hardest to convince, but even her doubting questions tapered off as Jon and David nodded emphatically, their faces sincere. Bethany Brown knew her daughter wasn't given to lying. Abby wasn't sure how much of the story her parents believed, but they seemed to be taking her concern for their safety seriously when they heard what had happened at the Buchans' house. It would have helped if they could have seen what Calder did to Jon's car, but the old Mustang had already disappeared. Whatever spell had been cast seemed to be working; as they had traveled to the Browns' house, no one in Newcastle Beach seemed to notice the four people walking down the street, armed with swords.

"So now we're here," Abby finished, and looked at her family and Blanca Reyes expectantly.

Jon was sitting with his arm around his mother, who seemed reluctant to let him out of her sight. Based on the steely look of determination in her eyes, Abby was certain she would be making the journey to Cai Terenmare.

Bethany Brown exchanged a look with her husband and he nodded. Bethany took his hand, slipped her other arm around Abby's younger brother, and then turned back to Abby. "What do we need to pack?"

Abby breathed a sigh of relief. "Don't worry about taking clothes or food," she stressed. "There are plenty of supplies where we're going."

"So much for hoarding toilet paper," Jon said under his breath.

Abby shot him a warning look. *Not the time to be messing with me, dude,* she thought. He mouthed *Sorry,* and she continued. "I don't know when we'll be back, but only take the few mementos you can't live without. We have to hurry. The Kruorumbrae will be here soon."

ಬಂಗಚಬಂಗಚಬಂಗಚ

Michal was getting a little freaked out. It seemed much darker than it should have been in the trees, like the moonlight was somehow unable to penetrate the canopy. She kept hearing little scurrying sounds—as if the spider web hadn't been creepy enough. *There had better* not *be rats in here,* she thought.

Obviously Joe was toying with her now, but the joke was on him, because this little game of hide-and-seek was not going to win her affection. He was *this* close to blowing his chance with her, never mind how cute he might be. This was not worth it. She was annoyed, but she was also starting to feel a little scared, and she wasn't even sure why. If Joe came out right now, she might still forgive him. She heard the snap of a twig behind her and twisted in the direction of the sound. "Joe?"

Nothing. No response, no one there, nada.

Now the leaves crackled in front of her—she turned back quickly, the hair rising on the back of her neck. "Joe? Come on Joe—this is *so* not funny." Her voice sounded overly loud as she tried to convince herself there was nothing to fear.

Again, nothing but silence. Even the weird little scurrying sounds seemed to have stopped.

Then, out of the corner of her eye, she spotted movement, and she whirled toward it. "Joe! Stop being such a—" Michal stopped midsentence. There was a young man standing there. His face was gaunt, handsome, and his eyes were dark, charismatically intense. "You're not Joe," she said simply.

"No. I'm not," he replied. He stepped toward her and took her hands, pulling her toward him.

She let him—it didn't occur to her to do anything *but* step into his embrace. As he drew her into his arms, Michal stepped through a mess of trailing brambles, grazing her ankles and shins on the sharp, prickly thorns. They were just scratches, but deep enough to bleed. She didn't feel any pain.

Then, from off to her side, came a low growl. In her trance, Michal turned to find herself face-to-face with a sleek, jet-black panther with a silky pelt and glowing red eyes. It was staring down at her from the fork of a tree. The fur between its shoulder blades was standing on end, and its muscles were tensed as if it was ready to pounce.

"Lucia, dear," the young man purred, "play nice."

The large cat leapt to the ground. Lying on the sand next to where it landed was Joe, his blank, glazed eyes staring up at the night sky, his face pale like the full moon. And then Michal saw blood...so much blood. That was when she started screaming.

ಬಗಬಗಬಗ

Shortly after Michal ventured into the grove, Monroe looked up from writing in the sand and saw hundreds of strange lights. The tiny red, glowing dots were illuminating the hedge, almost as if someone had strung a net of lighted faux holly berries across them. *A bit early for Christmas*, Monroe thought absently, picking at the driftwood log she was sitting on, her mind unable to grasp what she was seeing.

She realized that the lights were accompanied by the sound of scurrying feet, and the noise was getting louder. Whatever Marisol had seen in the bushes was back and had brought friends. Lots of them—and they were coming her way. Monroe stood up, her fight or flight response taking over and telling her that flight was the most reasonable course of action.

Then she heard Michal screaming, and there was no "all systems go"—only a girl frozen and confused by her fear.

ಬಗಬಗಬಗ

Grabbing Monroe's hand, Marisol propelled her into motion, moving her away from the bushes as hundreds of black cats poured fluidly through the branches, except they weren't cats—not quite. They seemed to be, at first, but they moved like liquid and all together as one being—like black oil and smoke at the same time. Then they changed and didn't look like cats at all, but something else, something unreal with gnarled limbs, black spiky fur, and gnashing teeth; something lethal.

All around Marisol, her friends were screaming, running, trying to get away, but the oily smoke was everywhere at once. The only place to avoid the creatures, the only safe place, was the grove, and yet, how could that be, when that was where the screaming began? But Marisol knew that was where they had to go.

Marisol and Monroe burst into the grove, clawing their way through thick vines, plowing through the brambles, moving away from the beach without rational thought. Marisol only knew they had to keep going, had to get away from the thing that was coming, that was consuming everything like a dark, hungry fog.

Ahead of them, more red eyes glowed in the darkness of the grove. Then Marisol saw Michal lying on the ground, her long blond hair splayed out around her, her eyes pleading with them for help, right before she was dragged by her ankles into a tangle of dark brush.

Monroe began to scream. The sound was muffled when something black and furry jumped down from an overhanging branch, straight into her face, knocking her to the ground.

Marisol picked up a driftwood branch, wielding it like a club, and began beating the thing that was on top of her friend. She hit it with all her might, and the creature yelped and scurried away, dragging a long prehensile tail behind it. Carrying the branch in one hand, Marisol pulled Monroe to her feet with the other and helped her run through the grove to a set of stairs etched into the stone retaining wall that bounded Newcastle Beach. Marisol knew that these steps led to the inn's gardens, and hopefully, to safety.

The girls ran as fast as they could. Monroe was a little slower because she was wounded. Marisol could see deep gashes on her shoulders and across her collar bone, but luckily the thing had missed her jugular. The creature's claws, if that's what they were, had sliced her cheek though, and that seemed to be bleeding the most. Monroe seemed to be more in shock than pain, however, and Marisol guessed that the adrenaline coursing through her body was pushing her to keep going. She would feel the pain later.

Up ahead, Marisol saw the familiar lights of the inn's swimming pool, and just beyond that, the lobby. Running over to the pool's guest services cabana, Marisol snatched a towel and helped Monroe apply pressure to her cheek to stop the bleeding. She helped her friend get inside the lobby, and told the front desk staff to call for medical assistance.

"You'll be okay now," Marisol said. "I'll be right back—I have to go help the others."

"Marisol—no!" Monroe cried, reaching for Marisol's hand. "Don't go back out there—please don't! It's still out there!"

Marisol hesitated. She couldn't help but recognize the irony. In spite of all the times Michal had made snide remarks regarding Monroe's intelligence, Marisol had to concede that Monroe was the smart one when it came to common sense and safety. Still, someone had to get back out there and try to save their friends.

Marisol made a decision. "I *have* to, Monroe." She let go of her friend's hand and hefted the heavy piece of driftwood against her shoulder like a baseball bat. As she walked toward the front door of the inn, Marisol looked back once more to reassure Monroe. Then she headed outside, down the inn's front walk, and back onto the sand.

The beach was empty. The bonfire was still going, and a few coolers had been tipped over in the chaos, but no one was there. No people, no monsters, nothing but the full moon lighting the empty expanse of shoreline.

Marisol ventured out onto the sand a little further, hoping to find someone, anyone, alive, dreading a more gruesome discovery. Her terror threatened to paralyze her, making her stomach cramp like it was tied in knots. Taking a deep breath, she tried to force the fear aside and then discovered that she also felt supremely *aware*, all of her senses finely tuned to note every detail of her surroundings. *Probably an adrenaline high,* she reasoned.

The sand was littered with footprints, but it was too loosely packed to determine whether they were made by human feet or not. There were far too many impressions to find a discernible trail leading to someone who might need help.

Marisol studied the dark grove of trees where the trouble had started. She shuddered, thinking about the thing she and Monroe had encountered. Was Michal still in there? And if so, was she even alive? If she was, Marisol might be her only chance for survival, but it seemed like a very, very bad idea to go in there alone, in the dark. Just looking at the grove made her guts squirm. It would be smarter to go back to the inn and get some help rather than trying to find Michal on her own. That was, if there was anything left to find.

"Looking for someone?"

Marisol froze. The voice had come from behind her, somewhere between where she stood on the beach and the safety of the inn. She had no doubt it was not a human voice. Her grasp on the driftwood branch tightened. She turned, slowly.

*No sudden moves*, she thought to herself. *You can't let it see your fear.*

Sitting on its haunches was a creature the size of a German shepherd. It looked much like a lean, black cat except for its disturbingly humanoid face and long, twitching tail. One side of its face looked scarred, as if it had been burned. It was smiling as though it knew a secret. The coy smirk broadened into a Cheshire cat grin, although not quite as mad. Not just yet, anyway.

"Feeling pretty brave tonight, I see," it said. Its breath smelled like rotten meat and sulfur. "Too bad that big ol' stick won't help you. You can hit me all you like, but I think I'll stay around for a while." The creature cocked its head to the side, showing Marisol the large cavity in its skull where her weapon had found its mark. The hole was disappearing, filling in with a mass of black fur.

Marisol's mouth dropped open and the creature's grin grew a little wider. The cat thing chuckled to itself, as if it enjoyed the look of disbelief and horror on her face. She shut her mouth, trying not to show weakness.

The cat got to its feet and walked a slow circle around her.

Marisol followed the creature with her eyes and held tightly to the driftwood branch. Her weapon might be useless in the long term, but it could still buy her a little time—*that* she could see very clearly.

"My, my, my," the thing purred, looking her up and down. "Little Marisol...all grown up now, aren't you?"

Marisol didn't answer. She didn't know how this thing knew her name, but she had a feeling that responding wouldn't help, and the creature couldn't care less if she *did* answer. It had a story it wanted to tell, and she was going to hear it whether she wanted to or not.

"Oh yes, Marisol. I know you. I know you very well. Are you still afraid of the dark?" The creature waited for a response.

Marisol held her tongue.

"Not much of a chatterbox, are you? I'll bet you can scream real well though—oh yes, I'll bet those lungs are *niiice* and healthy. You used to scream so well when you were scared, back when I lived under your bed."

Marisol's eyes widened in shock and recognition.

The thing smiled—*that* was the reaction it had wanted.

Marisol quickly composed herself and tried to make her face look expressionless.

"Oh, such fun we had! Your pretty madre loved her stories, didn't she? *My* personal favorite was El Cucuy—she'd always tell you that story when you'd beg, 'Please, please, please just one more glass of water,' before beddie-bye. You were *so* annoying. She'd tell that one just to shut you up. Then you'd lay awake for hours, so scared that I was going to pop up like a jack-in-the-box. And sometimes I *did!*" The Cheshire cat grin was full-on crazy now, those red eyes swirling with madness.

Images from a half-forgotten nightmare flashed in Marisol's mind. *No, no, no,* she thought, shaking her head. *It wasn't real, it wasn't real...*

As if reading her mind, the thing continued. "Oh, but it *was* real. And where's madre now, my *dulce*? Did you finally manage to annoy her so much she left for good?"

"Shut up, shut up, SHUT UP!!" Marisol shouted, clocking the thing in the head with her weapon, knocking it off its feet. She started running toward the inn.

The creature was back on its feet in seconds, pursuing her. "Yes, oh, *yes*," the thing growled hungrily. *"Run, run, run, fast as you can..."*

ဆက္ဆက္ဆက္

The Browns' minivan was almost to the old mansion when Jon noticed something was amiss. A terrified girl was racing toward the Newcastle Beach Inn. Something was chasing her. It was difficult to see what it was exactly—the dark form seemed to meld with the shadows so that it was almost invisible. Jon didn't need a positive ID to guess what it was and what it wanted. He had encountered that kind of monster before. But he did recognize the girl.

"That's Marisol!" Jon shouted. "One of the Shadows is after her!" He could see Marisol try for the inn's front door and then change directions, veering back to the sidewalk. She leapt away from the Shadow's long claws, and it slammed into the door. As the blur of black resumed its chase, Jon could see that a long crack had formed in the carved wood. "Stop the car!" he yelled, grasping the handle to open the van's sliding door.

"Dad! Stop—please!" Abby pleaded. The van skidded to a halt as Abby's father hit the brakes. Abby looked around the vehicle, which was already full with her family, David, Cael, and Jon and his mom. "Make room guys—she's coming with us."

ဆက္ဆက္ဆက္

Marisol saw the van jerk to a stop, and was amazed to watch the door slide wide open. Jon was waving at her, frantically shouting her name. She flew toward him and threw herself into the van, landing on his lap with relative grace as he yanked the door closed, the creature still in pursuit.

Abby shouted, "She's in, Dad. Hit it!"

Abby's father hit the gas.

"Are you okay?" Jon asked, looking her over.

"I am now. You have impeccable timing," Marisol huffed, trying to catch her breath. She put her arms around his neck, relieved to be safe, for now, at least. The creature was still out there. She remembered the feeling of its hot, putrid breath on her skin, its snapping jaws inches from her heels as it chased her. Her heart pounded as wildly as a prey animal's thinking about it. Because that's what she was to that creature. Prey.

She looked around at the others in the vehicle, wedged tightly into the minivan's middle and back seats. "Hey, Abby...David," she said slowly, still in shock. She felt her whole body trembling. Apparently Jon did too. He stared at her, a question in his eyes. She managed a weak smile and wrapped her arms tighter around him, trying to stop shaking.

"Hey Sol," David said from his position between Abby and a kid in the back. "Welcome to the crazy van."

"Thanks," Marisol said, swallowing, trying to slow the beating of her heart. "You saw the giant cat monster chasing me too, right? Or am I the crazy one?"

"Yeah. We saw it," David assured her. "That's why we're all crowded in here like it's a clown car—we're trying to get away from those things."

"Well, they were all over the beach, and everyone was running away, screaming and freaked out, but they're gone now, except for the one that was after me," Marisol said.

"Any idea where they went?" Jon asked.

"None, which is really scary, because I think they eat people...they must have gotten Joe, and I saw one drag Michal into the grove. And one of them wounded Monroe really badly—but she's safe now in the inn. That thing came after me when I went back out to look for the others. Wherever those creatures went, we should head in the opposite direction and get help," Marisol finished in a rush, finally taking a breath.

The woman sitting beside Jon was thin with tousled, dark, shoulder-length hair and Jon's brown eyes. The look on her face seemed to be one of shock or horror. Maybe both. Marisol was painfully aware of how crazy she must sound. She turned to the woman and held out her hand. "Hello. I'm Marisol Cassidy, by the way."

"Nice to meet you," the woman replied, shaking Marisol's hand. "I'm Jon's mom, Blanca Reyes. Are you sure you're okay? That creature didn't hurt you?"

"No, but it would have killed me, I think, if it had the chance. Thanks for the lift," Marisol quipped, her voice quivering a little. She tried a smile again, willing herself to calm down.

"Anytime," David replied. He seemed annoyingly calm, as if homicidal cat monsters were yesterday's news. Marisol stared at him in disbelief. "So, introductions...Abby's dad is driving, this is her mom and brother, and this is Cael." David gestured to the man riding shotgun, but didn't elaborate on who Cael was.

"Hello," she said politely.

The man seemed tense, his eyes focused only on the road ahead. He didn't even turn around to acknowledge her. *Not a big talker, apparently.* He seemed to be wearing some kind of armor, as were Jon, Abby, and David. *Weird,* Marisol thought.

The others nodded their welcome as Abby's father drove through the open gates of the tall stone fence encircling the old Spanish colonial mansion.

*Why are we going here?* Marisol wondered, taking in her surroundings with wide eyes. Although the old house was right across from the inn, people avoided it like the plague. Supposedly it was haunted, and she was pretty sure there'd be no one there to help them or the others she'd left behind.

As they passed the ruins of an overgrown garden and a reflecting pool, Marisol looked back. The creature that had somehow escaped from her nightmares and chased her down the street had stopped at the estate's iron gates and was sitting nonchalantly on its haunches. It wasn't following them.

*What's it waiting for?* Marisol pondered. She could see those red eyes glowing in the darkness. "What *is* that thing?" she asked.

"Long story," Jon answered, "but here's the quick and dirty version. It's a shape-shifting monster called a Shadow."

"A *Blood* Shadow," Abby added. "A Kruorumbrae."

"It knew my name," Marisol murmured, with fear in her voice. As she glanced behind again, she saw that the terrifying creature still remained at the gate line. It was watching, staring, as if it had all the time in the world to retrieve its prey.

# FIGHT OR FLIGHT

"**W**hy is that car upside down?" Marisol asked as Abby's father continued up the driveway past an overturned SUV. Mr. Brown parked the minivan by the mansion's front door.

"Those shadow things have already been here. I don't want to weird you out, but you're going to have to come with us," Jon said.

"I'm already weirded out," Marisol replied, shifting uncomfortably on Jon's lap. Now that she knew she was sitting next to his mother, she felt a little awkward. She hoped Ms. Reyes was okay with a girl using her son as a chair.

On the other hand, Jon didn't seem self-conscious about the seating arrangement at all. In fact, he seemed quite happy about Marisol being so close and had wrapped his arms around her waist.

Marisol looked at him. "It's been kind of a strange night. Where are you guys going?"

"Somewhere...less dangerous than here. Newcastle Beach isn't safe for us anymore," Jon explained. He tugged open the door of the van and Marisol slid off his lap, exiting the vehicle.

She looked at the overturned car, shuddered, and crossed her arms, feeling a chill more from fear than the cool autumn air. She turned to see Jon step out of the van and offer his arm to his mother as she followed him.

*A gentleman.* Marisol smiled.

"We need to leave town fast. Do you trust me?" Jon asked, looking into Marisol's eyes.

She stared back at him—his gaze was intense. "Yes," she said, uncrossing her arms. "My parents are both out of the country so they won't even know I'm gone. But what about my friends? We have to get help for them."

"*We're* the reason the Kruorumbrae are here. They're looking for us. Once we leave, they'll follow, and Newcastle Beach will be safe again—for now, at least." Marisol shivered, remembering her earlier thought that her sense of safety was only temporary. "Come with me," Jon pleaded. "There's no time to tell you everything yet, but I'll fill you in as soon as I can." He took Marisol's hand and she let him lead her into the dark depths of the mansion.

The others grabbed their bags and followed them into a hall with one tall, gilded mirror. The rest of the place was a dump. Around the mirror were the remains of other mirrors, all shattered, their glass shards scattered across the floor.

Marisol looked up to see that the dome in the ceiling had been destroyed as well.

The man David had introduced as Cael took charge. "Quickly, now—David, you and Abby take her family through, and I will follow with the others."

David nodded and grabbed the small black suitcase Abby's mother was holding. He held out his arm for her and she took it, timidly. She looked curious and frightened at the same

46

time. "It will be all right, Mrs. Brown," David said. "I promise." They stepped through the glass and disappeared.

"Whoa," breathed Marisol. "What the hell?" She looked over at Blanca Reyes. "Sorry, Ms. Reyes."

"No, it's okay. I was just thinking the *exact* same thing," Jon's mom said, smiling. "Oh, and please, call me Blanca. 'Ms. Reyes' sounds like an old lady."

"You got it," Marisol grinned.

Abby stood between her father and brother and took their hands, guiding them through the mirror.

"Jon, what *is* that?" Marisol asked.

"It's a door to a kind of parallel universe," Jon said.

"Ah," Marisol nodded. "And we're going through it?"

"Yep," Jon replied.

"And we'll be safe from those shadow things?" Marisol asked.

"Yep," he repeated.

"All right then." She took his hand and Blanca's. "Let's do this."

"I like this girl, Jon," Blanca grinned.

"Me too," he agreed. "Let's get out of here." At that, he led them through the portal.

&#8498;&#x2063;&#x204A;

Cael took one last look around to make sure they weren't being followed. Although he was certain Tierney would use the silver hand mirror to return to Cai Terenmare, he didn't want the dark lord using the Caislucis portal. He stepped through the glass. On the other side, he saw Eulalia hugging David, Abby, and Jon fiercely, and then greeting the newcomers.

He felt his breath catch. He'd known her for so long and yet she still managed to take his breath away. He could hardly believe he was home with this stunning woman and that she was finally ready to be with him. For the first time since she'd told him she was marrying Ardal, he felt a sense of peace.

When Eulalia saw Cael, she went to him, placed her hands on his cheeks, pulled his face to hers, and kissed him.

"I promised I would return them safely," he said, feeling an uncharacteristically wide smile spreading across his face.

"And you delivered," she returned, kissing him again.

"Marisol," David began, "allow me to introduce my biological mother, the Dowager Queen, Eulalia. Cael is a knight of the highest honor—the head knight, if you will, in charge of protecting our kingdom."

Marisol hesitated, nodded to Cael, and then curtseyed to Eulalia. "I'm honored to meet you, Your Majesty."

"Welcome to Cai Terenmare, Marisol." Eulalia smiled warmly and took Marisol's hands in greeting. "I hope you will be very comfortable here."

"Thank you," Marisol replied.

"Come," Eulalia said. "Let us go to the banquet hall. There is much to speak about." She turned to Cael and took his arm, leading her guests away from the mirror. Her guards returned to their posts, securing the portal.

ಬಂದ ಬಂದ ಬಂದ

"So, David," Marisol whispered as they followed the queen. "When you say 'our' kingdom, and the queen's your mom, that means you are—"

"Yep," David replied. "I'm king. They call me the Solas Beir here, but essentially, it means king."

"Okay..." Marisol said, nodding slowly.

"It's weird, isn't it?" David asked. He looked unsure of himself, a strange contrast with the mannerisms of the confident boy she'd known growing up.

"Yeah...but like I told Jon, it's been kind of a crazy night," Marisol said. "It started out so normal, hanging at the beach with our friends, you know? And then, everything just hit the fan—there were monsters everywhere, attacking everyone." She grabbed David's arm. "David—I think Michal might be dead."

David stopped walking and looked at her. "I'm so sorry."

"Me too. She wasn't always the nicest person, but she *was* a person. She didn't deserve that," Marisol frowned. She suddenly felt overwhelmed by a sense of loss, thinking about all the people who had been sitting around the bonfire, friends who might have suffered Michal's fate.

"No, she didn't. Tell me more about Monroe. What happened before you left her at the inn?"

Marisol choked back a sob and cleared her throat, fighting the urge to cry. "That thing that was chasing me cut her up pretty badly. She'll be okay eventually, at least physically. Emotionally, I don't know," she added. "That shadow monster—it knew things about me...I used to have these terrible nightmares as a kid. Now I wonder if they were nightmares or if there really was something in my room with me."

"I don't know—maybe it *was* with you somehow, in your dreams. The Kruorumbrae—they're tricky. And they lie," David told her.

"Did you ever have dreams like that?" Marisol asked.

"Once—a long time ago," David replied. "I don't really remember—and I think my experiences were different from the other kids in the neighborhood."

"Oh. Yeah, I guess so." Marisol looked around at the stone walls and vaulted ceiling of the corridor leading to the banquet hall. Colorful silk banners lined the walls. "How long have you known about this place?"

"Not long. I was introduced a few days ago, when Abby told me about it. After the Autumn Ball I came here with her and Jon," David said.

"Ohhh," Marisol turned to Jon. He was looking at her anxiously, probably because she had almost started crying. She smiled to reassure him. "So *that's* why you didn't call me."

Jon smiled back. "Yeah, sorry about that. I was a little busy."

She kissed Jon's cheek. "Forgiven."

&#8526;&#8450;&#8419;&#8526;&#8450;&#8419;&#8526;&#8450;&#8419;

Cael knew Eulalia was right—there *was* much to speak about. They needed to help the newcomers make sense of their new surroundings.

Abby's family and Jon's mother sat down at the long, elaborately carved banquet table looking dazed, glancing around the room as if they couldn't believe their eyes.

Cael studied the girl they'd rescued on the way to the portal. She seemed to be adjusting better than the others, suspending her disbelief and accepting the strange turn her life had taken. He was impressed. He settled into the chair beside Eulalia as servers moved about, providing a meal. Then he took her hand. "You and I need to discuss the implications of

Tierney's escape from the Wasteland and formulate a plan to stop him now that he is free."

"Indeed," she replied. "You saw evidence of his return?"

"I am afraid so," Cael said in a low voice. He nodded toward Marisol. "His minions attacked the girl and her friends."

"It will be difficult to protect our world from discovery by the humans," Eulalia noted solemnly.

"I suspect Tierney will return to Cai Terenmare soon," Cael predicted. "Even he can appreciate the need to keep the existence of our world a secret."

"I hope so," Eulalia said. "Still, I shall advise Riordan Buchan to stay here with his family a while longer, since the Kruorumbrae are running amok. He would not dare risk his family's safety."

"Where are the Buchans?" David asked, overhearing the mention of their name.

Eulalia turned to him. "They are with Gorman in the library. They will be happy to hear you have returned."

Riordan Buchan and his family had agreed to become guardians of the portal now that he had inherited the mansion.

Gorman, the small, earthy indigo man who served as the kingdom's historian and librarian, was teaching Riordan, Cassandra, and their children about the history of the Buchan clan and what might be done to protect the portal once they had dealt with the Blood Shadows.

Cael steered the conversation back to the topic that was most pressing in his mind. "It seems unlikely that Tierney will attempt a breach of the castle via the mansion's portal—he is not a fool who would enter the fortress by smashing a hive of bees. Instead, he will use the silver hand mirror to cross over and then gather his troops, who have been scattered across the kingdom since the time of his arrest. I predict that once his forces are united, he will launch his attack. This means that we must organize our own forces and strengthen them with support from the oracles at the outer edges of the realm."

"Yes," Eulalia agreed, "but that will not be easy." Then she turned to address the newcomers. "Although David is Solas Beir and the rightful heir to his father's throne, he has been raised as a human, and this has undermined his authority. Some consider him an outsider with much to learn."

At this statement, David winced, but his mother gave him a reassuring smile.

"Those of the Light who reside in the region nearest to our home have welcomed him," Eulalia continued. "He has already made strides in winning their hearts by presenting himself with humility, promising to serve his people. Many of them attended the coronation." Cael noted the way she gazed at David, her pride for her son shining brightly in her eyes. "After so many years of waiting for his return, they would not have missed the crowning of the Solas Beir. But for those who did not witness his return, some convincing of his valid claim as heir will be necessary. Faith might be a virtue, but there will always be those in the kingdom who won't believe until they see with their own eyes."

Abby's parents and little brother, Blanca, and Marisol sat with furrowed brows, trying to process the new information as they listened intently to the queen.

"And how far does the kingdom reach?" inquired Marisol.

Eulalia squeezed Cael's hand, looking to him to explain the geography of Cai Terenmare.

He nodded at her and turned to the others. "The ivory castle in which you are seated is called Caislucis. It is perched on a cliff overlooking the Western Sea and surrounded by ancient forests. Caislucis is also the dwelling of the Solas Beir's council and other key leaders and advisors. It is a hub for politics and the symbolic center of the kingdom, even though it is not the geographic center of the vast continent of Cai Terenmare. This castle also houses a great library and serves as the kingdom's university. Along the edges of the forest are the Great Plains, where the lives of those in the Light mirror the world of your preindustrial human ancestors. The plains are dotted with small farming and ranching communities."

"It is within these humble villages," interjected Eulalia, "that David's work will start. There, he will begin proving his worth and winning the loyalty of his irresolute subjects by using his power to help those in need."

"Then, there is the matter of the oracles, whose realms lay on the outer boundaries of the kingdom," Cael remarked.

"Yes," confirmed the queen. "During the reigns of past Solas Beirs, the four oracles have either been loyal to the Solas Beir or impartial in matters of those in the Light. The oracles are like forces of nature, and there is a mutual respect and elemental balance between their power and that of the Solas Beir. However, as the power of the Kruorumbrae has increased, this balance has eroded, and relationships with the oracles have become precarious. There is no guarantee that they will show loyalty to a new Solas Beir, much less one who has not lived in their world."

"I believe David would do well in meeting with the Northern Oracle first," Cael advised.

"I know this is a lot of information to absorb," David said, scanning the faces of Abby's parents and Jon's mother.

Cael took a moment to observe the newcomers. They did look befuddled. Blanca gave Jon a questioning look. Jon tried to reassure his mother by putting his arm around her.

"It's all right," Marisol said. "Keep talking. We'll catch up." She caught Cael's eye and smiled. He nodded and returned her smile, encouraged by her response.

"The Northern Oracle lives in the isolated northern region of the kingdom," Cael continued. "She and her colony have little contact with others, but they have been consistently loyal to the Light, dedicated to the pursuit of discipline and self-reliance through a stoic lifestyle and edification through the ancient texts. She guided my fellow warriors and me in our search for the Sign of the Throne, the symbol of the Light that was the key to David's return. She also helped me vanquish the Western Oracle, a narcissistic monster with a blood thirst rivaling that of her serpent-limbed daughters, the sirens.

"Like the Blood Shadows, the sirens preyed on those in the Light and were a constant threat to those living in the sea. They murdered my comrades. They almost killed me as well, but I was able to destroy them. With the assistance of the merpeople, who had fallen victim to the sirens for many generations, I survived and was able to return the Solas Beir's sigil to Caislucis." Cael studied the faces of his listeners. They still wore expressions of disbelief, but at least they seemed less shocked by their surroundings.

"The sea king's daughter, Nerine, saw Cael safely home," Eulalia added.

"Because of her kindness and her loyalty to the kingdom, I recommend her for the post left vacant by the demise of the former Western Oracle," Cael suggested. "Nerine attended

David's coronation and, politically, it cannot hurt his cause to have one of his own in a powerful position."

"I agree," David replied. "Is this something I need to run past the court council?"

"If you wish, I can speak to them on your behalf," Cael said. "I am sure they will agree, and we can then send word to Nerine regarding the nomination. If she accepts, she will gain power over the seas stretching from the beaches below our castle to the cliffs along the Eastern Sea, where the Eastern Oracle holds court in his city."

"Thank you, Cael," David said. "I can think of no one better than Nerine for that role, and I appreciate your recommendation to me and your offer to speak about it to the council. Please move forward on that."

Cael bowed his head respectfully. "Yes, Solas Beir."

"I am concerned about the loyalty of the Eastern Oracle," Eulalia divulged. "It is rumored that those in the Light and those of the Shadows dwell side by side in his city. I do not understand how that can be possible."

The realm of the Eastern Oracle was located far from the western coast, and it was a stark contrast to the pastoral communities surrounding Caislucis. Separated from Caislucis by an enormous desert, not as vast as the Wasteland, but just as barren—and actually referred to as *the Barren* by locals—the city of the Eastern Oracle would be difficult to travel to. David's father had closed all the portals within Cai Terenmare, as well as those leading to the human world, and communication had been limited. Eulalia had never met the current Eastern Oracle. As a general rule, only the Solas Beir met with oracles, and the Eastern Oracle was a pious traditionalist.

"Even with the extraordinary circumstances of the assassination of David's father, the Eastern Oracle was not willing to meet with me or any of the ambassadors I had hoped to send, because I am a woman. There has been almost no communication with the east since Ardal's death," Eulalia explained. She looked at David. "I am worried that David will have great difficulty winning his loyalty, even though he holds the crown."

"Perhaps if David gained the support of the Southern Oracle first, that would influence the Eastern Oracle to join our cause," Cael mused.

"Perhaps," Eulalia replied. The Southern Oracle was more of a wild card. Like the Western Oracle, he was rumored to be narcissistic and loyal to no one. "He seems unwilling to engage in the political conflict between those in the Light and the Shadows. Like the Northern Oracle, the Southern Oracle and his people are isolated, but not by distance and harsh, frozen terrain. He lives in the center of a thick rainforest, one with sprawling foliage that will make the journey treacherous, if not deadly, since many of the plants guarding his village are poisonous, carnivorous, or both. Legends describe horrific beasts and phantoms lurking in that dark forest, and as is often the case in this world, such stories have a nasty tendency to be true."

"Great," David muttered. "Well, I guess I'm up for a challenge."

Abby squeezed his hand. "Me too."

Cael glanced at Abby's mother, who looked horrified. "Fear not," he assured her. "I will travel with the Solas Beir and your daughter to ensure their safety."

Bethany Brown nodded, but did not look any less worried. She gave Abby a stern look that said they would be having a discussion later.

Cael found he could not blame her for worrying, considering Abby had almost died once already.

"I visited the Southern Oracle's village many years ago, when Ardal was still alive," Eulalia said. "Traveling by portal, we avoided the dangers of the rainforest. I enjoyed the warm hospitality of his people, who embrace the dangers of their forest, revere them even, and in doing so, value their lives more. I remember the Southern Oracle as charismatic and full of life, and I suspect that he holds the same philosophy as his people. Perhaps that is why he seems loath to get involved in politics."

"Indeed." Cael nodded in agreement. "Choosing sides comes with serious consequences. But if David can win his loyalty, it will be a great victory for the Light."

ꝏꝿꝏꝿꝏꝿ

As David prepared for his journeys to the oracles and waited for word from Nerine, he began his training in earnest. As the new Solas Beir, and with the magical powers that came with his heritage, he had already gained experience with his abilities to fly and heal, but needed to learn about politics and combat. Eventually David would be able to weaken his enemies sufficiently so that he could end them by simply speaking a word, though this would take much time and dedication to his training.

Until he gained that level of mastery, however, it was time for school—and not just for David. Abby had much to learn about being a c'aislingaer, slang for cai aislingstraid—one who walks in dreams. And since she, Jon, and Marisol were not about to be left behind when David traveled to the outer realms of his kingdom, they too had work to do. They met with Gorman to learn about the history and politics of the kingdom, and David and Abby each had individual sessions with Eulalia to learn more about their abilities. David met often with Obelia and the other six council members, learning on the job, as it were.

&#8440;&#1011;&#8440;&#1011;&#8440;&#1011;

At the large, round table in the room adjacent to the Great Hall, David met with the council to discuss the latest news of the realm.

Obelia scanned a piece of parchment before addressing the Solas Beir, Cael, and her fellow council members. "Solas Beir, reports have been coming in about several villages in the Great Plains being ravaged by Shadows. With rumors of Tierney's escape, those in Darkness are growing bold again."

David sighed. "It seems there's no rest for the weary."

Fedor of the Great Plains spoke up. "Your Majesty, I believe it is imperative that you meet with the plainspeople soon if you hope to win their trust."

David looked at Cael. "What do you think, Cael?"

"I agree," he responded, "but I would be hesitant to have you put yourself at risk again without combat training."

As Solas Beir, David didn't need Cael's approval. He could have gone anyway, but he trusted Cael's judgment and submitted to his guidance.

"All right," David said. "When can we start?"

&#8440;&#1011;&#8440;&#1011;&#8440;&#1011;

The more Marisol came to know Cael, the more she admired him. Cael supervised the combat training himself and coached her, David, Abby, and Jon on military strategies. He was pleased with their progress, and praised them often. Cael seemed to understand that while David could easily break the class curve by virtue of being Solas Beir, Marisol and his other human students also needed encouragement. He had high expectations, but he was fair. He recognized hard work, and that his pupils understood what was at stake.

For a girl who had shied away from conflict her whole life, Marisol found that she was quite adept at the logic involved with strategies for battle, and not too shabby with the hand-to-hand stuff either.

When she knocked Jon flat on the training lawn—again—Marisol apologized. "Sorry! It's only because I took mixed martial arts when I was a kid." He was sprawled on the ground, trying to catch his breath after getting the wind knocked out of him. "My mom was a little paranoid about the paparazzi," she explained.

"No—don't be sorry," Jon said, looking up at her and rubbing his jaw. "My aching pride and swollen face aside, it's kinda hot to have a girlfriend who kicks butt."

"Am I?" she asked, extending her arm to help him up.

Jon brushed himself off. "Hot? Two words—last one's 'yes.'"

Marisol laughed. "No, you ginormous dork. Your girlfriend."

"Uh," he faltered. "I actually thought we'd already established that, considering the, um, quality time we've been spending together. Sorry—I assumed…"

"Well, you never actually asked me," she pointed out, putting her hands on her hips.

"Oh. Easy enough," Jon countered. "*Will* you be my girlfriend? Don't leave me hanging—please say yes." He flashed his big, brown, pleading-puppy eyes.

Marisol grinned. "Two words—last one's 'yes.'"

೫ಆ೫ಆ೫ಆ

David was surprised to learn that aerial combat might come into play. He *had* been rather pleased with himself when he learned to fly on his first official day as Solas Beir, but he had assumed that the purpose of that power was simply transportation. Fighting while in flight seemed a bit more complicated. Erela, the tall, enigmatic councilwoman with billowing, white wings, volunteered to train him.

David had thought of Cael as stoic, but working with Erela brought new meaning to the concept. Cael would never be mistaken for a joker, and he was not known for his winning smile (although David was seeing a few more smiles these days, thanks to the time Cael was spending with Eulalia). Nevertheless, Cael *was* capable of emotion—he had just been trained to keep it in check. David wasn't so sure about Erela. She was intelligent, but seemed to have a strong moral compass that lacked in compassion. She noted when he did well in his exercises, but there was an emotional flatness to her feedback— you couldn't exactly call it praise. It was simply information.

Her response to his failings was more difficult to discern. It was almost like there was a dark undercurrent there, but whatever it was, it was secured under lock and key. Her grey eyes were those of a cold, calculating killer—not because she was cruel, but because she *was* a predator.

Gorman had told him a story about gryphons—those proud eagles with the bodies of lions. They were symbolic of nobility, strength, and protection, and renowned for being judicious. No one would mistake them for being cuddly. David thought Erela might be like that, only a different species of predator. The word "valkyrie" came to mind, but even that didn't seem to be the correct classification for her. He didn't know *what* she was, or how she had come to serve on his council. He was certain, however, that it was better that she be for him than against him.

ಬಂಛಬಂಛಬಂಛ

Whereas Erela was unemotional, Fergal was warm and engaging, showering his students with passionate praise. Cael recruited the tiny aquatic faery to teach fencing. His enthusiasm was incorrigible—David and his fellow trainees couldn't help but enjoy the dance of the sword with him cheering them on.

Fergal was not to be underestimated. The stories of how he had valiantly assisted in the Solas Beir's return made him a living legend, and with his lightning quick swordplay, they were not tales anyone would doubt. Fergal was fearless, and above all else, held himself to the highest standards of honor. He had the soul of a true knight, even though he was the smallest soldier in the kingdom and resembled an amphibian—Fergal's skin was a mottled green and his hands and feet were webbed.

Exhausted from their latest whirlwind sparring session, Fergal and his students lay on their backs in the grass, gazing up into the gnarled branches of an ancient tree. Sunlight filtered through leaves that gently turned on the breeze, dotting their faces with dancing, botanical shadows.

"Fergal," David said, tucking his hands behind his head, "when you shape-shift, you become a frog, right?"

"Yes, Your Majesty. So I do," Fergal replied.

"How does that work?" David questioned.

"I beg your pardon, Sire, but that is a strange question," Fergal remarked. He propped himself up on his elbows. "I never gave it much thought. It seems perfectly natural—I will myself to change and I do. Simple as that."

"Can you show us?" Abby asked. She sat up and crossed her legs, staring at the faery expectantly.

"Of course," the small faery nodded. Standing up, he straightened his periwinkle waistcoat, plucking a stray blade of grass from the jacquard silk. He blinked his large, gold-ringed black eyes and shivered slightly. His faery form melted away instantly, lingering as ash in the air, leaving a tiny, chirping frog. Abby held out her hand and he hopped into her palm. Then he blinked his eyes again, his body quivered slightly, and the process reversed, leaving Fergal standing in the frog's place.

"Brilliant!" Jon exclaimed.

Marisol applauded, a look of childlike delight lighting up her face.

Fergal took a dignified bow. "Thank you." He leapt gracefully from Abby's palm to return to his place under the tree.

"That was amazing!" Abby said. "So, I've been meaning to ask you, Fergal...Eulalia becomes a white doe, and I know that white symbolizes royalty here. Is her doe white because she's a noble?"

"A keen observation," Fergal smiled. "The answer is yes. Eulalia is of noble heritage, and all the members of her family have had white totems."

"But what about Eulalia's sister, Lucia?" Marisol asked. "Isn't her panther black?"

Fergal nodded gravely. "Indeed. But this was not always so. Lucia once had the ability to become a powerful white panther. After she feasted with Tierney, she grew in strength and power, but her totem changed," he answered. "This is not to say, however, that all the black-colored animals you find in Cai Terenmare belong to the Darkness. The ravens of Caislucis, as you know, are creatures of the Light." Fergal turned to David. "As heir to the throne, your father was born to nobility as well, of course. Your father's spirit bear was white, and your form, whatever that may be, will be white also."

"So the last Solas Beir became a polar bear?" Jon asked.

"No, not a polar bear," Abby answered. "A spirit bear— it's a type of black bear with white fur that was revered by the indigenous people of Canada."

"Know-it-all," Jon smirked. "And how do you know this?"

"My fellow know-it-all Ciaran told me about it," Abby said to Jon. She turned to Marisol. "He's five and he *really* likes animals."

Fergal chuckled, nodding in agreement. It was no secret he was very fond of the Buchan children. "I too have heard a few of Ciaran's animal stories," he smiled. "They are quite informative."

"Oh, all right—I take it back," Jon said. "Ciaran is not a know-it-all."

Abby ignored Jon and continued. "Anyway, Ciaran's dad is into legends and culture. Riordan told me that across the mythology of our world, white animals are often considered sacred, and it's supposed to be good luck to see one."

"I concur," Fergal said. "Although not every white animal in your world is one of us disguised in spirit form. Often, white animals in your world simply lack pigment. Just as not every black cat is evil, contrary to human superstition. Not that the superstition is not at times grounded in truth, as you all have witnessed from your own encounters with the Kruorumbrae."

"But then, most of you shift into something that looks like the regular, naturally colored form of an animal, like your frog?" David asked.

"Correct. All the better to blend in, no?" Fergal gave David a sly wink.

"Very clever, my friend. You just want to keep us on our toes," David smiled.

Fergal grinned and leapt to his feet, brandishing his sword. "It is all part of my secret plan to make better swordsmen of you. En garde, Solas Beir."

## C'AISLINGAER

Abby was dreaming. She had always had vivid dreams, but in Cai Terenmare, her dreams had taken on a quality that made it difficult to know the difference between her visions and reality.

In her dream, she was running from something dark, but she felt so small, like she was running on tiny legs. As fast as she might be, she could never outrun the gathering darkness that loomed over her like a storm. Her vision was blurred as if there were a dark fog around her, and she began to cough as thick black smoke filled her lungs. She was suffocating on some kind of evil vapor. Then, out of the darkness came a shape filled with light, and the smoke began to clear. It was a white lion. "David," she said, and woke up.

ജ‍ഓ‍ജ‍ഓ‍ജ‍ഓ

In his room, David was also dreaming. "Abby," he whispered, and reached for her in his sleep.

ജ‍ഓ‍ജ‍ഓ‍ജ‍ഓ

Sitting up, Abby looked around her room. Her nightmare had been terrifying, but the image that stayed with her was the lion—she had felt such a sense of peace about him, that he was powerful and good. *Could it be him?* she thought. She didn't know for sure if the lion was David's totem, but something about the way the lion moved reminded her of David's presence and the peace she felt when he was near.

Her thought was interrupted by something rustling. It startled her at first, but then, more curious than afraid, she got out of bed to investigate. The sound seemed to be coming from her balcony.

As Abby passed under the ivory arch into the crisp night air, she could smell the ocean in the breeze. Perched on the carved marble railing of her balcony was a black shape. Two eyes rimmed in gold peered at her from the darkness.

"Brarn," she whispered.

The raven nodded as if in acknowledgment and flew to her outstretched hands. She stroked his feathers affectionately and brought him into her room. "How did you get here?" Abby asked, thinking he wouldn't answer, but asking just the same.

The raven cocked his head at her and she laughed.

"Never mind," Abby said. "Oh sorry, I mean, 'nevermore.' If I put you down on my chair, will you still be here when I wake up in the morning?"

He answered with another cock of his head, so she put him down on the wooden-spindled chair beside her bed. "All right. Good night, Brarn. See you in the morning."

"Morning," Brarn croaked in his raspy voice. "Good night."

"Exactly," Abby murmured sleepily, pulling the warm blankets back up to her shoulders.

He was still there when she woke several hours later, and she brought him downstairs to the banquet room to show the others.

Eulalia, Nysa, and Fergal seemed especially happy to see him. "I am glad he has come home," Eulalia said. "I was worried about him staying in your world."

"Me too," Abby replied. "How *did* he get here?"

"Ravens have always had the uncanny ability to transcend the boundaries of our worlds, so long as a portal is open," Eulalia explained.

"So now that we restored one, he's back in business," Abby concluded.

"It appears so," Eulalia agreed, smiling.

Brarn had joined Fergal and Nysa in sitting on top of the breakfast table. They communed as old friends, sharing the meal without needing to say anything at all.

ဆက်ဆက်ဆက်

"I think I had a dream about you last night," David said.

Abby and David were sitting on an ornately carved wooden bench outside Eulalia's chambers, waiting to meet with her for a discussion on dreamwalking. Eulalia thought it would be helpful for them to practice walking in their dreams together, in preparation for their upcoming journeys.

"I don't remember all of it," David began, "but it seemed like you were very frightened of something—you were running—and then I reached for you and told you everything would be okay."

"That was what I dreamed about too! Well, it was something very similar...do you think we made a connection?" Abby asked.

"Could be," he said, slipping his arm around her. "Do you remember any more of your dream?"

She nodded. "There was this black darkness that was coming for me, and it was all around me, like smoke. I was trying to run from it, but it was choking me."

"Ugh—sounds horrible," David grimaced.

"It was," Abby confirmed. "But then everything was okay because you came to me and pushed the darkness away. Well, I *think* it was you—it felt like your spirit—I think I saw you in your animal form."

"Really? That's awesome!" David's face lit up with excitement. "Tell me I was something fierce, and not pathetic—like a tiny mouse. Or a hamster."

Abby smiled slyly. "Something fierce, huh?"

"Yes, please." He had a hopeful look in his eyes.

"Well, I'm very sorry to disappoint you, but you were a..." She paused for effect.

"What? What was I?" David asked. He looked worried.

"You were a weasel."

"What?!" His mouth dropped open in surprise, and then he frowned. "That's not cool."

Abby shrugged. "Sorry, kid, I don't write the future, I just see and say." She patted his hand sympathetically. "On the bright side, weasels *are* pretty fierce, aren't they? Or is that wolverines? You were definitely weasel-*ish* though—very, very tiny and rodentlike. Actually, now that I think about it, maybe you were a ferret. I saw one in a pet store once. It seemed friendly."

David stared at her. "You have *got* to be kidding me."

Abby grinned. "Totally am."

"Really?" The hopeful look returned to his eyes.

"Really," she said, nodding. "I saw a white lion."

"Now *that* is wicked cool." David smiled to himself.

Abby laughed and playfully punched his arm. "Yeah, dude. That's *wicked* fierce."

"You little tease." David reached for her, and she slid away from him, giggling. "And then you make fun of me?" He scooted toward her and she tried to escape, but she was laughing too hard. He caught her and pulled her back to his side of the bench, then scooped her onto his lap, pinning her against his chest. "There. That's better. Now, to think of a punishment for your impudence..."

Abby tried to wriggle free and gave up. His strong arms were like bands of steel. "Are you going to torture me?" She tried to look repentant, but could tell by his knowing smile that he wasn't buying it.

"Hmm, there's a fun thought," David said, raising an eyebrow. He leaned in close and his lips brushed her neck. "No, love, I think I'll save my revenge and serve it cold," he murmured, slowly running his fingers up and down her arm. "You won't see it coming."

She froze, transfixed by his touch. "Ohhh, scary," she managed.

He pulled back to look at her, and then his face erupted into a smug grin, as if he were very pleased with the effect his touch had on her. "Just you wait," he whispered. He meant it as a threat, but she kind of liked his idea of revenge. And judging by the cocky look on his face, he knew she liked it. She leaned into his touch, hoping for more, but he laughed and kissed her nose, releasing her. "Someone's coming," he said.

Abby heard the click of footsteps echoing off the stone floor of the corridor and slid off David's lap just before Eulalia rounded the corner.

"Hello!" the queen exclaimed. "I am so sorry I am late."

"No worries, Mom," David said. "We had plenty to chat about to keep us busy."

Abby tried to stifle a giddy laugh, and it came out as a giggle-snort, which made David burst out laughing.

"Oh?" From the perplexed look on the queen's face, Abby guessed she was wondering what she had missed, but thinking perhaps it was best not to know.

"Yes," David said. "Little Miss Giggles over here may have dreamed about what animal I will change into."

"That is fantastic. What did you dream, Abby?"

Abby cleared her throat, regaining her composure. "He was white lion full of the Light, vanquishing the Darkness."

"Oh." David smiled dreamily. "Sounds even cooler when you say it like that."

Abby thought his smile was a little goofy and that he was probably thanking his lucky stars not to be turning into a rodent. He looked endearingly dorky.

At the sight of David's funny smile, Eulalia looked confused again, and for a moment seemed tempted to ask her son why he was acting odd. Then she turned to Abby instead. "That would be wonderful, Abby. There are stories in the human world that white lions are divine messengers, ushering in eras of peace and prosperity. I hope it is true."

"That would be nice," Abby agreed, trying hard to ignore her distractingly cute but dopey boyfriend and focus her attention on the queen. "I'm all for peace and prosperity."

Eulalia nodded. "As am I." Then she smiled shyly. "Not to change the subject, but I also bring news. There is a reason why I arrived late today."

"Oh? Does it involve Cael?" Abby asked.

"It does." Eulalia's smile grew bright. She suddenly seemed to be having difficulty containing her own giddy laughter.

"Oh really...?" Abby smiled back. There could only be one reason for the queen to smile like that.

Eulalia nodded. "Yes. He asked me to marry him."

"Oh!" David exclaimed, surprised. "Congratulations!" He jumped up from the bench and hugged his mother tightly.

Abby joined him in the hug. "Congratulations, Eulalia. This has been a long time coming."

"Yes, we are so thankful to be reunited after so many years apart."

David pulled back, his brow furrowed with concern. "But with the journey coming up, you'll be separated again, at least until we get back."

"Yes, this is true," Eulalia agreed. "That is why the wedding must wait until after you return, and of course there will be much to do while you are away. In the meantime, we must focus on your journey. I would like to hear more about your dream. Come, let us continue this discussion in my chambers."

Abby and David followed Eulalia into the sitting room of her suite. In contrast to the more spacious room containing her bed and dressing area, this room was small but cozy, with an oriel window offering a magnificent view of the Western Sea.

Once they were seated, Abby recounted what she remembered from both dreams and asked the question that was on both their minds: were the similarities in the dreams mere coincidence, or had she and David really made a connection?

"It is difficult to say," Eulalia began. "The dreams have similar themes and content, but are different enough that I cannot say for sure if you actually communicated with each other. Let us try a different approach. Choose a location that has meaning to you both and focus on that image as you fall asleep tonight. As you dream, try to make yourself aware that it is a dream, and then meet each other at that location. Try to remember as much as possible, but do not tell one another your dreams. I will want you to each tell me separately so we can see if a true connection has been made."

"All right," David said. "I'm not very good at remembering the details, but I'll try. I'll write down the dream as soon as I wake up. Where should we meet, Abby? Where we first danced?" He took her hand and squeezed it.

Abby smiled, remembering that night. "The steps by the beach…sounds good," she said. "That's a special memory for me. I think there's enough of an emotional connection there to draw us together."

"Yes, that is exactly the kind of place you need," Eulalia agreed.

"It's a date," David said.

೩಄೩಄೩಄

The session was interrupted by a gentle knock on Eulalia's chamber door. "Come," she called.

David looked up to see Cael enter hesitantly. "I do not wish to intrude," he said.

"Cael! Congratulations!" Abby jumped up and pulled the knight into a hug.

David chuckled at Cael's look of surprise. Cael was, as a rule, not the huggy type, but the emotional armor he'd kept so close over the years had just about melted away now that he was free to express his love for Eulalia, and now that he had four protégés who were becoming like children to him. David smiled as he watched Cael laugh and hug Abby back.

David's relationship with Cael was still more formal, but mutual respect was growing day by day. Standing, David went to shake Cael's hand. "I'm very happy for you both. These last few weeks—you've helped me so much by mentoring me that it already feels like you're part of my family. It's an honor to make it official."

"The honor is mine, David. Thank you." Cael smiled, and then, since he was apparently on a roll with the hug thing, pulled David into an embrace. "I hope you know that I will always love your mother, and will ever keep her safe, so long as I have breath."

"I do know that. And I know you've done your best to care for her in far less happy circumstances than this. You have both sacrificed so much—I hope we will have better days ahead," David said.

"And alas, that brings me to my reason for interrupting you. I, too, hope for better days, but they seem to be far off just yet," Cael stated.

"Oh no," Eulalia said, concerned. "What happened?"

"We received a report that Nuren, a village on the Great Plains near the South Forest, was attacked last evening," Cael reported. "It was mostly livestock that were taken, but…"

"How many villagers?" Eulalia asked.

Cael looked at his feet. "Six," he said gravely.

"Six," Eulalia breathed. "The Kruorumbrae have grown bold in the knowledge that their master has returned. We must quickly go to offer our condolences and see what can be done to help."

"Yes," David nodded. "That should be our first priority. I imagine we should take some of our own stock to ease the loss and replenish other supplies as well. Cael, what other damage was done?"

"Some buildings were destroyed. I do not wish to sound callous, but this may be an opportunity for you, David, to use your powers to assist them and win their trust," Cael proposed.

"No, you make a good point," David replied. "I can help them rebuild and tend the wounded. That's why I'm here, isn't it?"

"Yes, dear one," Eulalia said, taking David's hand. "That is why you are here."

"All right then—it's decided," David declared. "Abby, can you pass on the news to Jon and Marisol? They should join us so they can see what we're up against. Mother, could you please make the arrangements for supplies? Cael and I will go brief the guard."

"Of course," Eulalia said. "We shall meet at the stables in one hour."

Taking Eulalia's hand, Cael kissed it tenderly as they headed for the door. To David it seemed like a kiss that expressed both Cael's love for her and his fears about dark days to come—dark days that might already have come. David stayed back a moment with Abby.

"You did well," Abby whispered, placing her hand against his cheek.

David knew she was trying to be supportive but couldn't help but think that her gesture might mirror the sentiment of Cael's kiss. His own fears about the future were overshadowing the present. He placed his hand over hers and then brought her hand to his lips to kiss her palm. "I'm trying. Abby—I don't know what we'll find at that village. I'm afraid it may be worse than Cael let on. Six people gone—that's a huge loss. No one there will be untouched by the tragedy. I'm worried for them...I'm worried for *us*."

"Well, we can't change what's already happened, but we can keep working for those better days. This is where we start—pulling the people together, strengthening each other," Abby replied, lacing her fingers through his.

"You're right. We'll keep working for that," David said. He squeezed her hand and looked into her eyes. "In the meantime, though—what am I supposed to say to these people? 'I'm sorry for your loss' doesn't quite cut it. It sounds pretty empty when I'm supposed to be this powerful leader but I can't bring back the six they lost. I can't heal that hurt."

Abby stared back at him and then wrapped her arms around his neck. "No. You can't. But you know what it's like to lose someone."

He nodded and looked away, avoiding her gaze so she couldn't see the sadness in his eyes. "I do know about that," he whispered. His adoptive parents were gone, and even though he had Eulalia, they had left a void in his heart. There were still moments when it seemed impossible to believe that he couldn't just call Margaret Corbin and tell her about his day, as he had regularly done when he was away at college.

"All you can do is your best to heal the villagers' other wounds. And keep fighting so that this doesn't happen to other people," she added. Abby rested her head against his chest. "I know it feels empty, but just being there with them, in this moment, that's something. Maybe somehow this loss will inspire them to stand up and fight with you when it comes to that."

"I hope so." David swallowed. His fears were threatening to choke him. Fighting a wave of emotion, he placed his hand gently under Abby's chin, lifting her head to look into her eyes. Then he tilted his head down toward her and kissed her hard.

After a moment, Abby pulled back to study his face. Her eyes widened with concern. "Hey, now," she said softly. "What was that for?"

David tried to cover his fear with a smile, but Abby held his gaze. Given her look of determination, he decided it was best to answer honestly. "I just have this fear that when we enter this fight, I'll end up losing you. No matter how hard I try to keep you safe," he said.

"Well, David Corbin, you may be the Solas Beir, but you are just one man, and there are greater things at work here than you. Keeping me safe is not your job."

He stared at her, shocked. "It's not? I kind of thought it was."

Abby put her hands on her hips. "Nope. Your job is to stand up for your people and to serve the Light. So is mine. At some point, we've got to trust that no matter what happens, the Light *will* prevail, even if it means we have losses of our own."

She smiled. "Besides, remember what you told me when we met? Carpe diem."

"Yeah, but Abby…I was talking about recreational cage diving—which is a totally different animal than what we're currently dealing with," David countered. "What happened to the girl who said she didn't see the point in risking her life for no good reason?"

Abby kissed his cheek. "I found a good reason. The best reason. You."

"Well then, you're crazy to be willing to die for a slob like me," he laughed.

"Crazy is what makes me so darn irresistible." Abby grinned. "You know you like it."

"That I do." He kissed her and took her hand. "Come on, then. We're burning daylight."

"Yep, lots to do. Villagers to woo, monsters to slay…"

ဆေ၁၈ဆေ၁၈ဆေ၁၈

Within the hour, two small armies had been gathered: one to help the villagers of Nuren, and one to stay behind to guard Caislucis, in case the attack on the village was meant as a trap to leave the fortress vulnerable. Abby watched as Cael gave the castle guards their final instructions and then dismissed them to return to duty.

Fearing an ambush, Cael further divided the group that would be traveling to the village. The larger group, led by Phelan, Cael's second in command, and Fergal, swordsman extraordinaire, would travel by way of the main trade road leading to the Great Plains. Cael would lead the Solas Beir's party eastward through the forest.

"The Kruorumbrae will not expect two groups," Cael explained, holding the reins of his mount. "If something should happen, the unaffected group can circle around and give aid with a surprise attack from behind."

"The villagers will, however, expect to see a member of the royal family in the group that travels the trade road," Eulalia said, settling into her saddle. "I will travel with Fergal and Phelan."

"I would feel better if you were with me," Cael said.

"I know," Eulalia replied. "But if either of us is in danger, the other will sense it—and this way, you can focus on training your students."

"The queen will come to no harm, sir," Phelan said. "You have my word."

Fergal leapt from his perch on Phelan's horse to the queen's, brandishing his sword in agreement. "And mine."

Cael looked from Phelan to Fergal. "I will hold you both to that," he said. He looked up at Eulalia, then took both of her hands in his own and kissed them. "Safe travels, my love."

"And for you as well," she smiled, leaning down to kiss his cheek. She turned her horse's head toward the road and led her group away.

"She'll be fine," David reassured the knight as he watched them go.

"I hope so," Cael said, swinging up into his saddle. "Come. The village is not far, but there is much to do."

"Villagers to woo, monsters to slay…" Abby whispered to David.

"Shush, you," David whispered back. He chuckled as he nudged his horse forward.

Abby heard the rush of wings and was surprised to see Brarn landing on her horse's neck. The horse did not seem at all disturbed by the arrival of a second passenger. "Good girl," she said, stroking the mare's neck. She nodded to Brarn. "Hey, you. Nice of you to join us."

The raven seemed to be searching for a comfortable perch and finally settled on Abby's saddle horn. He looked up at her with a kind of beaky smile, if it could be called that. She wasn't sure if ravens smiled with their beaks or their eyes, but Brarn's eyes seemed to twinkle as if he were happy to be a part of the expedition.

"You have a friend," Marisol said, her horse matching pace with Abby's.

"One from our world," Abby smiled. "Did you know that Brarn is the one who first led me to Eulalia?"

Marisol looked perplexed. "Huh. How'd he do that?"

"You know the labyrinth at the old mansion?"

Marisol nodded. "Ah, yes. The spooky tangle of overgrown weeds we drove past the night we came here."

Abby smiled, remembering. The labyrinth *had* looked spooky that night. "Yeah, that. Well, Brarn led me through that tangled mess to the queen," Abby said.

"Wow," Marisol breathed, her eyebrows raised in surprise. "Smart bird."

"He's pretty amazing." Abby beamed down at Brarn. "He also helped Fergal deliver the Sign of the Throne to David."

"Impressive," Marisol replied. "And I thought it was a bad omen when he showed up—I guess I need to rethink that."

"I think you might," Abby agreed.

They had been riding through the woods in silence for a while when, suddenly, Brarn broke from his perch and flew toward a sunny break in the trees.

"We are coming to the edge of the forest," Cael announced, gesturing to the open field beyond the archway of branches.

Brarn circled the field, then shot upward to the top of one of the trees. Abby followed him with her eyes, and gasped as he landed on a branch next to something that seemed to be dripping red liquid.

"Stop!" Abby cried. "Brarn's found something!"

"Is that blood?" Marisol asked, horrified.

They heard the swish and snap of feathers as Erela landed on the path in front of them at the edge of the field. She set her feet apart in a fighting stance and looked around, scanning the woods for signs of an impending ambush. She watched Brarn circling above her and then frowned when she saw what he had discovered in the tree. With one great flap of her large wings, she launched herself into the air to retrieve it.

"Whoa—she makes quite an entrance, doesn't she?" Jon said. "Where'd she come from?"

"She flew over the forest," David answered, dismounting. "I think being under the canopy makes her feel trapped."

"Hmph. The claustrophobic angel," Jon muttered.

Erela carried Brarn's find to David and Cael. It was a decapitated goat—the head was nowhere to be found.

"Holy headless goats, Batman," Jon said.

"How'd that get all the way up there?" Abby asked.

"I know what did this," Marisol said. Everyone turned to look at her.

"What?" David and Abby asked in unison.

Marisol blushed as though she suddenly felt embarrassed to have so many eyes focused on her. "Well, I mean, we've got a goat, and it's been totally drained, right? And whatever attacked it had to be able to jump really high to put it in a tree. So…it had to be a *chupacabra*."

"Yeah, but the blood drained out because it's missing its entire head!" Abby pointed out. "Doesn't that seem, I don't know, a *tad* overzealous?"

Marisol shrugged. "Maybe the *chupa* was really hungry."

"Um, I don't think chupacabras exist, guys. They don't, do they, Cael?" David asked.

Cael shook his head. "No. Not in this world at least."

"I was thinking velociraptor," Jon whispered to Marisol, making little clawing motions with his hands.

Marisol stifled a giggle. "Inappropriate," she hissed under her breath. But Abby could see that she was smiling.

Cael turned to Erela. "What do you think?"

"It is a message for me. They want me to know they are watching," Erela said.

"Have they chosen a side?" Cael asked.

"I do not know," Erela said. She and Cael exchanged a dark look and she walked away, toward the village.

"Cael, she's not talking about the Kruorumbrae, is she? *Who* sent her a message? Who is watching?" David asked.

"The Daughters of Mercy," Cael replied. He turned to follow Erela, leading his horse by the reins.

Jon swung down from his saddle. "The Daughters of Mercy? They sound like nuns."

"I don't think so," David contemplated. "They sound a little more dark side to me."

"You haven't met many nuns, have you?" Jon asked.

"I've met a few. They were nice," David said, helping Abby dismount.

"Well, I guess you had a different sampling than I did. All the nuns I ever met went *totally* dark side on me," Jon recalled. He took Marisol's reins while she swung her leg over her horse's neck, grasped the saddle horn, and hopped neatly down from her mount.

Abby laughed. "Hmm, I wonder why. Shall I list your offenses against the church?"

"Ah, that won't be necessary," Jon scowled, narrowing his eyes. He shot Abby a look of warning. He turned to Marisol. "Nor is it necessary to ask for details. Especially not from my mom."

Clucking her tongue, Marisol shook her head and took back her horse's reins. "You are a *bad* boy, Jonathon Reyes."

"I'm sorry," Jon said.

"Don't apologize," Marisol smiled. "I like it."

Jon grinned. "Oh, *really...*"

"Yes. But to get back to the subject at hand," Marisol replied. Ignoring Jon's pout, she turned to David and lowered her voice. "She's an angel right? Maybe the Daughters of Mercy are angels too—you know, like the Angel of Death? That's New Testament dark side, isn't it?"

"Old Testament," David corrected her. "And I don't think she's an angel. I was thinking more like a valkyrie."

"Aren't they supposed to hang out on battlefields or something, taking the valiant dead to Valhalla?" Jon asked.

David shrugged. "Maybe...look, I don't know *what* she is exactly."

"Betcha five bucks she's an angel," Jon offered.

"All right, I'll take that bet and your money, Reyes," David said, clapping him on the shoulder. "But I promise you, my friend—she is *not* an angel. Come on, let's go chat with the villagers."

ဆလဆလဆလ

Abby saw that Eulalia had already arrived with her troops; she was talking with the two Nuren eldsmen and the eldswoman who served as village leaders, ambassadors, and at times, peacekeepers. Gorman had been teaching Abby and her friends about the politics of the region surrounding Caislucis. She noted that each wore long robes over his or her clothes and a medallion around the neck, signifying their role. David, Cael, and Erela joined the discussion while Abby, Jon, and Marisol stood back and surveyed the village.

"Looks like this place got hit by a tornado," Abby said. Structures that appeared to have once resembled a barn and some kind of tower had been almost leveled. Some of the villagers were clearing the rubble, while others worked with the castle guards to distribute supplies and care for the new livestock. Abby approached a woman working near the destroyed buildings. "Do you need help here?" she asked. "My friends and I can work on clearing this out."

"We would be grateful for your help," said the woman. She had dark skin and wore her hair bound in a colorful scarf. The skirt of her printed, ankle-length dress was smudged with dirt. She smiled wearily and handed Abby a pair of leather gloves. Jon brought over a small cart and Marisol led the horses to graze in the field. Returning, she picked up a spade and joined Abby and Jon.

As Marisol shoveled away debris, Abby and Jon began placing heavy stones into the cart. "We're emissaries of the Solas Beir," Abby said to the woman. "I'm Abby, and these are my friends Jon and Marisol."

"I am called Yola," the woman said. She looked as though she had not slept at all; her eyes were dark and full of worry.

"Was anyone in these buildings when they fell?" Abby asked.

"There were sheep and goats in the barn, but none of our people, thank the Light," Yola said. "The other building was the granary—much of our food and the grain for our stock were stored there. It is a great loss to us."

"I'm sorry. Did you see it happen?" Marisol asked.

"No—I did not see it myself, though I heard it. When the creatures came, it was already dark, and most everyone was inside for the night. There was a terrible sound, like the wind, and hellish screams, the likes of which I have never heard and hope never to hear again. The creatures were attacking our animals, and the screams of those they took echoed throughout our village. Then everything shook as the buildings fell. There was a crash, like thunder—and then all was silent.

"I was terrified to leave my home, but I thought perhaps people might need my help. I searched, but I could not find anyone wounded. As people emerged from their homes, we were able to identify the missing. Those who were taken were either guarding the village or doing their last chores of the evening. Had this happened during the day, more of us would have been lost," Yola explained.

Jon hefted a stone into the cart. "Have they found any of them yet?"

"No. They vanished, as did the creatures that took them," Yola said.

"And everyone else is okay? I mean, no one else was wounded?" Abby asked.

"We are all relatively unscathed, yes." Again, Yola smiled wearily. "I fear, though, that I shall never see my brother again."

"Oh! I'm so sorry," Abby said. In her surprise, she had almost dropped the stone she was holding, but Jon helped her ease it into the cart. "Thanks," Abby said to Jon, then turned back to the woman. "Your brother was one of the taken? Oh, Yola, I am so very, very sorry."

"He should not have been among them. He volunteered for the night watch when someone took ill," Yola said. She cast her eyes downward. "I should not have said that."

"Why?" Abby asked, putting her hand gently on Yola's shoulder.

Yola looked up into Abby's eyes, fighting back tears. "He would not want me to think that way. Daudi is very brave. If he is still alive, he will do his best to return to us. And if he met his end, he would be honored to do it in someone else's place. To speak otherwise is to dishonor him."

"I see. I pray he is still alive," Abby said. "Yola, will you come with me to speak to the Solas Beir? I know he will do all he can to find out what happened to your brother and the others."

"Do you really think he can help me find my brother?" Yola asked.

"I hope so." Taking Yola's hand, Abby led her to David, who was still deep in conversation with the village leaders.

ЮСЗЮСЗЮСЗ

Out of the corner of his eye, David saw Abby and a woman walking toward him. He gestured for them to join the discussion. "Abby," he said, "it sounds like, besides the six who are missing, no one was injured in the attack or when the buildings collapsed."

Abby nodded. "Yes—we were just talking about the same thing. David, this is Yola. Her brother is one of the missing."

David took Yola's hands in his. "Yola, I am so sorry about your brother. I promise I will find out who did this."

"Was it the Kruorumbrae?" Abby asked.

"I'm starting to have my doubts, based on what we've heard about the attack. Yola, please forgive me for speaking frankly, but I don't want to keep information from you, and I hope what I share will not bring you more sorrow," David said.

"I understand," Yola nodded. "Please—I am grateful for anything you can tell me. If my brother is alive, I will do whatever I can to help bring him home."

"All right," David said. "What we know so far is that this attack was different than past Kruorumbrae raids. While the Blood Shadows do prefer to attack at night, they do not usually destroy buildings. They also would not just take the people who were outside; they would have entered people's homes and taken everyone they could find. They have raided several villages north of Caislucis, and the Kruorumbrae were not deterred by closed doors.

"It's strange there is no sign of the people who were taken. Our guards have been searching the areas surrounding the village for evidence of the missing, and there is nothing there. The Kruorumbrae are, if anything, consistent. If they had come to feed, they would not have taken people and left the bodies of your livestock. Forgive me, but they would consider that a waste of food.

"The other thing is that goat we found in the tree—that is the strangest part to me. There is simply no precedent for it. Yola, what I'm saying is that, while I don't want to give you false hope..." David paused, suddenly unsure if he should finish his sentence. The woman took a deep breath and urged him to continue, patting his hands. "I think your brother was taken by something other than the Kruorumbrae," David continued. "There is a chance he may still be alive."

"Oh, please, let it be so!" Yola cried.

Abby put her arms around the woman. Then she turned to David. "If this wasn't the Blood Shadows, then who was it? And why would they take Yola's brother and the others?"

"We're still working on that part. We don't have any answers yet, but we might have some ideas. I think it is more important than ever that we talk with the oracles," David said. "Yola, I promise you and your people—I will send you news as soon as I can."

"Thank you, Solas Beir," Yola said.

"You are welcome. I truly hope we can find him and the other five." David surveyed the village. "It looks as though the supplies have been distributed to everyone, but we could really use a place to store them, couldn't we? Let me see if I can help with that. Abby, can you join me for a moment?"

Abby nodded. "Of course."

David put his arm around Abby and guided her toward the field where the horses were grazing. He kept his voice low. "I need your help."

"What can I do?" she asked.

"I'm going to use my power to rebuild the buildings that were lost, but I have no idea what the impact will be on me," David whispered.

"Do you think using power will make you sick like when you healed Nysa?" Abby whispered back.

"No—I don't think it will be that, exactly, but I'm worried I might pass out or something. Not a real confidence booster for them to see me like that."

"No, I suppose not," she agreed.

"Let's bring our horses over, and could you just stay close to me? I have a feeling I'm going to be pretty exhausted. I'm going to need some help staying on my feet," David explained.

"Just lean on me if you feel faint, and I'll keep you propped up until we can get you on the horse. I won't let you fall," Abby promised.

"Thanks. I appreciate that." He took the horses' reins and led them back to where Yola and the elders were standing, then passed the reins to Abby. "Okay—here goes nothing..."

"Good luck," Abby whispered.

David looked around. Everyone had stopped what they were doing. Although the adults all looked relatively young, they were diverse in appearance and dress. Like Yola, some of the women wore long, colorfully printed dresses, while others were dressed more like Abby in leather leggings and billowing shirts. Most of the men wore colorful tunics with loosely fitted pants, but a few were dressed in long robes. All of them were staring at him. *No pressure, folks,* he thought.

Holding out his hands and closing his eyes, David focused on what the buildings should look like. He imagined them coming together, stone by stone, beam by beam. He felt warmth radiate from his hands and heard the sound of stone grinding as it moved. He kept his eyes closed, letting go, trusting that everything was happening as he saw it in his mind's eye. He felt an intense pressure building inside his head, which began to ache. Then, as if he had released a breath, the pressure left him. He heard applause and cheering and opened his eyes.

The buildings were standing as if the damage from the night before had only been a bad dream. *That wasn't so bad,* David thought. *I wonder if I could do something similar to find the missing villagers. If I could just see them in my mind...*And then he teetered back a step, overwhelmed by exhaustion.

He slumped against Abby. She put her arms around him to keep him steady, and Cael reached out to help. Cael had been watching David intently and had moved closer when David started to look faint. Together, Abby and Cael helped David into his saddle, bracing his legs in case he should slump over again.

The only other person who seemed to notice that something was amiss was Eulalia. Judging by the concerned look on her face, she too had noted the toll using his powers was taking on him.

Everyone else was still looking stunned that the pile of rubble was gone as if it had never existed. By the time their attention turned back to David, he had managed to sit up straight in the saddle and put on a winning smile to mask how drained he was.

"You are the true Solas Beir," Yola exclaimed, walking over to David and taking his hand in both of hers. David smiled and squeezed her hands, and Yola pressed his hand against her cheek in a gesture of gratitude. At that, the villagers began cheering again.

David was too exhausted to speak, so he kept smiling. Yola let go of his hand, bowing slightly before she rejoined the other villagers. David gave them a diplomatic wave, and the queen stepped in to say a few last words before they returned to the castle.

They headed back up the forest road, with Abby and Cael flanking David in case he needed them. Eulalia joined them this time, leaving Phelan and Fergal to lead the other group back across the Plains. As the trees closed in around them, Eulalia nudged her horse to pull alongside of Cael's.

"Well, how did I do?" David asked her.

"You were perfect," his mother smiled.

"Thanks."

"How do you feel?" she asked.

"Terrible," David sighed, "but I'll be okay, once I get some sleep." He was weary, but they still had a long ride home. "I'm glad we were able to help."

"I think what you did today went a long way toward earning the trust of the Plainspeople. I imagine the story of how you rebuilt their village will spread far and wide," Eulalia noted.

"I didn't rebuild their village," David yawned. His eyes felt heavy with fatigue, but he managed to keep them open and focused on the forest path. "I just raised their barn."

"Nevertheless," Eulalia smiled, "it was spectacular."

ಬಂಡಬಂಡಬಂಡ

When they arrived back at the castle, Abby and Cael helped David off his horse and up to his room. He was leaning on them so heavily that they were bearing most of his weight, nearly carrying him. He looked exhausted, his eyes half closed.

"I need to make security rounds with Phelan," Cael said, helping David sit down on his bed, "but do you need anything before I go?"

"I have him, Cael," Abby reassured him. "Thanks for your help."

Cael nodded and closed the chamber door behind him.

David lay on his bed, too tired to change his clothes. Abby pulled off his boots and then sat beside him, stroking his hair. "Why don't we get you under the covers?"

"Okay," David yawned. He rolled to his side so Abby could pull the covers down and then rolled back the other way, so she could pull them up over him.

Leaning in, Abby kissed his forehead, caressing his cheek. "I should let you rest. Sweet dreams." She turned to go.

He reached out and grabbed her hand, his grip surprisingly strong, considering he was so tired. "Stay with me. Please?"

Abby looked at the chamber door for a moment, considering. "Okay," she agreed, and lay down beside David. She wrapped her arms around him, pulling him closer.

She lay awake, watching him, listening as his breathing deepened when he drifted off. She was worried about him. He was new to using his power, and he was getting stronger, but it seemed like he had paid a heavy price for using it in the village. What kind of price would David have to pay when they finally went to battle? What toll would facing Tierney take?

Abby closed her eyes, but when she opened them, she was no longer lying next to David. She was no longer in the castle. She was sitting on the steps at the beach below the Newcastle Beach Inn, wearing the gown she had donned the night of the Autumn Ball. The crests of the waves were glowing bright white in the light of a full moon.

"Is that seat taken?"

Abby looked up to see David coming down the steps as he had that night, dressed in his suit. "All yours," she said, smiling.

"For how long?" David asked.

"For always," Abby said.

David took her hands and helped her to her feet, pulling her close to him, like he had done that night. Then he grinned. "Fancy meeting you here, stranger. I like this dream."

She laughed. "Me too. Let's stay a while."

"Only if you dance with me again," David bantered.

"I think I can manage that."

There was no music this time, but it didn't matter. Abby settled into his arms happily and they shuffled around, her head nestled against his shoulder and her eyes closed.

A moment later, a shriek pierced the air—it sounded like a woman's scream, and yet somehow also like the screech of a bird of prey, honing in on dinner. It made Abby's skin crawl.

"What was that?" she whispered.

The night sky seemed to darken. "Look," David said, pointing at the moon above the ocean. A dark, winged figure was silhouetted against the circle of white.

There was a rustle behind them, and Abby looked over David's shoulder to see thick, black smoke rolling down the steps like a low fog. "No," she said. "Not again."

David whirled around, saw the smoke, then looked up at the sky again. The winged thing was diving toward them. He turned Abby to face north, pointing her in the direction of the old mansion. "Get to the portal. Run, Abby. Run!"

Abby started to run, but turned back. David had vanished, and in his place was the white lion. The lion growled a warning to her as the smoke gathered in drifts around their ankles. Then she turned and ran.

☙ℭ☙ℭ☙ℭ

At that moment, David startled awake as Abby sat bolt upright in bed, letting out a gasp as if she had been held underwater and was desperately trying to breathe.

He sat up beside her and wrapped his arms around her, and she crumpled into his embrace. He lay back down, pulling her with him so that her head lay on his chest. Her skin felt cold, so he pressed her closer, trying to warm her up.

"Shhh," he said as he stroked her hair, breathing in the clean scent of her soft skin. "It was just a dream. It wasn't real."

"No," she said, trembling against him, "but it will be. Something very bad is coming. I saw..."

"No, don't," David interrupted, placing his hand on her cheek. "Don't tell me your dream, Abby—remember, we're supposed to tell Eulalia first. Then we'll know for sure if we made a connection. Even though we both know we did."

She looked up at him, her eyes wide. "Then you saw it too?"

"Yes. But don't talk about it now. Close your eyes, okay? I'll help you fall back asleep."

Abby looked doubtful. "I don't think I can sleep anymore."

"Just close your eyes. I'll distract you."

Abby reluctantly closed her eyes.

David focused on enveloping her within his warmth as he returned to stroking her hair. Before long, her breathing deepened, and he kissed the top of her head before drifting off again himself.

Hours later, he awoke to a soft kiss on his cheek. "Good morning," Abby said.

David smiled. "Hmm, good morning. I like having you here with me when I wake up."

"Me too. How do you feel? I was really worried about you last night. Yesterday was exhausting for you."

"It was, but I'm good now. I think having you close helped." He felt strong and refreshed, with none of the dizzy fatigue that had overtaken him after he used his power.

"It helped me too—especially after that nightmare," Abby admitted.

"Yeah, that wasn't too fun, was it? I think we need to go have a chat with my mom, and with Cael too. I need some answers about those Daughters of Mercy."

ഇരു ഇരു ഇരു

After finding the queen and sharing their dreams separately, David and Abby went with Eulalia to speak with Cael in the armory.

"You are right, David," Eulalia said as they walked. "You and Abby made a clear connection this time. You seem to be making progress."

"What we saw in the dream—is that going to happen?" Abby asked.

"Perhaps not exactly, but there seem to be noteworthy elements. The figure you saw in the sky does bear a striking resemblance to a Daughter," Eulalia said.

"What are they?" David queried.

"I can answer that question," Cael interrupted, stepping out from the armory. "But not here. Come with me to the library. There is something you need to see."

He turned down a hallway and led them to a large room with floor-to-ceiling shelves laden with scrolls and books. They followed him to the area that housed maps and Cael selected one, unrolling it on a large table.

"This is a map of Cai Terenmare," Cael began. "Here you see the castle in which we stand, the forest that surrounds Caislucis, and the Great Plains on the western edge of the Barren. To the north of the desert is a stronghold used long ago in the war against the Kruorumbrae, and further north still, lies the Northern Oracle's territory.

"The Southern Oracle's territory, as you might guess, is south of us, in the center of a rainforest. Here, on the eastern border of the desert is the city of the Eastern Oracle. There have been rumors of late that the Blood Shadows have been gathering near the city. Here," he pointed to a spot inside the boundaries of the Barren, not far from the city, "is the Eye of the Needle. It is a rock formation resembling a tower. At the top is a cave that forms the Eye. That is where the Daughters of Mercy reside.

"Now, as to what they are…they look like beautiful winged women, but they are not women. They are predatory in nature, but pride themselves on being just, preying on those who have committed some wrong. Like some of the oracles, they have a history of remaining neutral in the battle between the Light and the Shadows. However, over the years, they have begun to reveal a darker side and are no longer preying only on the unjust."

"Is Erela one of them?" David asked. He thought about the way Erela had behaved during training—his intuition about her predatory nature had been spot-on.

"She used to be," Cael answered. "She dissented when the choice of prey began to change, and was cast out."

"Do you believe they were responsible for the attack on the village?" David asked.

"Yes, I do," Cael stated. "But, until now, they have remained on the eastern side of the Barren. The question is, why have they attacked a village on our side of the desert, and what have they done with those they have taken?"

"How do we find the answers to those questions?" Abby asked. "Can't we just have Erela talk with them and find out what's going on?"

Cael looked at Abby. "I am afraid it is not that simple. Were Erela to return to the Eye of the Needle, the Daughters would surely tear her apart," he explained.

"Oh. So that won't work," Abby said.

"No, it will not," Cael agreed. "The Daughters of Mercy are *not* known for compassion, whatever they may call themselves. However, the oracles may have the answers we seek. If we can win them to our cause, we may also convince the Daughters of Mercy to join us. Perhaps then they will release the villagers."

"*If* the villagers are still alive at that point," David noted. "Seems like we're risking their lives in seeking out the oracles first—they may not have the luxury of time."

"Nor do we," Cael said. "But I see no other options. I do have good news, however. I received word from Nerine this morning. She accepted the nomination to be the new Western Oracle and is coming with a small cohort of her kinsfolk for the induction to the post. Her messenger said they will arrive tomorrow, soon after our training exercise."

"That's great," David said, smiling. "One down, three to go. Well, two, assuming the Northern Oracle is still with us."

"Excellent," Eulalia exclaimed. "We must make preparations for tomorrow's ceremony. I must also speak to you further about your latest dream. David, now that you have dreamed about changing to your animal form, are you ready to try the transformation?"

"I suppose so. Fergal makes it look so easy, but honestly, I don't know where to start," David admitted.

"Well," Cael said dryly, "the library is certainly not the place to begin. I imagine Gorman would object to you running amok in here."

Stunned, David and Abby exchanged a look. They both stared at Cael for a moment and then burst out laughing.

"Did you just make a joke, darling?" Eulalia asked, hiding a smile.

"Yes, I believe I did." Cael seemed a little surprised himself.

"You *are* working your magic on him, Eulalia," Abby quipped.

Cael grinned—another rarity for him. "Oh, come on then—out to the training lawn." He grabbed Eulalia's hand and led the way.

As they walked together, David and Abby continued their discussion of dreamwalking with Eulalia.

"So in the dreams, I can't really change the outcome, can I?" Abby asked. "I've heard about lucid dreaming, and that's the idea there, that you take control...but this is different, isn't it? I can't make the Shadows I see disappear, much as I'd like to."

"Yes," Eulalia confirmed. "Your goal is not to control the dream, but rather to observe so you can see what the future might hold. However, you *can* connect with another dreamer, and push that person with your mind as you communicate in the dream. In that sense, you do have control, and you may in some way affect the future."

"What do you mean, 'push them?'" Abby queried.

"When you are awake and someone is experiencing a strong emotion, you feel it, do you not?" Eulalia asked.

"Yes. Like certain times when I interacted with Lucia, or the way I could sense the Kruorumbrae's desire to feed. It was physically draining," Abby said.

Eulalia nodded. "Exactly—you feel the emotion and you absorb it. There is a physical effect. But you can also push back, influencing the other person. If, for example, the person was angry and you wanted to calm them, you would first discipline yourself to be calm. Then you would project that emotion onto your target, pushing them in the same way their anger pushed you."

"Oh man, it's like a Jedi mind trick," Abby said, passing under the archway that led to the training lawn.

"It totally is," David smiled. He stopped walking and waved his hand in front of Abby. "These are not the androids you're looking for..."

Abby laughed. "Wish I'd known about this before. I could have bent all kinds of people to my will."

"Abigail Brown, sociopathic mastermind," David grinned. "I suspected as much."

"Yeah, you have no idea," Abby laughed, elbowing him. "I'll be trying that evil little trick on *you* when you least expect it."

"Hmph." David crossed his arms and pretended to be annoyed. "We'll see about that, Master. Now, if we're done focusing on you?"

"But of course, my liege. Proceed," Abby said, bowing.

"Finally. Sheesh," David added, sighing dramatically.

He turned to see Eulalia and Cael exchange knowing smiles as they watched the banter between him and Abby. He wondered if they ever had conversations like that. They seemed so serious sometimes, but maybe things had been different before they became responsible for an entire kingdom. He hoped that he and Abby would never lose that sense of playfulness, even in the face of an oncoming war.

# TRANSFORMATION

When they made it to the training lawn, David took a deep breath. "All right then. How do I start?"

"Focus as you do when you use your power at other times, and think about becoming the lion. Let the feeling of that flow through you," Eulalia said.

"Okay, got it. Become the lion—simple enough." David closed his eyes and concentrated for a moment. Then he opened one eye again. "Wait—same process for changing back, right?"

"Correct."

David opened both eyes and looked at her seriously. "And when I change back, I'm not going to be standing here naked, am I?"

Eulalia laughed. "No—not at all. This is not a physical transformation—it is spiritually based, with an outward manifestation that is physical. It is as if the animal form surrounds you."

Abby put her hands on her hips. "Quit stalling, Corbin."

"Okay. Just checking." David squeezed both eyes closed again and concentrated. He expected to feel the usual warmth radiating throughout his body, but he felt nothing. He squeezed his eyes tighter, waiting for something to happen. After a few moments, he opened them again. "Nope. Nada."

"Try again," Eulalia encouraged.

David closed his eyes and focused, but nothing happened. "Sorry—I don't think this is working. Maybe I'm not a lion after all. Maybe I'm destined to be that ferret."

"It was a weasel, actually," Abby grinned.

David narrowed his eyes at her. "Thanks. That's very helpful."

"Weasel?" Eulalia asked.

David shook his head. "Never mind—it's just an Abby thing, created for the sole purpose of tormenting me. I'll try again, but maybe if I saw one of you do it first? Cael, do you mind?"

"Happy to oblige," Cael nodded. In an instant, he transformed into a beautiful wolf.

"A wolf," David grinned. "Of course he's a wolf—I guess I could have seen that one coming. And he makes it looks so easy, doesn't he?"

Cael transformed back. "But, I am not a white wolf—just a common grey one."

Eulalia took his hand. "You are anything but common, love."

Cael smiled and held her hand to his lips, kissing it gently. "Thank you, my sweet."

"I have a thought," Abby uttered hesitantly.

David looked at her, raising his eyebrows. "A helpful one this time?"

Abby rolled her eyes dramatically and then smiled. "Yes, dear. A helpful one. Whenever you changed forms in my dreams, it was in reaction to me being in danger. Maybe that's what's missing. You don't have the same incentive."

"Okay, so what do you suggest?" David asked. "Should we have Cael wave a sword at you?"

Abby shook her head. "No—I was just thinking that you could focus on that thought and channel how you might feel if I were in a dangerous situation."

"I remember how I felt when I thought Calder was going to kill you after I went through the mirror. I certainly felt like I could do some damage then," David said.

"Yes—see, that's good. Use that."

"All right." David closed his eyes once more. He relaxed his breathing and focused on an image of Calder springing up from his muscular hind legs, vicious claws and teeth going for Abby.

David could feel the air around him change, rippling against his skin as if he were standing in a column of hot vapor. Then he opened his eyes and looked down to find that his hands had been replaced by large white paws. He stretched, testing his muscles, and then sprang into motion, bounding down the length of the training lawn.

ဆဟဆဟဆဟ

At the far end of the field, Jon and Marisol were sparring. They heard a loud roar and turned to see an enormous lion bearing down on them. Marisol deftly leapt clear, but Jon had an episode of deer-in-the-headlights syndrome, freezing in place.

The white lion pulled up short, inches from Jon's face. To his credit, Jon didn't scream. To his dismay, his reaction was not exactly awe-inspiring. The sound coming from him was a toneless "Nyaaaaaaaa," accompanied by a half raised hand that flopped about like a dying fish.

The lion transformed back into David, and then he looked at Jon quizzically. "Nyaaaa?"

Jon narrowed his eyes. "Don't say it. I am *well* aware that my fight or flight response needs a little tweaking."

"A little?" David asked, raising an eyebrow.

Jon nodded. "Yes. Just a smidge."

David laughed. "Sorry for exposing a chink in your armor—I guess I got a little carried away with the lion thing."

"Don't worry about it," Jon said, looking at Marisol, who was trying to hide a smile. "I think she found it endearing."

Marisol grinned. "I did, actually. You are completely adorable."

"Thanks," Jon said. "That's what I was aiming for."

"Oh, you are *always* adorable, Reyes," David chimed in, elbowing Jon.

"Aw, thanks, Corbin. Because, you know, it's your opinion I *really* care about," said Jon, punching David in the arm.

"How could you not? I'm a very important person," David smiled, rubbing his arm. "Seriously though, I'm sorry for practically mauling you. Come on—Cael and Eulalia have updates for us. Nerine will be coming to accept the post as Western Oracle, and we need to prepare for the ceremony."

ര‍യ‍ര‍യ‍ര‍യ

"Given that David made significant progress yesterday with his ability to transform, I would like to revise today's training exercise," Cael announced. "Rather than splitting you into teams, I want Abby, Jon, and Marisol to run into the forest and hide, while David tracks you using his animal senses."

"We're going to play hide-and-seek?" Jon asked.

"A version of it, I suppose. It is not just about David, though—I want you to use what you have learned about stealth to avoid being found. If he finds you, return here to wait for the others," Cael instructed.

"Sounds good," Marisol smiled.

"Excellent," Cael said. "Oh, and David? Try not to eat your friends when you find them. Ready…set…run!"

"Wait—what? Is he serious?" Jon asked, hesitating. Marisol and Abby had already dashed into the forest.

"No, man, he's joking," David laughed. "Cael and a sense of humor—I know, it's a wild concept. Better hurry, though. I won't bite you…too hard."

"Not cool, dude," Jon said, and ducked into the trees.

ဆဟဆဟဆဟ

Marisol had a plan for how to disguise her scent. She darted in the direction of a nearby stream. She sloshed in the shallow water and zigzagged from bank to bank several times before coming to a large tree overhanging the water. "This will do nicely," she said, climbing up high into the branches. The leaves obscured her completely.

ဆဟဆဟဆဟ

Abby ran in a different direction and circled a few trees to confuse David. Then she encountered a stream. She crossed to the other bank by teetering along a row of algae-covered rocks and then paused, trying to decide on a good hiding place.

Catching movement out of the corner of her eye, she turned to see that Brarn had joined her. He sat perched on a tree limb, watching her. "Hey there," she said. "Any suggestions?"

The raven cocked his head in answer and then took flight, gliding low in front of Abby.

"Déjà vu. Last time I followed you like this, you led me to Eulalia. Wonder where we're headed this time."

Brarn flew over a small dip in the forest floor, which was carpeted in ferns, and then up over a hill, swooping under mossy branches, banking left and right as he navigated a maze of trees. It was all Abby could do to keep up with him. Finally the raven settled on the low branch of a tree in front of a solid mass of green. But it wasn't solid—not quite.

"It's another labyrinth," Abby whispered to herself. "This really *is* déjà vu." Just ahead of her was the entrance. "Shall I go in?" she asked the raven. "For old times' sake?"

Brarn stared at her with his dark, gold-rimmed eyes.

"Not talking, I see," Abby observed. "All right, wish me luck." She stepped into the labyrinth and followed the path that wound around inside. It was more challenging than the smaller maze of hedges at the old mansion, but after encountering a few dead ends, she found herself in an open circular area that seemed to be the labyrinth's center. There was a low stone bench on one side and a flat stone circle in the center. She studied the stone circle—there seemed to be some kind of writing on it—runes, perhaps. The strange carvings were so worn, she couldn't tell. Then she heard a rustling movement behind her, and turned around.

Jon didn't really know where he was going, so he ran one direction and then turned and ran the other way. He walked along fallen logs and hopped over the stream. At one point, he came across a series of tree stumps, so he climbed up on one and jumped from stump to stump. *Gotta throw David off,* Jon thought. *I can't be the first one he catches.*

He finally came to a hill. There was some kind of small, fern-covered valley below, and a flat rock jutted out from the top of the hill, creating a stone lip that might make a great hiding spot.

But first, Jon would have to do something sneaky. He crept to the edge of the stone ledge and looked down—the drop looked to be maybe six feet, and the ground was soft. He jumped down and walked through the ferns until he reached the point where the stream cut the valley in two.

Then, he very carefully walked backward, placing his feet in his footprints until he was back to the point where he had landed. Here the ground was pretty scuffed up, but he didn't think it mattered. It might actually help. He turned and leapt into the small alcove under the ledge, and hunkered down in a patch of ferns. He smiled to himself, satisfied with his strategy. From here he could enjoy the show.

David was enjoying his new form. He could run and run and his muscles did not seem to tire. Everything was different, more vibrant somehow—all his senses seemed magnified, especially his sense of smell. He could smell the three of them; Jon's path seemed less focused than Marisol's or Abby's.

He sensed that Marisol might be nearby—her scent was the strongest. He followed her down one side of the stream, and was temporarily confused when the trail ended, until he realized Marisol's strategy. He crossed the stream and sought her scent on the other side, tracking her back and forth until he came to a large tree. He found her scent on an exposed root that arched over the stream, then traced it up the bark of the tree. Looking upward, he thought he saw a slight movement, and his ears confirmed that someone was in the tree.

David slipped back into his regular form. "Very clever, Sol. But I've got you treed."

"Darn," Marisol said. "And I thought I was being so smart." She climbed down.

"You *were* smart. I'm very impressed," David said. "All right, off you go to hang out with Cael, and off I go to find Abby and Jon." He changed back into a lion and crossed the stream, backtracking to a point where he had picked up Jon's scent.

David smiled as he caught on to Jon's stump-hopping trick and broke into a run as the scent got stronger. Standing on the stone ledge, he could see the soil disturbed below, and footprints leading away. *You were tricky, Jon. But not tricky enough,* David thought. He leapt from the ledge and followed the footprints, bounding over the stream. Here he lost the scent. He looked back across the water. There seemed to be a small cave under the ledge—it looked like some kind of gaping mouth.

David paused, trying to decide if he should investigate or try to pick up Jon's scent along the bank. Then he picked up on another scent.

ᏎᏨᏎᏨᏎᏨ

In his hiding place, Jon was holding his breath. He clasped his hand over his mouth for fear David would hear him. He watched the lion follow the footprints, jump over the stream, and then pause and look back as if contemplating the alcove. Jon froze. *You can't see me,* he thought. *Go away.* Then David did just that, tearing off at full tilt into the trees, as if repelled by the force of Jon's thoughts. *No way,* Jon thought. *Did that actually work?*

ᏎᏨᏎᏨᏎᏨ

Out of the shadows of the labyrinth, a massive beast emerged. He was bigger than Calder had been, but while Calder had been a hairless, muscled brute, this feline creature was lean, muscled in a way that was beautiful and terrible at the same time. He had the look of a sophisticated and efficient killer—covered in thick, shiny fur with black-on-black stripes. He approached Abby with a menacing deliberateness, bearing long, primeval fangs.

"Hello, Rabbit," the creature said as he circled her slowly. "I've been waiting for you."

Abby could feel the beast's hot breath on her skin. *Don't show fear,* she thought, planting her feet in a fighting stance and drawing herself up to look taller, brawnier. *Look him straight in the eye. If you're going to die, at least have a little dignity about it.* She stared into his eyes and spoke his name: "Tierney."

The creature stared back, eyeing Abby's clenched jaw and defensive stance, and then he smiled apologetically. "Oh, I'm so sorry," Tierney said. "I forget this face can be, shall we say, rather off-putting. Allow me to present a more pleasing visage." His form changed, melting away like smoke, leaving black ashes lingering in the air. In the creature's place stood a handsome young man with dark eyes—nothing like the beast he had just been.

*Don't be fooled by the illusion,* Abby told herself. *He's the same monster he was before—it's just a mask.* She stood her ground, infusing her voice with authority. "On the contrary. You *know* that face is off-putting. That's why you wore it."

To her surprise, Tierney started laughing—not a mean, condescending laugh, but one of genuine, unguarded amusement. It wasn't quite the response Abby had expected.

"Well, now," he chuckled, "you are a surprisingly perceptive one. Do you know why I'm here?"

"I assume it's to get to the Solas Beir by killing me," Abby said.

"Oh, come now, Rabbit, I'm hurt. I have absolutely no such plans. None at all," Tierney replied.

"I have trouble believing that—your reputation precedes you," she said.

"Well, dear Rabbit, a reputation is really quite subjective, don't you think? And you must concede that *your* sources may be a bit biased when it comes to me." He began circling her again, looking her up and down. "Actually, I'm here because I heard a very interesting story about *you.* And I must say, I think there's more to you than I was originally led to believe. I heard that an ordinary human girl rescued the Lightbearer by killing a Blood Shadow—and not just any Blood Shadow, mind you, but one of the strongest among us. And I wondered to myself, an *ordinary* human girl? How can that be?"

Abby noticed that Tierney used the term "Lightbearer" rather than David's formal title of Solas Beir. She didn't think it was an accident. In fact, she was certain that Tynan Tierney never said or did anything that wasn't calculated. "What is it you want, exactly?" she demanded, putting her hands on her hips.

"Only to see if the story was true. I can see now that you've been underestimated. Clearly, you are no ordinary human girl. You are turning out to be *much* more interesting than I thought you would be, pretty little c'aislingaer," he said.

Abby glared at him. "Thanks, but you can't fool me into falling for flattery."

Suddenly Tierney stepped close to Abby, his arms pulling her to him, his breath on her neck as he whispered in her ear. "No, indeed I cannot. For I have met many a fool, and you are not one."

He was so warm, and his touch made her skin tingle, much to her chagrin. She fought to show no response, reminding herself to keep her guard up.

He continued, his lips almost grazing her skin as he talked. "What I want, Abigail, is to show you the truth—to help you see my side of the story so you can decide for yourself if my so-called reputation is deserved." He pulled away suddenly, his head cocked to one side as if he had heard something.

Abby heard nothing.

Tierney turned back, his dark eyes on her. "Your boyfriend is coming. Better not let him catch you fraternizing with the enemy. Until we meet again, little Rabbit." Taking her hand, he held it to his lips, kissing it with a disarming tenderness. Then he was gone—not in some magic puff of smoke, but simply not there anymore.

Abby heard the crack of a twig breaking as someone approached. Rather than feeling a sense of relief, she felt oddly guilty, like she had been caught in the act of doing something wrong. She had just survived what should have been a lethal encounter with a monster, but instead of being frightened of Tierney, she found herself attracted to him. And that terrified her.

"Abby?"

She heard someone calling her name and had a dizzying sense of being outside herself. Someone was touching her, as if they were trying to shake her awake. Her eyes were open, but somehow they weren't. She blinked and found herself in David's arms. He was cradling her on the ground, his hand supporting her head.

"Abby? Are you all right? Did you faint?" David asked.

"I—I don't know…I was running during the training exercise, and I saw this labyrinth—I ran inside…" She was so dizzy—bile was creeping up her throat. She fought back the urge to vomit.

"Labyrinth?" he asked.

Abby nodded. "Yes, and it was so dark, and I—"

"Abby—there's no labyrinth here."

"What?" She sat up in David's arms and looked around. The labyrinth was gone. She was lying in the center of a flat, circular meadow in the middle of the forest. The nausea left her, but her head began to ache.

David's eyes grew wide as he stared at her. "There's blood in your hair." He pulled his hand away from her head—there was blood on it too. "Abby, you're hurt—the back of your head is bleeding. Did you fall?"

"What? No, I..." *Did all that really just happen?* she asked herself. *Was that a dream?*

"It's okay, sweetheart—I've got you now. You don't have to talk. There's a stone here with your blood on it. You must have fallen and hit your head. Stay very still for a moment," David urged, supporting her body in the crook of one arm as he placed his other hand over the wound, applying gentle pressure.

He closed his eyes in concentration and she felt heat come from his hand. The dull ache at the back of her head faded, but she noticed that he winced as her wound was transferred to him. He ran his hand over the back of his own head and it came back bloody.

Abby felt guilty. "David, you didn't have to do that—I'm sorry. I would have healed in no time with just a bandage."

He shrugged. "Eh, it's fine—I heal fast. The blood's already stopped, and I can hardly feel the pain. That was just a small thing—I'd go through a whole lot more than a knock on the head to heal you. Besides, I need practice. Healing is much harder for me than flying or even transformation—there's more visualization involved in focusing my energy to repair a wound, and more of a personal price paid for using power. But don't worry about me—I can handle it. How are *you* feeling?"

"Much better. Thanks," Abby said. She smiled. "You're kind of handy like that, you know. I think I'll keep you around."

"Good—I'll hold you to that." David frowned. "I'm worried about how confused you were when you came to—maybe you were having a vision or something. Let's get you home and make sure you're really okay. I think we need to talk to my mom." He scooped Abby up in his arms and started back toward the castle.

"You don't have to carry me—I can walk. I'm fine. Really."

"Shh," David said. "I was *trying* to be romantic. You're stepping on my hero moment here, woman."

"Oh. Sorry." She kissed his cheek. "You may proceed."

He grinned. "That's more like it." He held her tightly as they headed homeward.

Abby looked back over David's shoulder. The ground seemed flat, but there was something strange about it—something she wouldn't have noticed at all if she didn't know what to look for—something better seen from a high vantage point. Slightly raised above the rest of the meadow were small mounds of grass, mimicking the pattern of the labyrinth.

ဆ〜෪ဆ〜෪ဆ〜෪

"Shouldn't they be back by now?" Marisol asked.

"I would think so," Cael agreed. "Come, let us do a bit of tracking ourselves."

Cael changed into a wolf and sniffed the ground, picking up a trail. Marisol followed him into the woods. When they came to the stone ledge over Jon's hiding place, Marisol silently signaled for Cael to stop, running her fingers through his fur. Placing a finger to her lips, she pointed to the scuff marks on the ground below, and then to where she thought Jon might be hiding.

The wolf seemed to smile, then nodded. He launched himself off the ledge, letting out a vicious growl as he landed on all fours in front of the entrance to the alcove.

Marisol heard Jon's involuntarily yelp, and she began laughing so hard she had to sit down on the edge of the stone lip for fear of losing her balance. When she saw Jon storm from his hiding place and glare up at her, she rocked back and forth, laughing even harder.

"Not funny, you guys," Jon said. "Not funny at all."

Cael changed back and chuckled. "I am sorry, Jon. We simply could *not* resist."

"*Great* hiding place," Marisol grinned. "You did much better than I did. David found me right away."

"Thanks," Jon said, grumpily crossing his arms.

"Your trail was very clever, Jon," Cael remarked. "I commend you—you seem to have outwitted the Solas Beir."

"Not you though," Jon said.

"Actually, I only followed your scent. It was Marisol who caught on to your trickery."

"Knew there was a reason I went for the smart girl," Jon muttered. "Even though she is *incredibly* mean."

"Sorry," Marisol said, smiling. She hopped down from her perch and pecked Jon on the cheek. "Forgive me?"

"I suppose," Jon said. "So where are David and Abby?"

"That's what we were wondering," Marisol said.

"I saw David pass by some time ago," Jon said. "He crossed the stream and then took off. Maybe he smelled Abby and went to find her."

"Where did he cross?" Cael asked.

Jon pointed, and Cael changed back into a wolf, sniffing the ground. He crossed the stream and circled the area, and then raised his head and bounded off into the trees.

"Guess he's caught their scents," Marisol said. "Come on." She took Jon's hand, and they ran after Cael.

When Abby and David arrived at Caislucis, they saw Eulalia making preparations for the new Western Oracle's confirmation ceremony. Dressed according to tradition for affairs of state, she was wearing an elegant white gown and her delicate silver tiara.

She was accompanied by several aides who were clad head-to-toe in white and feverishly taking notes. A petite Asian woman Abby had never seen before was talking with the queen. Her scarlet shift and black leather leggings seemed very bold among all that white.

"What happened?" Eulalia asked, hurrying over when she saw David carrying Abby into the Great Hall.

"She had a little accident during the training exercise," David said. "She fell and hit her head on a rock in the meadow."

"Let me see," Eulalia said.

"It's all right," David said, setting Abby on her feet. He kept his hands around her waist as if he still weren't certain she could stand on her own. "I healed her. But she seemed a bit disoriented when she came to, so I wanted her to take it easy."

"I'm fine." Abby stepped away from David's protective embrace to prove it. "Really—I just blacked out, I guess, and had some kind of dream, or vision, or something."

"What was your vision?" the newcomer asked.

"I...uh...it's difficult to remember," Abby began, suddenly unsure if it was the best idea to share her vision in the presence of a total stranger.

"Forgive me." Eulalia beckoned David and Abby to follow her to the center of the hall where she had left the woman standing. "Introductions are in order. This is my son, the Solas

Beir, and our cai aislingstraid, Abigail. David and Abby, this is the Northern Oracle."

David bowed formally, and Abby followed suit with a respectful curtsey.

"Welcome, Northern Oracle," David said. "We are greatly honored by your visit."

The Northern Oracle smiled. "A bit surprised too, I imagine. I must apologize for the lack of notice that I was coming."

"It's a very pleasant surprise," David said. "I am sure that the new Western Oracle will be honored to have you here as well."

"The queen has been telling me of your choice for the post—I think you have made a wise decision. I have not met Nerine yet, but of course the tale of how she rescued Cael has been told across the kingdom," the Northern Oracle commented.

"As have the tales about you and your people," David said. "Your valor in battle is legendary."

"You flatter me, Solas Beir," she said.

"Not at all," David said. "If not for your intervention at the Gauntlet, Cael would not have been able to obtain the Sign of the Throne, and I would not be here. I am eternally grateful to you."

The Northern Oracle smiled. "You have done well with your son, Eulalia. I can see already that he will be a gracious king, revered by his people."

"Thank you," Eulalia responded, beaming. "I am very proud of him. David, I was telling the Northern Oracle of your plans to visit each of the oracles."

David nodded. "Yes, I had intended to visit you in the north soon, but it seems you have spared us a long trip in coming to Caislucis instead."

"Indeed—it is quite a long journey. I had hoped to meet with you sooner, but I was delayed in coming. Nevertheless, let me assure you, Solas Beir, that we of the north have been ever loyal to the Light and will remain so," the Northern Oracle said.

"Thank you. We could not ask for better allies. Having you with us will go a long way toward an alliance with the Southern and Eastern Oracles," David said.

"We can hope," the Northern Oracle replied. "That is actually the reason for my visit. In the time just before you became Solas Beir, we were met with a series of attacks on our fortress, which is why I was unable to attend your coronation. The Kruorumbrae seemed to rapidly gain in numbers and strength. We were managing to hold them off, and then, suddenly, they vanished. Since then it is as though there were a veil over my visions, and I can no longer see my brothers to the south and east. I fear they too have been under attack."

"I hope all is well in their regions. We have had our own share of attacks, but it seems it is not just the Kruorumbrae we need to worry about," David said. "We believe that one of our villages was ravaged by the Daughters of Mercy."

The Northern Oracle frowned. "Could it be that they were pursuing the Kruorumbrae? I cannot imagine the Daughters of Mercy would attack someone who had committed no wrong."

"We fear that they did just that," Eulalia replied. "It is unprecedented, but they have taken captive a number of the villagers, seemingly without cause."

"I fear these are not isolated events," a musical voice echoed though the room. Abby turned to see a woman with smooth grey skin and long white hair entering the Great Hall.

"Nerine," David called, smiling. He walked over to the mermaid, who looked graceful in a sweeping white gown, having temporarily transformed her tail into legs. He took both her hands in his. "Thank you so much for agreeing to serve as the Western Oracle."

"I am honored by Cael's nomination, and happy to serve," Nerine said as she and David rejoined the others in the center of the hall. "And I am pleased to finally meet the Northern Oracle."

"Welcome, my sister," said the Northern Oracle. "Do you bring us news as well?"

Nerine nodded. "I do. There seems to be a great darkness rising once again, even from the sea. It is as it was in the days when the sirens preyed on my kind. Some of my people have gone missing, and there are tales of a beast that takes them. One with a serpentine tail."

*The creature I saw watching us,* Abby thought, in a flash of insight. "I think I've seen it. After David's coronation, he and I flew to Lone Tree Island. When we were leaving the island, I glimpsed something perched on the rocks, like it had been spying on us, but all I saw was a black-and-white striped tail as it slithered back into the sea. But if all the sirens are dead, what could it be?"

"I do not know," Nerine frowned, "but my people are very frightened. They say the old Western Oracle has risen to take her revenge."

"Surely that cannot be," Eulalia said. "Abby—what of your vision? Is there anything you can tell us?"

Abby looked from face to face, suddenly very uncomfortable to be in the spotlight. "Not exactly. Nothing related to the Daughters of Mercy or the sea. In my vision I entered a labyrinth and Tierney was there, waiting for me."

Eulalia and the Northern Oracle exchanged a dark look and returned their gazes to Abby. She felt her face grow red, which made her feel even more self-conscious.

"Did he try to hurt you?" David asked, taking Abby's hand.

David's familiar touch steadied her. Abby felt the flush in her cheeks fade as she met his gaze. "Surprisingly, no," Abby said.

"Well, what did he want?" David asked.

"He just...he said he just wanted to see if the stories about me were true. If the Shadows had underestimated me. And what's even weirder is he kept calling me Rabbit. Whatever *that* means," Abby finished.

"Hmm," David mused. He looked perplexed.

"Yeah. I know," Abby shook her head. "Weird."

"Abby, did you say there was a labyrinth?" Eulalia asked.

Abby turned to look at Eulalia. "Yes, I did. Why?"

"Because," Eulalia said, "there used to be one in the meadow. But it burned to the ground the night David was taken."

"All right then," Abby shivered. "I am officially creeped out." She caught herself, realizing she might not be speaking as formally as required, considering her audience. "On that note, please excuse me, but I've got to get ready for the ceremony. See you soon, Nerine. It was nice to meet you, Northern Oracle."

"I need to change as well," David added. "Nerine, Northern Oracle, thank you again for coming. I'm looking forward to the confirmation and the banquet. Please, if there is anything we can do to make your stay more comfortable, you only need to ask. We will see you again very soon." David placed his hand on the small of Abby's back and walked her to the corridor that housed their chambers.

ᛒᚷᛒᚷᛒᚷ

After David and Abby were out of earshot, the Northern Oracle discreetly pulled Eulalia to the side. "My dear queen, I do not mean to intrude on the affairs of your realm, but I sense there is more to that story than your cai aislingstraid was willing to divulge."

Eulalia nodded, her brow furrowed with worry. "Thank you, Northern Oracle. I do appreciate your concern. Perhaps she was shaken by her vision and her injury. I will speak with her about it later."

ᛒᚷᛒᚷᛒᚷ

That night, the queen observed Abby closely during the ceremony and banquet, but nothing seemed amiss. *Perhaps she was just shaken by the events of the day,* she thought. *The arrival of the Northern Oracle certainly took us all by surprise.*

Still, there was something that seemed off about Abby's demeanor. Eulalia could feel it, even if she couldn't say what it was.

ᛒᚷᛒᚷᛒᚷ

"What happened out there today?" Jon asked David while they were socializing after the banquet. "We looked everywhere for you guys, and finally Cael tracked you back to the castle."

"Abby took a bump on the head, so I healed her and brought her back here. Sorry to keep you guys waiting," David said. "I should have let you know, but we got distracted by our guests."

"Oh. No worries," Jon assured him. "Is she all right?"

"I think so. She was confused at first, but she seems okay now." David frowned. "Doesn't she?"

Jon looked over at Abby, who was standing on the other side of the room, laughing as she chatted with Marisol and Nerine. "Yeah, she seems fine to me," he said. "Why do you ask?"

"I don't know," David answered. "I'm just paranoid, I guess. Something bad happens to her and I blame myself for not being there to protect her. You know what I mean?"

"Yeah, man, I do," Jon nodded. "But trust me, that is *not* a road you want to go down. I could never keep her from getting banged up as a kid. And if you haven't noticed, she's pretty darn stubborn."

"Yeah," David chuckled. "I've noticed."

"I'll bet," Jon grinned. Then he grew serious. "The girl does what she wants, and there's no way you can protect her from everything. You can't be giving yourself a guilt trip about it."

"True," David agreed. "But what if I missed something when I healed her? What if I healed the gash on her head, but she has a concussion or something?"

"Man, you are going to make yourself crazy if you think like that," Jon said.

David groaned. "Too late."

Jon laughed, clapping David on the shoulder. "Yeah, well, lighten up, would you? We're at a party. Enjoy it."

ಬಂಗಾಬಂಗಾಬಂಗಾ

Abby opened her eyes and sat up in bed. She had to hurry—he was waiting for her, and in a few hours' time, the castle would be a hive of activity. She dressed quickly, and silently slipped out of her room, holding her shoes in one hand so she could pad quietly down a dark corridor and into a narrow passage.

Other than the spiders that spun cobwebs from its ceiling, no one seemed to know the passage existed or that it led to a door in the fortress wall at the edge of the forest. Nevertheless, she had placed a charm on both the entrance and exit so it would be hidden from prying eyes and to prevent anyone but her from using it. She didn't want to be found out, but she didn't want anything from the outside getting in either.

Once outside, she paused for a moment to slip on her shoes and look around, making sure she was not observed. Satisfied that she was alone, she stepped into the forest.

Here she treaded carefully, trying to position her feet on leaves and moss, avoiding mud. The last thing she wanted was to leave tracks, and it wouldn't do to soil her fine shoes either. It took time to reach the meadow—what path there had once been was overgrown. That was fine; the plants were healthy and would spring back, erasing her steps, hiding the night's activity.

Finally, Abby reached the meadow where the labyrinth stood. Again, she took a moment to look around, but no one was following her. She gracefully leapt across the long grass and into the entrance of the labyrinth.

Now, she relaxed. Here she would be hidden. Here is where he would be waiting. She knew the way well. She wound her way around, one hand stretched out to playfully caress the vibrant green wall formed by a towering hedge. She was excited to see him. It had been a while since she had been able to sneak out, but in the secret message he had left for her, he had begged her to come. He had said there was something he needed to show her.

Rounding the last corner, she saw him. He was sitting on the carved stone bench, gazing up at the stars, deep in thought. He was wearing a tailored suit, and he looked so handsome, his black hair ruffling slightly in the night breeze. Hearing her approach, he met her gaze with his dark eyes. He smiled.

"Tierney," she whispered.

"I was worried you would not come," he said softly, taking her hand and pulling her close to him.

"I promised I would," she said.

"So you did. Shall we?" He gestured to the round, flat stone in the center of the labyrinth.

"We shall." Somewhere in the back of her mind it occurred to her that she'd had a similar conversation before, but with someone else. She couldn't remember who. *No matter.*

She stepped onto the stone circle and the next thing she knew, they were standing in a different part of the forest. Before her was a tree stump, as tall as she was. On it was carved the face of a bearded man. His features were covered with the verdant fuzz of moss, accented by tiny scarlet and white mushrooms sprouting here and there on the bark. He was crowned in a thick fungus layered in ridges at the top of the stump.

She had not been here before, but she knew the name of this wooden man. "The Emerald Guardian?" she asked.

"Yes," Tierney said, laying his palm against the center of the stump man's forehead. "Place your hand over mine. We are going through."

She looked at him questioningly, then did as he asked. "They do not know about the Guardian, do they?" she asked as they stepped into the other world.

"No—and let us keep it that way," Tierney answered. He laced his fingers through hers and led her away from the tree they had just stepped through.

"Where are we?" she asked.

He chuckled. "At present, we are standing in a graveyard."

Around them stood marble stones of various shapes and sizes. Based on the moss and lichen that had seeped onto the surface of the stones, and the tall grass growing between the markers, this was an old graveyard, and one few people came to visit. Beyond the tombstones was a wrought-iron gate.

"Come—what I wanted to show you lies just ahead."

They passed through the gate and crossed a deserted country road. Tierney led her up a tree-dotted hill. At the crest of the hill, the countryside fell away sharply and transformed into something much different. A dark mass of factories stood silhouetted against the night sky, great smokestacks belching out black fumes. This, then, was not to be a trip for the sake of enjoying the scenery.

"You cannot see the stars anymore," he noted. "Do you see what they have traded for them?" Beyond the factories was an expanse of glittering lights stretching to the horizon.

She nodded. "What is this place?"

"It is legion," he said, with a small, sad laugh. "It is only one of many places where the trees are almost gone, the animals have fled, the waters are poisoned, and we cannot abide. The Solas Beir wants us to stop feeding on humans, but there is nothing else left to eat. They are locusts. In the few short years since he closed the portals, look at how much they have devoured."

"But you devour the humans," she said.

"Only so we can live. But without us, they are killing themselves. And if they succeed, we will be forced to feed on ourselves."

"Perhaps that is what he wants," she suggested.

A dark look crossed Tierney's face and, for a moment, she was certain he would hit her. She stepped back.

He studied her eyes. "Perhaps," he said. He took her face in his hands and kissed her hungrily, the heat behind it barely contained. Then he looked into her eyes again. "You know what I am. I cannot change that."

"I know," she said. "I never asked you to."

He kept her gaze a moment longer, and then a small, mischievous smile appeared on his lips. "Come," he said. "The night is still ours and we might as well enjoy it. When was the last time you danced?"

"It *has* been a while," she replied, returning his smile.

"There is one thing humans do well," Tierney said, looking down at the lights of the city. "They make the most of their short lives while they can." He took her arm, and they returned to the road, following it until they reached the edge of the city. They headed toward a busy downtown area bustling with nightlife.

Brightly decorated shop windows reflected the streetlights, and the people themselves were lit up with a contagious energy.

As if invigorated by it, she and Tierney laughed and picked up the pace, letting themselves be carried along in the vigor of beings with a limited shelf life. Her high-heeled shoes clicked against the sidewalk, keeping rhythm with the sounds of the city.

As they passed a window, she caught her reflection in the glass. She was wearing a dark, tailored coat that fell to her knees, one that fit in perfectly with the garments of the stylish young women they passed. Peeking out from underneath her matching cloche were strands of long blond hair.

*Lucia,* she thought. *I am Lucia.* She woke up with a start.

"No," Abby said. She was alone in her room, but she said it out loud anyway, as if speaking the word would make it true, warding off the chance it wasn't. "No. I'm not. I'm nothing like her."

ಐೞಐೞಐೞ

Abby and Eulalia were sitting across from each other in the small parlor of the queen's chambers. The afternoon light was bright, streaming in through a window of leaded glass, which was opened slightly on its iron hinges. On the wall, tiny rainbows formed from the light filtering through the beveled glass. An ocean breeze wafted in, stirring the sweet-smelling blossoms sitting in a vase on the small table between the wooden chairs, which had scrolled arms and cushions upholstered in a rich damask that felt luxurious against Abby's skin.

"Abby, I wanted to discuss your development as a cai aislingstraid. Is there anything you wish to tell me before your journey?" Eulalia asked. It was the last session they would have before Abby traveled with David to see the Southern Oracle.

Abby ran her fingers along the soft cerulean fabric of her chair. It was the same color as the sea outside. "Um, it's going well, I guess."

"You do not sound convinced of that."

Abby looked up to see the queen studying her face with concern. "I'm just tired. I had another nightmare last night, and it was hard to get back to sleep," she answered, rubbing her eyes.

Eulalia nodded. "I am sorry. I know that can be difficult."

"No, it's fine," Abby said. "Maybe I'll sleep better tonight. It's just...can I ask you a question?"

Eulalia smiled. "Of course."

"Okay. Is it possible to see something through someone else's eyes? Like, you feel like you actually *are* that person, but you're just seeing it from their perspective? And if that is possible, are you seeing what has happened, or what will happen?"

"It depends. It *is* possible to see through the eyes of another, but as to the second part of your question...it would help to know more specifically what you saw," Eulalia said.

"I was afraid you would say that," Abby replied.

"Why? There is no reason to be afraid."

Abby frowned. "I'm not so sure about that." She shared her latest dream with Eulalia, leaving out that she had felt attracted to Tierney. "Here's the thing—it was easy when I just thought of him as evil. But if I really was seeing things through Lucia's eyes, I guess I can kind of understand her, uh, motivation. Maybe there's more to him than I first thought. I almost feel bad for him."

Eulalia was silent. She rose from her seat and stared out the window at the sea.

Abby waited anxiously for Eulalia to respond. The fact that she didn't was disconcerting. She let the seconds tick by, trying to be patient and allow Eulalia the time to process whatever it was she was thinking about.

Finally, after several frustrating minutes, Abby had no choice but to break the silence—if she didn't get an answer soon, she thought she might go mad. "All right, so please, just tell me. Have I gone to the dark side?"

"No. Not yet," Eulalia said softly.

"But I'm walking a dangerous line, you mean?"

Eulalia turned to face Abby. "I did not say that."

"Okay. Well, tell me this. What Tierney said, about his survival being threatened and about us humans destroying everything...I mean, he kind of does have a valid point," Abby said. "Doesn't he?"

Eulalia returned to her chair and took Abby's hands. "It is not that he does not have a valid point. And I do believe that, yes, it is possible you were seeing something that did happen, and that you saw it from my sister's perspective. Certainly, if that is the case, it would make sense that you would have felt her emotions and that you would now possess a greater understanding of what appealed to her about him. But what Tierney said—valid as it may sound, is a half-truth. He speaks of the humans destroying themselves, but you must remember that he is also destructive. He is a predator, and what he says or does is not for the good of humanity. You must remember that everything he does is to serve his own interests first, even if there may be a benefit to others."

"Okay, I see your point. But how do we know for sure what he thinks? Is it possible that he believes he is right and that, in his mind, his actions are justified?" Abby asked.

"I am certain he *does* feel justified. Most people who go to the 'dark side,' as you are fond of calling it, do not behave the way they do because they think they are wrong. I am sure Tierney does feel that his perspective is the right one, and that is why he is able to pursue his goals without the burden of guilt," Eulalia explained. She stared into Abby's eyes. "And that is why I fear for you, Abby. You cannot simply accept what I say as true. You must discover the truth for yourself or he *will* turn you to his side."

"But I do believe you. And trust me, he will *never* turn me to his side," Abby insisted.

Eulalia gave Abby a sad smile. "I know you think so, but you must also understand that Tierney is relentless. If he wants to turn you to his way of thinking, he will pursue you until you fall. My sister also faithfully served the Light, and even she fell."

"I am not her."

"No. You are not. But I say again: you must discover the truth for yourself; otherwise you will always have doubt. Promise me this—when you go to visit the Southern Oracle, ask him to take you to the Blood Altar," Eulalia said.

"I promise—I will. But what will I find there?" Abby asked.

"You will see Tierney for what he truly is."

# THE RAINFOREST

"Abby!" David called as she was leaving Eulalia's chamber. He was jogging up the corridor.

"Hi," she said, closing the door behind her.

"So you're done with Eulalia?" he asked, taking her hand.

"Yep—we just finished our chat." She hoped she sounded more positive than she felt.

David didn't seem to notice. "Great—good timing then." He laced his fingers through hers and kissed her forehead. "I was hoping to catch you. Cael and I finished prepping for our trip. He and the other two have gone to fill their packs and say their goodbyes. You and I should do the same. Cael wants to leave at first light."

"So we should get to bed early tonight so we are well rested, I take it?" Abby asked.

David nodded. "Yes. The horses can take us to the edge of the rainforest, but after that, we're on our own. It's just too dense for them. We have a long walk ahead."

"That we do. All right, I'll go say goodbye to my family and finish packing." Abby suddenly felt very tired, thinking about the trip. No, that wasn't it exactly. She was emotionally exhausted from her conversation with Eulalia, and thinking about packing just added to that.

"I'll come with you," he said. He studied her face. "Abby, are you okay?"

"Yeah, I'm fine," she lied.

David looked up and down the empty hallway and then led Abby to an alcove of arched windows with a view of the Western Sea. "Abby," he said. "Talk to me. Please." His eyes were wide, pleading.

"What do you want me to say?"

David furrowed his brow in frustration. "I'm worried about you. Ever since you hit your head, you haven't been yourself. Does your head still ache?"

"No, I'm fine," Abby repeated.

"Well, then, why does it feel like you've been so distant lately?" he asked. "Did I do something wrong?"

"No," she said. "No, that's not it at all."

"Well, what is it then? Tell me," David pleaded, placing his hand gently on her cheek.

Looking up at him, Abby could see that he was genuinely concerned about her—that he was trying hard to be helpful. She sighed. "I'm just really tired. I haven't been sleeping well at all. Lots and lots of nightmares."

It seemed like every time she closed her eyes she was haunted by either Tierney or the Kruorumbrae. She couldn't help but feel a sense of doom about the journey to see the Southern Oracle. She hoped that was just the sleep deprivation talking, and not an actual premonition.

After her conversation with Eulalia, when she confessed that she could understand Tierney's way of thinking, Abby felt frustrated, humiliated, and yes—she had to admit—*frightened* by Eulalia's reaction. But she wasn't about to make the same mistake with David. Besides, it would only hurt him, and that was the last thing she wanted to do.

He caressed her cheek, still staring intently at her. "All right, well, how about this: let me stay with you tonight. I'll keep the bad stuff away."

"I don't know…"

"Abby, we'll be camped out next to each other every night on this trip anyway. Are you worried about what your parents might think?" David asked.

Abby shook her head. "No. They've pretty much treated me like an adult since we got here. They've been surprisingly cool about me going on this trip." She smiled. "Not that they've had much choice in the matter."

"Yeah, we haven't exactly asked their opinion, have we? But they've been nice to me—I think they might actually approve," he grinned.

"They do. They think you're great for me."

"That's a relief. Okay, then—if it's not about your parents, what are you afraid of?" David questioned.

Abby looked down at her feet, unsure of how to answer him. For a second, she was tempted to tell David about her conversation with Eulalia.

*I know what you're afraid of, Rabbit.* Tierney's voice echoed in Abby's mind. *You're afraid you'll say my name in your sleep and he'll find out about us.*

Abby shivered. *Get out of my head,* she thought. She prayed that Tierney's voice was only her imagination, and that he couldn't actually read her mind. "There is no *us*," she muttered.

"What?" David asked, startled.

"Sorry," Abby said, frowning. There was no way she could tell David the truth about her dreams of Tierney. Not ever. "I was talking to myself, not you. Arguing with myself, actually. See—I'm so sleep deprived, I've lost my mind." Making a decision, she forced herself to meet David's concerned gaze. "Okay. Please stay with me tonight—if anyone can protect me from the bad stuff, it's you." She smiled at him.

"Always," David vowed, pulling her close and kissing her. He stared into her eyes. "I will *always* keep the bad stuff away from you."

"Is that a promise?" she asked.

"Yes," he said. "It's a promise. Nothing will ever hurt you as long as I'm around."

☙❦☙❦☙❦☙❦

David woke Abby with a soft kiss on her forehead. She'd slept peacefully once she was nestled against him—or so he hoped. "Mornin', sunshine," he whispered.

"Good morning," she whispered back sleepily, kissing his cheek.

"Any bad dreams?" he asked.

"Not one, thanks to you. You've sold me on this being together thing. I don't ever want to fall asleep without you again," Abby said.

He smiled. "You will never have to. Like I said, I will always be here for you."

She returned his smile. "Good. Because you're stuck with me now."

"Just how I like it. Ready for our little adventure?"

She yawned and then sat up and stretched. "Yeah. I think a change of scenery will do me good."

"I think so too." David looked toward the window. The dawn sky was suffused with pink and coral. "Let's hurry—I'm sure Cael is already saddling his horse. Early riser."

"Too early," Abby groaned.

David laughed. "I know. Come on," he said, and kissed her cheek.

ಊಞಊಞಊಞ

After getting up and grabbing a bite to eat, Abby and David headed to the stables to join Cael, Jon, and Marisol. They quickly finished up their last-minute packing.

Abby noticed that she and Marisol had picked similar clothes for this adventure: tight-fitting pants and billowing shirts cinched with belts. Abby had been wearing dresses more often since coming to Cai Terenmare, but still felt more comfortable with pants when training or going out riding. Apparently Marisol did too.

Abby stroked her horse's neck. She made one last check of her pack, grasped the saddle horn, and swung up into the saddle.

"Everyone ready?" Cael asked.

"Yep—let's go," Abby said, smiling brightly.

"You're awfully chipper this morning," Jon muttered, climbing up into his saddle. He tugged on his pack to make sure it was secure.

"I'm excited," Abby replied. "Aren't you?"

"I will be once I wake up. I'm so not a morning person," Jon complained.

David chuckled as he, too, mounted his horse. "No whining, Reyes."

"Yeah, come on, Grumplestiltskin," Marisol teased, cocking her head to the side. Her long hair fell over her shoulder.

Cael looked around to make sure everyone was ready. With a nod, he nudged his horse to move out. David, Abby, Jon, and Marisol followed suit.

"Personally, I'm with Abby on this one," Marisol said. "I can't wait to see what's in the jungle. Will we see any animals, Cael?"

"We might," Cael said. "But remember, be careful not to touch them—some have a rather nasty bite. The same goes for the plant life."

Marisol frowned. "Oh yeah, I forgot about that part. Well, that's no fun."

"Now who's the grumpy one?" Jon asked. Grinning, he nudged his horse into a gallop.

Marisol laughed and hurried to catch up.

Abby started to follow, but then saw a dark shape pass over head. Brarn circled briefly before landing on her saddle horn. "Not this time, my friend," she said, stroking his feathers. "If we encounter carnivorous plants, I don't want you perching on them. Go home to Eulalia."

The raven cocked his head at her. "Go on," Abby said firmly. "I'll see you when we get back."

Brarn bobbed his head and took to the air, flying back toward the castle.

"You two have bonded," David noted. "I think that bird may like you even more than he likes my mom."

"I guess it must be because I rescued him from a Shadow cat once," Abby explained.

"He is not one to forget a favor," Cael said. "I daresay he would follow you to hell and back."

"Let's hope it never comes to that," Abby said. "Come on, we'll never catch those two if we don't get a move on." She nudged her horse into a trot, and Cael and David kept pace with her.

∞⊂3∞⊂3∞⊂3

Abby shifted in her saddle, trying to stretch out her back and neck. They'd been riding for hours, and her thighs had started to ache.

"Anyone else have a sore butt?" Jon asked.

Cael gave him a look. "Best enjoy the ride while you can, Jon. Once we reach the tree stump called the Emerald Guardian, we go on foot."

"Why is it called that?" Marisol asked. "Is it covered in jewels?"

"No—it is just very green," Cael replied.

"It used to be a portal once," Abby added, "a long time ago."

Cael turned to look at her. "How do you know that?"

"I saw it in a dream," Abby admitted. She realized the others were staring at her as well. "I'm right, aren't I?"

"Yes," Cael said. "It was a portal. One favored by Tierney. Ardal closed it when he discovered that fact."

"Ah. That part I didn't know," Abby lied. *It may be best to keep these things to myself,* she thought.

Cael stared at her for a second, then turned to the others. "It used to be that a journey to the outer edges of Cai Terenmare could happen in the blink of an eye. Now that the portals are closed, we have to use more conventional means, which is why we will soon be traveling on foot."

"And there's no way we can reopen the portals to speed things up?" Marisol asked.

"Oh, we can," David interjected, "but we won't. We can't risk Tierney gaining access to them again."

The group rode on in silence as the forest around them grew thicker and began to change from a landscape of ferns and moss-encrusted evergreens to a vine-covered wonderland. The horses began to tread carefully, stepping through the creeping foliage.

"We are almost there," Cael announced. "See ahead?"

Rising from the vines and encased in moss and fungus was the carved tree stump Abby had seen in her dream.

"It's a dude," Jon said. "With a green beard."

"Indeed." Cael smiled, and then grew serious. "And this marks the boundary of our forest. From here, we must be on the alert at all times. The Southern Oracle's rainforest is not a hospitable place. We are fortunate to be traveling during the dry season. Were we to enter the forest during the wet season, this journey would take us much longer, and I shudder to think what creatures we might encounter in the flooded undergrowth."

Solemnly, the group dismounted, taking their packs.

"Will the horses stay here or go back?" Abby asked, patting her mare's neck.

"They will stay. There is water nearby, and plenty for them to eat. They will be content here until we return," Cael affirmed.

After gathering their supplies, they traveled on without their horses. The vines twisted and thickened into a tropical canopy of dark green that blocked out the sunlight. Then the sun started to set, and what little light there was began to rapidly fade.

"We should camp here for the night," Cael said, inspecting a small clearing centered among the roots of several gigantic trees. He hunkered down and dug a shallow pit for a fire.

"I'll help you," David offered. He closed his eyes and in his mind's eye, he could see the dry branches littering the ground rise and settle into a neat pile in the middle of Cael's pit. He flicked his wrist and heard the crackling noise of flames. When he opened his eyes, he could see they had begun to burn brightly with a blue-edged flame.

"Nicely done," Abby said.

"Thanks," David smiled.

Marisol crossed her arms and stared out into the encroaching blackness of the jungle. "It's not so bad. Nothing scary just yet."

As if on cue, a long, lonely howl pierced the air. Jon shot her a look. "You were saying?"

Marisol frowned. "Yeah, okay. I stand corrected."

"Those who dwell in this forest are more restless at night," Cael said. "But so long as we have the fire and keep watch, we should be fine."

"Should be?" Jon asked. "Great. Well, I'm wide awake. Guess I'll take first watch."

Marisol peered into the darkness and shivered. "Yeah, I think I'll stay up too," she said, taking Jon's hand.

"Very well." Cael laid out his mat under one of the trees. "Wake me when you feel tired. Oh, and keep your satchels packed—remove only what is absolutely necessary, and return it to your pack as soon as you are finished using it. We may need to leave in a hurry. Swords at the ready," he added, tapping his scabbard lightly. Then he lay down, closed his eyes, and within a moment was softly snoring.

Jon shook his head in disbelief. "Dude can sleep anywhere."

"Shhh, he's probably a light sleeper," Marisol warned. "Here—sit with me back-to-back so we can keep watch."

Nodding, Jon rolled a log over for Marisol to sit on and then settled in behind her, his hand on the hilt of his sword.

David and Abby laid out their sleeping mats side by side. "G'night guys," Abby said drowsily, curling up on her mat.

Jon looked over at her. "Et tu, Abby?"

"She hasn't been sleeping well," David explained. "Hopefully she can get some z's tonight." He lay down with Abby and pulled her close. "I'm here with you," he whispered. "No bad dreams."

"No bad dreams," Abby whispered back. She yawned and settled into the crook of his arm. "Love you."

To David's surprise, she drifted off almost as quickly as Cael. "Good night, Abby," he whispered, kissing her forehead. "I love you too." Then he fell asleep as well.

&#8199;&#8199;&#8199;

David woke with a start. Somewhere in the night a woman was screaming.

"Abby," he murmured, and tried to sit up. Then he realized that Abby was still fast asleep in his arms. He raised his head to look for the others and was shocked at the complete darkness around him. The fire had gone out. He closed his eyes and focused his power to relight it.

"Ahh!" Jon yelped, when the fire blazed high in front of his face. He had been kneeling in front of the pit, trying to get the dead fire started again.

Marisol and Cael were on their feet, back-to-back, swords held out in front of them, eyes scanning the forest.

"Sorry, Jon," David said. "You okay?"

"Fine—just singed my eyebrows," Jon grumbled, rubbing his forehead. He stood and drew his sword.

Abby woke and looked up at David. "What's going on?"

"We were about to wake Cael to take the next shift when the fire blew out," Jon explained. "That's when the screaming began."

"What do you mean, the fire blew out?" David asked.

"One minute it was nice and toasty, the next it was out cold," Marisol clarified.

A woman's scream pierced the air again. It was impossible to tell where it was coming from. It sounded close at first, then further away, then close again, from somewhere on the other side of the clearing.

"Sounds like a banshee," Abby whispered, clutching David's arm. "It's horrible."

"It's *La Llorona*," Marisol gasped.

"What?" David asked. He stood up and pulled Abby to her feet. They drew their swords as well.

"The Witch of the Ditch," Jon replied. "The Weeping Woman."

"It's a ghost story from Mexico that my mother told me," Marisol explained. "There's this legend about a beautiful woman who drowned her children to be with the man she loved. But he left her, so she killed herself. After that, she was doomed to wander the Earth, searching for her dead children. People say she comes out at night near rivers, and that if you hear her wailing, you'll die."

"And there you go," Jon said. "We're done for."

"Not quite yet, Jon," Cael replied. "I have never heard such a sound, but if the creature meant to attack, it would have. For now, we stay on our guard. No more sleeping tonight."

"No rest for the wicked," Abby teased.

David looked at her and smiled. "I thought the saying was no rest for the *weary*."

"I like my version better," Abby quipped. "Seems apropos."

&#8414;&#8413;&#8414;&#8413;&#8414;&#8413;

Morning was a long time coming, but when the canopy turned from black to green tinged with grey, the screamer fell silent, vanishing with the darkness.

"I'm exhausted," Jon said, sinking down to sit on a log by the fire.

"Yeah, me too," Marisol agreed, joining Jon. "I think that little adrenaline rush is finally leaving my system."

"Why don't you guys sleep for a bit? You too, Cael," David said, stoking the fire. "Abby and I will keep watch and wake you in a few hours."

"We will not get far today if we do that," Cael objected.

"True, but if you don't get some rest, you won't be ready if that thing comes back tonight," David argued.

"Touché. Come on, Sol," Jon said. Standing, he took Marisol's hand, pulling her to her feet. Then he led her over to their as-yet-unused sleeping mats.

"Yeah, I'm game," Marisol agreed. She rubbed her eyes and let herself sink into a tired heap on the mat. "C'mon, Cael. I know you're tired too. Don't be all stoic about it."

Cael smiled. "Stoic? I think you have mistaken me for someone else."

"Yeah, see—you're actually making a joke. You *must* be tired, tough guy," Jon said.

Cael nodded. "I am—a bit. David, no more than three hours, please. We will want to put some distance between ourselves and our visitor."

"You got it." David said.

"Sleep well, guys," Abby said. She looked around the clearing and found a few more pieces of wood to add to the fire.

"I can do that." David stepped in to help her.

"No need to use power when you don't have to," Abby said. "You should conserve your energy in case we need you tonight. It's not like you got much sleep either."

"I'm fine," he insisted. "If you want, you could take a little nap too—I don't mind keeping watch."

"Sounds tempting, but if I sleep now it will be harder to rest tonight," she replied.

"*If* we get to," David countered.

"With any luck, our screamer will get bored and bother someone else," Abby said.

ဗပဗပဗပ

Hoping to put some miles between themselves and the previous night's intruder, everyone pushed themselves to exhaustion during the day's hike. As evening came and they made camp further into the rainforest, Cael volunteered for first watch.

"You sure?" David asked. "I don't mind staying up a little longer."

"Now who is being stoic?" asked Cael.

"Point taken," David agreed. "Abby?"

"Yeah, I could use some sleep," Abby said. She joined him on their mats, settling into his embrace with her back to him. He wrapped his arms around her, pulling her tight against his chest.

"You as well, Jon and Marisol," Cael instructed. "I will be waking you soon enough."

Marisol nodded sleepily and dragged Jon over to their mats. Soon they too were fast asleep.

Cael settled into a spot where he could watch for trouble. He realized that the last evening's visitor had rattled him—his muscles already felt tense in anticipation of the next round.

Hours later, the night was still blessedly silent. He woke Jon and Marisol for their shift.

Jon's hand immediately flew to the hilt of his sword as he startled awake. When he saw Cael's hand on his arm, he relaxed slightly, but didn't release his grip on the sword. "Is it back?"

"No. We seem to have lost it," Cael informed him.

"Thank goodness for that," Marisol said, relieved. "That was so creepy. If I never hear that sound again…"

"Yes," Cael nodded. "I think we are all in agreement about that."

ဆၢၺၢၺၢၺ

Abby woke up cold. She reached behind her for David—he was still there. She could hear him breathing steadily, fast asleep. She looked to the fire. It was still going. Whatever had bothered them the night before seemed to be gone—or, if it was still lurking about in the dark, it had run out of things to scream about. Sleepily, she closed her eyes and rolled over to snuggle up to David, face to face. In his sleep he stirred slightly and draped his arm over her. She nestled her cheek against his warm chest and began to drift off.

"Hello, Rabbit."

Abby's eyes flew open. She found herself looking not into David's blue eyes, but Tierney's, which were so dark and intense, they were almost black. She recoiled and tried to wriggle away, but his arms were around her, holding her close.

Tierney grinned. "Please, don't get up on my account. It wouldn't do any good anyway—I'm in your head."

Abby glared at him. "What do you want?"

Tierney studied her clenched jaw and laughed. Apparently the enraged look on her face filled him with delight. *I'm so glad to be a source of amusement,* she thought angrily.

He reached out and caressed her cheek. "Don't be mad, love. I wanted to see you, of course."

"What did you do with David?" she asked.

"He's still here, lying beside you," Tierney said, gesturing to his body. He was wearing David's clothes. "If it makes you feel better, I could wear his face too."

"No," Abby said quickly. "No, don't do that."

"Why?" Tierney asked, feigning innocence. "Would that bother you, dear Rabbit?"

"No, no, I..." she said.

Tierney raised his eyebrows expectantly. "Yes?"

144

Abby looked into his dark eyes. "I want to see you as you are," she said firmly.

"Do you, now? How very interesting," Tierney replied.

ഓരോയ്യോയ

Abby sat bolt upright, her heart beating fast. She sucked in a breath of air, and breathed out slowly, trying to calm herself.

David opened his eyes and looked up at her. "Abby? What's wrong?"

"Nothing," Abby lied. "Just a bad dream." She looked around the camp. Jon and Marisol were sitting back-to-back, eyes trained on the forest around them. She could see Marisol's hand resting on the hilt of her sword. "Everything's okay—just go back to sleep," Abby said, settling in next to David, gently brushing the hair off his forehead.

"Okay," he mumbled. "Love you." David closed his eyes and drifted off again.

"Love you too," Abby whispered. She spent the remaining hours of the night staring at his sleeping face, afraid to close her eyes, terrified of what she might see.

ഓരോയ്യോയ

As he woke to take the next shift, David saw that Abby was awake. He reached over and tucked a stray curl behind her ear, noticing that the dark circles under her eyes seemed worse than ever. "No offense, sweetheart, but you look like you're exhausted. Did you have trouble sleeping again?"

"A little bit," Abby admitted. She sat up and pulled her knees to her chest, staring into the branches above them.

David followed her eyes. Morning was coming; the darkness around them had faded to a dull grey. He sat up and rubbed her back. "What happened? Bad dream?"

"Something like that."

"Want to talk about it?" David asked.

"No. Not really," she said, avoiding his gaze.

David looked at her tired eyes and decided not to press the issue. "Okay. No pressure. But if you want to talk later, I don't mind." Were her dreams so terrible that she didn't want to relive them by talking about them? Or...was it something else? Was she hiding something? David felt frustrated. He wished she would talk to him, let him help her with whatever was going on.

"Thanks," Abby said. She smiled wearily. "For the record, it's not because I'm trying to be stoic about it."

David put his arms around her. "I know. But you don't have to carry it alone. I know it's got to be pretty bad if you don't want to talk about it."

Abby rubbed her temples as if her head were aching. "It's just—sometimes it feels so real. Like I can't tell anymore when I'm dreaming and when I'm awake. I feel like I'm going crazy."

"I'll let you know if you are. And you're not, by the way," he said. He slipped his hands under hers and took over massaging her temples.

She relaxed and closed her eyes, letting her hands drop to her lap. "Thanks—that's good to know. David?"

"Yeah?" He stopped the massage to show he was listening.

She opened her eyes. "Just...just promise me that if I say anything in my sleep, don't be offended, okay? Just know that it's a dream, and I can't always control it. It doesn't mean anything. Okay?"

*What's that supposed to mean?* he thought. She was definitely hiding something. But what? What could be so terrible that she'd keep it secret from him? David stared at her and then started rubbing her temples again. "Okay. I'll try to remember that. I can't imagine what you could possibly say that would offend me, though."

"Well, I'll try my best *not* to say anything like that," Abby promised.

"Look," he said, taking his hands from her face. The dull grey above them was growing greener. "It's almost morning anyway, and the others need a little more sleep. Why don't you get some more rest?"

"Don't think that's going to happen," she said.

"It's okay. Just lay your head in my lap. I can keep watch."

"All right. Maybe the light will keep the nightmares away." She laid her head on his thigh and closed her eyes. Her face relaxed again as he stroked her hair.

David watched her slip into a deep sleep. The dark circles under her eyes seemed to lighten as her breathing deepened. She almost looked like a child.

It worried him that she was keeping the dreams to herself. Weren't they supposed to be connecting, working together? It seemed like they had been making good progress with dreamwalking, but now she had shut him out completely. There was something she wasn't telling him, but he feared if he pressured her, she would pull away from him more than she already had. *What happened to us, Abby?* he thought. *Where have you gone? And what are you hiding?*

ဟဢဟဢဟ

Abby woke to soft whispers. At first, she feared that David was gone and she was trapped in another dream. Then she realized that the others were already awake, and David was talking softly to Cael on the other side of the camp. Immediately she knew the hushed conversation was about her.

"I'm worried about her," she heard David say. "I'm losing her, and I don't know what to do about it."

"All you can do is be there for her," Cael replied. "She will talk when she is ready. She still loves you. Of that, I have no doubt."

"I hope so," David said. "I can't do this without her. I'm not that strong."

Abby saw Cael place his hand on David's shoulder. "You are stronger than you know."

Abby closed her eyes and pretended to be asleep again. After a short while, she gained the courage to sit up and pretend she hadn't heard their conversation.

She spent the day walking beside David, being overly polite, trying to hide her anger. She wasn't sure why it bothered her so much—it made perfect sense that David would feel that way, considering how she'd been acting, and it also made sense that he would consult with Cael. Who else would he talk to? Jon? Marisol? David had grown close to them, but they wouldn't understand like Cael, who had his own c'aislingaer he worried about.

Abby didn't know if Eulalia had shut Cael out during her years with Ardal, but Cael probably understood the toll Abby's nightmares were taking. After all the years of waiting to finally be with Eulalia, he was well acquainted with the need for patience. Abby understood all this in some logical part of her mind, but another part of her felt betrayed.

Night had fallen yet again, and she lay on her side, studying David's face in the firelight. He was fast asleep, but she could see that he seemed to be having a nightmare of his own. His brow was creased, and she could see the movement of his eyes under the lids. *I'm so sorry,* she thought, and kissed his forehead. He stirred, and his face relaxed. He was still deep in his dreams, but whatever storm had been raging in his mind seemed to have quieted.

Over his shoulder, she saw movement. She sat up, staring into the darkness of the jungle. Had the screamer found them? She looked back to the camp fire. It was still burning brightly. Jon and Marisol were keeping watch, their backs to each other, as usual, their fingers intertwined as they talked softly, keeping each other awake. They too were staring into the darkness, but seemed relaxed, unaware that anything might be amiss.

Abby, on the other hand, felt her body tense up as she became aware that they were not alone, that someone, or something, was watching them, veiled in that curtain of darkness, just out of the firelight's reach. And whoever it was whispered one word. Her name.

She knew who it was. *Tierney.*

With this realization came a surprise. She was no longer afraid. She was angry. *This ends tonight,* she thought. *No more secrets, no more hiding.*

Standing up, she took one last look at David, who was still sleeping peacefully, completely unaware that she had left his side. She was thankful for that. Whatever happened next, she didn't want him to know about the dreams with Tierney. She had never meant to betray him, and she felt guilty enough as it was. She stepped out of the firelight and into the darkness.

In spite of the blackness of the night, she could see Tierney moving just ahead. She snuck away from the campsite to follow him, her hand on the hilt of her sword, ready for whatever he had planned. He led her through the trees to a place where there was a break in the canopy, and the moonlight streamed through, lighting his handsome face.

His hair was as dark as David's, but longer and wavy. He was a little taller too, and had olive skin. The biggest difference between them, though, was their eyes. It wasn't just that Tierney's were so dark; there was something older about them, timeless and ancient at the same time. And while she could tell what David was thinking just by looking into his eyes, it was impossible to read Tierney. Not that she cared what Tierney was thinking. She just wanted to put an end to this madness, to make him stay out of her head and leave her and David alone.

He stepped up on a large, flat rock and nonchalantly leaned against a low branch in a tree. Guarded, Abby followed his gaze to the pond that lay below his perch. The water was so calm and still that the pond seemed unreal, like mirrored glass. Giant lily pads rested on its surface, and a single, sweet-smelling, white flower sat in the center of each; the flowers glowed like tiny moons.

"It's beautiful here, is it not?" Tierney asked. He looked at her and smiled warmly.

Abby had been expecting him to intimidate her, to threaten her. Not this. She felt her resolve falter as he gestured for her to join him, to sit and enjoy the view, it seemed. She had come prepared for a war of words, prepared to die fighting if it came to that. She had not considered a peaceful outcome.

Silently she stepped closer, joining him on the rock. She leaned against the trunk of the tree, trying to mirror his calm stance, but she was unwilling to let her guard down. She could feel his eyes on her as she crossed her arms over her chest.

"I didn't frighten you this time, did I?" he asked.

"No," Abby said. "You didn't." She didn't want to look at him. She stared out at the pond instead, and came to a decision. If Tierney was going to play at peace, she would play nice too, at least until she had the answers she needed. She turned to look at him. "I had a dream about you," she said.

"Did you? I'm flattered." His dark eyes burned into hers. "Tell me, little Rabbit. What did you dream?"

Abby uncrossed her arms and put her hands on her hips. "Why do you keep calling me Rabbit?"

Tierney grinned to himself. "You will find out soon enough."

"Fine," she said angrily. "But that is *not* my name."

"All right then, Abigail. Tell me your dream," he said softly.

Was he actually apologizing? Abby wasn't sure. She wasn't sure about a lot of things all of a sudden. She felt her guard slipping away as she lowered her arms to her sides. "You showed me a city, and how my world was being destroyed by my own people. You said we're locusts, and without you to prey on us, we would destroy ourselves completely," she recounted.

Tierney stared at her. "There is truth to that. You humans do have a tendency to self-destruct, don't you? I know you think I'm a monster, Abigail, but without me, humans would have killed themselves off long ago. You don't know how many times my kind have saved the human race from itself."

"So enlighten me. I want to know."

"Do you really?" A small smile played on his lips as though he were amused by her boldness. "Well, then, as you wish, dear girl. Long ago, before we were barred from your world, those like me provided a valuable service to your kind. You were at each other's throats all the time, warring, preying on one another. We targeted the most vile among you, those who preyed on innocence, and we thinned the herd, as it were, removing those who would have poisoned you all. You were like rats, multiplying, greedily competing for food, killing each other with disease. Was not the loss of a few worth the salvation of many?"

"You did us a *service?*" Abby spat, incredulous. "Call it what you will, but you're still talking about killing people. If we are rats, you are snakes."

Tierney chuckled softly, his dark eyes twinkling in the moonlight. "Oh, humans. One serpent leads you astray, and you are forevermore biased." He took a step toward her, his hands clenched at his sides. "I am not a snake, but I *am* a predator. I cannot deny it, I cannot switch it off. This is what I was made to be. A killer."

Abby stood frozen. His eyes were intense—she couldn't look away.

"But Abby—that does not mean that you and I are enemies." He suddenly pulled her to him and kissed her.

*Abby. Not Rabbit. Not Abigail. Abby.* The way he said her name was so tender, so intimate. She knew she should pull away, that if she let him kiss her she really *was* turning into Lucia. But she didn't.

◦◦◦◦◦◦◦◦

David stirred in his sleep and reached for Abby. She wasn't there. He woke up, suddenly desperate to feel her beside him, to know she was safe, instantly aware that something was horribly wrong. In a flash, he was on his feet.

He was the lion again, searching for her scent. He bounded off into the darkness, leaving Jon and Marisol by the fire. Startled into their own awareness that something was wrong, David heard them calling for Cael to wake up as he left the campsite.

David sped through the forest after Abby, his white fur almost glowing against the darkness. He could feel her and something else—something that might take her from him.

As he broke from the trees, he saw her, dazed, teetering on a rock above a moonlit pond. Surrounding her, in an ever tightening circle, were dark, squatting shapes with red eyes and gnashing teeth. *Toads,* David thought, in a flash of recognition. They were monstrous, bigger than any amphibians he'd ever seen, with ridges on their heads like horns, and great lumpy warts covering their slimy skin. But there was something else too, something with Abby, a shadow encircling her like smoke.

David changed back into himself and took flight, launching himself toward Abby. The toads leapt into the air, jaws snapping at him as he scooped her into his arms. Pressing her tight against his chest, he rocketed up into the sky, away from the shadow thing, away from the creatures that wanted to feed on her. And then, when he looked back from high above the pond, there was no sign of the shadow, only the toads that were a nightmare come to life.

David held Abby close, flying through the trees. Her eyes were shut—she was fast asleep. He was angry with himself. How could he have slept through her sleepwalking into that mess? How could he not have known the danger she was in until it was almost too late? *Never again,* he thought. *I will never fail her again.*

He landed by the fire and set her down gently on her mat. "Abby," he said. "Abby, please come back to me."

"What happened?" Cael asked.

"She was sleepwalking, and these toad things almost got her. And now I can't wake her up." David felt helpless. Abby was alive, but she seemed lifeless. Had those things poisoned her somehow? He scanned her body for any sign she'd been bitten.

His thoughts were interrupted by a rustling sound coming from the direction of the pond. It was getting closer. Fast.

"What is *that?*" Marisol asked, stepping into Jon's arms. In the darkness, hundreds of red lights blinked on and off. "Oh no—please, no. Not again."

Jon pushed Marisol behind him and drew his sword. Beside him, Cael drew his.

The rustling sound grew louder, and a dark shape flew in the air toward Cael's face. He neatly sliced the monster toad in half. It sizzled and melted into a pool of dark slime at his feet.

"It's *huge,*" Jon exclaimed. "Is that thing for real?"

"'Fraid so," David said. "Climb that tree, Marisol. I need you to take care of Abby."

Marisol nodded and climbed to a large branch, hopefully out of the toads' reach. David flew up and nestled Abby between Marisol and the tree's thick trunk.

"Hold on to her," David said. "Don't let her fall."

"I won't," Marisol promised, wrapping her arms around Abby's limp body.

David landed between Jon and Cael and drew his own sword. The toads were everywhere, surrounding them, leaping at them. David's sword was a blur of silver, cutting them down. In the periphery of his vision, he could see Jon and Cael slashing at the toads, trying in vain to stop the tsunami of fanged amphibians.

"Climb!" Marisol shouted from the safety of the tree. "It's hopeless! There are too many!"

"Do it," David ordered, slicing a toad flying toward Jon.

"Not without you," Jon called, stabbing a toad inching toward his feet. It popped like a water balloon filled with slime. Jon jumped back to keep the sizzling goo from slopping over his boots.

"Go, Jon. I can fly. You can't," David said.

"Valid point," Jon agreed, surveying the unending amphibian mass pouring into the camp from the darkness. "Cover me."

David and Cael kept the toads at bay while Jon threw himself into the tree, scrambling up to perch in the fork of a large branch near Marisol and Abby.

"You next," David told Cael. "I'll keep them off you."

"All right," Cael said, and followed Jon. But as he pulled himself up, a toad leapt through the air and latched onto his thigh, sinking in its teeth. Cael stabbed it with his sword and kept climbing as the toad disintegrated into black sludge.

Seeing that Cael was out of the fray, David rose into the air. Sheathing his sword, he held out his hands, feeling the heat build. Then he focused his energy and incinerated the toads.

They began to melt as the heat rippled across the swarm, leaving only a handful hopping around the campfire. These he targeted one by one, until none remained. He circled the camp, making sure he had eliminated any strays.

The night was quiet again as David landed on the ground. The sleeping mats and packs were covered in thick goo.

"I think our mats are done for," he called up to the others. "But we might be able to salvage some supplies from our packs."

"I say we get them in the morning," Jon said, clinging to his branch. He scooted closer to the trunk of the tree and wrapped his arms around it. "I don't know about you, but I'm staying in this tree tonight."

"I don't blame you," David replied. "Marisol—how's Abby?"

"I can't believe it," Marisol said, shaking her head, "but she actually slept through all that."

"That's not good," David frowned. *Why isn't she waking up?* he wondered. What if he hadn't gotten to her in time and those toad things had poisoned her? She hadn't been bitten, as far as he could tell. He considered the way the creatures' guts had sizzled after making contact with the silver swords. It was possible that even touching the toads might be toxic, that poison could be secreted through the skin, like a poison dart frog in the Amazon. There was no way to know if she'd touched one. What if he was going to lose her just like he'd lost his parents? What if a vision of her own death was what she'd been hiding? He felt himself freezing up with fear and forced it aside. If he wanted to help her, he couldn't afford to think like that.

"Let me take her." David flew up and retrieved Abby from Marisol's arms. He settled down on an adjacent branch, balancing Abby in his arms while scooting backward to lean against the trunk of the tree. "Abby," he said, his voice faltering. He stroked her hair. "Abby, please. Wake up."

Abby stirred at the sound of his voice. "David," she whispered. Then she took in her surroundings with wide eyes. "Why are we in a tree?"

Laughing with relief, David pulled her closer to him, holding her tight. When he let her go, he felt a tear roll down his cheek.

"What happened?" Abby asked, looking concerned. She brushed away the tear. "You're scaring me."

"I thought I was losing you," David answered, and kissed her forehead. "But everything's okay now."

"Not quite," Cael called out from one of the lower branches. "We may have a problem."

ಬಚಚ ಬಚ ಬಚ

In the morning light, Cael asked David to inspect his wound. He had managed to climb down the tree on his own, but now, sitting on the ground with his back against the trunk, he wished he had taken David up on his offer to fly him down. He felt dizzy from the effort of climbing down, and exhausted from yet another sleep-deprived night. Gingerly, he probed the injury on his thigh. The skin around the bite was hot, festering from the venom.

"I can heal this." David placed his hands over the wound.

Cael grimaced. Even the most gentle touch sent searing pain up and down his leg.

"That is a generous offer, but I cannot let you do that," he said through clenched teeth, shoving David's hands away.

David stared at Cael's face and then placed his hand on Cael's forehead. "But you're burning up with a fever," he said. "Why shouldn't I heal you before the infection gets worse?"

Cael closed his eyes in an attempt to block out the pain. "Because," he managed, "the venom of a toothed toad is particularly potent, and I have no idea how it might affect you when you take my wound. We need your strength for whatever horrors may lie ahead."

"He's right," Jon said. "If you hadn't toasted those toads, we'd all be, well..."

"Toast," Marisol finished.

Cael smiled at this, in spite of his pain.

"If you took on your wolf form, would that somehow expel the poison?" Abby asked.

"A brilliant idea, but I am too weak at the moment to try," Cael admitted, opening one eye. "Not to worry, though. This is not the first time I have had something nasty take a bite out of me."

"Well, then, what can we do?" Marisol asked.

Cael noticed that Marisol's gaze was trained on the long scar running from his jaw to his neck, the remnant of a wound acquired from an earlier encounter with monstrous beasts. That time it hadn't been toads, but the bite had left him similarly feverish and had taken a long time to heal. He didn't want to think about what kind of scar the toad bite would leave. "If we could just make it to the village, they may have an antidote," he said. "I imagine they have seen this kind of wound before."

"I'll carry you," David said. He stood up and brushed the dirt from his knees. "We'll try to cover as much ground as we can before dark."

Abby picked up her pack and David's, and Jon grabbed Cael's and his own.

"Nasty," Marisol said, scraping dark slime off her pack with a stick. She glanced at the mats, still lying in liquid toad.

"So much for those. They've been marinating in that stuff. Definitely toast."

"Is there anything worth saving in the packs?" David asked.

Marisol opened her pack, and a dank stench filled the air. "Ugh! That goo leaked inside." She plugged her nose, using her stick to probe the pack's contents. "No—nothing to salvage here. My food is ruined."

"The other packs seem okay," Abby said, taking a cue from Marisol and using a twig to scrape them clean. "A little slime, but I think they were on higher ground, so they didn't get as soaked. Don't worry about food, Sol—we'll share." She tossed her pack to Marisol.

"Thanks, Abby." Marisol scrunched her nose in disgust, eyeing the blob of toad slime that had dripped onto the toe of her boot. She flicked it off with the stick. "Not that I'm very hungry now."

"Let's go," David said. "It gets dark fast around here. I'll try not to bounce you around too much, Cael." He slipped into his lion form, and Jon helped Cael onto his back.

ᏊᎳᏊᎳᏊᎳ

"I have a feeling we are getting close," Cael said. "It seems like we made good progress today." He was lying on the ground, close to their newest fire pit.

"How are you feeling?" Abby asked, gently laying her palm on his forehead.

Cael's fever was worse, but now he had the chills as well. "Horrid," he said, a wry smile on his lips.

159

She reached into her pack and pulled out a piece of flatbread. "Do you feel like you can eat this?" she asked.

"I would rather not," Cael replied. "I have a feeling we shall see it a second time if I do."

Abby frowned. "Well, let's at least try a little water, and see if you can keep that down." She held a leather cask to his lips. "It won't help to get dehydrated."

Cael drank a few sips. "Thank you, Abby."

"Of course," she said, patting his hand. "Rest now."

Cael did as instructed and closed his eyes.

ଃଠ୯ଃଠ୯ଃଠ୯

David had circled the camp in his lion form, looking for signs of predators. Slipping back into his regular form, he snuck up and took a look at Cael's wound, careful not to wake him.

"We'll have to watch him closely tonight," he said to Abby. Jon and Marisol had busied themselves gathering dry branches to add to the fire. "If he gets worse, I'll have you guys spend the night in another tree, and I'll carry him to the village and come back for you."

"I don't like that idea at all," Abby said, crossing her arms. "Who knows what's waiting out there in the dark? How would we be able to help if something attacked you?"

"Well then, I'll fly him there. I have half a mind to do that anyway, considering how that wound looks," David replied. "But, after last night, there is no way I'm leaving you unless I absolutely have to."

Abby uncrossed her arms. "I've wanted to talk to you about that," she said quietly, staring out into the trees to avoid his gaze. "I'm so sorry. This is all my fault."

"How is it your fault? You were sleepwalking."

"I was, but I wasn't," Abby said, looking at her feet. "I thought if I kept it to myself, it would be better—that it would only hurt you if you knew. But I was wrong. Because of me, Cael got hurt, and things could have been so much worse."

David placed his hand under Abby's chin and lifted her face so he could see her eyes. "Abby—when I found you, you were practically comatose. Those toads were about to feast on you, and there was some sort of shadow surrounding you. How is any of that *your* fault? I don't understand."

"It's Tierney," she said. "He's been haunting me—my dreams, my head. He's been trying to seduce me to join him."

David felt like he'd been kicked in the gut. *So that's what she's been hiding.* He took Abby's arm and led her to the far side of the campsite, out of earshot of the others. "And when you say 'seduce,' you're not speaking metaphorically, are you?"

Abby shook her head. "No. I'm not."

David stiffened and let go of her arm. She started to reach for him and he backed away from her.

"David, I'm so sorry...I should have told you."

He gave her a hard look. "When did this start?" he asked. "It was that afternoon, wasn't it? When you thought you were in the labyrinth."

"Yes," Abby nodded, biting her lip. "I talked to Eulalia about it." Her eyes were filling with tears, pleading with him, begging him to understand.

He fought the urge to comfort her or ask why she'd gone to his mother for help instead of coming to him. "Go on."

Abby choked back a sob and looked down at the ground again.

He felt guilty for feeling angry. "I'm sorry. I didn't mean that the way it sounded. Tell me what Eulalia said. Okay?"

She looked up at him. "Eulalia was worried that I was starting to relate to Tierney, like Lucia did. She told me to ask the Southern Oracle to show me something called the Blood Altar."

"I haven't seen anything like that listed on the Cai Terenmare maps," David said. "What is it?"

"I don't know, but she thought it would help me see the truth of what he is, so he couldn't trick me anymore."

"Then we'll go see it together," David said. He took both of Abby's hands, and turned them over to kiss each of her wrists. He looked into her eyes. "I will do whatever it takes to break his hold on you."

She started crying in earnest. "I'm so sorry I hurt you. Can you forgive me?"

David pulled her into his arms, cradling her against his chest. "Abby—there is nothing to forgive. Whatever you may have said or done in those dreams, it wasn't your fault. He was manipulating you." He caressed her cheek. "You still love me, right?"

She looked up at him. "With all my heart."

"That's all I need to know." He kissed her forehead. "Abby, when all this is over, when we win this war and we don't have to worry about something bad happening to each other—I want to be with you for real."

"You *are* with me for real," Abby insisted.

David smiled sadly at her and then pressed his cheek against her forehead. "I know, but here's the thing. You scared me last night—I saw those toad things and I thought I wouldn't be able to reach you in time. I thought they were going to kill

162

you. And then, when you didn't wake up right away, I was afraid you'd been poisoned. It was like the thing with Calder all over again. I know there are no guarantees, even without all these stupid monsters trying to kill us every bloody second, but...I need you to be mine." David got down on one knee and looked up into her eyes. "Marry me."

Abby stared at him wide-eyed, and then bent down and kissed him hard, cupping his face in her hands. "Yes!"

"Yes?" he asked, just to be sure. "I mean, I know this isn't the most romantic setting and I don't even have a ring..."

"Yes," she said, kissing him again.

He kissed her back, feeling a sense of simultaneous relief and elation. Then he stopped, a silly grin plastered on his face. "Are you just kissing me now to shut me up?"

She nodded and grinned impishly. "Do you have a problem with that?"

*No, I don't have a problem with that,* he thought. After days of feeling distant from her, things finally felt right between them. She was back to her old self. He didn't want her to ever stop kissing him. "Not in the least." He pulled her down to sit on his knee.

She wrapped her arms around his neck and kissed him again. When she finally pulled away, she eyed him seriously. "I promise you, David, when this is over, nothing will ever come between us again."

"Good," David said, nudging her to her feet. She got off his knee and he stood up. "But if this turns out to be one of those long, drawn-out wars, please marry me sooner rather than later. I'm not really up for decades of waiting like Cael, you know?"

"Agreed," Abby said. Then she frowned.

"What?" he asked.

"I wish we could run away together right now. But I know we can't."

David looked at the jungle surrounding them and laughed. "No, I guess not. We have a job to do. And even if we didn't, I don't think people would be happy if they were denied a wedding."

"You're right. Our mothers would kill us. But it doesn't have to be some big thing," Abby added.

"Oh, I don't know about that," David chuckled. "Affairs of state are kind of a big deal around here. My coronation was a pretty fancy shindig, remember? I'm a little scared to see what a wedding is like."

Abby groaned. "Yeah, me too. Guess we'll find out when Cael and Eulalia have theirs."

"Yep, guess so." He pulled her close, wrapping his arms around her. "So, how do I keep you safe tonight? I could hold you close to me like this, and refuse to let you go."

"Not if you have to leave with Cael, you can't." She looked around and pointed to a vine hanging from a tree. "Tie me to the tree so I don't go wandering off. That way, if you have to leave, I'll stay put."

David tugged on the vine—it was strong. "That might work, but then what if something attacks us again and you're stuck there?"

"Jon and Sol can untie me if you're not around." She grinned. "But if you're still here, then you'll use your super-cool laser powers to burn through the vine and whisk me to safety, right?"

"I'm not Superman, you crazy, beautiful girl," David smiled. "It's not like I go around shooting laser beams from my eyes, you know."

"No, you only fly, shoot blue fire from your hands, and turn into a lion. How silly of me," Abby quipped. "Look, I'm willing to take the risk."

"This is a terrible idea, Abby."

"More terrible than me sleepwalking into a mess of those toads again?" she asked.

He shuddered. "No. I guess you're right. I'll get the vines."

# THE SOUTHERN ORACLE

With Cael out of commission and Abby in her own restricted state, night watch duties became a bit more complicated.

"We'll each take a turn," David said to Jon and Marisol, "but we won't have partners to back us up, so don't be afraid to wake one of us if you need to."

"It'll be okay," Jon said. "I'll go first, and Marisol, you take next shift. We'll save David for last in case something happens and we need him before his turn."

"Works for me," David said. "I could use a little shut-eye after toting Cael all day. He doesn't look like much, but he's no lightweight."

Marisol laughed and playfully punched David's arm. "Shut up. He'll hear you."

"I did," Cael said, and croaked out a dry laugh.

"You were meant to," David said. "Just making sure you're sticking around."

"You are not rid of me yet, Solas Beir," Cael replied.

"Good," David smiled, and offered Cael some more water. "I promised your betrothed I'd look out for you, and I have no intention of disappointing her."

ℬ☙ℭ✠ℬ☙ℭ✠ℬ☙ℭ✠

David took the water over to Abby. "Sure about this?"

"Yes," she said. She strained against the vines, testing to make sure her bonds were secure. She looked at him and smiled, trying to reassure him. "Good—nice and tight. I'm staying right here tonight."

"Okay, then. I'm right here, sleeping next to you." David sat down beside Abby and caressed her cheek. "Sweet dreams, my love."

"You too," she said. "I love you, David."

"And I love you," he said, and kissed her. He laid his head in her lap and drifted off.

Abby watched David sleeping, wishing her hands were free so she could hold him, but knowing her restraints were for the best.

Jon sat slightly away from them, his eyes trained on the forest, his gaze turning to Marisol time and again. "Seems a bit barbaric," he said to Abby.

"What?" she asked.

Jon turned toward Abby. "You, tied up like that. But after last night, I don't blame you. Or him. If I'd seen those things about to attack Sol, I would've lost my mind."

"You're in love with her?"

Jon stole a glance at his girlfriend, who was sleeping peacefully. He smiled. "I guess I am."

For the briefest of moments Abby felt a twinge of regret, but it was quickly overshadowed by both a sense of relief and joy. She wouldn't have to worry about lingering jealousy between Jon and David, and Jon had finally found someone worthy of him. She'd grown to like Marisol and couldn't imagine a better match for her best friend. She smiled. "Have you told her yet?"

He frowned. "No. I keep waiting for the perfect moment, but we've been a bit busy."

"There is no perfect moment, Jon," she urged. "Seize the day."

He nodded. "Yeah, I probably should."

"If it helps, she loves you too," Abby said.

"How do you know?" Jon asked, his eyebrows raised. "Did she say something?"

Abby shook her head and grinned. "No. But I see how she looks at you."

ಬಀಬಀಬಀ

Jon woke Marisol, gently kissing her forehead.

"Morning," she said, stretching sleepily.

"Not quite yet," he whispered, settling down beside her. "Just time to trade places. Sorry."

"It's okay." She kissed Jon's cheek. "Sleep tight."

"Thanks." He squeezed her hand.

She stood up to go.

He sat up. "Wait. Sol?"

Marisol turned back and knelt down beside him. "Yeah?" she whispered.

Jon pulled her close and kissed her.

168

"What was that for?" she asked.

"I…just couldn't sleep without it," Jon said. "So, thanks."

"Glad I could help," Marisol smiled, and went to sit on a log where she could see the forest better.

*Should have told her,* Jon thought to himself, annoyed that the voice in his head sounded a lot like Abby's. He peeked over at Abby—she was fast asleep, still sitting with her back against the tree, the vines wound tightly around her, with David resting his head in her lap. *Shut up, Abby voice,* he thought. *I know, okay? So back off.*

ಬಞಬಞಬಞ

Marisol felt like she had been watching the trees forever. *Longest night ever,* she thought. But at least it was quiet. That was a nice change.

Out of the corner of her eye, she caught movement. *Great,* she thought, *spoke too soon.* She leapt to her feet and whirled toward whatever was moving through the forest, drawing her sword on instinct. Then she froze.

Someone was there all right. It was her mother.

As Marisol's mind tried to make sense of what she was seeing, Esperanza Garcia put her finger to her lips and motioned for Marisol to follow her. Then she turned and walked into the forest, disappearing in the darkness.

Marisol walked to the edge of the camp, to the end of the firelight's reach. "Mom?" she called.

There was no answer. But then, farther into the trees, she could clearly see her mother. Esperanza turned back and gestured once again for Marisol to join her. *Hurry,* she seemed to say.

Marisol hesitated. *Could be a trick,* she thought. *You don't know what's really out there in the dark, do you?* Her inner voice had an authoritarian tone, almost like Cael's when he was in his teaching role. *Yeah,* she argued with herself, *but it's my mom. I* know *it. I can feel it.*

She heard the Cael voice again. *Then ask yourself this: how did she get here?* Marisol considered that and made a decision. *Only one way to find out,* she thought, and stepped outside the fire's circle of light.

Once she was standing in the darkness, Marisol began to feel doubt. What if it *was* an illusion? What if her mother weren't there after all? Then, up ahead, Marisol saw her mother again.

"*¡Andale, mija!*" Esperanza hissed, impatiently waving Marisol forward. Yes, that was definitely her mother. Marisol had heard that little catchphrase her whole life. It was usually followed by nine words: "You are going to be late for school! Again!" Not this time though—for Marisol, school was out indefinitely.

She hurried to catch up. "*¿Mami? ¿Es tú?*"

"*Sí, mija. Es mí.* Oh my darling—you've been missing—I am so glad I found you," Esperanza said, taking both of Marisol's hands in hers, looking her daughter over, inspecting her for any sign of injury. "Are you hurt?"

Marisol stared at her mother, who was fussing over her like she was five years old again. "No, I'm fine. But *Mami,* how did you find me?"

Apparently satisfied that Marisol was in good health, Esperanza met her daughter's gaze. "*Es muy extraño*—you will never believe it, *mija.* I was working late at the museum, and I found a mirror—except it wasn't a mirror, it was a window. I saw your face. I reached for you, and suddenly, I was here." Esperanza pulled her daughter into an embrace.

After all the fighting about the divorce and then their separation when Esperanza moved overseas, it had been a long time since Marisol had hugged her mother. It felt good, like maybe there was hope for mending what had become a very strained and painful relationship.

Marisol pulled back and saw that her mother was weeping. It surprised her. She tried to remember the last time she had seen her mother cry, and she couldn't. "Oh, mom—I'm *so* sorry. I didn't mean to make you worry."

Esperanza wiped her face with the back of her hand. "It's all right, *mija*. Everything will be okay now. But we can't stay here—this is an evil place. Can't you feel it?"

Marisol nodded. "Yes, *Mami*. It's a very scary forest."

"*Sí. Muy malo.* But the mirror—it must be magical. It brought me to you, so maybe if we go through it again, we can get out," Esperanza suggested. Taking Marisol's arm, she tugged her along further into the dark rainforest.

Marisol looked back toward camp as she trailed behind her mother. "But *Mami*—I can't leave. My friends need me."

"They *do* need you, *mija*," Esperanza agreed, tightening her grip on Marisol's arm. "Monroe has been worried sick. She called and told us that Michal was dead, and oh, my daughter...we thought you were too. But I knew, I knew *en mi corazón*, that it wasn't true. We must go—everyone will want to see you. They will be so happy."

"I know they will, but you will have to tell them I'm all right. My friends here need me more," Marisol insisted. Her arm was starting to ache where her mother was holding onto her with an iron grip. "I can't just abandon them."

Esperanza stopped abruptly and turned to face her daughter, letting go of Marisol's arm. "I see. But you can abandon your own mother?"

Marisol flinched like she had been slapped across the face. Then her shock was swallowed up by the anger she had been fighting to control since her mother left town. *Yeah. Just like you abandoned me and Dad for a guy closer to my age than yours,* she thought. But she could never say that out loud.

That was the thing about Esperanza Garcia. Even if Marisol were to voice her anger, her mother would still get her way. There was no escaping it. In spite of all the anger and hurt, even in spite of those moments when Marisol thought she might truly hate her mother, she still loved her. Some bonds could not be broken.

"All right, Mom," she sighed. "Show me this mirror."

ಐೂ೮ಖಐೂ೮ಖಐೂ೮ಖ

Jon woke reaching for Marisol. She wasn't there. Then he remembered it was her turn to be on watch. He sat up.

She was nowhere in sight. "Sol?" he called.

No answer. Something was wrong. Jon leapt to his feet. In the soft dirt near the fire he could see scuff marks in front of the log where she'd been sitting, and that she had walked to the edge of the camp. Her tracks were among the scattering of leaves littering the ground. Definitely her boots, judging by the markings on the soles. She had stopped there and looked out into the trees. He could tell by the way her feet had left tracks— the perfect outline of her soles standing side by side, imprinted in the dirt. Then? He could just make out the tracks she'd left as she stepped into the trees.

"Sol!" he shouted into the darkness.

No answer.

Jon turned to David. "David! Wake up!"

David was in a deep sleep, his head still in Abby's lap. But Abby opened her eyes. "What's wrong?"

"Marisol's missing," Jon explained. "I have to find her. Wake him up, will you?" He grabbed a branch sticking out of the fire and rushed into the darkness, waving his torch, trying to follow Marisol's trail. "Sol!" he shouted. "Marisol! Answer me!"

ဆလ၁ဆလ၁ဆလ၁

"*Mira, mi hija*," Esperanza said. "The magic mirror."

Marisol had not been sure what to expect, but she was certain it wasn't this. In front of her was a perfectly ordinary-looking oval mirror framed in plain dark wood, and inside the glass, she could clearly see the corridor of the Guggenheim Museum Bilbao. Across the hallway, hanging on the wall, was a Warhol. This was no dream—the painting was real. One step through the glass, and she could touch it.

ဆလ၁ဆလ၁ဆလ၁

Jon was seeing things clearly too. But the scene before him was one of horror, not wonder. Some lady was trying to convince Marisol to step into the yawning oval of a mouth, one that belonged to a nasty-looking carnivorous plant.

Once those fang-fringed jaws enveloped her, Marisol would slowly be digested in the plant's acidic juices. It would not be a pleasant way to die.

173

"Sol!" Jon screamed. Dropping his torch, he launched himself at her, knocking her to the ground.

The plant's jaws snapped shut, and Marisol seemed to waken from a daze. The torch still burned faintly where it lay. In the light from its embers, she took in the plant with wide eyes, not quite understanding.

"*Mami?*" Marisol asked.

"*Sí, mija.* I'm right here," the lady replied.

*Her mother?* Jon thought. There *was* a resemblance there. It wasn't that he didn't know who Esperanza Garcia was. He couldn't stand in the checkout line at the grocery store without seeing her face plastered on the cover of some sleazy tabloid magazine. But Marisol almost never talked about her, so in his mind, the Esperanza Garcia who had been a model, and the woman who was his girlfriend's mother, were not the same person.

Esperanza reached out for Marisol, beckoning to her, and the hairs on the back of Jon's neck stood on end. Something about this woman was all wrong, and it wasn't just because she had tried to lure her daughter into the maw of a flesh-eating plant. Following his instincts, Jon got to his feet and blocked the woman from putting her hands on Marisol.

The woman glared at him. "Do *not* keep me from my daughter," she said.

"That's not your mother, Sol," Jon said. "It just looks like her." He drew his sword and held it out in front of him with both hands. Marisol got up and stood behind Jon, looking unsure.

"Don't listen to him, *mi hija*. You know it's me," the woman said.

A dark shadow passed over the woman's face, and she looked up into the canopy, her attention drawn away from Jon and Marisol. Then she let loose a high-pitched shriek that made Jon's blood run cold.

Marisol covered her ears with her hands and pressed against him.

He shifted his grip on his weapon, moving to hold the sword in one hand and wrap his other arm firmly around Marisol. *La Llorona,* he thought, tightening his grip on the sword's hilt. *The screamer has returned.*

The woman's form seemed to waver and blur as though she were standing in a column of mist. Then Jon's view of her was obscured when a solid mass of blackness crash-landed on top of her, something that came from the trees.

ഇരുഇരുഇരു

"David, wake up! We need you!" Abby cried. She would have shaken him awake, but with her arms bound, the best she could do was stretch out one finger to tap his forehead.

David opened his eyes and looked alarmed when he saw Abby's face. "What's going on?" he asked. He scrambled to his feet, fully alert.

"Marisol is missing and Jon ran off to find her. You have to help him," Abby said.

"What about you and Cael?" David asked.

Abby looked over at Cael. He had not awakened—he seemed to be in a feverish, fitful sleep, fighting the infection ravaging his body.

"We're fine. Just go!" Abby said.

"Okay—be back as soon as I can," David called out as he sped off into the darkness, changing form mid-leap.

Between the shrieking and a low growling noise, it was impossible to hear anything else, and Jon's view of the woman was almost completely blocked by the dark shape doing the growling. Something about the woman's form had changed though, because she had sprouted a long, serpentine tail. It uncoiled, disappearing into the trees beyond, and then reappearing suddenly in a blur of black and white, smashing into the creature on top of her.

Jon pulled Marisol to the ground and lay on top of her, shielding her as the tail whipped around wildly, knocking into the trees around them. Jon couldn't hear the crack of the breaking branches over the woman's shrieking, but he could see the tree limbs falling around him.

The end of the tail slammed into the dark shape again, and the creature leapt away, clinging to the trunk of a tree. It seemed to be some kind of giant panther, with jet black fur and glowing golden eyes.

Esperanza Garcia was gone and in her place was a horror—something with a grey, dappled upper body like a toad and a face that vaguely resembled an old woman's. Below her waist was the tail of a snake. The lamia had raised her paddled tail above her head, preparing to smash the panther, when the big cat launched itself at her face.

Jon seized the opportunity to jump up and pull Marisol to her feet. "Run," he said.

The white lion David joined the battle just as Jon and Marisol disappeared into the trees. The first thing he saw was a black, panther-like shape attacking a snake woman. *Tierney,* he thought. He growled and took a swipe at the giant cat, digging his claws into the creature's shoulder.

The cat yowled in pain. It turned its head, looked at him, and ran off into the forest.

The lamia watched it disappear and turned to David, smiling. "Thank you, Solas Beir. He *was* rather annoying, wasn't he?" Then she whipped her tail at David, flinging him against the trunk of a tree.

ಬಂಡಿಬಂಡಿಬಂಡಿ

"Cael!" Abby cried. "Cael, please wake up." If Cael weren't so sick, he would already have been on his feet, sword drawn.

She was terrified—she could hear someone screaming in the trees. It had to be whatever had kept them awake that first night, and it sounded like it was getting closer. She had no idea where David and the others were, or if they were okay.

If only she weren't bound. If only Cael would just wake up and untie her. She strained against the vines, but it was no use. David had been very thorough. *Exactly which evil spirit possessed me to think being tied up in a haunted forest was a* good *idea?* she thought. *Not one of your brightest ideas, Abby. Not bright at all.*

She heard a low growl and saw a dark shape approaching from the other side of the camp. It looked like a huge jaguar with black-on-black spots, and it was slinking toward Cael's still body.

"Leave him alone!" Abby shouted. The cat turned its gaze toward her, and again, she wished she weren't tied to a tree. It was coming toward *her* now, and there was nowhere for her to hide.

The jaguar crept closer until she could feel its hot, feline breath. Then the vines went slack.

೫ೞೞೞೞೞ

David's head was spinning, but he got to his feet. The lamia packed quite a punch with that scaly tail of hers. He saw the tail whizzing back toward him and crouched low before it could give him another lashing. It crashed into a section of tree trunk above him, raining splinters of bark onto his mane. The tail seemed to be her primary weapon—the rest of her, the more human-looking parts, seemed pretty weak. If he could just take the tail out of the equation, he would have the upper hand.

The tail was coiled up, ready to deliver the next blow. *It's now or never,* he thought, as the tail uncurled again and came flying toward him. She was aiming low, so he leapt up, launching himself off the trunk of a tree, and landed on top of the tail as it swept past. She whipped her tail back angrily, but he sank his claws into her reptilian flesh and held on.

*This is going to be one wild ride,* he thought. And he was right. He felt himself slam into a tree again, and heard the snap, crackle, and pop of breaking branches as she tried to shake him off. The trunk of the tree was mercilessly unyielding against his back, but after several minutes of being thrashed against it, David could feel things changing. The snake woman's enthusiasm and vigor lessened, as though she were tiring from trying to lift her tail with his weight on it.

David smiled grimly to himself. *Taking the wind out of your sails, am I, sweet pea?* He sunk his claws in deeper and bit the tail. He could feel a heat building in his paws, searing her flesh. The lamia started shrieking, and her tail slumped to the ground like a dead thing, twitching slightly.

Retracting his claws, David moved away from the tail and slipped back into his human form. He walked over to the lady end of the lamia and stood staring at her while she continued her shrill, senseless screaming. She was as annoying as a three-in-the-morning car alarm. "Oh, shut up," he said, and punched her squarely in the face.

She did. Dazed, she stared back at him, blessedly silent. Then she hissed, turned, and slithered off into the darkness, like a naughty child who had been shamed into obedience.

David watched to make sure she was gone, then hurried back to camp, shifting into a lion so he could run faster. The first thing he saw when he arrived was the black cat. It was crouching over Cael's body and snarling up at Jon and Marisol, who had climbed a tree. Abby was nowhere to be seen.

David launched himself at the giant feline, flipping it on its back, pinning it to the ground with his front paws.

"David—no!" Cael cried, trying to sit up. But he was too weak to even manage that, and he collapsed onto the ground as his elbows slid out from under him in the soft dirt.

The large cat underneath David dissolved into a man with dark hair and skin and a lean, muscled body. He was wearing nothing but a loincloth and a grin.

"Greetings, Solas Beir," he said.

"David," Cael croaked. "*Please* do not eat the Southern Oracle."

Immediately, David slipped back into his human form. Red-faced with embarrassment, he stared at the man before him. He had tried to kill the very person he'd hoped would become his ally. "My deepest apologies, Southern Oracle. I mistook you for someone else."

David stood up and helped the man to his feet. Then he reached for a cask and knelt to help Cael take a drink.

"Oh? And who might that be?" the Southern Oracle asked, frowning as he brushed dirt from his skin.

"Tierney," David said, avoiding the man's stern gaze.

"Forgive us, Southern Oracle," Cael intervened, "but we have been haunted by many a horror these past nights. The journey to your village has been rather treacherous."

"And I see that you have not arrived unscathed," the Southern Oracle noted, crossing his arms. He looked up at Jon and Marisol, still in the tree, and smiled widely. "You can come down now. I promise not to eat you."

"Thanks," Jon said. "We appreciate that." He climbed down to join the others.

"It appears I, too, was mistaken," the oracle said to Cael. "After your Solas Beir attacked me instead of the lamia, I assumed you lot were a threat to the safety of my village. I—"

"Where's Abby?" David interrupted. He looked around frantically; he could feel himself growing panicked. *Maybe she hid*, he thought, trying to reassure himself. *But how could she if she was tied up?*

"She was gone when we got here," Marisol said, swinging down from her perch. She narrowed her eyes at the Southern Oracle. "You didn't eat her, did you?"

David's eyes widened with alarm as he looked from Marisol to the Southern Oracle.

The Southern Oracle laughed. "No, my dear, I did not. I fear, however, I may have given her a terrible fright. Do not worry—she did not go far." He peered around the tree with the vines that had bound Abby. "Come on out, little one."

The head of a white rabbit hesitantly peeked out over a tree root. The Southern Oracle chuckled and knelt down. "Come on, now. I will not bite."

The rabbit hopped out from behind the tree. It stuck out a front paw as if it were studying it, and then looked up at the people towering above it. "Oh, you have *got* to be kidding me," it said.

David's mouth gaped open in shock. "Abby?"

"Yeah," the rabbit answered. "It's me."

"Oh." He sighed with relief. She was okay. Mostly.

"Yep," Abby the rabbit said. "Of course, *I'm* the one who turns into a pathetic fur ball."

"I wouldn't call you pathetic," David said, not even bothering to hide his smile. "You're kind of adorable." He picked her up.

"And fluffy," Marisol added, stroking Abby's soft fur.

"*Not* helping," the rabbit growled. "Guess we know why Tierney had that little nickname for me. I'm going to *murder* him the next time I see him."

"Well now. *You* are a pleasant little one," the Southern Oracle laughed, scratching behind Abby's long ears. "I apologize for not introducing myself properly. I am also known as the Jaguar King, for reasons that may be most apparent to you."

"Quite," Abby said, squirming in David's arms. She hopped to the ground and turned back into her human self. "Never thought I'd be turning into an animal too." She scrunched up her nose as if it itched, sneezed, and brushed away the fine white hair that had been tickling her. "And apparently I'm allergic to myself. *Fantastic*."

"That was quite impressive," the Southern Oracle smiled.

"Really? Because that's not quite the word I was thinking of," Abby countered.

"My dear girl, to be human and be able to transform yourself? That is *most* impressive. Never mind that the form seems diminutive. Every creature serves a purpose, no matter the size," the oracle said.

"Don't forget about Fergal," David added, taking Abby's hand. "He's wicked with a sword and he's little too."

"I'll try to remember that as I hop around. Maybe I'll slay my enemies with lethal cuteness," Abby scowled.

"Perhaps you will," the oracle chuckled. "I have no doubt you would be quite fearsome in battle." He reached up into the tree and pulled down some leaves from a parasitic plant attached to the tree's trunk. He walked over to Cael, knelt down, and pressed the leaves to Cael's wound. "Here, my friend. This should help you."

Cael winced at the oracle's touch, and then his face relaxed as the swelling in his leg eased. A nasty-looking greenish pus began to ooze from the wound. "Oh, that is foul," Cael groaned, covering his nose. "Most foul indeed."

"Indeed," the oracle agreed, nodding. "But we must leech out the venom." He looked up at Marisol. "You, girl—what is your name?"

"Marisol," she replied.

"Ah, yes. A lovely name," the Southern Oracle said. "You climb well—grab a few more of those leaves to take with us. There is another plant higher up."

Marisol scampered up the trunk of the tree and reached for a plant. The oracle watched her and then shook his head vigorously. "No, no—not that one. Never that one. That plant will kill you. The one beside it."

"But they look *exactly* the same," Marisol said, exasperated.

"Not to me," the oracle replied. "There are subtle differences not easily discerned by the untrained eye."

Marisol shot him a look and took leaves from the correct plant, avoiding the deadly one. She jumped down and brought them to the oracle.

"Thank you, dear," the Southern Oracle said. "Do you have a pack to keep them safe? I am traveling a bit light, as you can see."

Marisol nodded, keeping her eyes on his to avoid having to acknowledge what served as fashion in this part of the kingdom, David assumed. Then she looked up into the canopy, which had faded from black to grey. "It's almost dawn."

"Yes," the oracle said. "My village is not far. If we start now, we should arrive in time for dinner. Shall we be off?"

"Sounds like a plan," David said. "Cael is still too weak to walk, though. I'll carry him."

"Good," the oracle said. "I would, but you seem to have damaged my shoulder in our earlier battle with the lamia."

"Oh—I'm sorry about that," David apologized. "Abby told me that Tierney appeared to her as a black panther, so I assumed, incorrectly…"

"He appeared to her and did not kill her," the Southern Oracle mused. It was a statement loaded with questions.

Abby shrugged. "He wasn't in a killing mood."

"Intriguing," the oracle said.

"He looks different than you—you have spots and he has stripes, like a black tiger," Abby clarified. She glanced over at David and then turned back to the oracle. "Not that it would be easy to tell the difference in the dark. But he also has long fangs, like a saber-toothed cat."

The oracle nodded. "Indeed, he does. And I am surprised you did not become more intimately acquainted with them."

"He just wanted to chat," Abby said.

The Southern Oracle stared at her, his eyes intense. "About what, pray tell?"

Abby shifted uncomfortably under the oracle's gaze, and glanced back over at David. David nodded for her to continue. "He was trying to get me to see his side of things...and to recruit me," she admitted.

"Well, dear Abby, I can see there is much more to you than just a small white rabbit. I will be interested to learn more during our visit," the oracle said.

"May I heal your shoulder before we go?" David offered.

"I would like that. It has been a long time since I have held counsel with a Solas Beir, and longer still since I have seen one heal." The Southern Oracle presented his shoulder; long, red claw marks stretched all the way from the joint to the blade.

David placed his hands over them and felt the heat flow from his palms. He winced as the wound transferred to his body.

"Ah, that is much better," the oracle sighed, flexing his arm and shoulder. "Well done, Solas Beir. You have your father's healing hands. Now, please, allow me to be the one to carry our friend."

David tried to ignore the burning pain in his shoulder. "Thank you," he said, his jaw clenched. "I'd appreciate it."

The oracle helped Cael to his feet, and Cael cautiously tried putting weight on his injured leg. "I thank you as well, Southern Oracle. I am feeling better, but I can still feel venom in the wound."

The oracle slipped his arm around Cael, supporting him. "Have no worry, my friend. In a few days' time, the wound will be healed completely. It was fortunate that I encountered you in this part of the forest. The healing plants grow in abundance here. Now, come. My people will be excited about your arrival. We do not have guests very often."

The oracle shifted into his jaguar form, and then Jon helped Cael onto the oracle's back before they started off into the forest.

Marisol scooped up Jon's and Cael's packs and followed.

Abby picked up her pack and David's, studying David as he carefully tested his shoulder. "Are you okay?" she whispered.

"Yeah, I'll be fine," David whispered back. "I guess my claws did quite a number on the Southern Oracle's shoulder." He had a feeling he'd be paying for that particular mistake all day. His body seemed to take longer to mend itself with larger wounds; minor ones tended to heal almost instantaneously.

"What do you think of him?" Abby asked.

David pondered for a moment. "He's not quite what I expected. At least he doesn't seem too put out by our horrific reception of him. That was less than ideal."

"Yeah—what a train wreck. Thank goodness he has a sense of humor," Abby said.

# THE BLOOD ALTAR

The village was not quite what David had expected either. Given the Southern Oracle's clothing, David had envisioned a smattering of rudimentary huts in a clearing. Instead, he was pleasantly surprised when he was greeted by a sophisticated network of ornately carved spherical tree houses linked by suspension bridges.

Laid out below on an outcropping of stone was a plaza with a breathtaking view of a magnificent waterfall. Below the waterfall's dramatic plunge was a series of pools, each with its own smaller waterfall cascading into the next pool, stair steps forming a river that widened and flowed eastward. In shallow areas, water coursed over black rocks carpeted in green algae.

When they stepped out of the perpetual grey-green twilight that defined daylight in the rainforest, David found the vivid emerald greens of the trees and turquoise blue of the sky stunning. The brightness of the sunlight made his eyes water.

The villagers were no less colorful, garbed in clothes dyed in every shade imaginable, almost as though they were reflecting the rainbow formed by the mist of the waterfall.

186

Some, like the Southern Oracle, were more scantily clad, but others wore modest one-shouldered sarongs. No one, male or female, was wearing pants or shoes like David and his fellow ambassadors. In the hot, humid air, this made perfect sense.

It had been days since David and his friends had bathed, and sleeping in the dirt had not helped with personal hygiene. David could feel his clothes clinging to him. He could only imagine what he must smell like; he had become immune to his own stench.

The Southern Oracle seemed to notice David's discomfort. "Have no worry, Solas Beir. There is plenty of time to make you beautiful before the feast," he chuckled. He motioned for several of the villagers to join him in the plaza. "Take our guests to the pools—they could use some rejuvenation after their difficult journey," the oracle commanded. Then he grinned. "And give them something more suitable to wear."

The villagers nodded and smiled. A couple of the women cheerfully took Abby and Marisol by the hand and escorted them to steps leading to the pools above the plaza.

As David watched the girls walk away, he turned to the oracle. "Forgive me for asking, but is there anything we should watch out for in the water? I don't mean to seem overly cautious, but given all the dangers we encountered in the forest, the toothed toads that took a bite out of Cael…"

The oracle nodded. "It is an understandable question. But do not worry—the botos will take care of you."

David didn't know what botos were, but he thanked the oracle and followed half a dozen men down the steps to the lower pools. He noted that there was something strange about their appearance. They looked human, yet there was something beautiful and otherworldly about them. Their smooth, dark skin had an iridescent, pinkish sheen in the sunlight. In the center of their foreheads, at the edge of the hairline, there seemed to be a small, circular indentation.

David's suspicions were confirmed when he reached the water and saw the villagers swimming. They moved through it as smoothly as fish. A young boy dove into the pool, and when he broke the surface, David understood. These people, the botos, were river dolphins. They slipped in and out of dolphin form as they played in the water, taking human form when it suited them. There was a contagious joy about them as they splashed about.

The pools were deeper than they seemed, and the water was warm, as if it were fed by hot springs rather than the cool rush of a waterfall. David settled in against the rock wall of the pool, scooting down into the water until his chin grazed the surface. He sighed contentedly as the warm water soothed his aching, sleep-deprived body. Jon and Cael followed suit.

"You know all the crap we went through to get here?" Jon asked.

David and Cael looked at each other and back at Jon. "Yeah," David said. "What about it?"

"Totally worth it," Jon sighed. "I may stay in this pool for the rest of my life."

"Don't fall asleep in here," David laughed. "You'll drown."

"Nah," Jon said. "You heard our friend, the Jaguar King. The botos will take care of me. I don't have a care in the world." He closed his eyes and rested his head against the pool's edge.

"Nor do I," Cael agreed, and closed his eyes as well.

David smiled. The water was working its magic on him too; for the first time in days—weeks even—he was feeling optimistic. He was sure their new friend would become an ally.

And as if things couldn't get better, beautiful singing started coming from the pools above them. The voices of the female botos drifted down, inspiring the men to harmonize with their voices.

The music was not just beautiful—it was healing. The water vibrated with it. David could feel the music resonating through his body, mending his injured shoulder. He closed his eyes and tried to understand what was happening—the word "echolocation" came to mind. He knew the term referred to animals from the human world, and that it didn't quite capture what he was experiencing, but it was close enough. It would do.

ಬಲ3ಬಲ3ಬಲ3

Abby and Marisol were thrilled to trade their sweat-soaked clothes for beautiful multicolored sarongs. The boto women adorned them with necklaces made from stone beads. Abby recognized some of the gems—turquoise, carnelian, and even bits of hardened coral. "So beautiful," she said, rolling a carnelian bead between her fingers.

Marisol smiled at Abby as a boto woman combed and braided Marisol's long hair, inserting more of the beads as she wove the hair into an intricate bun that seemed to be the preferred style in the village. In the course of their journey, the girls' hair had become matted messes caked with oil and dirt. In an attempt to be practical, they had both pulled their hair back into braids, just to get the thick, heavy locks off their sweaty necks, but that had been a lost cause aesthetically speaking. "It just feels so good to be clean," Marisol said. "I didn't want to leave the water, but I can't wait to eat."

"Yes," Abby agreed. With the promise of a feast and a safe place to sleep, she felt better than she had in days.

They met David, Jon, and Cael on the stone plaza as the moon was rising. The tree houses had taken on a soft glow, and looked like pale orbs floating in the treetops.

"It's like a Christmas tree," Jon mused.

"Well, maybe a more tropical version of one," Marisol said. She smiled as Jon slid his arm around her waist.

"Beautiful, are they not?" the Southern Oracle asked, stepping out onto the plaza's pavers.

"Very. Why do they glow like that?" Abby asked.

"Fish oil," the Southern Oracle replied. "We use it to waterproof our homes. If you peer down into the river tonight, you will see the light of the golden carp illuminating the water. In the daylight, they look as though they have bronze scales, but in the dark they are quite stunning. Come—the feast awaits." He gestured to a long one-story building near the plaza.

It too had intricate, glowing carvings on its beams and corbels. Its open doorway was draped with swags of fuchsia and orange blooms that reminded Abby of hibiscus flowers. She couldn't tell what they smelled like though, because the smell of barbequed meat wafted out of the longhouse, overwhelming her senses and making her mouth water.

In the center of the building was a large fire pit with roasting meat skewered on a series of rotating spits. Above the fire, smoke drifted out into the night sky through a square hole in the roof. Several villagers moved along the long, rectangular tables, serving their guests. The feast consisted of wild boar, a myriad of fruits Abby had never heard of, and some kind of roasted jungle rodent.

"Do not worry," the Southern Oracle assured her, patting her hand as she stared at her plate. "It is not rabbit meat."

Jon tried it. "It's good," he said. "Tastes just like—"

"Don't say it," Abby stopped him. But he was right—it was good and it did taste like chicken. She tried to think of it that way rather than whatever it was that scurried and scavenged in the dark rainforest. At least it wasn't toad.

&#8414;&#x2767;&#8414;&#x2767;&#8414;&#x2767;

After the meal, there was music and dancing, and the botos' voices sounded as beautiful accompanied by instruments as they did a cappella.

Finally, late into the night, the Southern Oracle invited David and his friends to join him in his home high above the plaza.

"Thank you so much for your hospitality, Southern Oracle," David said, sitting on a short, wooden stool. Abby and the others had settled on cushions on the flat hardwood floor of the spherical tree house. "We could not have asked for a more welcoming reception."

The oracle smiled, settling back into a woven chair that hung from the ceiling of his small, cozy home. "We do not have many guests, but we do love to entertain." He studied David's face and then leaned forward. "But let us hold counsel with honesty, Solas Beir. I know you did not come for the food."

"No, we didn't, even though the food alone would have been worth the journey," David said, smiling. "We come as diplomats. As the new Solas Beir, I felt it was important to meet with each oracle personally. And I seek you as an ally. The Kruorumbrae are rising again. The Kruor um Beir has escaped from the Wasteland and is gathering his forces. Many of our villages have already suffered from raids. War is inevitable. Because of this, I have appointed a new Western Oracle and I have met with the Northern Oracle, who has sworn her allegiance. We hope to gain yours and the Eastern Oracle's as well. With our united forces, we will be more than a match for Tynan Tierney and we will be able to bring peace to our kingdom again."

"I thought as much," the Southern Oracle replied, "but I must say no."

Abby, Jon, and Marisol collectively gasped, unable to contain their shock. David and Cael managed to keep their composure, but exchanged a look.

David felt alarm thud through his veins, and his head began to ache. He had the urge to put his head in his hands and rub his temples, but he resisted, keeping his hands in his lap, trying to appear unruffled.

"I recognize that my answer is not what you had hoped, and you wish to know why I have answered thus," the oracle said.

"Yes," David said, his voice sounding steadier than he felt. "I do."

Sitting back in his chair, the oracle held his hands palm to palm, staring at his fingers thoughtfully for a moment before meeting David's gaze. "You have seen our village. You see that we live peacefully. And while you have personally experienced the dangers of our forest, you can also appreciate that it serves as a barrier, protecting us from outside predators like the Kruorumbrae," he explained. "I have no reason to believe that the Blood Shadows will breach our borders. If we continue as we are, we will prosper. But if we join you, my people will suffer. I cannot risk provoking an attack."

"But the Shadows have already entered the forest," Abby said. "I saw Tierney there, and you yourself fought with the lamia. The Shadows are already encroaching on your borders."

"No, my dear, you are mistaken," the oracle replied, turning to look at her. "Those were simply illusions. The forest knows your fears and defends itself by creating physical manifestations to eliminate threats to its survival. It is alive, you see, not just as individual plants and animals, but as one organism. I have no reason to believe that Tierney was truly present. But I do trust you saw a version of him. Perhaps he *was* trying to recruit you, as you claim. But perhaps it is your fear of him, Cai Aislingstraid, that made your dreams come to life."

"And the lamia?" Abby asked. She was clearly angered by his insinuation, but she looked like she was managing to keep her emotions in check.

"I would say that illusion targeted *her* fears," the oracle said, nodding toward Marisol. "It would seem she has some unfinished business regarding her mother."

"Maybe I do," Marisol began, crossing her arms, "but I wouldn't call what happened an illusion. It was real enough to try to kill me. I get that the plant was using camouflage to lure me in—even in the human world, we have carnivorous plants. And maybe Abby did dream up Tierney, and the toads were just coincidental, part of the forest's efforts to exterminate us. But the lamia? That was something else entirely. Yes, she appeared as my mother, but do you usually encounter snake women in the forest? One with a tail like a siren's?"

"No," the oracle admitted. "That was a first. I have only heard of creatures like that coming from the sea."

"My point exactly. She seemed like she was out of her element, and she had been tailing us since the first night we entered your realm. So then, how do you know *for sure* that the Shadows are not in the forest already?" Marisol asked.

"I do not. But nevertheless, I cannot afford to help you. I am sorry. Please, stay with us as long as you wish. When you are ready to go, I will make sure you are well supplied and will send an escort to see you safely home," the oracle offered.

"Thank you—we appreciate that," David replied. It wasn't a lie. He really was grateful for the oracle's hospitality, especially since their supplies were all but gone. But the oracle's generosity felt like a meager consolation prize in the wake of David's failure to gain an ally.

He rose from his seat and gestured to the others to rise as well. "I see your reasons for not joining us. I can't say I'm not disappointed, but I do understand. It's very late, so we will retire to our own quarters now and let you rest as well. We still need to speak with the Eastern Oracle, so we will leave tomorrow, but we look forward to a time of fellowship with you and your people before we go."

"I look forward to that as well," the oracle replied.

ဆဣဆဣဆဣ

"I can't believe it," Abby sighed, after Jon closed the door to the guest tree house. "How could he say no?"

"I don't know," David said, deflated. "I hope it's okay with you all that I said we'd leave tomorrow. I know this place is beautiful, but there's no point in staying if he won't join us. We really need to move on and speak with the Eastern Oracle."

"You were right to say what you did," Cael said, putting his hand on David's shoulder. "I understand the oracle's reasons, but we must hurry and win what allies we can before Tierney makes his move."

"I think he's a coward," Marisol muttered, crossing her arms. Jon slipped his arm around her waist.

"I may agree with you, Marisol, but it is best not to voice that opinion beyond our circle. The Southern Oracle has his reasons, and they may be more complex than we know. We must respect his decision and preserve our relationship with him," Cael reasoned.

"How's your leg, Cael?" David asked. "Will you be ready to travel tomorrow?"

"Almost completely healed, I think. The healing plant and the pool did wonders for me," Cael answered. "For that I am very grateful to our host."

"Good," David said. "I don't want to push you and cause further injury."

"I will be fine," Cael assured him. "It is late—let us rest while we can before our journey." He pulled back the blankets on his bed and sat down.

David couldn't help but notice that Cael winced slightly as he pulled the covers up over his injured leg. The skin around the wound still appeared swollen, but otherwise Cael's rapid recovery seemed nothing short of miraculous.

ⓈⒸⓈⒸⓈⒸ

Abby tossed and turned beside David. The tree house rocked gently in the breeze and she should have been able to sleep. The low bed she was lying on was warm and comfortable. But sleep simply would not come. Finally she sat up.

"Are you okay?" David whispered, reaching for her. The others were fast asleep. "More dreams about Tierney?"

"No." She took his outstretched hand. "I can't sleep at all."

"Me neither." He sat up and rubbed Abby's back. "I'm so frustrated. I was sure he would come to our side."

"I was too." She slid her legs to the side of the bed and stood up. "I'll be back."

"Where are you going?" David asked.

Abby walked over to the door of the tree house, opening it quietly. "I have to ask him something."

"Abby—I don't think it's a good idea to push him," David cautioned. "Like Cael said, we have to respect his decision."

"It's not about that. Trust me on this, okay?"

He looked at her. "All right. Come back soon."

Abby nodded and slipped quietly out of the tree house.

When she made it to the Southern Oracle's small home, she knocked on the door. He answered a moment later. It didn't look like he had been able to sleep either.

"Ah, Cai Aislingstraid. I hope you have not come to try to change my mind," the oracle said.

"I haven't," Abby replied.

The Southern Oracle looked surprised and more than a little relieved. "Good, for I stand firm in my decision. I must do what is best for my people."

"And I respect that."

"I am glad to hear it. Well then, how can I help you, C'aislingaer?" he asked.

"Before we leave tomorrow, would you please take me to see the Blood Altar?"

The oracle stared at her silently for a moment. "Why would you want to see that?"

"The queen has requested that I see it," Abby explained, holding his gaze. "She thought it would help me learn more about Tierney's nature and how he thinks."

The oracle narrowed his eyes. "I am sure you would receive quite an education. More than you may desire. The Blood Altar is an evil place. My people are forbidden from going there."

"But *you* could take me."

"I am loath to do that," he said, studying her face.

Still looking into his eyes, she stood up straight and planted her feet. She had traveled this far, and there was no way she was leaving until she saw the Blood Altar. If she had to stand in the Southern Oracle's doorway all night to convince him, so be it.

The oracle seemed to understand she would not be deterred. He sighed heavily. "All right. I will take you. Meet me at sunrise in the plaza."

"Thank you, Southern Oracle," Abby said, and turned to leave.

"Do not thank me yet," he called after her.

ぬひぬひぬひ

The Southern Oracle was true to his word, and as the sun rose over the emerald horizon of the colossal trees, he was standing in the plaza waiting for Abby.

She came alone, even though David had wanted to come too. Now that he knew where the oracle stood on becoming an ally, their once-promising relationship was strained. David felt he could no longer trust the oracle, but she had persuaded him not to join them.

"I'll be okay," Abby had insisted. "My gut tells me he will be more open without you there. You are the Solas Beir, after all. I'm far less intimidating. And don't worry about what he said about the place being evil. He'll keep me safe."

David wasn't so sure. "What if he can't? Or won't?" he had asked. Finally, reluctantly, David had let her go, and Abby had rushed out to meet the oracle.

"Good morning, Cai Aislingstraid," the Southern Oracle said. "Did you sleep well?"

"I did, after our late-night chat," Abby replied.

"Good. I did as well. You do realize, however, that with this side trip, you will not be able to leave today, as your Solas Beir wished to do?"

"Yes—we talked about that, and he understood. He felt it was worth the time for me to see the altar," she said.

"Well then, let us proceed. The first part of our journey will be much too difficult for you to attempt on your own. We must climb to the top of the waterfall. You will be safer and we will go faster with you on my back. Is that agreeable to you?" the Southern Oracle asked.

Abby nodded. "Sounds fine."

"Excellent. Climb on up." The oracle slipped into his jaguar form, and Abby settled onto his back.

His fur was surprisingly silky. She plunged her fingers into his thick pelt, trying not to pull out the hairs, and pressed her thighs against his sides as she would on a horse. He was almost as big as one, and the experience was much like riding bareback, except that he was faster than a horse and much more agile. He scaled the rocks on the side of the waterfall as if they were nothing more than stairs, finding paths where she could see none and avoiding the slippery moss with ease.

Once at the top, the Southern Oracle paused and turned so Abby could see the village below. She felt a dizzying sense of vertigo, but it was thrilling to be so high above the canopy. From their perch, the tops of the trees were a patchwork of varying shades of green. Then the oracle turned and rushed off into the trees, twisting through them as if he were following a path. Perhaps there had been one once, but the jungle had long since overtaken it.

From time to time, Abby could hear the roar of the river as they neared the water, and then the oracle would turn away, making his way around large boulders and fallen trees. Under the canopy, it was difficult to tell how much time had passed. He was running fast—the trees became a blur.

Finally he broke out into an open place and stopped. Abby could see that the sun was high in the sky. They were next to the river again.

Before them was a second towering waterfall. Behind the spray, Abby could see the blackness of a cave. It looked like the gaping jaws of a monster, lying in wait to gobble her up. She felt the hair on the back of her neck rise.

Abby jumped down from the jaguar's back, and the Southern Oracle resumed his human form. He pointed to the cave. "The passage there is very low and narrow," he explained, "so it is best if we both travel on foot."

Nodding, Abby followed him to the cave's yawning black mouth. She stopped short of entering, suddenly gripped by a wave of fear. There was a heaviness to this place—she felt as if the air itself were pressing on her shoulders, threatening to push her to the ground.

The oracle turned back to her, sensing her hesitation. "Are you all right, my dear? We need not proceed if you have changed your mind."

"No," she said. "I have to see this. It's just that all of a sudden, I felt so much fear."

"You are right to be frightened," he murmured.

Abby shook her head. "No, it wasn't just *my* fear. It was like I was feeling what others had felt as they passed through here."

"You are an empath, then," the Southern Oracle realized.

Abby nodded. She had the ability to pick up on what others were feeling and was sensitive to places with a high emotional charge.

The oracle studied Abby and pondered this. "The queen had the same feeling when she came here."

"Eulalia came *here*?" Abby asked.

"Yes," the Southern Oracle replied. "And your perception of the place is correct. It is haunted by the fear of those who were murdered here. This is not a place that is kind to those like you and the queen. You must not let the fear overtake you. Take my hand. What you felt will get worse the further in we go."

Abby grasped his outstretched hand. "Thank you." She could feel his strength, and a sense of peace replaced the fear. "That helps a lot, actually."

The Southern Oracle nodded and led her through the passage. It was pitch-black, but he seemed to find his way easily.

Abby guessed having jaguar eyes was an advantage in dark places. It was an exercise in trust. She had to rely on him completely for navigation. She tightened her grip on him when she stumbled over a crack in the floor of the passage.

*He was right about the fear thing.* Abby could feel it pressing on her, encircling her, stealing her breath as she climbed the passage's steep incline. It didn't help that she could hear things in the dark—scurrying things, crawling things.

She felt something pass just in front of her eyes as it flew by. Squeezing her eyes shut, Abby tried to think happy thoughts. She found herself thinking about David's eyes, and focused on remembering exactly what they looked like. It helped block out the fear that threatened to crawl down her throat and choke her.

They must have turned a corner, because suddenly Abby could see light through the lids of her closed eyes. She opened them cautiously and found the Southern Oracle leading her out of the darkness and onto some kind of raised platform. She could see the blue sky and green trees around them again.

They were up high—higher than before, and the sun was directly above them now. She could see the waterfall below, and far off in the distance, an edge where the water dropped again, likely the waterfall near the village. They were on top of a ziggurat, which more closely resembled the stepped pyramids of the Mayans than it did the tomb of an Egyptian pharaoh.

Facing east, centered at the front of the platform, was a long stone table that could be nothing other than the Blood Altar. There was no mistaking the meaning behind the monstrous faces carved into the altar's sides or the shallow trough leading from the table all the way to the bottom of the pyramid and down to the river below.

The ziggurat straddled the river. The passage they'd used must have crossed underneath the river from the entrance on the north side of the waterfall to where they'd exited on the southeast corner of the platform. There was a terrible beauty about this place—the care that had been taken in creating the many carvings, and the purpose for them.

"How many people died here?" Abby asked.

"Thousands upon thousands," the Southern Oracle replied. "Tierney turned the river red with his lust for blood—with his greed for power."

"Tierney?" she gasped.

The oracle nodded. "Yes. Long ago, *he* was the Southern Oracle. There were portals in this place, leading to many kingdoms in your world. He presented himself to kings there, claiming to be a god. He had many names and took many forms, proving his claim as a deity through demonstrations of his power. He promised them prosperity for a price, and they were willing to pay it. But not with their own blood. They raided villages in neighboring kingdoms and brought their victims here. The tunnel we passed through was the last walk the blood slaves took before they met their end—before Tierney consumed their life force to become even more powerful."

Abby stared at the altar, then walked over to it. She hesitated, then placed her hands in the trough. The oracle cried out, but she couldn't hear him.

The world around Abby faded. Everything was red. She was caught in a dizzying whirl of countless faces, faces that had experienced unspeakable fear and sadness. But what she felt most was hunger, greed —and anger. How could humans do this to their own people? She looked down at her hands, covered in the blood that flowed freely from the trough. It was as the oracle had warned. She could see the blood coursing down the steps of the pyramid and into the red, red river. No wonder the forest was cursed. The land could never be clean.

Her vision cleared, and she turned to the Southern Oracle, her eyes blazing. "You were there."

He looked into her eyes, shrinking at her gaze. "Yes," he said quietly.

"You helped him. You know what we stand to lose."

"Yes," he whispered.

"And yet you will not help us defeat him," Abby said incredulously.

The Southern Oracle slumped to the floor of the stone platform, sitting on its edge. He stared at the river as if he could see that rushing line of red in his mind as well. He probably could. Abby did not think you could forget something like that.

"You do not know what you ask of me," he murmured, avoiding her eyes.

"Help me to understand."

"He is my brother."

Abby was stunned, but held her tongue.

The oracle continued. "It started with one kingdom. A handful of victims, a few sacrifices a year in exchange for the prosperity of the ruler and his subjects. Tierney was true to his promises—he ended a terrible drought, made crops flourish—it seemed a fair exchange."

"Was it fair to those who were sacrificed?" Abby asked.

"No. It was not. But Tierney never lied about what he wanted—the king understood his price. Then there were several kings, and soon there was a never-ending line of humans walking up that passage to their deaths. I was not innocent in the bloodshed—I cannot pretend I was. But I tried to stop it. I went to the Solas Beir. He removed Tierney from his position and closed the portals here. The sacrifices stopped. He appointed me Southern Oracle, and my brother never forgave me for my betrayal."

"You did what you had to do. It was genocide," Abby replied.

"I *know* what it was. But you cannot ask me to side against my brother again."

"He did this as the Southern Oracle. What do you think will happen if we lose and he rules Cai Terenmare?" she asked.

The Southern Oracle hunched forward, covering his face with his hands. He was silent for a long time, and Abby sat down beside him. Finally, he raised his head and looked at her, taking her hand. "All right," he said, sighing heavily.

"All right?" She searched his eyes.

"You win, C'aislingaer. I will align with the Solas Beir. What happened here must *never* happen again."

Abby smiled and kissed his cheek. "*Thank you*, King of Jaguars."

He smiled back and squeezed her hand. "You are a formidable opponent, Abby. I do believe my brother has greatly underestimated you."

"And I agree with the former Solas Beir's decision to make you Southern Oracle. You are a man of honor," she replied.

The oracle sighed and shook his head. "No. I am a man who has made many mistakes."

"But you learned from them. The old Solas Beir knew that. That's why he chose you to replace Tierney. He knew you would understand what was at stake better than anyone." Abby stood up and held out her hand. "Come on—let's go back to the village. But can we climb down the pyramid this time? I can't handle going through that passage again."

The Southern Oracle took her hand and got to his feet. "Neither can I."

# THE SIXTH COURTESAN

The courtesan stood looking out into the vast nothingness of the Barren. To the west was home. Due east was the city from which he had scarcely escaped. He considered himself lucky. Of the six of them, three had been used until their last breath had been taken from them. The fourth had put up a fight and had died for it, but her sacrifice had created the diversion that made his flight from the city's dungeon possible. The fifth—well, the fifth had been the hardest to leave behind.

He could do nothing for the others, but the fifth still lived, or at least he hoped she did. He had wanted to free her as well, but with the guards close at his heels, it simply wasn't possible. She was young, much too young to be left alone in that den of vipers, but there was nothing he could do until he found someone with the power to intervene. If he failed, the Shadows would feed on her, draining her completely. It was her face that drove him to press on. But even if he did fail and she was lost, many others like her lived in his village, young ones who could just as easily be taken. He could not let that happen. If he could not save her, he must honor her by crossing the Barren to warn the others.

He stopped to rest at the rock spire that marked the desert's border. The Eye of the Needle it was called, and around the steep rock wall of its base was a smattering of large boulders. He chose one and set down his satchel, opening it to check his supplies. Before the palace guards had given chase, he had managed to steal the bag and some food from the bazaar flanking the city's gates. He had stolen a leather cask as well. It had been half full, but now, after a good day's run to this place, it was almost empty. Ahead, the hot, dusty dunes of the Barren mocked him, asking him if he truly dared to venture forward with nothing but a few sips left.

He did not have a choice. He could not return to the city. He had heard there was a village on the southern coast, but getting there would still require travel through part of this desert. Even if he managed the journey, the place was rumored to be a vile rat's nest of bandits and cutthroats—not much different from the gang of slave traders he'd just left, really. Supposing he made it to Southport alive, he had nothing to trade for a voyage home except himself, so in all likelihood, the bandits would simply ship him north to the city of the Eastern Oracle again.

He thought of his sister back home in their village on the plains, and of an old saying she favored: "The Light will provide." The saying had carried them through to harvest during many years of hardship. He had to hope provisions would come this time too.

He slipped the strap of the satchel over his head and onto one shoulder, slinging the bag to rest on his hip, so the weight of it was distributed across his body. He adjusted the richly embroidered silk tunic that had been given to him upon his arrival in the city. The tunic was deep purple in color, the mark of the royal courtesans. One of his hands had been branded with a golden tattoo. It was a shape he knew well, one that served as the sigil of the Solas Beir, that of the Sign of the Throne. He traced the spiral of the nautilus shell and stepped away from the rock spire onto the hot sand. The Light would provide. It would have to, for there was nothing else.

The courtesan followed the sun as it journeyed west. He was unsure how many hours passed in the dizzying heat. He only knew that he had to keep to his path, west, always west, one foot, then the other, step after step.

Ahead, something shiny twinkled, glinting in the sunlight. As the courtesan approached, he was able to discern the stone basin of a well. Surely, he thought, it would be dry—he dared not hope otherwise. To his delight, the well was full and running over into the shallow trough that encircled it. He dipped a finger into the cool liquid and tasted it. The water was sweet. *How can this be?* There was an insignia carved into the white marbled wall of the fount, a woman with wings outstretched like a bird. The symbol was bounded by a simple carved circle.

The courtesan hesitated, remembering the creatures who had taken him, their harsh, bird-of-prey screams piercing the stillness of the night.

Above the image was a jewel, also enclosed in a circle. This jewel was the source of the twinkling light he had seen from afar. It was an amethyst, deep violet like his tunic, a stone of protection and healing. In spite of the resemblance of the carving to the winged creatures who had been his captors, surely this fount was his salvation, a sign the Light had indeed provided. His parched throat felt as though it were full of splinters, and the water was so very sweet.

He filled his cask and drank, then refilled it and drank again. A third time he filled it and then capped it tight for the journey to come. He wished he had more containers to hold water, but at least now he was refreshed. He ducked his head into the well. It felt so lovely to feel the cool water on his skin.

He still did not know how he would make it across the Barren without losing his way or his mind, but this gift of water had certainly improved his odds. He ducked his head again for good measure, to enjoy the coolness of the fount once more.

Suddenly, he felt a sharp pain pulse through the hand that had been branded and raised his head from the pool, startled to find a small reptile staring up at him. The creature was long, almost eel-like, with a ribbon-like tail and a rounded snout. Just behind its eyes was some kind of lacy frilled growth, not quite horns, but gills perhaps. It had small, stubby appendages. The creature's scales were a muddy red, almost black, and a lighter scarlet line ran along its sides. The tapered tail bloomed into a flat paddle, edged in black and white stripes. The thing hissed at him, revealing rows of teeth curved like cutlasses toward the back of its throat. The courtesan pulled his hand back—he could see a half circle of red dots next to the gold tattoo. The thing had bitten him.

☙ভাগ্যভাগ্য

"He changed his mind?" David asked in disbelief after the Southern Oracle left their tree house, having formally shared the news with the others. Cael, Jon and Marisol had joined the oracle to tour more of the village, leaving David and Abby alone.

"Yep. He sure did." Abby was beaming from her victory.

"I love you, woman. I really do. I don't know how you did it, but you are *amazing*."

"I *am* amazing," she agreed, grinning. "But it's a long story. I'll have to fill you in later. For now, he's hosting one last feast before we leave tomorrow."

"Great! Wow, I just can't believe it. I'm thrilled." David scooped her up in his arms and spun her around. The tree house swayed precariously.

"Whoa there," she laughed. "Dial down the enthusiasm. You're going to kill us."

With the news of the Southern Oracle's decision to join the alliance, the frosty tension that had so quickly developed between him and David melted. The feast ended with the promise of friendship and future visits.

After the feast, Abby shared her experiences at the Blood Altar with David and the others. She wanted them to understand the oracle's reasons for becoming an ally, and why he had said no initially. It was David who understood something no one else recognized, not even Abby.

"You pushed him," he said. "Remember what Eulalia said about you being an empath and being able to project emotions?"

Abby remembered. "You're right. I didn't even know I was doing it, but it's true. There was such a strong emotional echo in that place—it was overwhelming. But what surprised me is that it wasn't the fear that stuck with me, it was anger at the injustice of what happened to those people."

David nodded. "Righteous anger."

"Exactly," Abby agreed. "It was almost like I was standing outside of myself, watching as I focused that anger into a fine point, and then beamed it at him, burning it into him until his resolve evaporated. It was powerful."

"Sounds like somebody's got their own laser powers," David smiled.

"Guess so. Better not tick me off, Fly Boy," she said, punching his arm playfully. "I'll mess you up."

David raised his hands in surrender. "I wouldn't dare. So how about using that mind trick on Tierney? Think it could work?"

"Worth a try," Abby said. If the Southern Oracle was strong enough to once again stand against Tierney, maybe she was too.

With replenished supplies, they headed into the depths of the forest, accompanied by the oracle and his entourage. The horrors that had haunted them on the journey to the village seemed to have vanished, and with extra guards for the night watch, the group was able to travel more quickly than before.

Soon, Abby found herself saying a heartfelt goodbye to the Southern Oracle, as he left them safely at the Emerald Guardian. Though she had not known him long, she would miss him. She respected his courage.

The sun was setting once again, and the forest was getting dark. With the rainforest at their backs, everyone seemed to be in a lighter mood, as if a weight had been lifted from their shoulders. The familiar sounds of their own forest were comforting, and the sight of their horses, grazing as contentedly as when they had left them, made everyone ache for home.

Still, when Cael suggested they postpone the long ride to the castle until morning, no one objected. The fortunate turn of events with the Southern Oracle had buoyed their spirits, and for the moment, almost erased the sense of urgency driving their mission.

Exhausted, Abby had no trouble getting to sleep. Wrapped in David's arms, she felt warm and safe.

Spending time in the rainforest had been draining; even without the sleep-deprived nights, there had been a depressive shadow hanging over her, something intermeshed with the canopy itself. The heaviness of it made Abby feel as if her body were made of lead—even with the good news of having the Southern Oracle as an ally, there were times when it took all she had to keep putting one foot in front of the other. It was similar to her experience fighting fear in the passage at the Blood Altar. She knew the others could feel it too, but not as keenly as she did. She wasn't sure if that was because she was an empath, or because of her experiences at the Blood Altar. Either way, she felt cursed.

ЮСЗЮСЗЮСЗ

The courtesan stumbled down a dune and across the flat, dusty bottom of a lake that had been dry for centuries. Ahead were more dunes. They looked blurry, but the courtesan was unsure if this was because of the heat in the air, or if something was wrong with his vision. He was starting to suspect the latter. He looked back at the path he had taken, following his sandy footprints to the crest of the dune. Perhaps he *was* seeing things, because he seemed to have company.

The eel-lizard thing that had bitten him was stalking him now, hanging back several paces, just far enough away to stay out of reach. The courtesan stared down at the semicircle of angry, red dots on his hand. Next to them, the branded golden nautilus shell still lay flat on the top of his hand, but the skin around the tattoo was swollen. His hand was ballooning into something unrecognizable, a fleshy lump with pudgy sausage fingers. His throat felt swollen as well, and the dry splinters of thirst had returned. Each swallow was raw, agonizing. Attached to his belt was his cask, still nearly full. In the grip of his fever, he had found it too heavy to lift, and then, as his temperature rose, he had forgotten about it entirely.

The ground below the courtesan rolled like the deck of a ship, and through a dizzying haze of confusion, he wondered if the ground was actually moving or if the desert heat was slowly frying his brain. Or perhaps it was the eel-thing's venom crawling through his veins, killing him as slowly as he stumbled through this never-ending land of sand and more sand. There were many things he was unsure of, but of one thing he was certain: whatever was following him was growing.

ഓവേയവേയവേയ

It seemed to Abby like she had just closed her eyes when she opened them again. She looked toward the fire—nothing seemed amiss. Jon was on watch, his back to her. She was still lying in David's arms, and he was sleeping peacefully. Untangling herself from his embrace, she sat up.

She felt a presence—someone was watching her. She turned her head in the direction of the rainforest. There, crouching on top of the Emerald Guardian, was Tierney.

"Hello, Rabbit," he smiled.

She placed her hand protectively on David's back, pulling him closer to her.

213

"Shhhh," Tierney whispered from his perch. "Don't wake him up."

She glanced at Jon, wondering if she should warn him. She thought better of it. If she sounded the alarm, Tierney would either attack or disappear. Better to have this little chat, if that was what he wanted. She had a few things of her own to say.

Tierney noted her dilemma with amusement, one eyebrow raised, a sly smile on his lips. "Don't bother warning your friend. He can't see me anyway."

"I'm dreaming," Abby realized.

"Bingo." Tierney winked and cocked his finger like a gun, firing it at her. *Bang.*

The gesture would have seemed strange coming from anyone else in Cai Terenmare, but Abby remembered the dream she'd had seeing him through Lucia's eyes. He had been at ease in her old world, fitting in perfectly. She thought about what Fergal had said about blending in, and how easily Tierney transitioned between the formal speech of this realm and the casual cadence of her own. This guy had been around.

"I figured out why you call me Rabbit," she told him.

Tierney's sly smile widened. "Did you now? And how do you like it?"

"It's taking some getting used to," she admitted.

He chuckled. "Ah. I see. It wasn't everything you'd hoped for."

"On the contrary," she said, narrowing her eyes, "it was more than I'd hoped for, since I never expected to have that ability in the first place."

Tierney shrugged. "Still—you'd prefer something a bit more menacing, a little bigger, perhaps. Something like me. Don't deny it—I can see it in your eyes."

"Every creature serves a purpose, no matter its size," she insisted, repeating what the Southern Oracle had told her.

He feigned sympathy, clucking his tongue. "Oh, Abby, love. That's just something people say to be polite. Trust me—being a predator is so much better than being prey."

Abby scowled, irritated by his patronizing tone. "Yeah, well, some people would accuse you of overcompensating."

Tierney laughed, rocking back on his heels on top of the stump. Abby hoped he would lose his balance and fall off, but no such luck. He had the reflexes and agility of his feline alter ego. "Touché, my darling girl, touché. I understand you met the Southern Oracle. How is my dear brother?"

Abby gave Tierney the most cheerful smile she could muster under the circumstances. "Fantastic," she said brightly. "We've become the *best* of friends."

His arrogant smile turned frigid. "How very nice for you."

Abby's smile widened. She was pleased with herself for managing to irritate Tierney for once. "Yes, it *is* very nice. And I finally had the chance to see you for what you are."

Tierney leapt down from his perch, his eyes narrowed. "Is that right? Well then, I'm on pins and needles. Pray tell, dearest—what did you see?"

Abby felt fear rise in her throat, but forced it down, determined to end things with Tierney one way or another. She stood up and stepped over David's sleeping body, blocking Tierney from getting too close to him. She stared into Tierney's eyes, her feet planted, her fists clenched. "I saw the Blood Altar, and I know what you did. You said you preyed on us to save us from ourselves. But that's not true." Abby felt her anger glowing like an ember. She rolled it around in her mind, trying to focus it.

Tierney eyed Abby's defensive stance and stepped closer to her, tracing her cheek with his finger.

Abby felt her heart beat faster, but she willed herself not to react to his touch.

Tierney stared into her eyes, studying her face.

She saw his eyes move to take in her lips and felt his finger brush her bottom lip tenderly, as though he were remembering kissing her in the rainforest dream. When he looked into her eyes again, his were blazing with intensity.

"Isn't it true?" he asked. "I told you I was a predator. You know I must feed to survive. You can't *really* be surprised by that, can you?"

She glared at him. "That wasn't survival. That was a bloodbath."

He shrugged. "I suppose I *was* a bit greedy back then. Lesson learned. People do change, you know, and so I have."

Abby frowned. "Really? And how is that, exactly?"

He chuckled and kissed her cheek before she could protest. "You'll find out soon enough, love. See you soon." With that he disappeared.

Abby sat up with a start. David was sound asleep next to her. She looked at the Emerald Guardian. No Tierney. But there was something else. Just behind the stump was a stone door set in a frame that looked as though it had been chiseled from some ancient tomb and placed to stand alone in the middle of the forest. The door was propped open. Through the doorway, she wasn't seeing the dark forest, as she would have expected. There was daylight there. And sand. Lots of sand.

She stood up and walked over to the door. She didn't dare walk though—this might be one of Tierney's tricks, and who knew where she might end up? Instead she cautiously peered through the doorway. In the distance she could see a city with a high stone wall. The city seemed to rise in tiers, and at the very top was a tall, stone palace. There was something else as well. The smell of the sea.

She studied the door. It was void of decoration except for one image—a man with the head of a bird. She reached out to touch it and woke up.

"A dream within a dream," she whispered to herself.

&#128018;&#67;&#55357;&#57;&#56;

From her spot next to Jon, Marisol was staring at the cooling embers of the campfire, eating breakfast. In between bites of flatbread, she caught him staring at her. It made her feel warm inside.

They'd grown closer during the trip. It seemed as if there was something he wanted to say, but then he looked away, turning his gaze to the fire. There were things she wanted to say to him too, but if he felt the way she hoped he did, she wanted him to say it first. Maybe he would, once they finally had time alone.

She turned her attention to the discussion between Abby, David, and Cael, chewing slowly while listening to Abby recount the details of her latest dream. Part of the dream sounded very familiar.

"Tierney was being mysterious, as usual," Abby said, scrunching her nose in annoyance, "but I really think there's something to the dream about the door."

"As do I," Cael replied. "The city you described sounds like the city of the Eastern Oracle. You must have been viewing it from somewhere to the west, in the Barren."

"You said there was a bird man on the door. Can you draw him?" David asked. He pulled a quill, ink, and some parchment from his pack.

"Sure." She quickly sketched the image. The bird's head had a long, thin, curved beak.

"Looks like some kind of Egyptian god," Jon noted, peering over Abby's shoulder as she added some final details. "Isn't Horus the one with the bird head?"

"Yes, but Horus had the head of a falcon," Marisol said. She pointed to the bird man's beak. "That's an ibis. That's Thoth. He was the god of wisdom. He was associated with magic, writing, science, and the judgment of the dead."

"I didn't know you were into Egyptian mythology," Jon said, turning to Marisol.

"It's something my dad is into," Marisol explained. "But I know that door. There was a recent discovery—a new tomb was uncovered, and the archeologists are hoping it will shed light on the lost scrolls of Thoth. There's a creation myth involving him, where he wrote down all the knowledge of the universe. Supposedly the scrolls contain the secret to making gold and other magical spells, so the legend was big with alchemists in the Middle Ages."

"Do you think the scrolls exist?" Jon asked.

Marisol shrugged. "Who knows? Maybe. But there's this other creation myth about an Egyptian god named Ptah, which speaks to the power of words and knowledge. It's said he spoke the universe into existence, kind of like the Bible story in Genesis. Sometimes legends intersect across cultures, so maybe there's something to them."

"Eulalia mentioned something similar about the potency of words and how they're essential to my power as Solas Beir,"

David said, nodding. "Your Thoth story is an interesting legend, but how does it relate to the door?"

"It sounds like the door is a portal," Marisol reasoned. "Thoth was considered by some to be a messenger of the gods. Like Anubis, he was connected to the underworld. If the door is a portal linking our worlds, then maybe the Egyptians saw the shape-shifters here in their animal forms and that got incorporated into the legend. Think about it."

"If the door *is* a portal, that would explain why I dreamed about it," Abby said. "But how does that help us if the door is in Egypt?"

"It's not," Marisol smiled. "It's in Vegas."

"What? Are you serious?" Jon asked.

Marisol's smile turned into a grin. "Deadly serious."

"What's it doing there? Shouldn't it be in a museum?" Abby asked.

"It *is* in a museum. Sort of," Marisol added. "It's in a new casino."

"Wait. How does that work? And why would Egypt let go of a find like that?" Abby asked.

"Money," Marisol explained. "Let's just say the investors made a significant contribution to the folks in charge of the find. Antiquity is a family-friendly casino combined with a museum of history and science. The resort has kind of an archeologist-slash-eco-warrior theme. There's not just stuff on archeological finds; there are exhibits on conservation too. *Preserving our treasures of yesterday, today, and tomorrow*—that's the slogan."

"Neo Indiana Jones?" Jon asked.

"Yeah. More or less," Marisol said.

"Okay. I'll buy that. But isn't it a bit of a contradiction? I mean, how does the eco thing work in a city that celebrates material extravagance?" Abby asked.

"I know," Marisol frowned, "but the marketing team said it would appeal to young, educated couples with kids and money to burn. It's *edutainment*. Antiquity is the newer, friendlier face of Las Vegas. Plus the museum qualifies for a pretty nice tax break."

"Wait a sec," David interjected. "I'm missing something. How do you know so much about this, again?"

Marisol felt her face grow hot with embarrassment. "My dad. He's one of the investors."

"Oh. Now I get it." David patted her shoulder. "You know, my dad probably would have invested in that project too. He liked anything that was educational."

Marisol nodded, feeling less self-conscious. Abby could be a little self-righteous sometimes. Maybe it was easy to think that way when you'd never had money. At least with David, Marisol didn't feel like she had to apologize for having wealth.

"Okay, so say this door *is* in Vegas, and say it *is* a portal. If we could reopen it, would it take us to the Eastern Oracle? In theory?" David asked.

"It might," Cael nodded thoughtfully. "Yes, I believe it would."

"All right. So if we were to ride across the Barren, how long would it take us?" David asked.

"Weeks," Cael said. "Likely a full month."

"And by ship?" David asked.

"Not accounting for storms, or whatever monsters we might encounter, probably a month as well. Perhaps longer," Cael said.

"But what if we went back into the human world—how far is it to Vegas from Newcastle Beach?" David asked.

Jon grinned like he could see where this was going. "Ten hours, tops—if I'm driving."

"You're not driving," Marisol said.

Jon's grin faded into a pout. "Oh, you're no fun."

"You're not driving," she continued, smiling, "because we'll fly. If we borrow my dad's plane, we could be there in an hour."

"That decides it," David announced. "A one-hour flight is worth finding out if this shortcut is legit."

&#8368;&#8368;&#8368;&#8368;&#8368;&#8368;

Eulalia did not want them to go. During their visit with the Southern Oracle, the queen had been plagued by horrible dreams and feared that something terrible was imminent.

Abby's dreams of Tierney had only reinforced this idea. Eulalia was certain that Tierney still had a hold on Abby and cautioned that the door could be a trap. In the end though, Eulalia had conceded that the possibility of a shortcut was worth the risk, especially since the winds of fortune seemed to be blowing in their favor. An alliance with three of four oracles was more than the queen could have hoped for. Now, if only the Eastern Oracle would stand with them.

The royal guard passed through the portal in Newcastle Beach first, sent to thoroughly search the old estate for rogue Shadows. Satisfied that the Solas Beir would not be ambushed, Phelan and his soldiers crossed back to assure the queen that all was well.

Then, optimistic about the journey ahead, David, Abby, Cael, Jon, and Marisol said their goodbyes to family and friends and passed through the portal. It was just the five of them again, but their experiences in the rainforest proved that they worked well together. And, as far as being able to slip unnoticed into the city of the Eastern Oracle, a small party would have the advantage over an army. A small party fit better in the Browns' minivan as well. It was a short drive to the Santa Linda airport.

Marisol had been a bit concerned the pilot would object to transporting an heiress who had been missing for weeks, but she need not have worried.

৪০৫৪০৫৪০৫

After many years of working for Marcus Cassidy and Esperanza Garcia, Nick Connor knew how to mind his own business.

Nick barely raised an eyebrow when his employers' daughter showed up with a group of sword-wielding kids and an older guy who looked the worse for wear, dressed in some kind of fancy armor, as if they'd just come from Comic Con.

So Miss Cassidy was sowing some wild oats and wanted to party in Vegas superhero-style. At least they weren't wearing tights and capes. And even if they had been, Nick had learned not to ask questions.

Mr. Cassidy would probably be steamed the pilot had flown the girl out of state rather than deny her request and drive her straight home, but Nick wouldn't lose his job over it.

Cassidy and his ex had been pretty busy jet-setting all through the kid's growing-up years. The girl hadn't been abandoned exactly, but quality time had been at a minimum.

Anyone who worked for them knew that—it wasn't a big secret. And it wasn't a big surprise that the girl was rebelling now.

Maybe she was making up for lost time, trying to get some parental attention she'd missed in her early years. Still, rebel or not, Marisol had turned out all right. She was polite at least—she'd shown him the respect of addressing him as Mr. Connor. She'd even thrown in a please and a thank you. And surprisingly, her friends had behaved themselves on the flight; not the rowdy bunch he'd expected. These were small things, but they meant something to him.

ဆု�04ဆု04ဆု04

"What are you writing?" Jon had asked as they flew over the California border.

"It's a letter to my dad," Marisol answered.

Writing to her father was hard. The rest of her incredible adventure since she had left Newcastle Beach had been a cake walk compared to this.

Funny how easy it had been to let go of her life in her old world—how she now thought of Caislucis as her home. The lamia might have been lying when she was pretending to be Esperanza Garcia, but still, Marisol was certain her parents were worried about her. They probably *did* think she was dead. For that she felt tremendously guilty.

But up until now, there hadn't been an opportunity for her to communicate with them. It wasn't as if she could have gone back to Newcastle Beach immediately, not if the Shadow who had chased her was still waiting on the other side of the portal. Now, after the passing of so many weeks, and with signs that Tierney and his foul band of nightmare goblins were back in Cai

Terenmare, it seemed safe to cross over, and she could finally let her parents know she was alive and well.

In the end, Marisol decided to keep her letter simple. She told her father that she was sorry for worrying him, and that she loved him and her mother, even if she couldn't say where she had been, where she was, or where she was going. She told him that she hoped to return home when she could.

As Marisol left the plane, she handed the letter to the pilot. "Thank you, Mr. Connor. Could you please give this to my father?"

Nick Conner nodded, and Marisol felt a weight lift from her shoulders. She knew he would make sure her dad got the letter.

# ANTIQUITY

"You can't bring those in here." The burly security guard blocked Cael's entrance to the Antiquity casino. "Weapons are strictly prohibited." He pointed to the large sign posted at the casino's front doors, where the same statement had been spelled out in capital letters.

Jon watched as a puzzled-looking Cael studied the guard as if he did not understand a word the man was saying. For a warrior who *always* had weapons close at hand, this was truly a foreign concept.

Frowning, the guard pointed at the sheathed sword hanging from Cael's belt. "No swords allowed. *¿Comprende?*"

Jon intervened. He pulled at the hilt of his own sword. "It's fake, see? But don't tell anyone—we want people to think it's real. We're the entertainment."

The guard scratched his head, his thick eyebrows furrowed together in confusion. "What're yuh, sword-swallowing circus freaks?"

Jon concluded the guard was a few cards shy of a full deck, and gave him a diplomatic smile. "Yeah. Something like that." Then he grabbed Cael's arm and steered him away, into the noisy depths of the busy casino.

As they entered the chaos, bells began to ring. Lights were flashing and people were shouting excitedly—someone had just won a lot of money. Jon glanced back and saw the guard look toward the noise. David, Abby, and Marisol took the distraction as their cue to follow Jon and Cael.

"So, where's Thoth's door?" David asked, catching up. The group paused, and Marisol looked around.

"Follow me," she said, leading the group through the rows of slot machines and zigzagging around card tables.

Cael looked around the casino, bewildered. They passed a table where a bedazzeled Elvis, a lime-green alien, and a woman wearing a perilously low-cut red sequined dress were playing poker.

"Welcome to the weirdest city in America, man," Jon said to Cael. "You can wear anything, do anything, and it's all part of the show."

Cael nodded. He looked horrified.

"I'm not saying that's a good thing," Jon clarified.

"It's not just the patrons that are scary," Abby added. "Just look at that thing. It looks like it's going to eat that guy's soul."

"What thing?" Jon asked, looking around the casino.

"See the guy in the suit? The one who looks like he's a short elevator trip from jumping off the roof?" Abby asked.

Sure enough, there was a man holding his head in his hands, staring at the cards he had laid on the table. He looked like he'd just lost a fortune.

"Yeah. What about him?" Jon asked.

"Look at the woman standing next to him. She looks human, but her face...the look on her face..." Abby shuddered in revulsion.

"Abby," Jon said slowly, "there *is* no woman. Just the guy playing blackjack with the dealer."

"You can't see her? She's right there," Abby insisted, pointing. Jon stared at Abby like she had lost her mind.

"She's right," David said. "There *is* something there. I don't see a woman, but there's *something*—like some kind of shadow, but it has density—it's like a dark space that moves on its own."

"They are all around us," Cael confirmed, his jaw clenched.

"What are they?" Marisol asked, whispering. Wide-eyed, she stepped closer to Jon and slipped her hand into his.

"They are much like the Shadows. They feed," Cael explained, "but not until after the victim is dead. She will feed on him, but first she will drive him to kill himself."

"Shouldn't we do something?" David asked.

"There is nothing we *can* do," Cael answered. "He has already given himself to her will, whether he knows it or not."

"Maybe it's better not to know," Abby said.

"I would not wish for his fate," Cael replied. "But we must not tarry, lest they sink their hooks into us as well."

"Yeah, let's go," Marisol agreed. "I'm getting a little freaked out."

Marisol led them away from the casino floor and down a corridor that curved slightly, bordered by a bank of elevators on one side, and by a series of small boutique shops on the other. She pointed to a sign with a sepia-toned photograph of hieroglyphics etched in stone. "This way," she said, turning down a second corridor.

Ahead was an archway flanked by plaster pillars painted to look as though they too were covered in hieroglyphics.

Entering the museum, they were greeted by a ten-foot tall, garishly painted plaster sphinx.

"Classy," Jon said. Then, on the other side of the exhibit room he spotted what they had come for. "There it is. Let's do this."

ༀༀༀ

Abby watched as David paused to remove something from around his neck. The silver nautilus shell, once halved, was whole again, and hung from a long silver chain that had been hidden under the fabric of his shirt. "You brought it?"

Taking Abby's hand, David pressed the Sign of the Throne into it, closing her fingers over the sigil. "Yes," he replied. "We may not need it to open the portal, but I brought it just in case. Keep it safe for me, okay?"

"Of course," Abby promised.

David approached the stone door. It looked exactly as it had in Abby's dream, except that it was firmly closed in the freestanding stone doorframe. Behind it were some other exhibits.

"Last time they opened a portal, it was quite a show," Jon explained to Marisol. He nodded to the guards standing near the plaster pillars. "If that happens, those guards will be coming our way pretty darn quick."

Marisol and Cael exchanged a glance and wordlessly moved in front of David and Abby to shield them from view.

Jon took a quick look around to make sure there were no other guards in the immediate vicinity. Then he took his place by Marisol's side.

"I believe the guards will be the least of our worries," Cael said. He was staring out into the hallway between the pillars, his hand clenched on the hilt of his sword.

Abby followed his gaze. The hallway had grown dark. Even though she could see the glow of the hallway's ceiling-mounted light fixtures, a dense, impenetrable fog seemed to have settled at the museum's entrance, masking the light.

"Those things...they're coming, aren't they?" Marisol looked around frantically. "I can't see them, but I can feel them—it's like the air is heavy, and the temperature has dropped."

Abby too could feel the change in the air. Similar to what she had experienced at the Blood Altar, the air in this room pressed down on her shoulders and the back of her neck. It was almost as though the weight of the air would force her to her knees. She thought it might if it got any heavier.

The cold air was accompanied by a smell—a mixture of smoke and sulfur. It made her want to retch. She placed a hand over her stomach, as if she could hold in the bile creeping up her throat.

"Yes, they are coming." Silently Cael unsheathed his sword and positioned his feet, ready to fight. "I cannot see them as clearly as Abby can, but I can feel them."

Marisol stiffened, her fear apparent on her face. Then the tightness in her expression softened as she composed herself. She followed Cael's example, planting her feet and holding her sword out in front of her. Jon did the same.

Abby stared at the museum's entrance as the fog shifted, solidifying. They were coming all right.

The first entity to make an appearance was the woman from the blackjack table. Abby froze in horror as she felt the creature probing at her mind and realized she had an awareness of this thing's sentience as well. Abby wondered if the thing knew she could sense its thoughts. Then she got an answer, more as a wave of feelings than a thought articulated, but Abby understood just the same.

Oh yes, the creature was well aware of Abby's uninvited psychic presence, but it didn't mind the intrusion at all. It was not threatened by the fact that Abby was gaining knowledge about its methods; rather, it took pleasure from her fear as she came to understand its intentions.

Blackjack Lady had left its prey unattended for the promise of something—*someone*—a bit more tasty. Not that it wouldn't go back for seconds later. It had the man's scent now, and it didn't really matter if he stayed at the table or left the casino. It didn't matter if he ran away to Timbuktu. It would find him.

The entity's tight-fitting dress leaned toward sleazy, and should it choose to become visible to those it hunted, it would blend in perfectly with the average tourist out for a wild night on the Las Vegas strip. Though the creature appeared female, Abby somehow knew this was just an illusion as well, and that, depending on the prey, its gender might well change. Whatever this thing was, it wasn't male and it wasn't female. It simply *was*, and the thing's true form would stay hidden until it began to feed.

It was the face that offered a glimpse of just what that might be. It was human-shaped, but somehow those soulless eyes and the smile, that hungry, *hungry* smile, twisted the face into an expression of evil that frightened Abby more than anything she'd encountered before. More even than the Kruorumbrae themselves.

Something about that face revealed how relentless this thing would be once it got hold of you. For this thing, silver swords and protective circles were useless. It didn't play by the same rules as the Kruorumbrae. It had existed long before such rules were made.

The thing was getting closer, slow-shuffling its way to them, not worried about hurrying. It had all the time in the world. And it had brought friends.

Abby turned to David. "Need help?" she asked, trying to keep her voice calm. She didn't think he would find it terribly encouraging if he knew how frightened she was.

"Almost there," he said. He was focused solely on the door, ignoring everything else. He had covered the carving of Thoth with his hands, and light was seeping out from beneath his palms, radiating to the edges of the door, bathing it in a pulsating sheet of blue.

There was a tiny popping noise, and the door unsealed. David pushed it all the way open, and a handful of sand poured out onto the marble floor of the museum. "We're in!" he shouted.

David took Abby's hand, dragging her through the portal. The moment her feet touched the warm sand, the heaviness lifted from her shoulders. Abby turned to watch the others pass through.

"Thank goodness," Marisol whispered, almost diving through the door in her scramble to follow David and Abby.

Jon and Cael walked backward together, facing the places where the dark forms seemed to be gaining in density. Then Cael grabbed Jon's arm, and they quickly stepped through the portal.

ಬುಚ್ಚಬುಚ್ಚಬುಚ್ಚ

Jon shielded his eyes against the intensity of a midday sun and the harsh glare reflecting off the sand at his feet. Then he turned back to look through the doorway, and a scream caught in his throat.

"You see them now, don't you Jon?" Abby asked quietly.

He could feel Abby's eyes on him, but he didn't turn in her direction. As much as he wanted to look away from the portal, he couldn't wrench his gaze from the things shuffling toward the doorway. He feared that the second he looked away, he would feel long, cold fingers wind around his neck and tighten like a vise. From the murderous looks on the creatures' faces, this seemed like a perfectly valid fear.

"I see them. They look like people." Jon's voice cracked, and with great effort, he swallowed, trying to force back the horror that threatened his sanity.

"But they're not," Abby said.

"No. They're not," Jon replied. If he sounded calmer, it was a fluke. He was terrified.

"We should really shut the portal," Abby urged.

"Yes, we should," Jon said. He wanted to, but couldn't seem to make his muscles obey, to take a step closer to the door. His limbs felt heavy, like petrified wood. And he couldn't tear his eyes from what he was seeing. None of them could.

One of the creatures had almost made it to the portal. It vaguely resembled the woman in the low-cut dress Jon had noticed playing poker earlier. But that woman had definitely been human. He was fairly certain this thing didn't have a soul.

This must be what Abby had seen preying on the man at the blackjack table. The thing smiled as it reached for Jon, almost touching the sheet of blue light hanging in the doorway. Then it hesitated, the hungry smile frozen on its face.

Maybe it recognized the source of the light and thought it might get burned. Jon hoped it would. *Reach out and touch it,* he thought, his fear turning to anger. *Go right ahead. See what happens.*

Instead, the thing turned to Marisol and whispered her name. Marisol was frozen with fear. She stared back, speechless. She looked scared to death; her tan skin faded to a dull, lifeless grey.

The thing's smile stretched wider across its face. Then it spoke to her, and its rasping voice made Jon's skin crawl. "Remember all those nights you pulled the covers up tight over your head, and you were so, so scared you weren't alone? You weren't."

Jon looked from Marisol to the thing, and the last of his fear vanished, replaced by rage. He stepped protectively in front of his girl. "Yeah, that's old news. Shove off." He grabbed the edge of the stone door to slam it closed. It was heavy, and met with resistance against the sand.

Marisol seemed to come to her senses. She joined him in the effort, pressing her weight against the door. Together they heaved it shut. The blue light winked out as the edges of the door sealed against the frame, generating a small puff of air that stirred the sand at their feet. They stared at the door for a second, and then Marisol threw her arms around Jon and kissed him. "Thanks," she whispered.

Jon grinned. "Anytime."

ಬಿಂಬಿಂಬಿಂಬಿಂ

Abby sighed with relief and held the Sign of the Throne out to David.

"You can hold onto it if you want," he said.

"I think it's safer with you," she replied. "Your powers have gotten stronger. You didn't need the Sign to open the door."

David slipped the silver chain around his neck again. "I think you're right. I'm not even tired." He kissed her cheek, then turned his attention to their surroundings. The door was set into a towering rock spire. To the west was nothing but sand dunes, and to the east was a city, far off in the distance. "Where are we?"

Cael craned his neck to look up. "The Eye of the Needle."

"Guess the shortcut worked," Jon said, squeezing Marisol's hand.

"Thanks, Sol," Abby said. "That was brilliant. You just saved us a whole lot of time."

"Anytime," Marisol replied, beaming at Jon.

David studied the stone door. What was strange was that the symbol carved on the Cai Terenmare side of the door was different than the image of Thoth on the Las Vegas side of the door. *The human side*, he corrected himself, feeling that increasingly familiar sense of disorientation that came from trying to reconcile his so-called human life with this one. It was funny how he still felt human, even though he had never been

234

one. "Hey, guys—look at the symbol on this side of the door. Thoth has been replaced by a winged woman."

"It looks like Erela, doesn't it?" Abby asked.

Cael nodded. "The Daughters of Mercy guard this portal."

"Or it could be Isis," Marisol shared. "Protector of the dead."

"So why Thoth on one side, and Isis on the other?" David asked.

"Maybe whoever made the door thought it was a passage to the underworld," Marisol suggested. "To pass into the land of the spirits, Anubis had to give approval for entrance. Thoth was the keeper of knowledge, and also recorded the judgment of who was allowed to enter the underworld—in other words, he was the keeper of knowledge about who was allowed to pass through the door. It would make sense that his image was inscribed on the human side of the door. And maybe whoever crossed over to the Cai Terenmare side encountered a Daughter, and that reinforced the legend about Isis."

"If they encountered a Daughter, they really *would* be going to the underworld," David said. "And speaking of, where *are* the Daughters?"

"I don't know," Abby answered. "It's a little too quiet, isn't it?"

"It is," Cael replied. "I would have expected to see them circling the Eye, guarding the portal from above."

David tilted his head back to take in the narrow tower of stone. At the very top he could just make out the cave of the Daughters of Mercy. The rock spire reminded him vaguely of the Washington Monument, but perhaps a more primitive version of it, with rough granite sides rather than walls smoothed by a stonemason's hand. He couldn't be sure, but if pressed, he would have guessed the obelisk-shaped formation was at least five hundred feet tall.

The skies above the Eye of the Needle were empty, a bright, cloudless blue—the kind of sky that would have been cheerful if it weren't arching over such a lifeless place. In the soundless breeze, wisps of sand drifted over the small dunes surrounding them. To the west, both the dunes and the sense of desolation grew.

"I hate this place," Abby said. "Bad things have happened here. I feel like something evil is watching me, and the air stinks."

David scrunched his nose. She was right. The air smelled rank, like something dead and decomposing. "I don't like it either," David agreed, taking Abby's hand. "Let's get out of here."

"The city is nearly a day's walk to the east," Cael said. "We should reach it as night falls." He began walking toward the city in the distance. David and Abby followed.

ဆုၺ္ၾဆုၺ္ၾဆုၺ္ၾ

Jon watched as Marisol took one more look at the carving of the winged woman, tracing the wings with her finger. He held out his hand, and when she turned toward him, she saw it and slipped her hand into his. He grinned.

"What?" she asked.

"You," he said. "I like being with a girl who's smart *and* hot."

"Thanks," she smiled. Then she eyed him seriously. "But...if you had to choose between being with a smart girl or being with a hot girl, which one would you choose?"

"But I *don't* have to choose," Jon said, confused.

"But if you did?"

"Is this a test?" he asked hesitantly.

"Maybe," she smiled. "Humor me. So would you go with answer A, brains, or answer B, beauty?"

"Answer C. All of the above," he countered.

"You can't answer C. That's not one of the choices."

"Well, it's not a fair question, Sol," Jon argued. "I like everything about you. But if what you're really asking is, would I still like you if something terrible happened and you were no longer beautiful, then the answer is yes. I would still like you. Do I pass?"

Marisol kissed his cheek. "Yes, you pass."

"Good. Now let's catch up to the others," he said.

Jon started walking, suddenly aware that the others were far ahead, making tracks, and he and Marisol were still standing in a place that smelled like death. Even if the Daughters weren't home at the moment, he felt like prey.

"Okay," she began, matching pace with his fast walk, "but just for the sake of argument, what if something terrible happened and I wasn't smart anymore?"

"Don't push your luck, lady," he laughed, pulling her into a jog.

As they caught up with the others, Cael stopped short, holding up his hand.

"What is it?" Jon asked.

"Riders," Cael informed him. "From the city. They approach with great speed."

In the distance, Jon could see a cloud of dust sweeping toward them. "That can't be good."

## *CITY OF THE EASTERN ORACLE*

Twenty riders were galloping fast in full armor, carrying flags emblazoned with the crest of the Eastern Oracle, a red dragon. They reined their mounts to an abrupt halt several yards away from the travelers, and the leader of the party dismounted.

David's hand automatically dropped to the hilt of his sword. The man walked confidently toward him and removed his helmet. Then he dropped to one knee and bowed his head. "Hail, Solas Beir. I wish you peace and prosperity all the years of your reign."

"Thank you," David replied, surprised. "Please—rise."

The knight rose to his feet. "Thank you, Your Majesty." His shoulder-length, sandy-blond hair was secured with a black leather tie, and he had a neatly trimmed beard. A scarlet cloak was secured to the polished black chest plate of his armor with gold medallions, signifying his role as captain of the city guard.

In contrast, the uniforms of his soldiers were more utilitarian, suits of dull black armor with the crest of the Eastern Oracle embossed in red on their chest plates.

"My lord, the Eastern Oracle, sends his welcome," the knight said.

"How did he know we were coming?" David asked.

"My master sees much," the knight replied. "He sends his apologies. He had wished to greet you personally, but his attention was required for urgent business in the city."

"All is well, I hope?" David asked.

The knight nodded. "Very well, indeed. The oracle has asked that I escort you to lodgings prepared specially for your visit. We hope they will meet with your approval."

"I'm sure they will. Thank you, Sir...?"

"Hedeon. My name is Hedeon. If it please you, Sire, we have brought swift horses to carry you. You must be weary from your travels." Five of the riders dismounted and led the extra horses over, leashed to theirs.

"Thank you, Hedeon, we *would* appreciate a lift." David turned to Abby, smiling. *Luck is with us,* he thought. And then, as if he were hearing her voice inside his mind, he corrected himself. *No, not luck. Light. The Light is with us.*

Hedeon offered his arm to Abby, and she took it graciously, smiling at the knight. He led her to a beautiful mare. "For you, dear lady."

"Thank you, sir," Abby said, and climbed up into the saddle.

Cael found his mount, and Jon led Marisol to hers. In moments they were traveling again, quickly making their way to the city.

ಎಲಿಎಲಿಎಲಿ

A towering wall encircled the City of the Eastern Oracle. Cael had confirmed the details from Abby's dream at the Emerald Guardian, telling Abby and the others that the city behind it rose in tiers on the edge of a cliff, and the palace, perched on the highest tier, overlooked the Eastern Sea.

As they crossed the drawbridge at the city's gate, Abby gazed down into the dark water of the moat and wondered for a moment what lurked beneath. Probably nothing, she decided, since it smelled of sewage. She hoped the rest of the city smelled better.

She was not disappointed. Just beyond the gate was a market more magnificent than any she had seen in the western region of Cai Terenmare she now called home. Spices and perfumes filled the air, and a rainbow of lanterns and banners hung overhead between brightly colored tents and carts.

The bazaar seemed to be a circus as much as it was a marketplace. All manner of entertainers walked about, enticing extravagantly dressed customers into various shops. The expensive-looking fabric and elaborate designs of their clothes were a sharp contrast to the simple, homespun clothes of the villagers Abby had met on the Great Plains. She turned to Hedeon. "Is this a festival of some kind?"

"Nay, my lady," the knight replied. "I should like to say it was a celebration in your honor, but the market is always this festive."

Out of the corner of her eye, Abby saw a large figure looming over a shopkeeper. She turned in her saddle to get a better look. The giant goblin had a twisted grin and looked as though it could devour the tiny man in a single bite. "A Blood Shadow!" she cried.

"Do not be alarmed," Hedeon reassured her. "The Kruorumbrae live among us most peaceably here. You will find that the Eastern Oracle has managed to restore order in the absence of a Solas Beir." He looked quickly to David. "I beg your pardon, Sire, but in truth, we *have* these many years been without a king."

David shook his head. "No apologies necessary. I know that with my father's death there was a vacuum in authority. I'm sure the oracle did what was necessary keep the peace."

The knight looked relieved. "Yes, Your Majesty, that is it exactly. I have only the highest respect for Ardal. He was a great Solas Beir, as I am sure you will be. But in the days following his death, our people suffered. We are so far from your throne on the western shore, and our fair city was long plagued by the Darkness. The assaults on our walls increased tenfold when news of the Solas Beir's assassination reached us. It was imperative that my master use a strong hand to bring the Kruorumbrae under the same law we serve." Hedeon turned back to Abby. "Look again, if you will, my lady. Tell me, what do you see?"

Abby looked back. The shopkeeper was handing the Shadow a large goat, skinned and ready for cooking. Or for immediate consumption, if, as she assumed, the goblin would be taking his meat raw. The Shadow grunted his approval as he hefted the goat over one shoulder and gave the man several coins. Then the odd pair shook hands.

Abby turned back to Hedeon, shocked. "They are doing business. But how is this possible? I thought the Shadows didn't eat the same kind of food we eat—that they prefer *live* prey."

Hedeon smiled. "It is difficult to believe, but it is true. Under the new law, we are able to live among the Kruorumbrae.

They have signed a pact not to harm our citizens, and thus far, the truce remains intact."

"How long has the truce been in place?" David asked.

"Twenty years," Hedeon stated.

"And with the return of Tierney, the pact still has not been broken?" Abby asked.

"No, it has not. The Kruorumbrae dwelling in our city have kept their promise," Hedeon replied. "But I shall leave it to my master to explain the details of the law. We have arrived at our destination."

The knight gestured to a columned building at the end of the road. It was three stories high with a domed roof and lavishly decorated with carvings honoring past Solas Beirs. Abby watched David's eyes as he took in the carvings. He seemed to be in a state of awe.

"Your forebears, Sire," Hedeon explained. "On the other side of this great house is a space reserved for the chronicling of your reign. It will be an honor to bear witness to your noble deeds."

David nodded. "I only hope I can live up to the precedent set by my father."

"You will," Hedeon said. "Of that I have no doubt. Please, allow me to show you the quarters prepared for your stay." He dismounted and helped Abby off her horse.

Servants stood at the ready, sweeping tall double doors open to reveal an interior even more extravagant than the sculpted façades of the walls outside. In the center of the building was a circular room, and the underside of the dome was painted with a fresco displaying further exploits of Solas Beirs past. At the far end of the room were doors leading to a garden.

"There is a spring-fed pool in the garden for your pleasure," Hedeon said. "And each of the suites on the third floor has a separate room for bathing. The second floor houses the library and music room. There are implements for writing in the library, and should you need a message delivered, you have only to ask. The kitchen and dining areas are on the ground floor. The staff will be happy to serve you in the dining area or bring food to your rooms, should you prefer that. Court-appropriate attire has been readied and awaits you in your quarters. Is there anything else you might require for your stay?"

"No, these are magnificent accommodations," David said. "Please, give the Eastern Oracle our thanks. He has outdone himself in his hospitality."

"He will be pleased to hear that," Hedeon replied. "He looks forward to meeting you at court tomorrow. I will come at the tenth hour to escort you to the palace."

David smiled. "Thank you so much, Hedeon."

"Truly, the pleasure is mine, Sire." With that, the knight gracefully bowed and excused himself.

⊱⊰⊱⊰⊱⊰

David watched the servants close the doors behind the knight.

"Wow. This is amazing." Marisol craned her neck, looking up at the fresco. "What should we do first? Check out our rooms?"

"All right," Jon said. "But then we're in the pool. Then food and sleep, in that order."

"You got it," Marisol agreed, and they scurried off toward a spiraling marble staircase, laughing like excited children.

"David, may I accompany you and Abby to your chambers?" Cael asked. "It is not that I do not trust our host, but I would like to make sure your rooms are secure."

"Of course," David said. "Better safe than sorry."

Abby and David had adjoining rooms, and Cael's was several doors down. Cael was very thorough in his search for possible secret doors, traps, or poisons, even inspecting the rich, all white clothes laid out for the next day's appointment with the oracle.

"I am sorry," Cael apologized, completing his survey of David's room. "You must think me paranoid."

"Not at all," David replied. "If the oracle wanted to trap us, showering us with luxury would be a smart strategy."

"Razzle 'em, dazzle 'em," Abby murmured. She was looking out David's open window, her elbows on the sill.

David could hear Jon and Marisol laughing in the pool below.

"Yes," Cael said. "I believe we are safe for now, and I will retire to my own quarters for some sleep. But, I have a word of caution you may wish to pass on to our friends."

"What's that?" David asked.

"Although I am confident there is nothing in our chambers to harm us, guard your speech and behavior. Whatever we say or do is sure to find its way to the oracle's ears," Cael warned.

"Duly noted," David said. "Sleep well, my friend. We'll wake you for dinner."

Cael nodded and stepped out of David's room, closing the door behind him.

"Feel like a swim?" David called to Abby. He held up a pair of silky, knee-length trousers trimmed in velvet ribbon, apparently the Cai Terenmare equivalent of board shorts. No self-respecting surfer he knew would be caught dead in floral pastels, but David had no other options unless he planned on skinny-dipping. Which he didn't.

Abby burst out laughing. "Sure. Why not?"

David grinned, wondering what her suit would look like. Considering the formal manners of the Eastern Oracle, he had an idea their host had provided Abby with something modest. David imagined her arrayed like a Greek goddess, in a shortened gown that draped in all the right places.

It took a while for Abby to change, and David finally knocked on her door. "Ready?"

"No."

He winced. He could tell by the sound of her voice she was not amused by what she was required to wear. "How bad is it?" he called.

She opened the door. "Awful." She was wearing a high-necked, long-sleeved top tucked into high-waisted, ballooning pants in a fabric that matched his trousers. If the idea was to mask her figure via carnival-mirror distortion, the designer of the suit had succeeded.

David raised his eyebrows. "That's it?" He peered into her room, thinking there must be some other garment appropriate for swimming. The only other clothing laid out for Abby was the long-sleeved white dress and lace shawl she was required to wear to court.

She nodded, scrunching her nose in distaste.

"Wow. Well, the good news is, *you* are still adorable, in spite of your, um, fancy-pants outfit." He caressed her cheek and her smile returned. "And I'm pretty sure Jon and Sol look as..." He was about to use the word "ridiculous," but then paused, thinking about Cael's warning to guard his speech. "As, uh, *opulent* as we do," he finished, watching Abby's look of puzzlement change to alarm as she understood what he hadn't said and why.

ಬಿಊೞೞಉೞೞಉೞ

The courtesan knew he did not have much time to live. He had come to this realization between episodes of feverish hallucinations. In the grip of these paranoid delusions, he was haunted by winged women with frightening faces and hunted by ghoulish palace guards. During the times he felt most lucid, it was clear to him that he *was* being hunted. His reptilian companion had not given up the slow chase; it had patiently shadowed the courtesan in his trek across the endless, wretched sand.

He had faithfully followed the sun, and the golden orb now sat on the western horizon. But the courtesan had no clue if one day had passed or a thousand since he began this walk. He had no idea how far he had come. He was not even entirely sure of his name, or if he had one. All he knew was pain—his body was swollen with it, pregnant with venom that leaked slowly from the source of the wound in putrid dribbles of milky green pus, streaked with red.

The courtesan stumbled on, unsure of why he needed to keep placing one foot in front of the other. Finally it occurred to him that that he could not think of a reason. Not one. This struck him as being quite silly, and he began to laugh. Laughing hurt. Laughing made his weak legs tremble, so he rectified the situation by collapsing spread-eagle on the ground. He lay on his back, arms outstretched, hands clutching fistfuls of sand. He lay like that for some time, breathing in, breathing out, staring up at a dark blue sky, only beginning to twinkle with stars. *How pretty they are,* he thought.

ᏊᏣᏊᏣᏊᏣ

The thing watched the courtesan curiously. It was in no great hurry. It watched the man's chest rise and fall, steadily at first, and then less so. It waited until the last of the indigo had vanished from the sky, leaving a blanket of black velvet covered in diamonds. The creature did not care much for stars. It was far more concerned about things within its reach.

It approached the man lying on the ground, prodding his body with the end of its reptilian snout. Nothing. The courtesan's eyes were open, as if he were still watching the stars. Those eyes were the only thing vaguely resembling the man who had started this journey. The creature did not care about this either. It cared only for what had been marinating beneath that thin layer of flesh.

ᏊᏣᏊᏣᏊᏣ

The queen's screams echoed through her bedchamber.

"What is it, Your Majesty?" The handmaiden had been startled out of a dead sleep. Startled was an understatement—the girl had been frightened half to death, certain she would find the queen murdered on her watch. How could she have dozed off? Thankfully the queen still breathed, although she was as visibly shaken as the girl. The handmaiden quickly poured her mistress a glass of water. "Here, Your Majesty. Drink this."

"No," the queen replied, waving the goblet away. "No—I do not need water. I need Erela. Fetch her as quickly as you can."

The girl nodded and ran out the chamber door. The queen's vision must have been horrific indeed for her to ask for the winged woman. The handmaiden was terrified of the former Daughter of Mercy—most of the servants were. But Erela was a respected member of the court council, and no one dared voice their fears where they might be overheard by superiors.

Still, the girl must do as the queen commanded. She rapped lightly on Erela's door. The winged woman opened it immediately, as if she had been standing nearby, in wait for her midnight visitor.

The girl felt like a mouse under Erela's predatory gaze. The handmaiden bowed her head as a sign of respect, hoping the councilwoman wouldn't see the guilt on her face, for sleeping during her watch. The girl had the sudden urge to confess her mistake, as well as every other wrong she had committed during her young life. She took a breath, forcing back the compulsion. This was the unnerving effect the winged woman had on people.

"Is it the queen?" Erela asked.

"Yes, Councilwoman. She bids you come," the handmaiden replied.

There was a rush of wind, and the girl looked up to find herself standing alone in a dark doorway. The handmaiden ran back to the queen's chamber. She discovered the queen sitting up in bed, telling Erela about her dream.

"It is a bad omen, the man dying in the desert. You must go to them," Queen Eulalia said. "Only you are fast enough."

"I will depart with haste," Erela replied, her wings outstretched over the queen's bed. "What else did you see?"

"I saw the Daughters, silhouetted against the sun. They are coming for them—for David, for Cael. And Abby, oh, her face...her face..."

"What about her face?" Erela asked.

"It was the face of death," the queen gasped.

☙ⷼ☙ⷼ☙ⷼ

Abby woke to a gentle knock. She looked to the door that led to the hallway, but the knocking was coming from the door linking her room to David's. For a moment she worried that morning had already come and she was late for court, but the moonlight streaming through her window said otherwise. She got up and opened the door.

"Hey," she murmured sleepily, rubbing her eyes. "What's going on?"

David looked embarrassed. "Sorry to wake you. I can't sleep."

"It's okay," she said, yawning. "I just dozed off, but I haven't been able to sleep well either. I keep drifting off and waking up a few minutes later—probably because you're not here with me."

"I miss you too," he whispered. "I know we, uh, may have 'friends' around, but I can't sleep without you."

Taking his hand, she pulled him into the room. He shut the door and let her lead him to her bed. She curled up in his embrace. "Better?" she asked.

"Much." He brushed the hair away from the back of her neck and kissed her skin. "Mmm, your warmth is exactly what I needed."

She smiled, breathing him in. He smelled amazing. "David?" she whispered.

"Mmhmm?"

"That little exchange we saw in the marketplace—did that seem orchestrated to you?" Abby asked, keeping her voice low.

She didn't think anyone would be listening in on a conversation held in someone's bedroom in the middle of the night, but what if they were?

"Maybe." He was whispering too, as if he shared her paranoia.

"It just seems weird that we would see something like that moments after entering the city. It felt contrived. But what's really weird is that Hedeon seemed to believe it was real. I didn't get the sense that he was lying to us."

"Me neither. He seems genuine. But something *did* seem off to me about what we saw," David agreed. "Actually, there's something that's been bothering me since the riders found us."

"What's that?" she asked.

He hesitated. "It will sound arrogant..."

"You? Arrogant? Banish the thought." Abby chuckled softly.

"Ha ha. You're hilarious," he quipped. He swatted at her playfully, and she scooted away, laughing.

She rolled over to look at him. "Okay, sorry. I'm listening."

"Finally. Geez," he said, pretending to be annoyed, but smiling as he pulled her back close against his chest. "All right, here it is. So, Cai Terenmare has been without a Solas Beir for over two decades. Then, when they finally get one, and I decide to pay them a visit, the Eastern Oracle is too busy to greet me personally? He blows me off?"

"Well, you *did* come unannounced."

"Yeah, but he *knew* I was coming. Hedeon said that. And apparently, the oracle knew well enough in advance to make the arrangements for us to stay here and to send riders to meet us in the Barren."

Abby nodded. "Point taken. And see, that just reinforces what I thought before about things being orchestrated. The wonderful hospitality, having clothes ready for the five of us—it's a little over the top, like it's meant to dazzle us into not seeing what's really going on." She tilted her head up so she could look at him. "Tell me I'm not just being paranoid here."

"No, you're exactly right." He stroked her hair and was quiet for a moment, thinking. "Everything has been so tightly controlled about our visit—we haven't really seen the city, and Hedeon will be *escorting* us to the palace for another very limited, censored view of things. We're only seeing what they want us to see."

"It's the razzle 'em, dazzle 'em filter," Abby replied. "And Cael knows it too."

David nodded. "Yes, he does."

"Do you think Jon and Marisol know?"

"No. And I don't think we should tell them. We're going to have to put on a very good show of not knowing when we meet with the oracle. It will be hard enough for you, me, and Cael to pretend—the more genuine Jon and Marisol are, the better," David said.

ഇൗൽഇൗൽഇൗൽ

As promised, Hedeon arrived at the tenth hour to collect Abby, David, and their friends from the Hall of Solas Beirs.

Behind his entourage of guards was an armored carriage. Taking her seat inside the iron-clad carriage, Abby exchanged a glance with David, who raised his eyebrows in return. The carriage had no windows.

As Hedeon began to close the carriage door, David put his hand out and stopped him. "Hedeon?"

"Yes, Sire?"

"Is all this really necessary? An armored carriage and a dozen guards?" David asked.

"Yes, Sire," Hedeon replied. "It is for your protection."

"But you said the city was safe."

"Indeed, so I did. But you are the Solas Beir, and we must take every precaution to ensure your safety. There is only one road to the palace, and you would be much too vulnerable in the open, on horseback. We cannot risk an assassin's arrow," Hedeon explained. "I do apologize for the rough interior of the carriage, but have no fear. Your time in it will be short." He smiled and closed the door.

"Well, now. That was ominous," Abby whispered. The carriage began to roll along the cobblestone street.

"We'll play along," David whispered back, slipping his arm around her shoulders. "For now." He met Cael's gaze. Cael nodded, but said nothing. Marisol exchanged a look with Jon, and he took her hand.

*So much for keeping them in the dark. Now they know something is wrong too*, Abby thought. And now, since they were surrounded by the guards outside the carriage, a discussion would most certainly be overheard. There would be no opportunity to make sure everyone was on the same page. The time for that conversation had passed.

The carriage lurched suddenly, as if the horses were exerting great effort in pulling it uphill. Then the ride was relatively smooth again, aside from the occasional bump of the wheels against the pavers.

A thought occurred to Abby: *Maybe we should be overheard.* "I like your gown, Marisol," she said, a bit too loudly. "The embroidery is beautiful." She felt everyone's eyes on her. It was a silly thing to say in light of the current situation, but her instincts told her it was critical to keep up the façade that all was well. If the guards overheard two women prattling on about fashion, that was fine by her. The more clueless they appeared, the better.

Marisol stared at Abby, and then nodded silently, taking her cue. "Oh, thank you," she replied. The brightness in her voice didn't match the look of concern on her face. "I love your shawl. I've never seen lace like that. It's very well made."

Abby examined the lace, which was of the purest white, with delicate threads woven into intricate patterns. "Yes, I daresay the handiwork is better than anything we have on the western shore. The artisans in this city are masters. Perhaps we can commission them for our gowns for the royal wedding."

"The queen would be quite jealous if our finery rivaled hers," Marisol said, smiling. A little over the top, but at least now the look on her face matched the emotion in her voice. Cael raised his eyebrows, and Jon stifled a laugh.

"Well, then, we will have to bring her a gift as well," Abby said. "If her dress were embellished with so fine a fabric, she would outshine the stars."

"She already does," David added, as the carriage came to a stop. "But if you ladies need an excuse to visit the marketplace after our appointment with the Eastern Oracle, I suppose we can indulge you."

The harsh glare of sunlight filled the cabin when a guard opened its door. Abby ignored this and continued, as if she were perfectly at ease and not itching to escape her cramped iron cage. "Oh, could we?" She clasped her hands together in delight. "I know just the shop—I saw the *perfect* fabric there."

David stepped out of the carriage and helped Abby down. "Of course. Anything for my beloved."

Abby turned to Hedeon. She focused her emotions toward him, trying to project only a sense of calm. *All is well here,* she thought. *All is well.* "Oh, Hedeon—would you be so kind as to escort us to the market after our meeting with the Eastern Oracle?"

"Oh yes, please. We want to make the most of our time in the city." Marisol gave the knight her brightest smile.

Hedeon smiled back. "I would be honored, my lady. Now if you please, the Eastern Oracle awaits." He offered Abby his arm, and she took it, rewarding him with a demure smile. Then the knight turned and led her into the palace.

With its high, vaulted ceilings and stained glass windows, the palace almost looked like a cathedral. "Beautiful," Abby breathed.

"Indeed. This is the crown jewel of our fair city," Hedeon boasted.

ଧଓଔଧଓଔଧଓଔ

Marisol paused to gaze at the windows before she followed her friends. Hedeon was leading the group past more guards in the palace foyer, and then up a grand staircase. At the

254

top of the stairs was a gilded mirror. Marisol stopped in front of it to look at her dress. The embroidery really *was* beautiful. She wasn't sure what the episode in the carriage had been about, but her gut told her it wasn't just that Abby had been nervous and trying to make conversation.

When Hedeon had closed the carriage's iron door, Marisol had been bathed in a wave of claustrophobia. But it was more than that. She had a bad feeling about this whole city, and she was pretty certain Abby did too. For now, it seemed important to keep up the ruse, even if Marisol didn't know exactly why.

"Sol?" Jon motioned for her to join him. The others were already turning down a hallway.

Marisol smoothed her skirt and looked in the mirror once more before going. *Not bad,* she thought. *Wait. What's that?* In the mirror's reflection, she could see movement in the palace foyer below. The guards flanking the doors were as still as statues, but something dark scuttled quickly across the marble floor. Something that looked all too similar to the thing she had encountered on the beach, the night she'd entered this world.

Startled, she whirled around, but saw nothing. The guards remained at their posts, and the foyer was void of other inhabitants.

Jon took Marisol's hand. "What's wrong?" he asked.

She took a breath to steady herself. "Just a trick of the light, I guess. But for a second there, I thought I saw the creature from my nightmares—the one from that night on the beach."

He scanned the foyer and frowned. "Come on," he said, placing his hand on the small of her back. "Best not to linger."

As Jon guided her toward the hallway, Marisol looked back over her shoulder. Nothing seemed amiss. At least nothing that she could see. But after the experience with the things in the casino, Marisol had learned she couldn't always trust her eyes.

ဆလၢဆလၢဆလၢ

Abby looked back down the hallway to see Jon and Marisol rounding the corner. She and the others had stopped just outside the imposing double doors of the court room. Guards were posted on either side, flanking the entrance.

"Ah, there you are," Hedeon called, as Jon and Marisol hurried to catch up. "We thought you had gotten lost." In his black armor and sweeping red cloak, the knight looked broad-shouldered and intimidating. Abby felt tiny standing next to him.

"Apologies," Marisol smiled sheepishly. "I got distracted by the beauty of the windows in the foyer. Jon had to retrieve me."

"I see," the knight replied, his face stern. "Please do stay with the group though—the Eastern Oracle has a strict policy about guests, and the guards can be quite harsh about unaccompanied visitors."

*I bet,* Abby thought, taking in the stony-faced guards flanking the doors.

"Now that we are all here, I must brief you on court protocol." Hedeon turned to David. "Sire, you and your knights will join me in meeting with the Eastern Oracle." The knight turned to address Abby and Marisol. He smiled, gesturing to a room on the other side of the corridor. Its doors were open wide and a smell like freshly baked pastries wafted out into the hallway. "Ladies, across the hall is the hospitality parlor where you will wait until our discussion is finished. As our honored guests, you are welcome to partake in a variety of delightful diversions. The parlor attendant will see to any needs you have. She is an amusing woman—I am sure she will keep you entertained."

Abby exchanged a panicked look with David. Despite Hedeon's warm demeanor and reassuring tone, the idea of her and Marisol being separated from the guys filled her with terror, more even than she'd felt in the iron carriage. With Cael's warnings echoing in her mind, this sounded like a trap. She imagined the doors to the oracle's court slamming shut and then armored guards dragging her away to be locked up in some windowless tower, never to see David and the others again.

"Abby and Marisol can't go in with us?" David asked, clutching Abby's hand tightly.

"My deepest apologies, Your Majesty. Women are not permitted in the court of the Eastern Oracle," Hedeon said.

"But they are our equals," David protested, frowning. "Marisol is as skilled in combat as any of my male knights, and Abby is my cai aislingstraid. And my betrothed."

Hedeon raised his eyebrows in surprise and stared at Abby. "She is a c'aislingaer?"

"Yes. Abby and Marisol are trusted advisors—I need them *both* by my side," David insisted.

Hedeon sighed. "Well, under certain circumstances, I suppose if the lady Abby is a cai aislingstraid, *she* might be permitted, but there are specific rules…" Abby felt a glimmer of hope for herself, but was frightened for Marisol. They couldn't leave her alone in this place.

"What rules?" David interrupted.

"She must wear the veil, and she must remain silent," Hedeon said. "Women are not permitted to speak in the presence of the Eastern Oracle."

"Not permitted to speak?" David asked, outraged. Abby could hear the anger in his voice, which had dropped an octave. He was choosing his words carefully, trying to control his rage. Anger would not help him win this battle.

"It's all right, David," Abby reassured him, placing her hand on his arm. She looked at Hedeon. "I can wear the veil, and I swear I'll stay quiet."

"Abby…" David began.

"No, it's fine," she said. She smiled meekly, hoping her own anger was hidden.

So the garment she thought was a shawl was actually a veil. She reverently removed it from her shoulders and placed it over her head, hiding her face. The lace did little to impede her vision, but judging by the look on Hedeon's face, her features were sufficiently covered. *Actually,* she thought, *this could work to our advantage. Maybe I'll be able to observe without* being *observed.*

"Marisol and I will wait across the hall," Jon announced, pulling Marisol toward the other side of the corridor.

Abby nodded in agreement, relieved that Jon would have Sol's back. She worried for him too, but given the oracle's bias against women, her main concern was for Marisol.

"Are you sure about that?" Marisol whispered to Jon.

"Solidarity, babe," he whispered back. "I'm not going in without you, and I'm *not* leaving you out here alone." Jon's tone of voice made Abby think something was not being said. And Marisol's relieved smile confirmed Abby's suspicions. She just hoped Hedeon hadn't seen the dark look in Jon's eyes.

"Yes, we'll just wait for you together." Marisol declared. She took Jon's hand and led him into the parlor.

Hedeon watched them go, seemingly oblivious. Abby prayed that was the case. The knight turned back to David. "That is settled then. They need not wait long—the Eastern Oracle prefers to keep his appointments brief. Are we ready to enter?"

David looked at Cael, who nodded assent. Cael had been awfully quiet this entire trip. Not that he was normally chatty, but still—Abby wondered what he was thinking. No matter; they would talk freely later. Abby's attention turned to David as he took her hand.

"Yes, we're ready," David replied.

"Very well, Sire." Hedeon turned to Abby. "And remember, you *must* remain silent."

Abby nodded in what she hoped was a submissive manner. "I understand."

"Good," Hedeon said. "Guards?"

The guards opened the doors. The windowless room was large and square. The wall behind the throne had two sets of double doors, one set on either side of the throne. The doors on the left were closed, but the ones on the right were open to a balcony. A soft breeze from the Eastern Sea drifted in. The smell of the moist air was lovely. Abby imagined that this room could get quite stuffy at times, even without the stiff rules of its chief administrator.

The Eastern Oracle's empty throne was made of dark, carved wood and sat on a similarly carved wooden dais overlooking the vast, ornate carpet stretching from the front of the dais to the court room's entry. Just beyond the four walls, the room was punctuated by an inner square made up of a series of carved marble arches supported by pillars. Both the entry and the throne were symmetrically framed by the pillars. It was a lavish room, but one ruled by strict order.

Hedeon gestured for the guards to close the doors and led Abby to stand on one side of the room next to the dark, paneled wall. "You will wait here until the audience with the Eastern Oracle concludes," he instructed.

She nodded silently. From here, in the shadows under the archway, her form would be obscured from view. *All the better to watch you, my dear,* she thought.

ಬಂಚ೫ಬಂಚ೫ಬಂಚ೫

"Solas Beir, you and your knight will stand here." Hedeon pointed to a spot in the center of the court's luxurious carpet, then marched over to the open door of the balcony and closed it ceremoniously. "I will inform the Eastern Oracle of your arrival." Hedeon walked behind the throne, exiting through the door on the other side, disappearing without another word.

In the silence, David looked over at Abby. *I'm sorry,* he mouthed. She nodded as if to reassure him, but he couldn't see the expression on her face because of the veil that covered it.

Cael placed his hand on David's arm. "Do not acknowledge her," he whispered. "Whether or not you agree with the man's philosophy, we must play according to his rules if we are to have success here."

"I know," David whispered back. "And I *will* play along. For now."

"Good," Cael whispered. "Remember what I said—be on your guard."

The door opened once again, and Hedeon emerged. He stood just in front of the throne and bowed formally to David and Cael. "Greetings to our most honored guests, the Solas Beir Artan, and his knight Cael. May I present my esteemed master, lord of our glorious city, the Eastern Oracle."

There was a swishing noise—the sound of silken fabric in motion. It almost sounded like the movement of a snake across sand. The Eastern Oracle emerged from his chamber wearing a high-necked scarlet robe that was tight around his thin chest and waist, and then blossomed into a full skirt with a regal train. He was attended by several clerks in long-sleeved black robes who nervously scampered behind him to keep his long train from catching on the carved wood as he mounted the dais.

The Eastern Oracle settled into his throne gracefully, then delicately raised his hands to adjust his headpiece, a matching square cap encircled with a gold diadem. His dark hair and beard were neatly trimmed, framing prominent cheekbones.

He placed his hands in his lap, all but the tips of his fingers disappearing into long, flowing sleeves embroidered with gold thread. It was only after this ritual that he favored David with a glance.

"Greetings, Lightbearer," the Eastern Oracle said. His voice boomed with authority, a surprise coming from a man so gaunt and pale that he seemed frail, almost sickly. There was something about his eyes that made him seem much older than the monklike young men who served him.

David noted that the Eastern Oracle did not address him using the formal title of Solas Beir, but ignored the possible slight. "Thank you, Eastern Oracle." He bowed and then straightened his back to stand tall, holding himself with dignity.

He had a feeling this man did not suffer fools lightly and would pounce at the first sign of weakness.

The oracle studied David through narrowed eyes. "I trust your stay has been pleasant, and my servant Hedeon has provided for your needs adequately?"

"Indeed he has. Your hospitality has soared far above all expectations. We offer our utmost gratitude," David answered.

"And what is it that brings you to our great city?" the oracle asked.

"You may be aware that Tynan Tierney has escaped from the Wasteland, and now builds his army."

"I have heard whispers and rumors of this," the oracle replied, waving his hand dismissively. "I also heard that it was the knight Cael who enabled the Kruor um Beir's escape."

Out of the corner of his eye, David could see Cael start at this accusation, but he said nothing, covering his initial shock with an impassive expression, his eyes stoically trained on the wall behind the throne. David kept his eyes on the oracle's.

"That rumor is false." David took a step toward the oracle. "Cael has ever served the throne of the Solas Beir with excellence and honor. It was because of Cael's loyalty and the sacrifices of his warriors that I was able to rebuild the portal and return to my birthplace. Tierney escaped because of an unprovoked attack by the Kruorumbrae on one of my subjects who came to my aid."

"I see." The Eastern Oracle settled back into his chair with a sigh, moving his hands to rest on the wide, wooden arms of the throne. He looked bored, absently drumming his fingers against the armrest. "And what has this to do with us on the eastern shore?"

David ignored the man's show of apathy. He took another step forward and infused his voice with authority. "*All* of Cai Terenmare would suffer should Tierney succeed in gathering his forces and resume his quest to seize the throne. The Southern, Northern, and Western Oracles have all made pacts promising me their loyalty. I now seek an alliance with you to once and for all put an end to the Kruor um Beir's evil."

The oracle's eyes widened in surprise, and he leaned forward, stilling the drumming of his fingers. Apparently David had finally managed to land on a topic worthy of the man's attention. "All *three* have pledged thus?"

"They have. May I count on you as well?"

The oracle scowled. "You most certainly may not."

"No?" David asked.

"No," he repeated sternly.

The look on the oracle's face was a mystery to David—was that fear in his eyes? Disgust? Hatred? Maybe a combination of all three?

"It seems to me that those who make a pact with your throne do not fare well," the oracle accused. "Is it not true that my dear sister, the late Western Oracle, was slain at the hands of the knight who now serves as your right hand? Only to be replaced with a lesser being?"

"Cael acted in self-defense after the former Western Oracle and her sirens murdered his crew and tried to take his life as well. He was on a diplomatic mission from the Solas Beir, and their aggression toward him was unprovoked," David countered.

The oracle laughed haughtily. "*Unprovoked?* Ah, Lightbearer, I see a common thread in your excuses, but your reasoning falls short. How could your knight be on a mission from the Solas Beir when the Solas Beir was dead? That order came from your queen," he scoffed. "It was *not* valid."

David felt anger blaze in his chest. So much for keeping emotions in check—the time for niceties had long since passed. "In the Solas Beir's absence, the queen's order was *equal* to my father's, particularly where my safety as the heir was concerned. And, with all due respect, Nerine has served more honorably in her short time as Western Oracle than your sister ever did."

The Eastern Oracle hissed, then resumed his composure. "Rubbish. *Nerine* is but a simple mermaid—her power will never be equal to my sister's," he said coldly. "But never mind that. Allow me to present a second example of how those who serve the Solas Beir fare. Is it not also true that your father removed Tynan Tierney from the post of Southern Oracle? What assurance do I, or any of the oracles, have that you will not do the same should we disagree with your policies?"

"Your example is moot," David replied, narrowing his eyes. He glanced down and realized he was clenching his fists. He forced himself to relax, uncurling his fingers; acting defensive was not helping. Taking a breath, he continued. "Tierney was not removed for disagreeing with my father—he was removed for slaughtering thousands upon thousands to feed his greed."

"They were simple humans. Your father lost sight of the proper order of things. He betrayed the powerful for the weak," the oracle spat.

"No. My father fulfilled his role in representing the Light by protecting those who could not protect themselves. And it cost him his *life*."

The Eastern Oracle glared at David, and then sighed dramatically, settling back into his chair. "Ah, young

Lightbearer, I see that we have reached an impasse. There are many things about which we do not agree."

"It seems so." David focused on projecting calm confidence. He maintained eye contact with the oracle.

The oracle looked away, studying his fingernails. He looked back at David. "Do you know that, in my city, the Kruorumbrae live among us, and my people have no reason to fear them?"

David hesitated, wondering where the oracle was going with this. He nodded. "That is what Hedeon told us."

The oracle raised his eyebrows, glancing in Hedeon's direction before turning back to David. "And do you believe it to be true? Have you seen anything to suggest otherwise?"

In the periphery of his vision, David could see Cael tense up, and knew what he was thinking. *Have caution in how you answer, Solas Beir.* "No. Quite the opposite," David replied. "We have seen only order in your city. But how can this be? The Kruorumbrae are well known for their insatiable appetites."

The Eastern Oracle smiled. "I have a system. You see, young man, in the void of power left by your father's death, *someone* had to take control, lest we be overrun by the Kruorumbrae. I established a system of courtesans to serve the needs of the Blood Shadows, who agreed to still their attacks against our citizenry. But I know you will not believe my words alone."

The oracle signaled to one of his clerks, who went to the door of the oracle's chambers. The clerk rapped twice on the door and a young man dressed in silken purple clothing entered the courtroom. "You must hear firsthand from those who dwell within the inner sanctuary of our city. Step forward, courtesan," the oracle commanded.

The young man moved in front of the throne and bowed to David.

"Tell me, Lightbearer," the oracle continued. "Does our young friend appear to be in good health?"

The courtesan took a step forward, turning slowly in a circle for David's inspection. David studied the young man carefully. He did seem healthy and strong, with a good complexion and clear, intelligent eyes. "Yes, he seems healthy enough," David replied. "What is the mark on his hand?"

The oracle looked amused, his eyebrows raised, a sly smile on his lips. "You do not recognize it?"

David frowned. "Of course I do. It looks like the Sign of the Throne, the sigil of the Solas Beir. But what does it mean in this context?"

"In this *context*?" the oracle laughed. "A fine dicing of words. But I shall indulge you, nevertheless. It means that this young man is a sacred son of our city. The courtesan class is elevated above all others. They have the finest quarters in the palace and eat the best food. I daresay they receive better nourishment even than I," the oracle chuckled, patting his perfectly flat belly. "They must, of course, because it is the blood of the courtesans that feeds the Kruorumbrae who dwell here. In exchange for their service, courtesans and their families live a life of luxury. Their family members bear a different mark, assuring that they will never be touched by the Blood Shadows."

"And what about the rest of the people who live here?" David asked.

"They too are protected. Under the law of the courtesans, our people have been safe from the Kruorumbrae," the oracle clarified.

"I see," David said.

"Good. I am most glad we understand each other," the oracle smiled.

"I do have one more question though," David said, returning the oracle's smile, "for him." He nodded toward the courtesan.

The courtesan turned to the oracle questioningly—it seemed he had not planned on having a speaking role. Or had been ordered to remain silent.

"You did say I would get to hear from him firsthand, did you not?" David asked innocently.

"So I did," the oracle frowned. He flicked his wrist at the courtesan. "Proceed." The courtesan turned back to David.

"Are you a courtesan of your own free will?" David asked.

"Yes, Sire. I am," the courtesan answered.

The Eastern Oracle beamed triumphantly. "You see, Lightbearer, under *my* system, we are living in a golden era of peace and prosperity, as golden indeed as the mark worn by the courtesans themselves. Why then, would I be so foolish as to disrupt that peace by joining your cause? Perhaps if *you* were to implement a similar system in the western realm and let go of this little war of yours, your problems would disappear."

The oracle was baiting him. For all his talk of peace, the Eastern Oracle wanted a fight with the Throne, and further discussion could only make things worse. David could see that an alliance with the Eastern Oracle would never be possible. The only question that remained was whether the Eastern Oracle was acting of his own accord or if he had already made a deal with Tierney.

"I see where you stand on the matter," David said. "Thank you for your time and hospitality. We will leave the city immediately and return to Caislucis, once we have gathered our belongings. Cael, Abby, let's go."

Abby moved from her place against the wall to join David and Cael in the center of the court. The Eastern Oracle looked startled. Apparently he had not noticed the presence of a woman. David boldly broke protocol, taking Abby's hand as they bowed together with Cael. Then the three of them turned and left the court of the Eastern Oracle without another word.

ᎥᏣᎥᏣᎥᏣ

The Eastern Oracle waited until the courtroom doors were closed. He turned to Hedeon. "Do *not* let them out of your sight," he commanded.

"Yes, my lord." Hedeon bowed to the oracle and then turned to follow the Solas Beir and his friends.

## RUN RABBIT RUN

"We're leaving," Jon heard David call as he stormed by the hospitality parlor, towing a veiled Abby. Cael followed a few paces behind.

Startled, Marisol looked up from the game she and Jon had been playing with the parlor attendant. She gave Jon a look of wide-eyed alarm, and they both rose from their chairs.

"Thanks," Jon said to the attendant, handing her the parchment cards he had been holding. Marisol placed hers on the marble-topped table in front of her. Jon grabbed Marisol's hand and they hurried to catch up to the others.

David, Abby, and Cael were almost to the top of the stairs when Jon and Marisol joined them. "How'd it go?" Jon asked.

"We'll talk in the carriage," David growled, charging down the stairs.

Jon raised his eyebrows. Apparently, the sooner they left the palace, the better.

෨ඏ෨ඏ෨ඏ

David watched the guards close the carriage door. He took a deep breath as the iron door clanged shut. Abby removed her veil and began to fold it into a neat square on her lap.

"Well?" Marisol whispered. "What did the Eastern Oracle say?"

"Pompous sack of..." David grumbled under his breath. Abby placed her hand on his arm and gave him a warning look. He glanced at Abby, sighed, and turned to Marisol. "He insulted Cael, my mother, my father, Nerine, and by proxy, pretty much everyone else associated with me. Then, he suggested I give up my *little* war and establish a system of glorified prostitution to solve *my* problems. I honestly don't know what I should be most offended about."

Jon let out a low whistle. "Wow. Super classy."

"I wouldn't call the courtesan law prostitution," Abby said quietly.

David turned to look at her. "It *is* though. Maybe not in the traditional sense of the word, but they *are* selling their bodies to the Kruorumbrae."

"As food," Abby clarified, looking from Marisol to Jon.

"Yes, as food," David said, disgusted by the thought. "Although who knows—why stop there?" He shrugged angrily. "And then, to mark them with the Sign of the Throne? The oracle has twisted a sacred symbol into something perverse. What I really don't get is why the courtesans do it—why would they voluntarily let those things feed on them?"

"Maybe they *don't* have a choice," Abby replied. "Maybe that courtesan was coerced into saying he choose it of his own free will. Or maybe he's doing it to protect his family. I would."

"You wouldn't if I had anything to say about it," David growled, his hands clenching into fists again. He stared at them as if they were foreign objects sitting in his lap, some distant manifestation of the anger and frustration boiling within him.

Abby covered his hands with hers, studying his face. He looked up into those beautiful cerulean eyes that he loved so much, and uncurled his fingers, taking her hands instead.

"I would if it meant protecting *you*," she said. "Is that really all that different from the time I protected you from Calder?"

David nodded. "Yes, Abby, it is. Calder was trying to kill us, and he almost succeeded. It was a life or death situation. But that's my point—it never should have come to that, nor should it come to *this*. These people shouldn't have to sell themselves to protect their families. They shouldn't have to live in fear."

"At least we know where the oracle stands now," Abby replied. "He drew his line in the sand."

"There's that, I guess." David sighed heavily—his meeting with the Eastern Oracle had been brief but draining, and he felt exhausted. He saw Abby's eyes widen with concern so he managed a weak smile. "Did you pick up on anything else from him? Anything about Tierney?"

Abby shook her head. "No, nothing. Except what we already suspected, that there's something he wants to keep hidden. I think the Eastern Oracle all but confirmed that with the way he was baiting you. It was like he was trying to make you angry so you wouldn't see what's really going on."

"Yes, I think so," Cael mused, talking to himself more than anyone else. David looked at him, wondering what else Cael suspected, and why he was being so quiet about it.

The carriage began to move, and then lurched to a stop. Outside they could hear raised voices. Abby's hand flew to her mouth—David grabbed her other hand and tried to calm the wild beating of his own heart.

"The Eastern Oracle commanded that I stay with our guests," David heard Hedeon say. "That is what I am doing. Now, if you please—open the door."

The guard grumbled something unintelligible, and then the door opened. Hedeon stepped inside, taking a seat beside Marisol. "Thank you," Hedeon said to the guard. "Now, please take us to the Hall of Solas Beirs." The guard closed the door, and in a few seconds the carriage began to move once again.

ᔿᐊᔿᐊᔿᐊ

Hedeon bowed his head respectfully toward the Solas Beir. "I beg your pardon for intruding, Your Majesty, but I would have a word, while I can."

The Solas Beir's gaze was intense, guarded. "All right," he said. "We're listening."

"First, I am sorry about what happened in court," Hedeon began, keeping his voice low so he would not be overheard by the guards outside. The rolling wheels of the iron carriage were loud on the pavers. He hoped they would mask any sounds within the cabin. During the trip up the hill to the palace, he had been listening carefully from outside the carriage, and he had not been able to decipher the conversation within until the carriage had stopped. Still, it was best to whisper. "I know the meeting did not go as you wished."

"You can say that again," Jon muttered.

Hedeon looked at Jon and then back at the Solas Beir. "Second, I am not here to keep an eye on you," he continued.

"You're not?" Marisol questioned.

272

"No." Hedeon shook his head and then thought about it. He smiled at Marisol. "Well, that is not entirely true. The Eastern Oracle *did* command that I follow you, so I *must* accompany you until you are out of the city. As you may have guessed, there are areas of the city he does not wish for you to see."

"Yeah, why is that exactly?" Jon asked.

"Jon." Marisol shot him a warning look.

Hedeon placed his hand on Marisol's arm briefly, and then removed it when Jon narrowed his eyes threateningly. "It is all right, Marisol—your friend asks a valid question. The Eastern Oracle censors your view because he is invested in keeping the status quo," he whispered. "I am sorry, Solas Beir. I lied to you before about there being peace in this city. Kruorumbrae *have* preyed on the people who live here. The courtesan system has decreased the number of incidents, but it has not eliminated the problem. And since we received word of Tierney's escape, the number of attacks has increased."

"Why are you telling us this *now*?" the Solas Beir asked. "And why should we believe you?"

"I understand why you may doubt me, but I knew your father. He was a good man and a just king. Before he was crowned Solas Beir, we served together in the wars against the Blood Shadows at the stronghold on the northern edge of the Barren. You showed great courage in standing against the Eastern Oracle. You proved your worth as a leader, Sire, and that was when I knew I could trust you," Hedeon said. He looked down at his feet, and then up at the Solas Beir again. He smiled. "Seeing you speak in court today...it was as if I were seeing your father once again."

"Thank you. That means a lot to me," the Solas Beir said. He still looked guarded, but smiled slightly.

"You are most welcome. You value equal treatment of all your people, just as your father did," Hedeon continued. He hesitated, unsure of how the Solas Beir would react to what he needed to say next. "Your Majesty…when you go to war, as I know you must, know that not everyone in this city agrees with the Eastern Oracle's archaic policies. There are good people here who would join your fight if they were not afraid that open resistance would endanger their families. Please do not judge them based on what you saw today."

"I will try not to," the Solas Beir replied. He reached out and placed his hand on Hedeon's arm. "And I do understand that you are taking a risk in telling me the truth. I appreciate your courage."

Hedeon smiled warmly, relieved. "Thank you, Your Majesty." He took the Solas Beir's hand and reverently pressed it to his forehead to show his gratitude and respect. Then he let go of his king's hand and looked around at the Solas Beir's friends. "Now, let us retrieve your belongings and get you out of the city. We will stop in the market to replenish your supplies, and the ladies can browse the fabric shops. We do not want to arouse suspicion about how much you know, so I would advise that you keep up your ruse and not be too quick to leave."

"You *knew* that was an act?" Abby asked. Her eyes were wide with surprise.

Hedeon chuckled. "Yes. The behavior I observed when you emerged from this carriage was quite out of character from the two young women I met on the road at the Eye of the Needle. You were much more guarded then. But fear not—most of the guards are new, and have been conditioned to turn a blind eye to the antics of the upper class."

"What happened to the old guards?" Cael asked. "Were they executed?"

"No, just dismissed. In implementing the courtesan system, the Eastern Oracle brought in new guards. He knew the old ones would object," Hedeon explained. "In fact, we were recently ordered to recruit a fresh batch of guards, although I do not know why. Perhaps some of the guards installed at the time the courtesan law was established had doubts as to its effectiveness. I know I have."

"How is it you have remained?" Cael asked suspiciously, narrowing his eyes. "The oracle must have known about your loyalty to David's father."

"I was able to keep the Eastern Oracle's trust when he needed someone to train the new recruits," Hedeon replied, unable to meet Cael's gaze. "When you deal with devils, you must sometimes act as one. I am not proud of what I have done, but I hope to make amends now that we once again have a Solas Beir. For now I will do my best to keep the guards from following you when you leave."

ဆာဝ၁ဆာဝ၁ဆာဝ၁

*Easier said than done,* Abby thought. Things had gone smoothly in retrieving their packs and securing horses. Hedeon had accompanied them to the bazaar, but was suddenly called away. There were reports of a prisoner escaping the palace dungeon, and as head guard, Hedeon was needed to coordinate the search.

"Tell Garvan that as my second in command, he should begin the search, and I will join him shortly," Hedeon had said, addressing the page sent to retrieve him. "The Eastern Oracle asked me to personally accompany the Solas Beir until his departure from the city. That is my first priority."

"With all due respect, sir, given the circumstances, priorities have changed," the young man replied. "His Honor the Eastern Oracle commanded me to fetch you. He said your presence was required in the dungeon immediately."

"Yes, yes, all right," Hedeon sighed, waving the page away dismissively. "My apologies, dear ladies, but I serve at my master's prerogative. I must take my leave."

"Is it a dangerous prisoner?" Marisol asked. She looked frightened. Abby wondered if Marisol knew something she wasn't saying. There hadn't been time to ask her if she and Jon had gleaned anything useful from the parlor attendant.

Hedeon also seemed to pick up on Marisol's fear. Smiling, he patted her hand to comfort her. "Fear not, my lady. I will leave two guards with you." To the guards he added, "The ladies of the Solas Beir's court are not to be disturbed as they visit the market. They are buying fabric for the wedding of the queen. Protect them, but do not interfere in their business."

"Yes, my lord," one of the guards replied.

Abby and Marisol exchanged a look. They could see that David, Jon, and Cael were waiting patiently by the gates with their saddled horses, trying to play the role of bored aristocrats indulging their ladies' fancies. "Look at that fabric over there," Abby said, pointing to a shop across the bazaar's courtyard. "Let's visit that tent." She took Marisol's arm and did her best to look excited about the reams of colorful silk. Following dutifully, the guards stood at attention on either side of the tent's entrance.

"Look—that has to be the finest embroidery in the kingdom," Abby said loudly, leading Marisol away from the guards, toward the back of the tent.

"So," Marisol whispered. "How long do you think we need to do this before we can leave?"

"I don't know," Abby whispered back. "I suppose we should buy something, though, so we don't tip them off. We have to look legit, but the sooner we're out of this city, the better I'll feel."

Marisol nodded. She still looked scared.

"What is it, Sol?" Abby asked. "You look like you've seen a ghost."

"I think I did," Marisol whispered. The color drained from her face. "Back in the palace, I could have sworn I saw the Shadow that chased me the night we left Newcastle Beach."

Abby's mouth gaped open. "Malden? He's here in the city?"

"I don't know for sure that I saw him," Marisol said, "but I did see the look on Hedeon's face. Whoever escaped *must* be dangerous. Why else would he be called away like that?" She clutched Abby's arm. "What if they captured Malden, but then he escaped, and now he's coming for me?"

Abby could feel Marisol trembling. She slipped her arm around her friend's shoulders. "Don't worry, Sol. None of us will let him lay a finger on you. If I get my hands on him, I will personally kick his teeth in."

Marisol smiled and gave Abby a hug. "Thanks." Then she raised a finger to her lips. "Shhh—incoming," she said. She nodded toward the shopkeeper, a small man who looked absolutely radiant about having customers.

The man bowed with open arms, apparently a sign of respect in this city. "Greetings, dear ladies. How may I be of assistance?"

Abby favored him with her brightest smile. "Greetings to you, sir. I was interested in the lace you have over there. I wonder how it would go with this." She held up a bolt of scarlet fabric.

"I shall fetch it for you," the shopkeeper smiled. "The lady has very good taste."

"That she does," Marisol said, mirroring Abby's warm smile. The man scurried away to retrieve several bolts of lace.

"Sorry I got us into this," Abby whispered. "I feel ridiculous. Worst idea *ever.*"

"Not the worst," Marisol grinned. "It's better than hanging out in Vegas with those soul-eater things."

"No kidding," Abby laughed. "But I guess we'll be seeing them again soon enough. *If* we ever get out of here. We..." She trailed off when a sudden movement derailed her train of thought. "Hey—did you see that?"

"What?" Marisol froze, her eyes wide with alarm. "Is it *him?*"

"No, it's okay, it's not Malden," Abby quickly clarified. "I thought I saw someone hiding over there, someone who looked human, I mean. See that tapestry? The one with the loom sitting in front of it?"

Marisol peered at the hanging tapestries lining the back of the tent. "I don't see anything."

"Keep that guy busy for me, would you?" Abby asked, patting Marisol's shoulder.

"Sure thing," Marisol said. She looked anything but sure. The shopkeeper was coming back, his arms full of fabric. "Hey, let me help you with that," she said with a forced-looking smile. Abby tried to avoid catching his eye as she slipped toward the back.

"But my lady," the man said, "I could not impose on you."

"I don't mind," Marisol said loudly. "Now that I think about it, that the blue silk over there might be better than the scarlet. Red is not really the queen's color." Abby saw that Marisol was steering the shopkeeper toward the front of the tent. She looked over her shoulder and nodded at Abby.

ᚱᚩᚷᚱᚩᚷᚱᚩᚷ

*Ah, the fickle whims of administrators,* Hedeon thought as he followed the page and made his way down the stone steps of the dungeon. *Fickle as the weather.*

This was not the first time the Eastern Oracle had sent him on one errand, only to interrupt him midtask with another demand. Nor was it the first time Hedeon had questioned the oracle's abilities to lead. The Eastern Oracle put on a good show of authority, as the Solas Beir had witnessed. But in truth, the man seemed rather unstable. He had a nervous facial twitch that he kept under tight control, something only Hedeon and others in the oracle's inner circle were privy to—and then, only during times of great distress.

Hedeon remembered first seeing the oracle's twitch after he delivered a report of a vicious attack on a citizen. The official report stated that the fight between the man and the Kruorumbrae had begun in a pub notorious for drinking and gambling. The truth was the attack was unprovoked and occurred nowhere near said pub, according to witnesses—who were, of course, bribed for their silence.

Lately that little twitch had surfaced more frequently, and not just within the inner sanctuary of the Eastern Oracle's chambers where he met with his advisors. And lately it was all Hedeon could do to keep some semblance of order in managing the guards. They were scattered all over the city, sent on strange and unrelated missions. Hedeon had begun hearing about the missions thirdhand from his soldiers, rather than receiving the commands himself and passing them down through the ranks. He found himself out of the official communications loop. The Eastern Oracle was no longer delegating tasks via his council members.

The court of the Eastern Oracle was in chaos, and silly, paranoid rumors were rampant. And then there was that odd little twitch. Hedeon wondered if his master was on the verge of losing his mind.

As he reached the bottom of the stone staircase and stepped toward the vestibule in front of the dungeon's narrow corridor of dark cells, Hedeon saw that his men had already gathered and were waiting for him. In the flickering torch light, he observed that they were outfitted as if going to war, armed to the hilt. *A little extreme*, he thought, considering the prisoner they were supposed to retrieve.

Then, as his soldiers turned toward him and drew their swords, he saw that someone else had already taken the role of commander. Hedeon's stomach dropped, and he thought perhaps the paranoid rumors he had easily dismissed were not so silly after all.

The gaunt figure standing before him wore a dark cloak with a hood that gaped wide at the sides. In the low light, the dark silhouette of the cloak resembled the hood of a cobra. And certainly the man wearing the cloak was just as dangerous as any venomous serpent.

Perhaps the reason for the Eastern Oracle's own increasingly paranoid behavior was because *he* had been making deals with devils. If so, the oracle had indeed gone mad. No one in his right mind would make a pact with the devil standing before Hedeon now.

Tynan Tierney pushed back his hood. "Hedeon, my old friend. I hear you have once again chosen to align yourself with the wrong people."

"I have made no alliance with you," Hedeon replied dryly, staring straight into the Kruor um Beir's unnaturally dark eyes.

Tierney laughed. "Indeed. That is exactly how you landed in your current predicament."

"Which is?" Hedeon asked.

"Soon to be discovered." Tierney smiled coldly. "Just as we will discover how much you shared with the Lightbearer. Take the traitor to the torture chamber. When you finish with him, he will either have confessed to his treason against the Eastern Oracle or be dead. Either outcome is fine by me." Hedeon felt despair seep into his veins.

Garvan, a soldier Hedeon had personally recruited and trained, stepped forward and took Hedeon's arm. He signaled for the others to assist him, and suddenly Hedeon was surrounded by his own men. He barely felt the pain shooting up his arms as they were wrenched roughly behind him and bound.

"Garvan," Hedeon pleaded, staring unbelieving at his protégé's impassive face. "I trusted you. Above all others, I trusted *you*."

Garvan refused to meet Hedeon's gaze. He grabbed hold of Hedeon's bound hands and forced him to turn about-face, marching him back up the stairs.

಄಄಄಄಄಄

Abby casually browsed the tables, making her way to the tapestries hanging along the tent's back wall. She looked back again—Marisol was good. Neither the shopkeeper nor the guards were looking her way. She peeked behind the tapestry.

A small girl, no more than eight years old, was crouched there. Her black curls were matted, and the dark skin of her face and arms, and the sleeveless grey shift she wore were covered in grime. She looked terrified.

"Don't be afraid," Abby whispered, holding out her hands nonthreateningly. "I won't hurt you."

The little girl remained silent. Her brown eyes were wild with fear. Abby hunkered down next to her, out of sight. "Are you hiding from the guards?" she asked.

The girl nodded. "If they find me, they will take me back to the palace. I do not want to go back. I want to go home."

"I'm Abby. What's your name?" Abby asked.

"Aziza."

"All right, Aziza. I'll take you home. Where do you live?"

"You cannot. My home is too far away," Aziza whispered. "Daudi said he would take me home, but he never came back."

"Daudi? Is that your father?" The name sounded familiar, but Abby couldn't remember where she had heard it.

The girl shook her head. "No. My father is at home, in my village."

"Okay. Well then, who is Daudi, and what were you two doing in the palace?" Abby asked.

"Not two. Six. We were taken by the winged women. Daudi got away from them. He said he would come back for me." The little girl looked like she was about to cry.

"Winged women?" Abby's mouth dropped open in shock as she remembered where she had heard Daudi's name. *The village on the Great Plains,* she thought. "Aziza—are you from Nuren?"

Aziza nodded.

"What happened to the other four? Are they still alive?" Abby asked.

The girl shook her head and started to cry.

Abby put her arms around Aziza. "It's going to be okay. My friends and I are leaving the city. We'll take you with us. We'll get you home safe."

The girl's body shook with sobs. Abby held her tightly. *What did they do to this kid?* Abby looked her over. Aziza didn't seem hurt—not physically, at least. There were no cuts or bruises on her arms or legs. She was barefoot and her feet were muddy. Her hands were dirty too, except for in one spot, where there was a gold tattoo, a mark very similar to one Abby had seen earlier in the day. "How did you escape?" Abby asked.

"A guard was taking me from my cell in the dungeon, but I bit him and got away. I crawled through the grate where they dump the garbage," the girl said. "I hid in the rubbish cart, but then I heard they were taking the garbage to be burned, so I rolled off the cart and crawled in here."

"You were very brave to do that, Aziza." Abby brushed the girl's matted hair away from her face. "Look, I'll get you out of the city, but I need to hide you. I saw a shop down the way that sells baskets. I'll buy a big one and we can smuggle you out. But I need to get my friends to help me. Can you stay here until I come back?"

The girl nodded.

"Okay. Stay quiet and hidden. I'll be right back," Abby said, hugging the girl. "I promise."

Rising, Abby headed toward Marisol and the shopkeeper. "Wow, those fabrics are beautiful," Abby said, praying her voice sounded calm. Her heart was beating wildly, and her face felt flushed. "Marisol, why don't you make your purchases? We're going to need some baskets to carry them home, so I need to step away and buy some."

"No need, my lady," the shopkeeper replied. "I have some here that you could take with you." He pointed to a pile of baskets near the till where he kept his money. None of them had lids.

"Uh, those are very nice, but do you have anything bigger?" Abby asked. "Maybe with lids to protect the fabric from getting soiled?"

The shopkeeper's eyes widened in interest. Abby could see what he was thinking—it was written all over his face. Bigger baskets meant a larger sale.

"I believe I do," he said, smiling to himself. "I will be but a moment, my lady." He excused himself and walked away.

"Oh no, I know that look," Marisol groaned, studying Abby's face. "What's up?"

"I found one of the missing villagers," Abby whispered. "But we're going to have to smuggle her out."

"Brilliant," Marisol muttered. "Remember when you said shopping was your worst idea ever? This trumps it. We're going to get caught." She stared at the shopkeeper who was rifling through baskets, looking for the largest one in his shop.

"I *can't* leave her. She's just a little girl," Abby said.

Marisol stared at Abby. "A kid? Are you serious?"

"Yes. I can't leave her," Abby repeated.

"Okay, you're right," Marisol agreed. "I'll keep this guy under my spell. Good luck."

The shopkeeper was coming back now, balancing two large baskets with lids. One of them was just large enough to fit Aziza. "I have these," he said. "Which would you prefer?"

"We'll take both," Marisol grinned, producing a bag of coins with a graceful flourish. "And the six bolts of cloth we discussed."

"Oh! Thank you, my lady! A fine purchase indeed," the shopkeeper exclaimed.

⠺⠛⠺⠛⠺⠛

David was starting to worry. It was all well and good that they were playing this little waiting game, this acting as though everything was fine and they weren't dying to bolt from the city. But the girls had been away for too long. Surely it couldn't take that long to make a few token purchases and get the heck out of Dodge.

Ah, there was Marisol, flanked by two guards, one carrying a huge basket, the other with his arms full of fabric. He chuckled to himself. He guessed the girls had done more than put on a good show.

"Where's Abby?" he asked, taking the basket from the guard.

"She's coming, but she took a little detour," Marisol said. She nodded subtly toward the guards who had accompanied her, and looked back into David's eyes, her face pinched.

David took that to mean the game was not quite over. He nodded and tried to contain his growing sense of alarm.

Marisol forced a smile. "Nothing to worry about. Can you help me load all this on the horses?"

ဆၠဆၠဆၠ

Marisol had managed to persuade the guards to help her carry her purchases, allowing Abby to slip away with an empty basket.

They almost didn't get away with it—the shopkeeper had insisted on loading the baskets with the fabric. Once outside the tent, Marisol explained to the guards that she would need to secure the baskets first, and then fill them. Why would she try to secure a heavy basket?

This seemed to make sense to the guards, and they followed her back to the city gate without questioning her logic. Of course, it helped that Marisol had flirted outrageously with them, making sure they were entirely focused on her and not Abby. As they walked, Abby found herself both impressed and disturbed by her friend's ability to manipulate people. She laughed to herself. Jon had certainly met his match.

It was in the middle of Marisol's charming of the guards that Abby made her silent escape, padding around to the narrow alley behind the tent. She looked around at the backs of the other colorful tents along either side of the row.

No one in sight. She laid her basket on the ground, removed the lid, and pointed the mouth toward the tent wall.

Then she lifted the bottom of the tent and whispered for Aziza to crawl inside the basket. The girl was quick and quiet, and Abby swiftly hid her from view as she tipped the basket upright and replaced the lid.

She had almost made it to the end of the alley when a large Kruorumbrae suddenly materialized in front of her and blocked her way. He almost looked human, but his brawny form and black eyes ringed in red betrayed his true nature.

"Excuse me," she said, pretending she didn't recognize him for what he was. She tried to slow her rapid heartbeat, to project only the image of a busy woman annoyed by a minor obstacle, one standing in the way of her completing an important task.

"What do you have in that basket?" the Blood Shadow growled.

Abby was dismayed to notice he was dressed like a palace guard. That could not be good. "Gifts for the queen," she snapped. "Now, if you please. There are people waiting for me." She moved to push past the Shadow.

There was a low chuckle behind her. Abby turned to find Malden sitting on his furry haunches, grinning and shaking his head. "Oh, girly, girly. You've never been good at lying." He narrowed his eyes. "Seize her."

Behind him appeared more Kruorumbrae guards. One of them wrestled the basket from her grasp, and another pinned Abby's arms behind her with superhuman strength. Pain shot like fire up her arms, and she prayed the guard wouldn't wrench them out of their sockets.

"How dare you?" Abby protested. She glared at Malden. "I am on a diplomatic mission with the Solas Beir. When he hears of this, you'll be sorry."

A tall figure emerged from a column of smoke. She pushed back her hood. "I think not. The Solas Beir has no authority in this city."

"Lucia," Abby gasped. *What's she doing here?*

"Open the basket," Lucia ordered.

The tall Kruorumbrae at her side did as Lucia commanded. Aziza was crouched inside, her eyes wide with terror.

"Ah, *there* you are," Lucia said, smiling coldly. "Take the prisoner back to the palace and get her cleaned up. She is a mess."

"No!" Aziza screamed. She kicked and clawed at the burly Kruorumbrae as he threw her over his shoulder. Her efforts had no effect—his grip on her was iron. He turned and carried the girl back toward the palace.

"Let her go!" Abby yelled. She gathered her anger into a tight ball and then pushed it out from her core in a frustrated scream. The Kruorumbrae in front of her were knocked backward, and the guard's grip on her loosened. Abby shook him off and set her feet in a fighting stance. The grin on Malden's face vanished, then returned, stretching wide as he saw his mistress calmly hold out her hand. An electric blue orb formed on Lucia's palm.

"Catch." Lucia threw the ball of energy at Abby.

Abby tried to block it with her arms, but the ball burst on contact, enveloping her in a wave of blue that crackled and popped as the electricity coursed through her body. She sank to the ground in pain.

"Get her," Lucia commanded. "She can join the courtesan."

Abby fought her way out of her haze of pain and tried to wriggle from the guard's grasp. It was no use. There was only one other means of escape. Closing her eyes, Abby called back the memory of being in the rainforest, when her arms were bound as they were now.

ಬಂಡಬಂಡಬಂಡ

David heard the screams and started running. *Abby.* He had to find her.

"The gates!" Marisol called after him. "The guards are closing the gates!" The commotion had alerted the guards at the city entrance, who were taking no chances with a prisoner on the loose.

"Go!" David yelled over his shoulder. "We'll catch up with you."

"I am coming with you!" Cael shouted, drawing his sword as he ran after David.

David stopped and held up his hand. "No, Cael. Get Jon and Marisol out. I've got Abby."

Cael hesitated. David could almost see what Cael was thinking as he considered whether or not to disobey a direct order. He would never abandon his king—it went again his code as a knight of the Light.

"*Go* Cael," David insisted. "We're right behind you."

Cael nodded gravely. "We will wait for you at the Eye of the Needle." He ran back and heaved himself up into his saddle. Jon and Marisol had already mounted their horses. "Come on," Cael shouted to them, and kicked his horse into a gallop. The gates were already halfway closed.

David launched himself into the air, landing on four paws as a lion. He ran toward the tent where he had heard Abby cry out. He could see a number of Kruorumbrae emerging from around the back side of the tent, chasing something small and white. The rabbit was running as fast as she could, and the Blood Shadows were close on her heels. She was able to outmaneuver them for the moment, but eventually they would catch her.

Roaring, David pulled up short, and then leapt at the Shadow closest to the rabbit, taking him down. The Shadow guard following him tried to jump over his fallen comrade, but David reached up, his lion claws finding purchase in the Blood Shadow's flesh. He slammed the second Shadow on the ground, and prepared to catch another. As he did, he heard Abby scream again. She had been hit by a bolt of blue energy, and lay enveloped in it, writhing on the ground, changing back to her human form.

David looked up. Malden and Lucia were standing behind a band of Kruorumbrae. Lucia had a pleased look on her face. David roared and leapt to shield Abby from another blow. His teeth clenched as the pain radiated across his flank. He changed back into himself, and then released his own volley of electric blue energy, incinerating three of the oncoming Shadows. Malden yelped and ducked under the edge of a tent.

Lucia met David's defiant gaze with a glare, as another orb formed on her palm. The orb grew big enough to envelop both David and Abby.

Abby had been weakened too much to survive getting hit again. Scooping her up in his arms, David launched himself into the air and the ball exploded on the spot where he had been standing a second before, leaving a smoking hole in the ground.

Below him, David could hear Lucia shouting at the guards to open the gate. She grabbed David's abandoned horse and leapt up into the saddle, calling for the Kruorumbrae to join her pursuit.

David flew over the city wall. Ahead he could see clouds of dust from his friends' mounts. They had escaped the city of the Eastern Oracle.

"David," Abby whispered. Her voice was hoarse. "Thanks for coming back for me."

"Always," he said, cradling her close to him as he flew toward the rock tower in the distance. "Are you all right?"

She wrapped her arms around his neck. "I'll live. But the little girl—the Shadows took her."

He glanced down at Abby. "What little girl?"

"That prisoner they were looking for. She was one of the Nuren villagers taken by the Daughters of Mercy. One of them, Yola's brother, Daudi, got away, and the other four were killed. But Aziza was imprisoned in the palace. They forced her to become a courtesan."

"No," David said, narrowing his eyes. "No, that is *not* okay. This will not stand."

"That's why we have to go back for her."

"I know—but we can't right now, not with Lucia and her cronies chasing us. Look." David pointed to the small army of Kruorumbrae bursting from the city gate.

Lucia rode at the front, leading the monstrous pack closer to the portal at the Eye of the Needle.

"If we don't go back, Aziza will die," Abby insisted. "She's just a little kid."

David looked at Abby's haggard face. Getting blasted by Lucia's orb had disoriented her, and he could see she wasn't grasping their current situation.

"Abby," he said gently, "I'm sorry. I promise you, once we get away from the Shadows, we'll rescue her. But right now, the best thing we can do is help our friends. *They* will die if we don't. Jon, Marisol, and Cael need us."

Saying their names did the trick, and Abby's eyes widened with understanding. "You're right," she agreed, nodding. "Of course you're right. But I promised Aziza I would get her out of the city. When we get back through the portal, we need to get help. We have to come back for her."

"We will," David vowed. "We'll come back and clean the Eastern Oracle's whole corrupted city. Things will change, I can promise you that."

# EYE OF THE NEEDLE

"**W**here are they?" Jon yelled. "Did they make it?" He dug his heels into his horse's sides, willing it to run faster.

Marisol glanced over her shoulder as she rode. "I see them! David has Abby. They're flying toward us," she shouted.

Cael scanned the sky. He reined his horse in to a trot and shifted in his saddle to get a better look. There was an expression of alarm on his face. "I cannot see them!"

Jon and Marisol slowed their horses to match pace with Cael's. "Look," Marisol pointed, "there!"

High above, Jon could make out a hazy silhouette. It was too high up and moving too fast to make out details, but it had to be David carrying Abby in his arms. Who else could it be?

Cael nodded, breathing a sigh of relief. "I never should have left them."

Marisol shot him a look. "You had no choice. Come on!" She goaded her horse into a gallop.

They were close to the Eye of the Needle now, but in the distance Jon could see riders from the city in pursuit—a lot of riders, based on the massive dust cloud in their wake.

"Looks like David and Abby invited friends," Jon frowned. "I hope they catch up to us before the Shadows do."

ꟊꟑꟊꟑꟊꟑꟊꟑ

Peering down, David knew they were cutting it close. As he landed at the base of the Eye of the Needle, the riders were fast approaching.

"'Bout time, slowpokes," Jon said, his arms crossed. He eyed Abby. "You okay?"

"Yeah, I'm good," Abby replied, disentangling herself from David's embrace. "Just got into a little scrap with Lucia and her beasties." Her voice was scratchy, but she seemed to have regained her senses. She was still weak though, and visibly shaking.

David watched her take two unsteady steps before he intervened and helped her ease into a sitting position on the sand. Lucia sure had done a number on her. Abby needed to rest, but she couldn't rest here, not with the Kruorumbrae on their heels.

"The little girl?" Marisol asked.

Abby shook her head. "They took her. I promised I'd save her, but I couldn't." There were tears in her eyes.

David bent down and kissed the top of her head, and then got to work. He walked over to the symbol of the winged woman and placed his hands over it. With his eyes closed, David focused on letting the power flow through him and into the portal.

Jon looked toward the city. "How much time do you think we have?"

David opened his eyes to turn and look at Jon. "We didn't have much of a head start before Lucia took up the chase."

Cael stared at the rising cloud of dust and frowned. "Not long. Minutes possibly. Swords at the ready."

David returned his focus to the portal. Blue light emanated from the palms of his hands, and around his neck, the Sign of the Throne started to glow.

He heard Marisol draw her sword. "Let's buy him as much time as we can."

After a moment, David let out a deep breath and the light coming from his hands disappeared. He backed away from the door and studied it. Then he unclasped the Sign of the Throne from around his neck and looked at it. Feeling a warm hand on his arm, he turned to see Abby next to him, her eyes wide with worry.

"What's wrong?" she asked.

"Nothing's happening," David said. "When I opened the door before, I could feel the boundaries between our worlds weaken." He could tell by the confusion on her face that further explanation was needed. "You know how when you push on a door that's stuck, you can feel it give a little, right before it pops open? It felt like that."

"So the door is stuck?"

"I don't know. I don't feel anything at all. It just feels...solid."

Abby took his hand. "Maybe if we tried it together? Like that first portal we opened?"

"Worth a try," David agreed.

"No pressure, guys," Jon called, "but we've got maybe two minutes here."

"Thanks, Jon," Abby retorted, rolling her eyes. "That's very helpful."

In spite of everything, David couldn't help but smile at her. She gave him a lopsided grin, and he felt warmth pour into him. As he had done when working on the portal in the Newcastle Beach mansion, he held the Sign in his open palms. Abby placed her hands over his, and David looked into her eyes.

There was a thrumming noise and blue light began to leak out from between their fingers. The light poured out onto the ground and pooled around the bottom of the door. There was a brief flash as the brightness of the light increased, and then the light was gone, extinguished like a blown-out birthday candle.

"What happened?" Abby asked.

"*Nothing* happened." David had been certain it would work. Frustrated, he returned the Sign of the Throne to its place around his neck. "Maybe it's us. Being exposed to Lucia's power like that—maybe it drained us."

Cael left his post watching for the Kruorumbrae to inspect the door. He ran his fingers along the groove between the door's edges and the stone frame. When he turned back to David and Abby, his face was grim. "I am afraid it is the door that is the problem. I should have seen this before—this portal can only be opened from one side."

"What?" David asked in disbelief. "No, that can't be. Can it?"

"I am sorry. I failed you, Solas Beir—I should have known," Cael said. "We never should have shut that door."

"But if we hadn't, those things from the casino would have followed us through," Jon called out, looking over his shoulder. "We *had* to shut it."

"You speak true, Jon, but now we have no means of escape save the Barren," Cael replied.

"Won't Lucia just follow us?" Abby asked.

"Perhaps. But the Barren is formidable. She may give up her pursuit," Cael considered. "She is no fool."

A scream pierced the dry, desert air. It sounded like a battle cry. David looked up to see the shape of a woman with wings, silhouetted against the sun. It looked just like the symbol on the portal.

"The Daughters of Mercy," Abby whispered, clutching his arm.

"Maybe they're coming to help us," Jon said. "We don't *know* that they chose a side, do we?"

"They chose," Abby said, trembling. "They didn't choose us."

"Maybe we can change their minds," David suggested. "Come on, Abby—I'll do the talking and you try to push them with your mind to come to our side."

Abby looked scared enough to jump out of her skin, but she wrapped her arms around his neck anyway. David lifted her into the air, flying toward the cave at the very top of the towering rock spire. The Daughters soared to meet them. They circled around David and Abby, and then dove down toward their friends.

ഇരുഇരുഇരുഇരു

Jon, Marisol, and Cael ducked in unison as a screeching Daughter of Mercy swooped low over their heads, her arms outstretched, her fingers curled into grasping, greedy talons.

Jon shuddered, remembering the banshee screams of the lamia in the rainforest. He waited until the Daughter had gained plenty of altitude before daring to rise. "Did you see her face? She looked like a corpse!"

Marisol's eyes were wide with horror. "That's not what I saw."

"On your guard, my friends," Cael shouted, tightening his grip on the hilt of his sword. "The Kruorumbrae are here!"

𐌑𐌂𐌔𐌑𐌂𐌔𐌑𐌂𐌔

David wrapped his arms more tightly around Abby's waist. She looked as petrified as the Eye of the Needle. "Keep projecting your emotions, Abby," he said, trying, despite his own terror, to keep his voice even and calm. "This will work. I know it will." It sure wouldn't work if the emotion Abby was projecting was her fear, but saying that out loud wouldn't help.

One of the Daughters stopped circling and floated in midair, directly in front of David. She flapped her great white wings lazily and stared into his eyes.

"I am the Solas Beir," David said. "I serve the Light. Join me—together we can defeat the Kruorumbrae."

The Daughter smiled—she had the face of a child, a look of sweet innocence unspoiled by darkness. Golden ringlets framed her cherub face. "Greetings, Solas Beir," she said, her voice musical and light as air. "What price would you pay for us to join your cause?"

David returned her smile in an effort to hide his disgust. *Mercenary,* he thought. *Mercenary with the face of an angel.* "I wish to bring peace to our land. You will be richly rewarded for fighting alongside us." As an afterthought he added, "There is much gold in Caislucis. Help us and it is yours."

The Daughter's face shimmered—now she looked exactly like Abby. Abby recoiled, gasping and clamping her hand over her mouth, as if she were trying to hold in her shock, or maybe a scream.

David feared she would let go of him and grasped her tightly against his chest. The muscles in his arms tensed and began to ache.

Abby looked up at him and seemed to recognize the strain she was putting on him. She wrapped both of her arms around his neck again, and he relaxed slightly.

The smile on the Daughter's face was Abby's. "We have already been richly rewarded, and care not for gold." Then her face changed again. It was still Abby's face, but her blue eyes turned black, soulless, not unlike those of the creatures waiting on the other side of the one-way portal. "David," she purred seductively in Abby's voice. "Come with me, David."

"No," David spat, shaking his head. "Never."

Suddenly, one of the Daughters slammed into him from behind, knocking the breath from his lungs, blindsiding him in an attempt to pitch Abby out of his arms. The first Daughter smiled wickedly and sank her talons into Abby's back, ripping at the fabric of her clothes, trying to tear her away from him.

Abby screamed out his name and tightened her grip around his neck, burrowing her face against his chest.

Gasping for air, David tugged Abby closer with the arm that was anchored around her waist. With his free hand, he released a ball of blue fire, forcing the Daughter with Abby's face backward. The Daughter's wings caught fire, incinerating in an instant. She fell into the fray below. Her sister released her hold on David's back and rocketed down, trying to catch her.

ಬಂಡಬಂಡಬಂಡ

"Seize them," Lucia ordered the Kruorumbrae. "I would prefer prisoners, but do what you must to subdue them."

Malden interpreted this last part very loosely. He'd subdue little Marisol all right, but her boyfriend would not get off so easy.

Malden had been riding in his Kruorumbrae form, that of a goblin boy, with a malevolent grin permanently seared on his face. The burn he had received from his last encounter with the Solas Beir had never healed. The nautilus shape of the Sign of the Throne was etched in his cheek, a blistering sore that still oozed black pus.

At his mistress's command, he leapt from his horse, landing on all fours in the shape of a black cat, now the size of a Great Dane—one with a prehensile tail and a disturbingly human face. His comrades followed suit, pouring from their mounts like so much dark sludge, solidifying into the stuff of nightmares.

Malden could see his pretty *dulce* standing between the Reyes boy and the knight, swords held out in front of them, their backs against the solid rock base of the Eye of the Needle. They were going nowhere fast.

ಬಂಡಬಂಡಬಂಡ

With the arrival of the Kruorumbrae, the Daughters of Mercy left their quarry on the sands below in favor of a

300

coordinated attack on the Solas Beir himself. David was surrounded. The Daughters were clawing at him from all sides, steadily wrenching Abby away from him. They pinned his arms and carried her off toward the cave. He could see her real face peeking out among all those twisted renditions of it. "Abby!" he yelled, and broke free, flying after her.

Abby was kicking at them as best she could, fighting to get free. But she was so high above the ground—what would happen if she escaped their grasp? There was nowhere to go but down.

David slammed into the mass of Daughters holding her captive, and managed to pull a few of them off Abby. He could see angry red lines all over her neck and back where those terrible talons had sliced her skin, and bruises forming on her arms from being rudely yanked from his embrace. He set another Daughter on fire as he struggled to reach Abby. "Let go of her!" he shouted.

"As you wish," one of the Daughters replied, and as one, they released their hold on Abby. She was falling so fast, and yet her eyes were locked on his—it felt as if time had stopped, as if she were frozen in midair and the ground were rushing up to meet her.

David dived for her, but he knew he wouldn't be fast enough. Abby shuddered as if embracing her fate—and suddenly she was gone. In her place was a white raven. David's mouth dropped open in a mixture of relief and awe. Then she was obscured from his sight as the Daughters surrounded him again. They were pinning his hands behind him, forcing him up against the rock spire.

David twisted his head to the side and caught a flash of white—Abby racing through the air with several Daughters close behind. They were herding her into the wide black mouth of their lair. One of them reached out, and for a moment, he thought the Daughter would catch Abby by the throat, but she was faster than the winged woman, and the Daughter's talon sliced her raven wing instead. He saw Abby falter, the injury to her wing throwing her off balance, but then she recovered before being swallowed up by the cavern's dark depths.

David managed to get a hand free and set another Daughter on fire, and then saw that one of them had turned on the others, fighting to free him.

*No, wait,* he thought. It wasn't one of the Daughters—it was Erela. She must have flown across the Barren to come to his aid.

It was a vicious fight—Erela had been cast out, and she was paying dearly for her rebellion, for daring to defy her sisters once again. Erela gave back as much as she was given, her own face a mask of fury.

Erela maneuvered behind one of her sisters. She broke the Daughter's neck in one swift motion, and then let go. The Daughter dropped from the sky like a stone. David wasn't surprised that Erela didn't stop to watch—she wasn't the sentimental type, after all.

She flew straight to David, pulling off one of his attackers and following the same, methodical protocol she'd used when disposing of her other sister.

David didn't mind—he quite appreciated her efficiency. He set another Daughter on fire, and then another, and found that he and Erela now faced but a single Daughter. The others they'd dispatched were lying, limbs askew, on the sand below.

"This one is mine, Solas Beir," Erela said. "You get the c'aislingaer."

"Thank you," David breathed, and shot up the rock wall to the Eye.

ᛒᚳᛒᚳᛒᚳᛒᚳᛒᚳ

"They're eating the horses!" Cael heard Marisol shout above the din of the battle. Over the shoulder of the Kruorumbrae he was fighting, he could see their horses collapsing and heard their primal screams over the guttural roars of the creatures that had taken them down.

"That's just wrong," Jon yelled, slicing through the gut of a Blood Shadow. "How are we supposed to cross the Barren now?" He punctuated each word with another hack of his sword through the creature's thick flesh.

"Win this battle and we will take theirs!" Cael shouted, beheading one monster and spinning to run his sword through another. He was still more skilled than his students, but they had learned much. Perhaps there was a chance they would live through this.

Or perhaps not. The Kruorumbrae who had been busy devouring the horses had finished their meal and abandoned the drained equine corpses to engage Cael and his young warriors. These creatures were larger than their comrades, and they were more powerful than ever now that they'd had a little snack. Cael felt searing heat and looked down to see one of the creatures grinning wickedly as it viciously raked its cruel claws across his torso. *I stand corrected,* he thought, sinking to his knees, watching blood gush from his gaping wound. *I may not live through this after all.*

"Cael!" Marisol screamed. She rammed her sword through the creature she'd been fighting and leapt over the one sprawled at Jon's feet—it was newly dead and still twitching.

The monster that had injured Cael was standing over him, its arm raised to swipe at Cael's head. Marisol raised her sword and brought it down smoothly. She severed the arm, relieving the beast of the need for its appendage as she sent the creature swiftly from its world into the next.

"Keep those things away from us!" Marisol shouted to Jon. "I've got to help him."

Jon grunted and nodded—he was too busy fighting to answer any other way.

Three of the bolts of fabric Marisol had purchased lay propped next to the now-defunct portal. She had set them there, meaning to grab them as she slipped through. Marisol stepped over Cael and retrieved one of the bolts. She eased Cael into a sitting position with his back against the rock wall. "Can you scoot forward a bit?" she asked, unwinding the cloth from its wooden spindle.

Cael grimaced and complied, his jaw clenched against the pain as Marisol wrapped the fabric around his waist, tightly binding his abdomen with it. She placed his hands over the wound, then pressed her own hands down on his, applying pressure to stop the flow of the blood. The blue silk turned red between their fingers. "Hold on," she cried.

"No promises." Cael smiled grimly. He knew he would bleed out long before the battle was finished.

"Don't you say that," Marisol chided him. "You're going back to marry Eulalia—even if we are making a mess of her pretty silk."

"She will have to forgive us," Cael responded weakly.

That was when Malden grabbed Marisol.

ᚱᚢᚷᚱᚢᚷᚱᚢᚷ

Abby was flying blind. Whatever advantage her raven eyes might have had over her human ones was rendered null and void in the darkness of the Daughters' cave. She had taken on this new form in full sunlight, and there was no time for her eyes to adjust to the complete blackness that now enveloped her. Not with the things that wore her face hot on her tail.

She twisted and wove between columns of stone, gliding over stalagmites and ducking under stalactites that seemed to appear from nowhere in the darkness. She felt them more than saw them—the way the air around her body changed as she flew close to the rock. She had been lucky so far, a few near misses, but whatever force was guiding her seemed to be keeping her from smacking into the cavern walls and out of the grasp of her evil clones.

If only *they* would collide with something solid. That would be helpful. Her injured wing was holding out, but for how long, she didn't know. Abby had no idea where she was or where she was headed—the Daughters of Mercy had every advantage in that regard. She was in their home.

The cavern could not stretch on forever, and that was a problem. Eventually, she would run out of room to fly. She could feel a sense of the walls growing narrower, pressing in on her body. She didn't think the sensation was a case of claustrophobia talking. She was sure what she was experiencing was real. The Daughters chasing her were funneling her into some kind of narrow passage—she would soon be trapped.

Maybe she could survive if she could find some kind of side tunnel—some hole small enough for her to squeeze into, where her pursuers couldn't reach her. Somewhere she could hide until David had the opportunity to kill them all and get her out of here. He *would* come for her—she refused to entertain the thought that the Daughters had killed him. If he were dead, she would feel it, and what she felt was that he was very much alive.

There, ahead—there was some kind of gleam, piercing the darkness. It was a tiny circle of bright light, growing larger by the second. She hardly dared to believe it, but sure enough, there it was. There was a hole in the rock wall—the daylight shining through drew her forward on its beams. She could just fit, and the Daughters wouldn't be able to follow.

Abby burst through the hole into the vivid blue of a cobalt sky. Then she saw the line on the horizon where the sky bled red, and her wings failed her. After that, there was only the falling.

ɞᘓɞᘓɞᘓ

"Stop," Malden ordered.

Jon froze—he had managed to protect Marisol and Cael from the other Blood Shadows, but this one had evaded his sword. Jon felt a sense of despair. Of all the nasty monsters in Cai Terenmare, *why* did Malden have to be the one to get past him?

The creature had Marisol in his grasp, one long, razor-sharp claw resting against her throat. Jon could see a scarlet bead form on her skin as Malden exerted pressure. "The girl comes with me," he purred, a smug grin on his ruined face. "We have unfinished business, don't we, *mija?*"

The creature began to drag her across the sand, back to where Lucia stood flanked by her bodyguards. Jon saw Marisol's eyes widen in terror, and in an instant, a number of things became crystal clear to him. Marisol had told him she had been plagued by horrible nightmares as a child. This monster was one of her bad dreams come true, her own personal Kruorumbrae bogeyman.

Malden was obsessed with her, and he meant to take her away so he would be free to abuse her without the risk of interruption. He wouldn't kill her. No, she would live, but some things are worse than death. Jon would die before he let that happen.

Bargaining with Malden was pointless—the creature had what he desired. Jon took his appeal straight to the top. "Lucia, please. Take me instead. You *must* have a hostage, and next to the c'aislingaer, I'm the Solas Beir's closest confidant. The girl is nothing."

The tall, burly Shadow at Lucia's side spoke up. "Why would we take hostages when we could kill you all now? Tierney would reward us well for ending the Solas Beir."

"No he wouldn't," Jon said, not breaking eye contact with Lucia. "He could have easily killed us when we were in the Eastern Oracle's court. But he didn't, because he doesn't want a war any more than the Eastern Oracle does. Tierney has something bigger in mind, and he doesn't want the Solas Beir dead just yet. He needs the Solas Beir to endorse his plan and sway the people to his side. Doesn't he?"

Lucia studied him silently. What was going on behind those dark eyes of hers? Was that a spark of recognition? Perhaps Tierney had been keeping something from her as well.

"Look," Jon continued, "the Solas Beir is busy at the moment, but when he's done with those Daughters, he'll come for you. You know he will. Let's avoid more bloodshed. Take me and walk away."

"Very well," Lucia said, narrowing her eyes. "Malden, release the girl."

Malden glared at Jon, and Jon wondered if the creature would comply. After a moment, the thing released his hold on Marisol, and she flew to Jon's arms.

"Jon, no. Please don't do this," Marisol begged.

Jon stared into her eyes and forced a brave smile. "I have to—I won't let that thing hurt you ever again. I love you, Sol." He felt a lump in his throat. "I wish I'd said that before now."

He held her tightly and gave her a kiss, realizing it would be their last. Once Lucia showed up with him instead of the Solas Beir, he *would* die. Of that, he had no doubt.

"I love you too. I promise—we'll come for you. I can't lose you. I can't." Marisol kissed him hard, refusing to let him go.

*One for the road,* Jon thought, feeling her warm tears trickle down her cheeks as she kissed him. He gently pushed her away, back toward Cael. "Go," he whispered, "before Lucia changes her mind."

Marisol gave him a last look and ran across the sand to Cael. Jon turned to the tall Shadow who had spoken and offered his hands, so the creature could shackle him. "I'm ready," he told Lucia.

She nodded, her face impassive. "Back to the city."

Jon saw her shoot Malden a warning look as he moved closer, intending to inflict pain as payment for the loss of his prize. Malden backed away, but Jon got the message loud and clear: *first opportunity, you die.*

ଧ୦ଓଧ୦ଓଧ୦ଓ

David hovered in front of the Eye of the Needle. Centered at the top of the cave's entrance was another symbol. It was similar to the one at the bottom of the spire, the winged woman enclosed in a circle, but this time the woman was absent. In this carving, the circle itself had wings.

"It used to refer to the righteousness of the Light," Erela said solemnly, floating beside him, "but the symbol no longer bears the same meaning for the Daughters of Mercy. My sisters have forgotten the path of the just."

David nodded and silently entered the cave, holding his hand out in front of him, palm up. A blue flame formed and flickered on his palm, illuminating the darkness. The air in the cavern was thick and acrid; he could feel it pressing down on him, threatening to choke him, to extinguish his light.

There was a noise emanating from the cavern's depths. It sounded like wings, but with the echo reverberating off the walls, it was difficult to tell if the sound came from one pair or many. David flew down the passage with Erela at his side.

The sound was all around them now. A pair of Daughters emerged from the darkness. Erela quickly ended one, and David set fire to the other. As the Daughter was consumed by the blue light, David saw something small and white at the far end of the passage. Against the blackness of the cavern walls, it almost glowed.

309

"Abby?" he called. He flew to her, but found only the smallest trace of his white raven. It was a single feather, lying on the floor of the passage. There was blood on it.

"Oh, Abby, no," he whispered. He picked up the feather and carefully tucked it into his shirt, next to the Sign of the Throne.

He heard the rustle of feathers behind him. He whirled around. "Abby?"

There was nothing. Then he heard the sound echoing from somewhere above him. Whatever was up there was masked by an inky blackness his light could not penetrate.

❧☙❧☙❧☙

"Above you, Solas Beir!" Erela shouted. She did not know if this Daughter of Mercy had been lying in wait or had managed to sneak past them in the darkness, but she had promised the queen she would keep the Solas Beir safe. She fully intended to keep that promise. She raced toward him.

The Daughter crouching upside-down on the ceiling was wearing the c'aislingaer's face. Her eyes were dark, empty—dead.

"What have you done with her?" David demanded.

The Daughter didn't answer. She simply gazed down at the Solas Beir with those soulless eyes and smiled wickedly, licking her lips. Her muscles were tense and her wings extended, the feathered tips almost touching either wall of the passage. She had the Solas Beir in her sights, and by the look on her face, she planned to rip out his throat.

❧☙❧☙❧☙

The Daughter dropped from the ceiling.

"Die!" David cried out, and the thing burst into flames. Bits of ash fell into his hair, and he brushed them away absently.

He flew to the end of the corridor, but there was no sign of Abby. The passage ended in a solid stone wall. He placed his palms against the rock—the surface was cold, unyielding.

"Abby was here—I *know* she was. But I can't feel her anymore. I can't feel her at all." Defeated, he rested his forehead on the wall between his hands. He didn't know what else to do. He felt hollow, numb.

Erela gently put her hand on his shoulder. It was an uncharacteristically compassionate gesture. Surprised, David turned to look at her.

"Come, Solas Beir," Erela said softly. "She is gone. We must help the others."

Resigned, David nodded and followed Erela out of the cave.

On the ground below, he could see his friends inside a semicircle of dead Shadows. Marisol was on her knees, tending to Cael.

As David landed on the sand beside her, Marisol looked up. "Where's Abby?"

David shook his head—he couldn't speak. He dropped down beside Marisol and pushed her hands away from Cael's wound.

"No, David," Cael said. "It is too much for you. If you take my wound, you will die."

"I don't care," David growled. He let the power flow from his hands. He winced as he felt a burst of heat in his own abdomen. He looked down to see blossoms of red soaking his shirt, just below the tip of the feather tucked inside. It was good to feel pain—it felt right somehow. It anchored him, kept him from falling into the black hole that appeared every time he pictured Abby's face.

Marisol stared at David, a pinched look on her face. She got up and went over to the remaining bolts of fabric by the portal. "We've got two of these left. The Shadows destroyed the ones we left on the horses, and I wrecked the other one bandaging Cael. So what's it going to be? Green or purple?"

David pointed at the deep violet cloth. "Better give me that one to bleed on. After seeing the courtesan in the Eastern Oracle's court, the last thing I want is to see my mother wearing a purple wedding dress."

"All right." Marisol knelt down to bind his wound.

David watched her unroll the fabric from the spindle and wind it around his waist. He sucked in his breath as she pulled it taut over the wound, biting his lip against the pain. Marisol stopped and studied his face, and he nodded for her to continue. "Where's Jon?" he asked through clenched teeth.

Marisol avoided his eyes and focused on tying a knot to secure the cloth. "He went with Lucia—he offered himself up to save me from Malden." Her eyes were shiny with the tears she was struggling to hold in.

David felt like he'd been kicked in the gut. He imagined how Abby would have felt about Jon being captured. The void he felt from losing her threatened to swallow his sanity. He had failed her completely. But if he couldn't save Abby, he would at least save Jon. He placed his hand on Marisol's arm. "I'm sorry, Sol. We *will* get him back." He tested the bandage, straining against it slightly. His abdomen throbbed with pain, but the wrapping was nice and tight. "Just give me a few minutes to heal."

"You will need more than a few minutes to heal from that wound," Erela said, eyeing his injury. "And the boy will be heavily guarded. We would be fools to try to rescue him now."

David peered up at Erela. She looked like a stone statue towering over him, her arms crossed over her chest. "I *can't* let him die," he pleaded. "Abby...Abby wouldn't have wanted that."

Marisol said nothing, but took his hand in hers. The sadness in her eyes matched the grief in his heart.

"Abby would want you to heal," Cael said softly, standing and unwrapping the soiled cloth binding his torso. "And so would Jon."

David felt rage blaze in his chest. "What Abby wanted was for me to go after the little girl they took. And I said no, that we'd have to come back for her later. If I'd done what Abby wanted, she would still be here with me."

"Then your other friends might have died," Erela stated, uncrossing her arms. "And you might have been captured in the city and lost her anyway. There is no way to know what might have been."

Cael placed his hands on David's shoulders. "The best way to honor Abby now would be to go home, gather reinforcements, and return to rescue Jon and the girl."

"All right," David sighed. "We'll go home. We'll get organized." He looked at Marisol. "And then we *will* come back, and we won't stop fighting until Jon and the girl are safe and we've freed every last courtesan. Are you with me?"

"To the end," Marisol said, squeezing his hand. Her eyes were still sad, but now David saw purpose in them.

"To the very end," Cael agreed, and Erela nodded her assent. "But for now, I will carry you west." He slipped into his wolf form as Marisol and Erela lifted David to his feet.

ဆဈဆဈဆဈ

Marisol salvaged a saddle and wiped it clean of equine blood. "I hope you don't mind, Cael," she said, slipping it over his back. "It's just that if David moves around too much, the wound will start bleeding again."

Cael didn't seem to object, so Marisol and Erela eased David into the saddle. Then Marisol went to see what other supplies she could salvage. There wasn't much, just a little food and a cask of water. After she transferred provisions from the others' packs into hers, she strapped the last bolt of fabric to her pack.

"We will trade off carrying you until you can fly again," Erela said to David.

"What about Marisol?" he asked. "She can't walk across the entire desert."

Erela looked surprised. "True. She can fly with me and scout ahead. My apologies, Solas Beir—I had forgotten she was human."

"It's all right," Marisol said, adjusting the pack on her shoulders. "I've gotten used to being in the minority around here."

Erela turned to her. "Do not think I forgot out of a bias against humans. I forgot because you fought valiantly today. You fought as one of us."

"Thanks," Marisol said, unsure how to respond to this new, softer side of Erela. To hide her embarrassment, she turned to David. "Here—drink this." She handed the cask to David, and then offered a drink to the others.

Cael didn't reply, but Erela shook her head. "Save it for yourself. You and the Solas Beir will need it more than Cael and me."

Marisol took a sip and secured the cask to her pack. "Well, if you change your mind, just ask." She slipped the straps of the pack back over her shoulders.

Erela shook her head again. "No, my friend, we have a long journey ahead, and if that is all the water there is, you must conserve it."

"I may be able to do something about that, once I'm better," David offered.

"Don't push yourself too hard, David. We'll be fine for now, as long as we get moving." Marisol took Erela's outstretched hand, and the former Daughter of Mercy lifted her into the sky.

## THE BARREN

Upon their return to the city, what was left of Lucia's army assembled outside the tall, imposing doors leading to the court of the Eastern Oracle.

"Take the boy to the dungeon," Lucia commanded the Kruorumbrae holding Jon's chains. The guard nodded assent and escorted Jon down the hall. Malden started forward, intending to follow them. "No," Lucia said. "If you lay one finger on the prisoner, I will kill you myself. Now, get lost."

Malden hissed at her. *Not if I kill you first, dearie,* he thought. He had been so close to having the girl all to himself, but Lucia had brought an end to his plans. The least she could do to make up for it would be to let him devour the boy.

Lucia narrowed her dark eyes and raised her hand. A bright blue orb formed on her palm. "Do *not* tempt me," she warned. "I am in no mood for your insolence."

Malden glared at her and scuttled away. *Later, sweetness,* he thought. *You can't protect him forever.*

ଚ୰ଓଷଚ୰ଓଷଚ୰ଓଷ

Lucia watched Malden run off in the direction of the palace's entrance, vanishing as he rounded the corner. The little wretch had grown bold. Perhaps she should have brought him to his knees to remind him of his place. She thought about calling him back and then reconsidered. The Eastern Oracle was conducting a meeting. If she could hear voices coming from inside the courtroom, those within would be able to hear Malden's squeals of agony. It wouldn't do to cause a scene. Not here.

Lucia covered her head with her veil and nodded to the guards to open the doors. She quietly slipped inside the Eastern Oracle's court, and the guards discreetly closed the doors behind her. The Eastern Oracle sat on his throne, and Tierney stood beside him, just in front of the dais. They had a visitor.

The sea hag's long, black-and-white banded tail wound in lazy curves around the room; the paddled tip nearly reached the door. Lucia noted a raw wound near the end of the tail—red, swollen stripes, like something had recently sunk white-hot claws into the lamia's scaly flesh, burning it, branding it.

Lucia had seen that kind of wound before. If she was right about the source of the injury, that wound was never going to heal. The sea hag would be forever marked. Lucia stepped carefully around the lamia's tail and walked the perimeter of the ornate rug to stand silently under the arches on one side of the room.

"I have done all that you asked of me," the lamia purred, her serpentine tail twitching like a cat's.

Although the sea hag addressed both men, her eyes were only on Tierney. Lucia did not like the familiarity with which she spoke—apparently this was not the first conversation between Tierney and the witch. While Tierney looked perfectly at ease and a small satisfied smile played on his lips, the Eastern Oracle's face was twisted in a mask of diplomacy that failed to cloak an expression of self-righteous horror and indignity in having dealings with a hag.

The old woman had slitted, serpentine eyes and a flattened reptilian nose. Squatty, toadlike arms sprouted from her sides, and the warty amphibian skin of her face and upper body resembled the inside of a rotting gourd, a contrast to the smooth scales on her reptilian tail.

Banded tail or no, no one would mistake such a creature for a siren. The lamia was one of the first horrors to come from the sea, a chimera born of covetous hunger, an ancient thing that had never been beautiful. This sea hag had long ago abandoned her siren kin's compulsive urge to feed, and had instead become the scheming creature standing before Tierney now.

The witch likely hoped to elevate her own status by doing tasks her superiors thought beneath them. Lucia was uncertain as to the specifics of those tasks, but she knew they must be vile for the sea hag to have the privilege of being called to court.

"The Sower is ready, my lords. All I have seen will come to pass," the sea hag crooned. "The false Solas Beir will fall, Ardal's true firstborn will take the throne, and the world will be as you wish."

"Well done, Meridoris," Tierney said, favoring the witch with a warm smile. "You will be handsomely rewarded when we succeed. In the meantime, however, a small gift to express our gratitude." He snapped his fingers and one of the guards brought forward a courtesan. It was the girl from the market.

Lucia was not surprised to see the girl wearing the uniform of a courtesan, but she *was* surprised Tierney would give her to a bottom-dwelling creature like the sea hag. Tierney had told

Lucia it was imperative that the girl be captured, and she'd assumed it was because he did not want critical intelligence falling into the hands of the Solas Beir. But he neglected to mention this part. Lucia thought about what Jonathon Reyes said, and wondered what else Tierney had failed to tell her.

The young courtesan seemed dazed, unaware of her surroundings. Had they drugged her to make her more compliant? Lucia wondered if the child had any idea what fate had in store for her.

The sea hag's eyes flashed hungrily, but she made no move to feed. She bowed slightly at her waist. "Thank you, my lord. I look forward to our future dealings. I shall eagerly await your word." Then Meridoris took the girl by the hand and led her out of the room.

A guard followed, walking behind the lamia's paddled tail as it coiled around the room and slithered through the exit. He closed the door once the witch was gone.

"You can relax now, Oracle," Tierney chuckled.

Lucia turned to see the Eastern Oracle let out a sigh of relief. "That was quite unpleasant. I shall be in my chambers if I am needed for further business." He rose from his throne, gathering the folds of his scarlet robe as he descended from the dais.

"I doubt there will be further unpleasantness requiring your attention today, Your Honor," Tierney smiled, crossing his arms.

"Good," the Eastern Oracle replied, scowling. Clearly he did not share Tierney's lighthearted view of the situation. Adjusting his red square cap, the oracle marched to the door leading to his chambers, and an entourage of aides followed in his wake.

One of the aides, a nervous, fidgety little man, seemed on the verge of coming unglued. In his hurry to vacate the room, he dropped his clerk's cap. A tall, muscled Kruorumbrae guard picked it up and held it out to him. The aide recoiled as if the guard might devour him, and then took the cap, muttered his thanks, and skittered away after his colleagues, hastily pulling the chamber door shut behind him.

Tierney grinned, watching all of this with great amusement. "He's not the most gracious of hosts, but the entertainment is worth the price of admission." He turned to Lucia. "Don't you think so, love?"

Lucia removed her veil and stepped out of the shadows to join him in front of the throne. "He does surround himself with amusing little people," she smirked.

Tierney laughed and vaulted up the dais steps to settle lazily into the Eastern Oracle's throne, irreverently throwing one of his legs over an armrest. "And how are things with our young Lightbearer?"

Lucia wondered what the oracle would think of Tierney abusing his precious throne, but kept her tongue. When delivering bad news to Tierney, it was prudent to proceed with caution. She frowned. "Artan still lives. He annihilated the Daughters."

Tierney raised an eyebrow. "*All* of them?"

Lucia nodded. "All but the traitor. But not before the Daughters took care of the c'aislingaer."

Tierney's eyes grew alarmingly dark and Lucia took a step back. Tierney studied her for a moment and then swung his leg down, shifting to sit up straight on the throne, gripping the ends of the armrests in his hands.

Lucia felt her heart beat faster in a mixture of fear and awe. He looked much more at home on the seat of power than the self-important oracle.

"Well, at least that task is finished. Pity the Lightbearer survived, but perhaps we will have the advantage now that our dear little Rabbit has left us," Tierney said, his eyes burning into Lucia's. "Was he very broken by the loss?"

"Quite," Lucia confirmed.

Tierney smiled and rose from his perch. "Excellent. Most excellent," he said, stepping down from the dais and taking Lucia's hands in his.

*So he's pleased by the loss of the cai aislingstraid. That's good,* Lucia reassured herself. "I brought you a present," she said, feeling more confident as she stared at her fingers intertwined in his.

Tierney's eyes widened in surprise. "Oh, really? Do tell."

Lucia smiled. "The Solas Beir's confidant. He sits in the dungeon as we speak."

"Hmm. That could be useful in getting our young friend to agree to our terms," Tierney murmured.

"Yes—I have a feeling the Solas Beir will surrender to you very soon." Lucia hesitated, unsure if she should continue. She looked into his eyes. He seemed pleased with her news. Perhaps he would forgive the boldness of her next question. "Tierney, what the witch said about the Sower...please, you cannot be serious about using him."

Tierney looked surprised by her question. "I am deadly serious about it."

"But once he begins, we will not be able to contain him. He could destroy everything. He could be your undoing," Lucia insisted.

Tierney narrowed his eyes. "I *can* control him."

"But he is an abomination—he should not even exist. We both know that."

"And *that* was Ardal's mistake," Tierney replied. "But his error shall render our victory. I shall wield the Sower like a sword. He will change everything." He smiled and stroked her cheek. "Besides, dear heart, every puppet needs a master."

"Yes, but which are you?" Lucia asked. Immediately she regretted it. She clamped her hand over her mouth, as if she could take the words back.

Tierney's eyes grew dark again. He studied her as if he were weighing a decision. "Dearest Lucia...you have so little faith." Eyes locked on hers, he took her hand from her mouth and turned it over, pressing her palm gently to his lips before letting her go.

Then he turned and opened the doors to the balcony that overlooked the Eastern Sea. He walked out into the evening air and placed his hands on the balcony railing. Silent, he stared down at the sea below.

Taken aback by his display of tenderness, Lucia watched him for a moment before following him outside. The sun had set and the first stars were glittering in the sky.

She placed her hand on his arm. "Tierney, I am so sorry. I spoke out of turn."

He turned and smiled sadly. He pulled her to him, cupping her chin. "Lucia, my love, don't you know that everything I did, I did for us? To change this world to be as it *should* be? To bring you to your rightful place as queen so we could finally be together?"

"I do know that," she whispered.

He searched her eyes. "It was always you and me." He paused, staring at the stars. "But look, now you've gone and shattered our dream. You've broken my heart."

She shook her head. "No. No, I..."

He nodded. "Oh, but you did. You said the child was hidden from you. You said you could not find him, and that's why I was forced to wait in the Wasteland."

"I...I can explain," Lucia stammered.

"No need." Tierney's smile was sad, bittersweet. "I see everything quite clearly now. It was all lies. The Lightbearer was not hidden from you. He was hidden *by* you. And as time grew short and Calder grew strong, he found out about your little lies, didn't he? He did not betray me. *You* did."

From the inky shadows on the far side of the balcony, Malden emerged, a patronizing smile etched on his face.

*So the little wretch has been flapping his jaws*, Lucia thought. She was furious. "Dog. Filthy, traitorous dog!"

Malden chuckled as he stalked boldly forward. "Filthy, yes. *Oh, yes.* Traitorous, no. Not to *him.*"

"Lucia," Tierney whispered.

She turned to him, pleading. "Tierney, please—"

Tierney cupped her face in his hands and kissed her tenderly. "I did love you," he said.

Then he tossed her off the balcony.

ᏦᏨᏦᏨᏦᏨ

Riding on Cael's back, Marisol spotted Erela in the sky. "She found something," Marisol told him.

Erela was flying back to them in a hurry. *Not as fast as she could fly though,* Marisol thought. Erela had been pretty speedy in coming to their assistance at the Eye of the Needle. She had been surprisingly patient of late, but still, it had to be killing her to have to slow down for the rest of them.

They were making better progress now that David had healed enough to travel as a lion, and Marisol was the one riding on Cael's back. David still couldn't fly, but whether that was because of the gaping wound healing in his abdomen or the one that remained in his heart, Marisol did not know. He wasn't the same without Abby. He seemed broken, hollow.

They had been traveling for days across the never-ending desert, and after their conversation around last evening's fire, David had kept running across the sand with them, but he had stopped speaking altogether.

The night prior, sitting around their campfire, they had been talking about the Daughters of Mercy. Marisol felt terrible for even bringing the topic up, but something Jon had said played over and over in her mind, and it was driving her crazy. Had she known what David had seen, she never would have asked the question.

Jon had said he saw death in the face of the Daughters, but Marisol saw something different. She saw Malden's face, and then her not-so-friendly neighborhood bogeyman really came after her. So was it a premonition? And if it was, did that mean Jon was going to die? Maybe it was already too late. Maybe he was already dead.

"It was not a premonition," Erela explained. "It was an attack strategy. The Daughters of Mercy, myself included, can sense your fears. We can assume the face of whatever it is you fear most."

"Oh." Marisol felt overwhelmed by a sense of relief that Jon might still be alive. "What did you see, Cael?"

Cael frowned. "I saw Eulalia. She was dead because I had failed her," he replied. Then he realized what was implied in that statement, and looked over at David. "I am so sorry, David—I did not mean to suggest that you had in any way failed Abby..."

"I saw Abby's face," David said, staring into the fire, his voice void of emotion. "But she wasn't dead. She was lost because she had joined Tierney."

After that, no one knew what to say, so they went to bed without another word.

Now Erela was landing gracefully in front of them, with none of the thunder or fury that usually marked her arrival. She wasn't the same either. Maybe it was because of the loss of her sisters, or maybe it was her connection to the Solas Beir. She bowed before the lion.

David slipped back into his regular form and finally broke his silence. "What did you find?" he asked.

"The sixth courtesan," Erela replied. "We should reach the body by nightfall."

೫೦೮೩೫೦೮೩೫೦೮೩

It was only because of the courtesan garb that the remains were recognizable. The body was little more than a dried-out husk, mummified. And yet, the dark violet silk still had a clean sheen, with only the slightest layer of dust, proving the man had died only recently.

Marisol felt the desert breeze pick up and stir the sand at her feet. Had there been a sandstorm since the courtesan died, they might not have found him at all. The dunes of the Barren shifted all too easily in the wind.

"It *has* to be him," David said. "Based on what Abby gleaned from the little girl, Daudi was heading west, and he would only have had a few days' lead on us when he escaped from the city. Apart from Aziza, no other courtesans escaped."

"Not that we know of, at least. It looks like he was trying to get back home. What happened to him?" Marisol asked. She picked up his leather cask and shook it—water sloshed around inside. "It's nearly full. But the way he looks—this seems a bit extreme for dehydration, doesn't it?"

Cael nodded gravely. "Indeed it does. He would not have died from his thirst. He would have suffered terribly from it, yes, but he would not have the same limitations as a human lost in this forsaken place. By the bite marks on his hand, I would guess he was attacked. Whatever it was seems to have drained him of his bodily fluids."

"There were footprints," Erela said. "The breeze has picked up and erased them, but there were reptilian prints leading to the body, and humanoid prints leading away, westward."

"A Shadow?" Marisol asked.

"Perhaps," Erela mused thoughtfully.

"But you don't believe that," David observed.

"If it were one of the Kruorumbrae, we likely would not have found a body at all, and certainly not in this state," Erela answered.

"I don't think we'll discover anything else about the culprit from looking at the body." David frowned. "I promised his sister, Yola, I would find him and bring him back to her. I was hoping I'd be returning him alive, but it looks like I've failed yet again."

Marisol put her hand on David's arm. "Stop it. You haven't failed anyone."

He turned to her with tears in his eyes. "But I have. I keep making promises I can't keep. I mean to keep them, but I fail."

"So stop."

David's eyes widened in disbelief. "What?"

Marisol put her hands on her hips. "Stop making promises and stop blaming yourself. It's not helping anyone. I know you think you failed Abby, but you didn't. And if she *were* here, she wouldn't blame you—she would be ticked off at you for blaming yourself. So just stop it."

"Okay," David whispered.

"No, it's *not* okay. Nothing's okay, but we are going to change that, starting right now." Marisol angrily threw down her pack and snatched the last bolt of fabric. She began unwrapping the cloth from the spindle.

"What are you doing?" David asked.

"You *did* find Daudi, and you *will* take him home to Yola. But not like this. This is too horrible for her to see. I'm wrapping him up." Marisol knelt to ease the body into the silken cloth. "Sorry Cael—guess Eulalia doesn't get any presents after all."

Cael hunkered down beside Marisol to help. "She would rather the gift go to honor one of our fallen."

Marisol watched as he expertly pulled the fabric tight around the body and secured it with a knot, then tucked the remnants of the knot back into the folds of the cloth. Apparently Cael had done this kind of thing before.

"Come," he said. "Let us take him home."

## *EPILOGUE: BROKEN*

In the days that followed, David found himself relying more and more on Marisol's strength. Daudi's village on the Great Plains was small, and it was no easy task to deliver his body to his sister, along with the news that four of those taken wouldn't be coming back, and the youngest remained in the hands of the Kruorumbrae.

No one in Nuren was untouched by this revelation of woe. Although it was not a comfort for the villagers to hear that the Solas Beir and his friends had suffered their own losses, there was camaraderie in shared sorrow. The villagers vowed vengeance on the Kruor um Beir when the time for war finally arrived. If nothing else, loyalty to the Solas Beir and his cause increased.

Delivering the news to Abby's family and Jon's mother was another matter entirely, and when the time came, David simply could not speak the words. Marisol became his mouthpiece.

Blanca Reyes was terrified for her son, and yet proud of him for saving Marisol from a horrific fate. David had feared that Abby's parents would blame him as he did himself. They didn't. Instead, they clung to the hope that since Abby's body had not been found, she might still be alive.

David wished he had that kind of hope. But he didn't. If she were still alive, he would have felt something. But he felt nothing, nothing at all.

Neither did Eulalia. She and Abby had shared a bond as empaths, and that bond was broken. "Perhaps she *is* still alive," Eulalia suggested. "I have long feared she would be seduced to join Tierney's cause. If that is the case, you may yet win her back."

David wished he could believe that as well. But he didn't. He spent his days avoiding everyone, seeking refuge in solitude. Since his return, he hadn't sat on the throne. He had abandoned that room altogether, and the council had taken to meeting without him. He couldn't sleep—not in his room, not in hers. Abby was everywhere, but not where he needed her most.

Only with the arrival of the newly appointed Western Oracle did he begin to feel something other than desperate anguish. What he felt was hate. His rage was not directed at Nerine herself, but at the reason behind her errand.

Through a blinding haze of anger, David listened as the mermaid recounted her story. "I witnessed Lucia being tossed from the Eastern Oracle's balcony like so much rubbish, falling like a meteor to the surf below," Nerine explained. "I quickly dove down and retrieved her from Eastern Sea's rocky bottom. Lucia was bleeding internally and barely alive, but I kept her from drowning. My guards and I then carried her west to Caislucis through the undersea caverns that span Cai Terenmare. Now, we give her over to your custody, to do with her as you will." At this, Nerine gestured for her guards to step forward.

The mermen gently laid an unconscious Lucia at David's feet to await his judgment.

In a former life, before he knew better, David would have fought off the hulking monster Calder to save his prodigal aunt, but now he hesitated. She was the source of all this heartache, after all. Perhaps it was best to kill her now before she could wreak further havoc on his miserable life. Or perhaps he should just let Lucia continue on the path she had chosen, let nature take its course, let her die.

*Heal her.*

The voice was in his head, the part of him that held onto memories of Abby and imagined conversations they would never have. He knew that. But it was *her* voice just the same. And if this was the only way he could ever be close to her again, he couldn't silence that voice by denying her request.

Kneeling, he placed his hands over Lucia's bruised, broken body. He let the power flow through him once more, taking her injuries for his own. In the terrible pain, he could hear Abby. He could hear her clearly.

*He's coming,* Abby said. *The Sower is coming.*

# CHARACTERS
*(in alphabetical order)*

**Abigail "Abby" Brown**: a girl with the ability to see the future and communicate with others through dreams. The daughter of Frank and Bethany Brown and sister of Matthew Brown, she was born and raised in the human world.

**Ardal of Caislucis** (AR-dahl of KASS-loo-sis): the father of David Corbin and the previous Solas Beir, also called the Great Bear King. Ardal was assassinated shortly after David's birth and before his kidnapping. (In general, people in Cai Terenmare use their city or region of origin as a surname.)

**Brarn** (rhymes with barn): the raven who guides Abby and is a friend to Queen Eulalia.

**Cael** (kayl): Queen Eulalia's champion and first knight of the castle, Caislucis, he is charged with ensuring the safety of the Solas Beir and the royal family.

**Cai Aislingstraid** (KIGH AY-sling-stride): a soul who sees, a person with the ability to see the future and communicate with others through dreams.

**C'aislingaer** (KIGH-sling-ahr): the slang term for Cai Aislingstraid.

**Cassandra Buchan** (BYOO-can): Professor of Psychology and Statistics at the University of Santa Linda, she's married to Riordan Buchan and is the mother of their children, Ciaran (KEER-ahn), Siobhan (sh'-VAWN), and Rowan (ROH-un).

**David Corbin:** the new Solas Beir (king) of Cai Terenmare, he grew up in the human world, and prefers his human name over his birth name, Artan. His adoptive parents, the Corbins, were murdered by Calder and Malden, Kruorumbrae.

**Eastern Oracle:** one of the four Oracles ruling the outer realms of Cai Terenmare, who work in concert with the Solas Beir to keep the balance between the Light and the Darkness. He governs the City of the Eastern Oracle, perched on the cliffs above the east coast of Cai Terenmare. The other Oracles are the Northern Oracle, the Southern Oracle, and the Western Oracle.

**Erela** (eh-REL-lah): a winged woman who serves on the Solas Beir's court council.

**Eulalia** (YOO-lahl-ee-ah): dowager queen of Cai Terenmare, widow of the last Solas Beir, Ardal, and birth mother of Artan (David Corbin), heir to the throne, and the new Solas Beir.

**Fergal** (FER-gahl) **the Valorous:** a shape-shifting faery, loyal to the queen. His spirit animal is a frog.

**Gorman:** a small indigo man who serves on the Solas Beir's court council and is the historian and librarian for Caislucis.

**Hedeon** (heh-DAY-on): head knight charged with the security of the City of the Eastern Oracle.

**Jonathon "Jon" Reyes**: Abby's best friend, neighbor, and the son of Blanca Reyes.

**Kruor um Beir** (KROO-or um BAIR): the King of Blood and Shadows, and the one who rules those who serve the Darkness.

**Kruorumbrae** (KROO-or-um-bray): evil shape-shifting creatures who feed on others, often referred to as Blood Shadows or simply Shadows.

**Lucia** (loo-SEE-ah): Queen Eulalia's sister, she assassinated Ardal and kidnapped Artan (David Corbin), betraying her family for Tynan Tierney, the Kruor um Beir. While living in the human world, she disguised herself as an old woman named Moira Buchan.

**Malden** (MAHL-den): a sadistic shape-shifter loyal to Tynan Tierney, who has historic ties to Newcastle Beach.

**Marisol** (mah-REE-sol) **Cassidy**: daughter of Marcus Cassidy, a wealthy businessman, and Esperanza Garcia, a former supermodel, she is friends with David Corbin, Michal Sloane, and Monroe Banagher.

**Meridoris** (MEER-ee-dor-ess): a sea hag and vile sorceress from the depths of the ocean.

**Michal** (MEYE-kahl) **Sloane**: a wealthy girl who is best known for being a bully. She and her friends, Marisol Cassidy and Monroe Banagher are referred to as "M Cubed" or $M^3$. Michal and her parents were close friends with the Corbin family.

**Monroe Banagher**: a wealthy girl who is friends with Marisol Cassidy, Michal Sloane, and David Corbin.

**Nysa** (NEE-sah): a water sprite called a nixie, loyal to the queen. Her spirit animal is the golden koi.

**Nerine** (NEER-ih-nee): a mermaid and daughter of the Sea King.

**Northern Oracle**: one of the four Oracles, she governs the Gauntlet and the Ice Mountain Territories.

**Obelia** (oh-BEEL-ya): head of the Solas Beir's court council. The other members of the council are Gorman, Erela, Eoin of the North Forest, Fedor of the Great Plains, Navit of the South, and Rodas of the East.

**Phelan** (FAY-lan): a knight, and Cael's second in command, charged with the security of Caislucis.

**Riordan Buchan** (REER-den BYOO-can): a writer, mythology enthusiast, and admirer of all things Gaelic. Married to Cassandra Buchan, he's the father of Ciaran, Siobhan, and Rowan, and the nephew of the real Moira Buchan, who was murdered by Lucia.

**Solas Beir** (SO-lass BAIR): ruler of Cai Terenmare. In representing the Light, the Solas Beir is endowed with great power and is meant to be a servant to the people. Solas Beir can be translated literally as Lightbearer, but this less formal term is used to refer to a future ruler who has not yet ascended to the throne. The term Lightbearer can also be used as an insult, referring to a ruler who is weak.

**Southern Oracle:** one of the four Oracles, he governs the Rainforest.

**Tynan Tierney** (TIGH-nan TEER-nee): the leader of the Kruorumbrae, creatures of the Darkness. He calls himself Kruor um Beir and seeks the throne of the Solas Beir. He is often referred to simply as Tierney.

**Western Oracle**: one of the four Oracles, she governed the seas and was mother to the murderous sirens. She, her daughters, and her island temple were destroyed by Cael.

**Yola** (YOH-lah): a woman from the village of Nuren, whose brother, Daudi (dah-OO-dee), was abducted along with five other villagers, including a young girl named Aziza (ah-ZEE-zah).

# PLACES AND TERMS
### (in alphabetical order)

**The Barren**: the vast desert in the center of Cai Terenmare, spanning from the Great Plains to the Eye of the Needle.

**Blood Altar:** a ruin with a macabre history located in the middle of the rainforest.

**Cai Terenmare** (KIGH TAIR-en-mahr): a parallel world to Earth filled with magic, shape-shifters, mythical creatures, and blood-thirsty monsters.

**Caislucis** (KASS-loo-sis): castle and city of the Solas Beir, perched on the cliffs above the Western Sea.

**City of the Eastern Oracle:** a large, bustling, walled city governed by the Eastern Oracle.

**Emerald Guardian:** a magical tree stump located near the northern boundary of the rainforest.

**Eye of the Needle**: a rock spire near the City of the Eastern Oracle.

**Newcastle Beach Inn**: a mansion built by Thaddeus Buchan as his home, and later deeded to the Newcastle Beach community. It sits across the street from his brother Samuel's mansion, which was damaged in an earthquake and is in ruin.

**Nuren:** a small village on the Great Plains.

**Pool of Healing**: a sacred pool within Caislucis that can heal almost any wound.

**Sigil**: a seal, signet, sign, symbol, or image with magical power.

**Sign of the Throne**: the sigil of the Solas Beir and an object of great power belonging to the Light. It is used to open and close portals from Cai Terenmare to other worlds.

**Silver Hand Mirror**: an object of power also used to open and close portals, but created and corrupted by Darkness.

**Southport:** a coastal town notorious as a haven for pirates and slave traders.

**Village of the Southern Oracle:** governed by the Southern Oracle, this tiny village stands in the center of a dangerous rainforest.

**The Wasteland**: a parallel world to Cai Terenmare that serves as a prison. In this endless desert where time is frozen, prisoners are compelled to count scarlet grains of sand for all eternity.

# THE SOWER COMES

## Book Three in the Solas Beir Trilogy

## Melissa Eskue Ousley

## THE WASTELAND

The girl sat beneath the cobalt sky, cupping the scarlet sand in her hands. She mumbled the numbers to herself, counting, counting, counting. She remembered nothing but her name. Sometimes she was called Abigail, and sometimes she was called Abby.

&lt;&gt;&lt;&gt;&lt;&gt;

David Corbin was trapped. Lost in a place where he wasn't awake, and he wasn't asleep. He remembered everything, especially the last thing, the part where he had heard *her* voice

1

telling him to heal Lucia—even though that was the last thing he had wanted to do. After all the lies, all the betrayals, he had wanted to see Lucia die.

But the healing wasn't for Lucia. It was for her, the one he had lost. Now Lucia had no more pain. He had taken it all. A part of him savored the agony that twisted his broken body—he was drowning in pain, but it helped him forget Abby's eyes. The problem was, he would heal eventually, as he always did. Before long, the pain would fade. Then he wouldn't be able to forget. Then, he would have to face Lucia. Already she had been calling for him.

ಬಚಿಬಚಿಬಚಿ

Lucia had been staring at the floor of her cell for hours, waiting. The other cells in the dungeon were empty. She had woken up alone, in the dark silence of the underground.

She suspected the other prisoners had been removed from the dungeon out of fear that she would bend their will to serve her own. Even the guards had kept their distance, afraid she might somehow infect their minds, reducing them to serve as her minions. The thought that she was so feared was amusing, considering her mind was still clouded from a death-like sleep. But there were benefits to having a bad reputation, and she didn't mind the solitude. There was only one person she wanted to speak to. He was too broken to come to her just yet, but he *would* come, and soon. She reached out to David again with her mind.

# ABOUT THE AUTHOR

**M**elissa Eskue Ousley lives in the Pacific Northwest with her family and their Kelpie, Gryphon. When she's not writing, Melissa can be found hiking, swimming, scuba diving, kayaking, or walking along the beach, poking dead things with a stick.

Before she became a writer, she had a number of educational jobs, ranging from a summer spent scraping road kill off a molten desert highway, to years spent conducting research with an amazing team of educators at the University of Arizona. Her interests in psychology, culture, and mythology have influenced her writing of *The Solas Beir Trilogy*.

www.MelissaEskueOusley.com
www.goodreads.com/MelissaEskueOusley
www.facebook.com/MelissaEskueOusley
Twitter: @MEskueOusley

30636050R10199